MW01007772

THE
INNKEEPER'S SON

THE JESTER KING FANTASY SERIES:
BOOK 1

K. C. Herbel

Epic Books Press
RICHMOND, VIRGINIA

Copyright © 2004, 2009, 2015 by K. C. Herbel.

All rights reserved. No part of this publication may be reproduced, distributed or trans-mitted in any form or by any means, including photocopying, recording, or other elec-tronic or mechanical methods, without the prior written permission of the publisher, except in the case of brief quotations embodied in critical reviews and certain other non-commercial uses permitted by copyright law. For permission requests, write to the pub-lisher, addressed "Attention: Permissions Coordinator," at the address below.

Previous editions of this book were published under the title: "With a Jester of Kindness"

Epic Books Press
P.O. Box 358
Quinton, Virginia 23141
www.EpicBooksPress.com

Publisher's Note: This is a work of fiction. Names, characters, places, and incidents are a product of the author's imagination. Locales and public names are sometimes used for atmospheric purposes. Any resemblance to actual people, living or dead, or to businesses, companies, events, institutions, or locales is completely coincidental.

Cover Artist: SelfPubBookCovers.com/Khonsu

Ordering Information:
Quantity sales. Special discounts are available on quantity purchases by corporations, as-sociations, and others. For details, contact the "Special Sales Department" at the address above.

Library of Congress Control Number: 2017937633

The Innkeeper's Son / K. C. Herbel. -- 1st ed.
ISBN 978-1-944314-02-6

In memory of my father, whom I still miss very much. To his father, the storyteller; to my mom, for always being there, and to my wife, my best friend in this world.

Book One

THE INNKEEPER'S SON

"It is not flesh and blood, but heart which makes us fathers and sons."

—FRIEDRICH SCHILLER

A Running Start

The silence of the forest was shattered by the thunder of horse hooves churning up the black earth of the King's Road. Two cloaked riders whipped their galloping mounts in a race against the setting sun.

As they passed a deserted crossroads, the larger of the two looked over his shoulder. "Hurry, the sun is almost down. We must reach shelter before nightfall."

Suddenly the tired mare under him slipped and stumbled. Its legs collapsed, and it rolled to the ground, hurling its rider further up the road. The second rider pulled up on the reins and turned around.

The fallen man grudgingly got to his feet and straightened the sword at his waist before shambling over to his downed horse. He looked back at his companion who pushed back the hood of his cloak, to reveal the smudged, sparsely bearded face of a youth.

The man spit the dirt from his teeth. "Go on, go on. I'm well."

The youth urged his jumpy, lathered horse forward. His large eyes danced from side to side above his quivering lips. "Are you quite sure?" he asked in a thin voice.

"I've taken harder falls in the lists."

"Yes, an old warrior like you must be quite used to it by now, but what of your mount?"

"She will survive. Old warrior? I am not an old …" The large man stopped and grinned. "Go on, I will follow immediately."

As the smirking youth turned his horse back up the road, the warrior brought the mare to its feet and inspected its legs. "Confound it!"

The youth again stopped his horse. The grin had escaped his face. "What is it? Is she lame?"

"What, this old battle-nag? Too stubborn for that, but she is wounded and look, she's spilled our provisions."

The large man tied a cloth around the mare's injured foreleg and bent to pick up the bread, fruit, and gold coins scattered across the road. He put a handful of coins into a purse and was reaching for a small loaf of bread when the cry of an infant erupted from his companion.

The dismounted warrior shot a fretful look to the younger man and then glanced about. As he eyed the woods, his free hand drifted onto the hilt of his sword. "Confound, it's nearly dark!"

The youth shifted in the saddle and pushed aside his grey cloak to reveal a very young, very small baby. "There, there, my little prince," he cooed. "What's the matter?"

At that moment, the youth caught sight of movement down the road they had just covered. All happiness drained from his face, and his back stiffened. His mount reared up, pawing the air with its forelegs.

The warrior's mare leapt into the air, kicking and snorting. Her master crouched low in the road with one hand solidly gripping the reins. The man's sharp green eyes searched the shadowy curtain of the forest beyond the naked blade of his sword.

The youth skillfully forced his startled mount back to the ground then pointed down the road. "He's found us! Run!" He dug his heels into his horse and charged up the road, cradling the baby.

The man hunkered on the road looked past his bucking mount in the direction the youth had pointed. His eyes fell upon the nameless crossroads, where a low, fog-like darkness crept through the trees. It billowed into view like black ink poured into clear, still water and hovered in the intersection. Thin, wispy tendrils probed in front of it, and into the woods on either side of the road, before melting back into the main body of darkness. Without warning, it shifted and started up the road in the direction of the two riders.

The warrior pleaded under his breath. "God save us." He yanked on the reins of his horse, demanding her obedience to his control. Then he put his foot in the stirrup, but the beast circled away from him. After a few hurried attempts, he managed to throw himself into the saddle. The frightened creature spun round and round beneath him as he paused to eye the gold coins still littering the road.

The youth shouted over his shoulder. "Hurry!"

"But the gold!"

"Leave it!"

"But we will need—"

"Leave it! Only the child matters!"

Without another moment's hesitation, the large man swatted the mare's rump with the flat of his sword and galloped up the road.

CHAPTER ONE

Fate Takes a Hand

The music of the crickets filtered through the air, soft and constant as the gentle hearts of the people who dwelled inside the warm wee cottages scattered haphazardly across the quiet valley. Small ribbons of white smoke curled out of chimneys, and the smell of supper being served at the inn was wafting through the air. Everything was just as it had always been, during this time of year in the Valley of the Yew.

John, the owner of The Valley's Finest Inn, was outside collecting the last armful of firewood. He always enjoyed this time of day, so he was in no hurry to get back inside to the kitchen. He reached down with his free hand and patted the tan hound by his side.

"There's a good lad." He looked to the west and watched the orange disk of the sun slip behind the distant hills. "What a sunset, 'ey Rascal?"

The dog seemed to smile in agreement and raised his head for a more effective petting. He nuzzled up against John's leg and almost knocked him over with his enthusiastic display of affection. A stick of firewood fell from John's arm, and Rascal scooped it up in his slobbering mouth.

"Good boy. Now come along and help me stoke the fire."

John turned and started inside. He looked around to see Rascal standing with his front paws spread far apart and his tail end wagging in the air. The dog looked at John then hopped to one side. John recognized the dog's mood and played along.

"Very well." He put down his load of wood at the kitchen door. "So you want to play now, do ya? I see that there stick means an awful lot to ya, 'ey Rascal? Tell you what: if I can get that stick away from ya—"

The dog dropped the stick and looked away from the inn. He perked up his droopy ears while tilting his head from side to side. The husky innkeeper looked up to see what distracted his canine friend.

Downhill, a piece, the road went into a thick grove of trees. John looked hard into the shadows of the small hollow. At last, he perceived someone coming out of the woods: two riders—in a hurry.

The riders were dusty and their horses lathered from a long hard ride. John brushed himself off and prepared to greet them. This proved to be a waste of time for they galloped directly up to him raising a cloud of dust. Rascal barked fiercely at the strangers and did his best to look twice his size and half his age.

"Quiet, Rascal!"

The dog skulked from his master's side, his hackles still bristling, and went to watch from inside the kitchen door.

When the dust settled and John had finished dusting himself off for the second time, he looked up and smiled at the new arrivals. The one closest to him was a large burly man. He wore a tattered brown cloak with fine chain mail armor peeking through in places. The other, a younger man, was slight of build and wore leather armor under a grey cloak. This one hung back, avoiding John's eyes. Both were unshaven and appeared to have been on the road for several days. In the gloaming, John still noticed the hilts of their elegantly crafted swords. The large man's sword looked heavy and broad while the smaller man's was long and narrow.

The big man shifted his weight in the saddle. "Are you the innkeeper?"

"I am John, the owner, milord."

"Well, John-the-owner, I see by yon sign, that this is 'The Valley's *Finest* Inn'. Is it so?"

"That is what they say."

"I would wager that they also say it is the valley's only inn."

John grinned, knowing that the game was up. "I am afraid milord would be richer for that wager, if he could but find the fool daft or drunk enough to take such a—"

The younger man cleared his throat. His large companion looked at him, raised his hand and whispered. "I know."

"Well then good John-the-owner, let us go into your inn and enjoy the finest this valley has to offer."

During this short conversation, John observed the slighter of the two men looking back in the direction of the road several times, as if expecting to see something or someone following them. John was just about to ask if there were to be others in the party, but decided to appear less observant and keep his nose out of business that might shorten it.

Putting his beak in the wrong feeder had been one of John's shortcomings in the past, but he discovered that sticking his nose into other people's affairs often hurt business, not to mention his nose. As his Gran always said, "Many a time a man's mouth broke his nose." So most recently, he had adopted an "anti-intrusion policy," which he strictly applied to strangers, and hoped for reciprocal consideration where his life and nose were concerned.

John led the way into the inn with the big man following close behind. Once inside, John showed the man the commons room and asked him to have a seat. The second man was nowhere to be seen, so John went to see if he needed assistance. As John got to the door he nearly collided with the slender man who was carrying a bundle cradled in the crook of his arm. John turned out of the way to avoid being plowed under and found the man's large companion standing behind him holding two plates heaped with food.

"Milord, please—!"

"We shall eat in our room."

John saw the urgency of acquainting them with quarters. "Do ye have a preference, milord?"

"A private room overlooking the stables."

"But milord would not be comfortable in that room."

"Nonsense! I can never sleep unless I know my mare is safe."

"Very good, milord." John picked up the key to the back room and motioned for the two of them to follow him up the stairs. While still on the stair, he asked, "Any special instructions for the stable boy, milord."

"Give them a good rubdown and a good portion of oats. Let them drink freely of the water. The mare has a cut on her foreleg, so have the boy put on a clean bandage. I'll be down later to examine it. Also, have the boy put some oats in a pair of bags for our journey."

"Very good, milord."

They reached the door to their room, and John opened it. The large man stepped into the room, looked about, then motioned for his companion to enter.

Once the slighter man slipped into the room, the large man stepped into the doorway, blocking John's entrance. He then handed John a small bag of coins. "We leave with the rising of the sun. Have our horses ready, and pack a cold breakfast and lunch."

John's eyes vainly searched past the large man. "Do you wish me to turn down the bed, milord?"

"No."

John turned to leave, and the man snared his arm. "One last thing." He took John aside in the passage. "Tell no one we are here, and bring up some warm milk in a short while."

"We have goat's milk, milord."

"Goat's milk would be fine."

John went downstairs with his suspicions highly piqued. However, he remembered his new policy and was determined to steer wide of the entire topic. This was not easy, for when he started fulfilling his latest guests' requests, he was met with a flurry of queries concerning them. A free pint of ale and a song easily distracted his nosy regulars, but nothing could deter his implacable wife, Moira. Her many years as an innkeeper had made her a well-established and much honored institution of local rumormongery. Fortunately for John, he didn't know much. However, this lack of information made Moira more persistent than ever.

"Well, did this mysterious stranger have money at least?"

John scowled. "Aye! He paid me in advance, and I'd imagine a lot better than the scrubby blokes we have blowin' through here half the time."

"You'd imagine? Ya mean you don't know?"

"Well you haven't given me much chance, now have ya?"

At this, John opened up the small bag of coins and dumped it on the table. Their eyes nearly popped from their heads when they surveyed the pile of gold and silver coins that lay on the table.

"Gaww! Did ya ever?"

"No. Not ever!"

"How much is it, John?"

"Don't know. But it's a kettle more than any other pile in this valley."

"Are those really … real?"

John eyed one of the yellow coins. He bit it then smiled. "Real gold!" He looked at the coin again. "He must mean for me to keep these for him. Zounds, put 'em back quick!"

They started to scoop the coins back in the bag when the back door opened, and in burst the stable boy. This so startled John that he dropped a few of the coins on the floor.

"Go milk the goat!" John barked at the boy.

The boy jumped back and hastily retreated out the door. John picked up the money and threw it into the bag. He wiped his forehead and tucked the bag into his tunic with a sigh.

John raised a warning finger to Moira. "Not a word."

Moira pretended to lock her lips and throw away the key. John was not greatly encouraged by this, but knew it was the best he could hope for.

By the time the goat's milk was ready, only one regular remained in the commons room. John ushered him out with a quick but hardy "g'night" and sent him on his way. He lit a lantern and toted the milk upstairs to his mystery guests. When he got to the door, it was slightly ajar, and he took this as an invitation to bring in the milk.

A young woman sat in the corner of the dimly lit room holding a baby. She spun around—her eyes and mouth open wide in astonishment. Leather armor of a masculine design hung loosely on her shoulders, but it looked like a costume on her as she breast-fed the small infant. John was taken aback by the sight of her and started to retreat out of modesty. However, his feet halted and tugged him to a stop in the doorway.

"Beggin' your pardon, ma'am, but what are you doin' here?" He kept his head bowed to give her an opportunity to cover her breast. She did so and without a word crossed the floor and took the milk from John's hand.

"Thank you. He was hungry and so I was pacifying him, but this is what he really needs."

John looked down at her waist as she closed the door. There on her hip was the beautifully wrought long sword he had seen worn by the slighter of the two mysterious riders. He urgently wanted to leave. The last time he had felt so prickly was just before he thrust his nose into the wrong place and got it bloodied. He glanced about in haste, feeling uneasy to be in the room, alone with the mysterious and well-armed woman.

The woman, seeing his discomfort, implored him to sit.

"Oh, I couldn't possible stay, I've so many chores to attend to."

He turned to the door and grasped the latch. A dagger appeared in the door just above his hand with a thud.

"On the other hand, I suppose this room could use a good tidying up."

The lady began feeding the goat's milk to the child. "Oh dear, I seem to have misplaced my dagger. Would you be so kind as to bring it over to me? I don't wish to disturb the child. You understand, don't you?"

John understood only too well what she meant, but he did not understand why all this was happening. Maybe, if he could just return the dagger and leave quickly without asking any questions, without any answers, without any shortening of his life.

"Please."

John fumbled momentarily with the blade and then removed it from the door with a tug. He was tempted to return it in the same manner in which it had found its way to the door, but thought better of this and started slowly across the floor.

Patiently the woman waited for him to approach. She reached out her hand, and John carefully placed the weapon in it. He recoiled, anticipating a possible attack.

"You silly man. If I meant you harm, you would already have felt my steel." Her words betrayed no emotion, and John felt that perhaps the blade would have been less chilling. He could not stifle a shudder.

The woman knit her eyebrows. "Good John, forgive my brutish manners, but I am not accustomed to dealing with such gentle folk. I am afraid that you have discovered a woeful secret, and now I feel that you—"

"I don't need to know anything, ma'am." John started for the door. "Now you take my gentle wife, she loves a good story. And the stable boy—"

"Shush and sit yourself down, John."

John knew that she wasn't going to let him go until she had explained everything. So he sat himself down and mentally prepared for his beating.

"John, as you have undoubtedly guessed, I am the very same man who came here earlier this evening." She gestured to the small bed-side table. Next to the candle, there was the beard of a man, without a face to hold it up. "There is the rest of my disguise. I'm afraid it was necessary to deceive you and your guests for our purposes—that is, for the purpose of keeping this child safe. I must keep this child a secret. I dare not tell you of the child's origins, even now, for fear that it may bring you trouble if you knew, and perhaps endanger the child.

"Put your mind at ease, good John, I have not stolen this child, but was charged with his safety. Let me just say that what I do for this child, is only what any decent person would do, if they but had the courage to take up the task."

She took a deep breath. "This child would be murdered by those who seek him, John. And that would surely be a foul deed, bringing great sorrow and suffering to ... Well, to many good people."

When John heard her speak his name, he felt as if she were on her knees pleading with him, as if he was the one with a cruel blow leveled at the infant. He looked into her face and saw the gentle tears of a woman rolling down her cheeks. At this moment of her weakness she was more beautiful than any he had seen before.

John found a handkerchief in his apron and offered it to the woman. "Here, gentle lady. I know now what this child means to you, and I will not let my mouth carelessly drop the strings of the bean sack."

The woman grabbed his hand. "Swear it, good John. Swear it! If not for this innocent babe, then for the goodness in your own heart, which I see is great."

John was taken aback by her demand of an oath, but he saw the way she cradled the child with such devoted love. "I swear – I swear it by the love that you have for the child."

"No! You must swear on your own love. I may be dead sooner than you have need to keep the secret from his enemies, and my love will not help you then."

John's heart nearly broke at the thought of this strange but gentle woman's death. Her tired red-rimmed eyes implored him, and he saw the truth of what she said. He looked at the child again, and the little one's sleeping face melted his heart. It was so innocent and vulnerable, and the woman's words made him aware that he did want to love this child.

John and Moira had only recently, after years of trying, been blessed by a child of their own. It occurred to John that their son William was not much older than this baby. At that moment his mind spun about, and he saw his own son, hunted by murderers, running for his life, innocent and helpless. He wanted someone to help his son, a hero to save him. His eyes met the lady's, and he saw in them the courage of just such a hero.

John knelt before the child and whispered. "Little one, I swear to you, by your innocence and by the love that I now feel for you that I will protect ya and your secret for as long as I have the strength to love."

The woman placed her hand on John's head. "Well spoken, noble John. Well spoken."

John felt odd at being called noble, but it also gave him a feeling of purpose—of strength—of nobility! He rose to his feet, bowed his head to the lady, and started to exit the room. There was nothing he could say. There was nothing he needed to say.

John stopped by the window. "Shall I open the shutters, milady?"

"No!"

John pulled away from the window, surprised by the sharpness of her tone. "But the night will be mild. The sky is clear."

"It will not remain so."

John felt a chill once again at the certainty of her gloomy prediction. He nodded to her and turned to leave.

As John reached the door, it opened abruptly, and in stepped the woman's large companion. His eyes took in the scene, and he glared at John. His hand flew swift as a hawk to draw the sword at his side and thrust it at John.

"No!" the woman shouted.

The broad gleaming blade of the sword stopped at John's chest. The large man, frozen in his stance, looked over at the woman with a puzzled expression.

She frowned at him. "You fool! You use your sword as most men do, too quickly and without thought. Do you think I would sit here and let him leave if I thought that he would betray us?" She paused and glared long into his eyes. A small line of blood ran down the broad blade of the sword. "And now you have wounded him. Do you not understand that to injure him is to injure the very people we do this for?"

The large man watched the blood run down the edge of his blade, and then he saw John's wide eyes and trembling hands. He lowered his sword and in one quick movement removed the blood and sheathed its elegant blade.

John sank to the floor. He put his hand over the wound on his chest and felt himself blanching.

The large man closed the door and stepped over John. As he crossed the room, the woman began to interrogate him.

"And where were you?"

"After the horses, I checked all the shutters and doors."

"And are they all secured?"

"They are now."

The man arrived beside the lady, and they began whispering. John stayed back near the door. In a few moments, the titanic man turned around. His face was red and drawn by lament.

"Good sir, I am afraid that I have wronged you, both in body and character. I have been too long at war. Please forgive me, and allow me to tend your wound."

John nodded, and the two strangers helped him to sit on the corner of the bed. The lady immediately went to work cleaning the wound, while her companion tore some cloth into strips. Once the wound was clean, the man began wrapping the bandage around John's chest.

Before they could finish, there came a loud creaking sound. The beams of the roof groaned and the shutters rattled.

John looked at the window. "A storm? That sure came up sudden."

The lady shook her head and whispered. "That's no storm."

Her companion nodded. "I hear no winds."

The noise increased as if a great weight were pressing down on the roof of the inn and squeezing in on its walls. The room darkened as the moonlight peeking through the shutters was snuffed out.

The warrior silently handed John the remainder of the bandages and stood. He then drew his sword and backed into the corner next to the window.

The shutters began to buffet violently. Suddenly one shutter unlatched and swung open a crack. The ruckus stopped and a ropelike stream of smoke snaked through the narrow gap. It blindly pawed at the floor and slowly crept toward the bed, drawing more of itself into the room.

The warrior raised one finger to his mouth and motioned for the others to move back. John leaned back and lifted his feet onto the bed. The woman took the child and quietly scooted to the far side.

The smoky probe hesitated and then moved towards the warrior. It inched right up to his foot, but he held his sword.

At that moment, the baby began to cry, and the tentacle coiled up into the air. It bobbed side to side, seeming to eye the child, and then it lunged forward.

Instantly, the poised warrior chopped off the alien limb. There was a flash of fire, and it flopped to the floor with a squeal. The darkness outside the window immediately lifted, retreating into the distance with a screeching howl.

John stared in amazement as the severed extremity transformed into adder heads, bat wings, and blood in the shafts of moonlight. These promptly sublimated into a sulfurous vapor and vanished.

John was hardly aware of his guest's hushed and anxious words to each other. He was still in shock as the warrior finished his bandage. The man looked John in the eyes. "Tis pity you cannot tell a soul about this fine battle scar, friend. Be content to wear it proudly yet secretly as a reminder of your oath to the child."

John got to his feet and bowed to them both. Amazingly they appeared unshaken by the supernatural events of the evening. As he backed out the door, John said, "I shall not forget my promise."

John jumped with a start as he bumped into Moira in the corridor. Abruptly he turned and closed the door, all but a crack.

"Your horses and supplies will be ready for you, on the morrow, my good *sirs*." He promptly shut the door, grabbed his wife's hand, and charged down the stairs—Moira whispering questions in his ear, and his mind spinning with all that had transpired.

CHAPTER TWO

Of Parting and Sorrow

The morning stars were winking out their last "good morrow" as the eastern sky began to glow with the promise of another day. The air was still, and a thick fog had descended on the low lands. The fog had silently crept its way up the road like a thief and surrounded the inn. It choked out the light of the early morning sun, making the whole of the first floor dark as night.

The baying of a hound, down in the hollow, broke the early morning quiet. Then another joined in, and another, until all the dogs in the valley were in chorus.

Rascal tugged at the end of Moira's apron, making her drop her basket of fresh eggs. He barked as he scampered to the door.

"Rascal! Ya miserable, good for nothing, trouble making, flea bitten … mangy …" Moira struggled for the right words to dismiss her sudden urge to have broiled leg of mutt for breakfast, but the only ones she could think of were the swear words of sailors, teamsters, and vagabonds. She pushed them all aside with an exasperated, "RASCAL!"

Moira went to the door, opened it, and shooed the anxious dog out with a swift foot to his rear; an unnecessary act, which only served to alleviate her frustration.

She yelled at the escaping hound as he galloped into the fog. "And stay out!"

John was in the commons room stoking up a good fire when the two mysterious visitors came charging down the stairs. Once again they looked like two men, except the woman's face was without whiskers. John could see fear in her eyes and wondered what could make such a brave soul afraid.

"John, we must leave immediately!"

"What's wrong, milady?"

Her large companion grabbed John's arm. "Good John, have you our provisions?"

"Why, yes. They're in the kitchen. But—"

"No time for explanations, John." The lady headed for the kitchen. "The Lord has provided us with a good alarm. Now we must make the most of it."

They all three entered the kitchen. John picked up their supplies and followed them out the back door.

Moira rose from cleaning up the eggs. "What's goin' on?"

"Just shush, and close your eyes, good wife. Just turn 'round and pretend ya never saw any of this."

Hastily John escorted his guests to the stables. The lady gently placed the infant into John's arms. Immediately she and the man began to rig their horses. They threw the provisions onto the back of the mare and mounted.

The lady leaned over and kissed John on the cheek. As she pulled away, John pulled back the blanket, which covered the infant, and gave him a kiss on the forehead.

"Good-bye, little one, I shall remember always."

As he handed the baby back to his protector, she said, "I know you will, noble John."

Once again John's mind filled with noble feelings and thoughts and prayers.

"But beware. His enemies are close at hand, and will certainly come here. Be brave, John. Be strong, for the child's sake. And may the Lord go with you."

"And with you," John responded. Somehow saying this simple three-word phrase never felt so important before, but John's throat tightened this time as he gave it voice.

With the baby safely cradled into a special pack, the lady turned her horse and urged it into a gallop. Her companion stopped and stared John firmly in the eye then solemnly nodded his head.

"He also serves … who runs indeed the finest inn in the valley." With this he smiled and reached down and touched John on his sword wound. "Courage, my friend. Your badge is hidden, let it shine through you and give you strength. God go with you."

John gripped the man's arm and replied, "And with you, friend."

Then the man gave a quick kick to his handsome mare and charged off. As John watched him disappear into the mist behind the woman, he remembered the pouch of coins they had given him.

John reached into his tunic, brought out the purse, and held it aloft. "Wait! You've left your money!"

"It's yours," came an answer from the murk, "for the finest night I ever had in an inn."

John started to protest but knew it would do little good. He put the bag back into his shirt and continued to stare into the dense fog. He could see no sign of his mysterious guests. They had been a mere hiccup in his life, and yet their departure left a void in his gut.

He was brought back to his senses by the loud howling of Rascal, who had come to his side. The hound paced back and forth, crying balefully. The other dogs of the valley were still strangely boisterous.

John turned his attention down the road towards the hollow. The fog was beginning to lift as the rays of sunlight penetrated and burned it away. He could make out the small clump of trees at the bend in the road, but beyond that was a blanket of white. He prayed that the fog would hide his recently departed guests from whatever enemies might be coming.

Several dark figures suddenly pierced the whiteness. They had arms and legs somewhat like men but were running on all fours, much in the way of a strange animal John had once seen in a traveling circus.

As they came closer, John could see that these were not ordinary creatures, but twisted, nightmarish monsters. Brown scraggly hair covered their bodies along with patches of ugly grey and pink flesh. Their hands and feet were longer than those of a man but constructed in a similar manner, with large black claws at their extremes. The ghastliest portions of this visage were their horribly contorted faces. They were something like barefaced men with long snouts and mouths full of jagged fangs. Occasionally their ugly, dirty faces came up from the mud to sniff the air.

John watched them for a moment, frozen in his tracks. However, the paralyzing fear soon became terror when men on horses came galloping through the curtain of fog behind the beasts. John ran into the inn, calling for Rascal to follow.

Moira was cooking at the stove when John came charging into the kitchen. It had been a long time since John had moved so quickly. She looked up in surprise. John held up his hand to signal her to stay quiet and listen, but at that moment Rascal came bounding into the kitchen.

"Get that scruffy mutt out of here!" she ordered.

John closed the door behind the hound and looked to his wife, who stood with her arms crossed impatiently. "Moira, don't just stand there!"

"Well what would ya have me do, your highness?"

"Here." He handed her the purse. "Hide this in the usual spot."

Moira stood with the bag in her hand, dumbfounded.

"Now, woman!"

John was not in the habit of calling his wife "woman" in that tone of voice, nor was Moira in the habit of answering anyone who did—that included her husband—but the fear in his eyes made her drop the matter and follow his order.

John ran into the commons room and continued right up the stairs into the room his recently departed guests had inhabited. Frantically he straightened up the room and opened the window. As he did, he saw that the creatures had almost reached the inn. Out of breath, John raced back downstairs. He stuck his head in his own bedroom and saw that little William was still sleeping in his crib then closed the door and headed to the kitchen.

Rascal was howling and scratching at the door. Moira, anxious to have the dog quiet, opened the door to let him out. Suddenly Rascal didn't want to go out. Instead, he backed away and ran whimpering into the pantry.

Moira frowned at him and shook her head. "What's the matter with the men in this house today? Yer all actin' –"

At that moment John burst breathlessly into the kitchen. He saw Moira at the open door and leaped towards her. "Close the door!"

John came into contact with the door, and his weight started to force the door closed. Suddenly the door exploded back into the room, knocking John and Moira to the floor. One of the monstrous beast-men was now in the doorway, crouched on the unhinged door. It snarled at John and smiled with its large drooling maw. Moira, horrified by the hideous visage, screamed and backed towards the pantry as the creature eyed her hungrily. Its eyes grew large as it saw the terror on their faces, and its smile broadened. John scooted back from the door with his eyes on the beast. Slowly it advanced on him, playfully stalking him, taking great pleasure in his fear. Finally it had John backed into a corner. It sniffed at John and then hissed, sounding something like a laugh. John's stomach turned as the odor of the monster's hot breath impacted his senses. With lightning speed the loathsome thing snapped one of its scabby hands around John's neck. Moira gasped out a small cry, which delighted the beast into snickering. Then it turned John's head to look him in the eyes. The creature smiled, showing every inch of its teeth, and brought one of its grisly hands up to its mouth. It licked its long black claws and slowly drew them back as if aiming at John's eyes. Moira closed her eyes and turned away. She was bawling hysterically and kicking her feet, which redoubled the creature's joy. John felt the creature's grip tighten as it prepared to take his life. Down came the claws of the creature, and John closed his eyes.

At that moment there was a loud snap. John felt the creature's hand loosen on his throat and opened his eyes. Its killing claws hovered, just inches in front of his face. The creature clenched his teeth and tried to bring them farther. They trembled but came no closer. It growled and hissed at John.

"NO!" growled a deep voice from the doorway.

The monster's head jerked back from John, and he saw a chain, around the creature's neck, pulling it back, and a whip around its wrist. Grudgingly the creature released John and pulled away from him.

John collapsed to the floor. Moira was still hysterical, and so he crawled over to her. He touched her shoulder, and she jumped away, then she cried in relief when she saw her husband alive. He took her in his arms and held her tight.

A dark figure filled the doorway and beat the ugly thing on the end of the chain leash. He then gave the beast a swift kick, which sent it sniveling to the corner by the stove. It spotted the broken eggs in the garbage bin and stuck its face into the gooey mess.

The figure ducked under the doorframe and crossed to the corner where John and Moira were cowering. As he drew closer, John could see that it was a man of enormous dimension. His features appeared chiseled and his entire body elephantine.

With one of his bloated hands, the colossus grabbed John and slammed him down on the large butcher-block table in the center of the kitchen. Quickly, while John was still stunned, the giant took two large carving knives and pinned his shirt to the table, burying the blades up to the handles in one swift move. Then he bent over John and breathed on his face.

"Where is he?" the giant demanded.

John didn't reply. He couldn't. His mind was a roaring, churning sea.

"Where is he?"

"Where is who?"

With one huge fat finger, the titan pressed on John's chest. John felt as if someone were standing on him. He let out a cough as the pressure continued. There was a sudden snap, and one of John's ribs broke.

"Now you tell me. Where little baby?"

The pain brought John back to his senses. He knew now what the giant was asking. He also knew that he couldn't tell him. These were the enemies the lady had warned him about. How had he allowed himself to become involved in all this? Why did the lady tell him anything? He grew angry with the mysterious lady and her companion. His family's lives were at stake here, and it was the strangers' fault.

"Where baby?"

"I don't know—"

"You lie!" With that, the huge mountain of a man proceeded to break another of John's ribs—then another.

Moira got up and started towards the giant. She wanted desperately to stop him from hurting her beloved husband any further, but then the ugly beast in the corner growled at her and she slid back down into the corner.

John's mind was racing. Why should he protect the strangers? After all, they had gotten him into this mess and then left him defenseless. What had happened to his "anti-intrusion policy"? Now the pain was starting to have the reverse effect. His mind was becoming cloudy as the pain in his chest grew.

"I – I—"

Without warning, all of the nonsense in John's head went away. All he could see was the infant, so tiny and innocent, so like his son. The words of his solemn oath to the child rang in his ears.

The huge man grinned. "You what?"

"I don't know what you're talking about."

Snap went another rib.

"Stop!" a new voice said from the doorway. "Don't want to kill him, yet."

John turned his face to the door. There stood a thin young man dressed all in black. He wore an odd tall hat and carried a gnarled, crooked cane.

"You not boss!" the giant said.

The raven-like man came to the table. "Yes, but I know how to make the man talk, remember? You will only succeed in killing him." As he spoke, his foreign accent became conspicuous.

The giant growled at the smaller man and then took his finger off John's chest. He backed away from the table and let the thin man in, next to John.

"You may leave now," the thin man said impatiently, "and take that *thing* with you!"

Dragging his feet, the giant took the monstrous beast and left.

With the monster gone, Rascal growled at the thin man from the pantry. The man approached cautiously then swiftly kicked the door of the pantry closed and latched it, leaving Rascal to claw and bark at him from within.

Another man wearing brown leather armor and a long sword appeared in the door and nodded to the man in black. "Sygeon."

The thin man tossed his head towards the opposite door. "Banarel, search the inn."

"No!" John said.

The thin man stared at John as the man he called Banarel drew his sword and charged into the commons room. "You are in no position to make demands of my mercenaries."

The man turned and paced the floor. He stopped beside John and breathed a heavy sigh. "You know, it's amazing. Most men would have already talked. Why haven't you, eh? Well, let us start at the beginning. What is your name?"

John did not reply.

"I said, what is your name?" The man then poked John in the chest with his cane.

"John!" Moira cried.

"John?" The man glanced at Moira. "John? Is that your name?"

"Yes."

"Good! You see now, that wasn't so hard, was it? Was it?"

"No."

"Good! Now where is the baby, John? Where is the baby?"

"I don't know."

"Where?"

"I don't know."

"Where?"

"I don't know. How many times must I say it?"

"Until I am satisfied, John. Until I am satisfied. Now, where is the little baby, John?"

"I don't—"

The shrill cry of an infant pierced the air.

"Not my baby!" Moira screamed as she jumped to her feet.

The man's head snapped around as Moira ran for the door, and he cut her down with a vicious stroke of his cane. He then pointed it at her. "You have a baby?"

Moira lay on the floor, her cheek split open from the brutal blow. Her entire body was shaking. She could hardly bring herself to blink but somehow managed to nod.

The man's eyes bore down on her, and then he cocked his head and listened to the baby's cry. "I have no interest in your brat." He turned on John and started to beat him, punctuating his words with blows. "I want – the baby – that came here – last – night!"

"Tell him, John!" Moira bawled. "If ya know, please tell him!"

"Yes, John. Tell me."

"I don't know."

"I grow weary of this game, John. But perhaps your wife would make for better sport or ... maybe your child—"

"No!"

"Then tell me, John."

"I can't."

"You can't remember, or you can't tell me?"

"I don't know."

"I see."

The thin man began to pace the room again. The mercenary, who had been searching the inn, returned to the kitchen. Though winded, he waited quietly with his black bulging eyes trained on John's interrogator.

"Find anything?"

"Couple merchants and a baby, but it's not the right baby."

"Yes, I know. And the merchants?"

"Sellin' ice in Hades."

"Good man, Banarel. Go outside with the others."

The mercenary nodded and exited the kitchen.

The thin man continued to pace. He stopped abruptly and stared at the floor. "Hello, what have we here?" He stooped down and picked something out of a crack in the floor. He inspected it and then walked over to Moira.

"Excuse me, madam, but are you in the habit of leaving bezants on the floor of your kitchen." He held out a gold solidus in front of Moira's face.

Moira could see that it was one of the coins that the two strangers had given them. "No, sir."

"Where did this come from?"

"I don't know, sir."

The man took his cane and put the end on John's chest. Then he looked at Moira. "Where?"

"Two gentlemen, strangers they were. Came through here and left."

"And these two gentlemen; did they have many bezants?"

Moira looked at John on the table, and the man pushed on his cane. John winced from the pain but looked at Moira and shook his head.

"Well?"

"Well … I don't know, sir."

"Do not lie to me, woman! Were they carrying many of these coins?"

"Yes, sir."

"Good! It must be them. When did they leave?"

"Don't tell him anything!" John cried.

The man struck John sharply with his cane then poked him for good measure. "That will be enough, John. You have got to learn to speak in turn." The man turned back to Moira. "Now, when did they go?"

"This morning, early," Moira answered.

"And which way were they going?"

"I don't know."

The man struck John hard.

"I don't know! I don't, I don't, I don't!" Moira went to her knees weeping. "Please, sir! Don't beat him anymore! Please!"

The door was darkened again by the large form of the giant.

"Beast find trail. Sygeon come now."

"Yes. I don't think we need to take up any more of your time. Good-bye, John. Good-bye, good madam."

With that the thin man stepped over the broken door and walked outside. Immediately John and Moira heard him yelling to his companions in a foreign tongue and then the sounds of horses riding away.

Moira ran to John and helped him from the table. She had to take off his shirt to get him free.

At that moment, the smell of smoke filled her nose. Moira looked to her stove, then to the door. The smoke came from outside. Moira ran out the door. As she cleared the building, she saw the roof of the inn ablaze with several small fires. The flames spread quickly in the thatch roof, and the black smoke became thick.

She cried John's name and sprinted back into the inn. A few seconds later, she dragged him outside then ran back in the kitchen door.

"Moira! Don't go in there!"

"I've got to get the baby!"

"Wait!" John reached for her, but it was too late. Moira had already disappeared through the thickening smoke. He tried to get up and follow her but stumbled forward and fell painfully to the ground. His strength waning, he crawled towards the door—facedown in the dirt. He heard a galloping horse to his right and glanced up just in time to see a heavy staff coming at his head. There was a loud crack. The kitchen roof collapsed, and so did John.

CHAPTER THREE

Phoenix

John's eyes fluttered open. Reluctantly his body began to move. And then—

"Moira! William!" He jolted up to a sitting position. The intense pain in his chest and head forced him to fall back. He looked about frantically. He didn't recognize his surroundings, but soon realized that he was in the tack room behind the inn's stable. He was lying on the small cot where the stable boy sometimes slept, under an old blanket. His head throbbed. His newest friend, the large companion to the lady, slept sitting against the wall. He was dirty and spattered with dried blood. His sword lay bloodied beside him, and cradled to his chest, sound asleep, was the troublesome infant.

Just then, there came a muffled thud from outside. The warrior's eyes snapped open and he shot a glance in John's direction, then to the door. He got to one knee with great difficulty, and gently handed the baby to John. Then he raised a bloodied finger to his lips to hush anything John might have wanted to say. Pain molded the contours of the man's face, but there was something more, like the anger in the teeth of a hungry wolf. The instant John made eye contact, a chill went through him, and he knew that the nightmare was not over.

The man crept towards the door—his bloodstained sword poised high. Silently he waited, like a viper, for his prey to enter. John watched him, fearful of what lay beyond the door. The blood was pounding in his head, and he forced himself to take a breath. The baby stirred in his arms and began to fuss. John pulled the babe close to him and stuck the tip of his littlest finger into the babe's mouth.

The seconds beat on like hours. The large man's sword started to quiver. His arms trembled with exhaustion and anticipation.

Crash! The wall next to John burst into splinters, and a horse came through it. As it cleared the wall, John could see that the horse and its rider were wrapped in elegant armor of the blackest steel. John's companion whirled around to face the intruder and was knocked to the ground by the horse's strutting forelegs. The horse and rider nearly filled the small shack, leaving little room for maneuverability. The rider urged the steed to trample the downed warrior. The horse put one of its heavy hooves on the man's chest and drove him back to the ground. With great skill, the rider held the mount steady and prepared to spear their victim with a cruelly barbed lance. The lancer rose up and aimed at the man pinned under the beast's hoof.

The prone man struck up with his sword and pierced the soft under-side of the horse. It whinnied and reared up on its rear legs. The dark rider's head struck a ceiling beam with a thud. The rider went limp and dropped with a crash to the ground.

Blood poured from the horse's belly wound. Its legs buckled, and it went to its knees before rolling on to its side. There was a moment of silence, then the horse let out a labored breath.

With a rattle, the dismounted rider sat up and pulled off the dark helmet, revealing a beautiful woman with short, light hair and pointed ears. She shook her head as if dizzy, then scanned around her. Her large, almond-shaped eyes were violet in color and glowed slightly in the dim light. They narrowed as they came across the baby in John's arms. Slowly, she slithered towards the baby, while slipping her dagger from its sheath.

Her eyes never wandered from the child, and her movements were like liquid moonbeams. John was horrified and hypnotized by the approaching visage.

The baby let out a cry. Suddenly John came to his senses and reached up to stop the deadly blow. He struggled with the woman, using every ounce of his strength to push her back. His ribs shrieked with pain, but he held on to her wrists. John rolled the crying baby onto the cot and tumbled to the ground with the woman. John's friend managed to grab her and held down her dagger arm. The woman kneed John's ribs and rolled over on top of the other man. She grabbed his throat and tried to bring her dagger down to him. The blade came closer and closer to his face as she put her weight behind it. She released his throat momentarily and punched him in the chest, where her horse had trampled him. The large man winced at the pain but continued to hold her at bay. She redoubled her attack on his chest, and his strength began to falter. She brought her blade a mere hair's breadth from his eye, then suddenly she straightened as if she had given up. With a dreadful scream, she came down with the black dagger. The man's strength could not hold her back any longer, and the deadly blade found its mark in his chest. The large man let out a groan as he expired.

John knew that he was next for her blade, so he pulled himself up and prepared to defend himself, but the woman didn't move. She just lay there, with a hand on her dagger and her head on the large man's chest. John found the man's sword and approached her with caution. He struggled with the sword's weight as he put it to her side. He gave her a push and jumped back as she started to move. She rolled over and lay motionless next to her opponent. Then John saw it—there in her side, between the plates of her armor—John's new companion had managed to plant his own knife.

The man suddenly gasped. By some miracle he was still alive. John knelt beside him and cradled his head. The robust warrior lay dying in John's arms. He coughed weakly, and a small line of blood ran from one side of his mouth. His chest was wet with gore around the black dagger planted there. The stranger who had become John's friend looked groggily at him and tipped his head towards the weapon in his rib cage. John drew the blade from his body and disdainfully threw it to the floor. Again John's friend gasped, and his hand grasped his chest. He smiled faintly at John as his life's blood flowed through his fingers. He clumsily reached into his tunic. A moment later he held out a bloody hand to John, who clenched it. John felt something pressed between their hands as the large man weakly squeezed. John squeezed back strongly, reassuringly, hoping to comfort the dying man. The man wheezed, then his lips silently mouthed several words. John leaned forward and listened, as the warrior whispered his last breath into his ear.

"His noble mother's." He gave a light squeeze to John's hand.

John felt the man's grip slacken—his body went limp, and he knew that it was over. The stranger, his friend, was dead. He let his lifeless hand drop to his side and released the body gently to the floor. He closed the man's eyes and painfully stood to look down at the calm, still face and body. Somehow the man didn't seem so large anymore—a mere shadow of the great warrior—as if when life had left him, all that remained was a shell, which shrunk like a corn husk in the sun.

John felt something in his hand and, remembering, looked to see what the dying man had thought so important. *What was it he had said?* A small ring rested in John's blood-smeared palm. "His noble mother's?" John wiped the blood from his hand and the ring. He looked at it briefly and put it into his purse. He would have time to examine it later, or so he hoped. For now, he had more pressing matters to worry about.

Exhausted, John picked up the babe and stepped out of the shattered shack. As he rounded the corner of the stable, he saw the smoldering, charred ruins of the inn. He fell to his knees, nearly dropping the baby. Suddenly tears poured from his eyes. He squeezed the baby close as his body shook, and he rocked forward onto his forehead.

"Moira, Moira," he sobbed into the dirt. "William."

John rolled onto his back and stared at the dark sky. The valley was still. He wished he were dead.

At that moment, a cold drop of water struck his cheek, and it began to drizzle. He didn't move until the baby began to cry. He stared blankly at the child, then slowly dragged himself to his feet. He glanced once more at the remains of his inn and hurried back to the stable.

The woman's vigorous assault had damaged the roof of the shack, and now it was leaking, so he hid in one of the stalls and waited. He waited for another attack, for the rain to stop, for his heart to stop pounding, for his world to stop churning. He hoped that the ordeal was over, but as he started to fade into unconsciousness, he was haunted by the thought that it might never be over.

* * *

John awoke to the cry of the baby. He had been waking up to it about this same time every day since the baby had come to live with him. That fateful day when they first met was now a memory five months old. Some nights he lay awake, wetting his pillow with tears for his Moira and the child he had lost. The baby was the only thing that took John's mind off them.

The strange journal he had found on Sir Sedgemore, the large man who died protecting the babe, was little comfort. From reading its tale, John could gather little about the child's history. Sir Sedgemore, Lady Enaid – his compatriot – and the child's mother were all apparently members of some noble court, and the father of the child was their liege lord. John got the impression that there had been some long-standing hostility between the clans of the mother and father, but being so far removed from any such court, John had no idea of their nationalities or troubles. John's limited reading ability made it difficult, but as he worked through the story, it filled him with sorrow, loathing, and finally fear.

According to Sir Sedgemore:

"Directly after the child's birth, my lord was poisoned against his wife, that most fair of ladies, and mother of his only heir. This villainous deed was perpetrated by his newest adviser—his cousin. No doubt accomplished with the aid of sorcery. That beguiling serpent! May he burn eternally in the pit of Hell for it.

"I now know that my lord was driven to madness, and thus, forgetting his great love for her, slaughtered his dear wife. He would have done like to their son, had she not received premonitions that such a horrible thing might come to pass.

"On the eve of that most foul crime, she managed to spirit the child away with the aid of her most loyal friends, Lady Enaid and myself. She then stayed behind, buying her son's escape with her life.

"And now, though I am surely named 'traitor,' I know I have done only what was right! I shall uphold my vow to the child's mother. In so doing, may I better serve my lord. My only regret is that I may never see my beloved wife and son again."

"With no ships leaving Dyven, we are forced to find another means to escape Lyonesse. Perhaps in the Bay of Lions we will secure passage to Damnonia or Albion. I only hope we reach his mother's people before our hunters can catch us. May God grant us speed!"

They must have been far from home. King William would never allow such wicked feuding and sorcery in his kingdom.

The journal ended abruptly with never any mention of who the mother's people were, or even where they might be found. So John had no choice but to take in the child, whom he had pledged to protect.

John eventually accepted the risks that came with taking care of the child. His story for the village folk was that Moira had saved their son, William, from the fire but died when she attempted to rescue two guests.

All told, five people lost their lives in the raid: Moira, William, the stable boy, and two unfortunate travelers, but no one would ever know that his son had died. John alone would mourn the loss of his child but knew that it must be. He held a private funeral for Moira and secretly buried their son in her arms. He then planted two heartsease flowers, Moira's favorite, on the site.

The night of the raid, shortly after the rain stopped, John had hitched up a horse and taken the bodies of Sir Sedgemore and his slayer to a secluded wood far behind the inn. Slowed by his injuries, John was most of the night burying them. The woman's elegant armor and weapons evaporated with the first light of dawn, which caused him great discomfort even when she was under many stones. From that moment, John was constantly on the lookout for suspicious characters.

Still, all this trouble paled when compared with the love in his heart for the babe. Its seed had been planted from the very moment he had seen the child and was now in full blossom.

John had come to accept the child as his own and was starting over. He had a new son, and their new inn would be open to guests soon. He worked hard and watched it go up day by day, board by board. Now it was almost complete. In the same way, his love for the child had grown. At first, he had tried to blame the boy for the death of his family and to keep some distance between them, but it is folly for a man lost in a stormy sea to push away the one thing keeping his head above water. And so John clung to the child, and each day made the child dearer to him.

He came to the child's crib-side and picked him up. "Now, what is it, wee one? Hungry again, are we? Well, let's see what we've got in the kitchen."

John took the child and talked to him as he prepared the milk. "Well, my boy, soon this inn of ours will be open again, and you'll have to help the old man with some of the chores."

The babe looked up at him with an expression of puzzlement.

"Well, maybe not right away, mind ya, but soon as you learn to get your own milk." John paused a moment in contemplation then continued. "I've also been thinkin' about your name. Five months is a bit long to be callin' someone 'wee one.' I guess I've been waitin' for ya to tell me your name, but if I wait too long, you'll be complainin' over a tankard of ale that you haven't got one.

"My first son's name was William, after our good king, and for your safety, that is the name you must carry. I thought, to avoid any curses, I should call you by your Christian name, but alas I've no way of knowin' what that is. So, I guess I must christen you myself and hope for the best."

John dipped his thumb into the warm water and touched it to the baby's forehead, making the sign of the cross. "I christen you, William. I don't think my other William would mind. You two are like brothers now. Oh yes, I mustn't forget. Holy God, bless this child, William, and watch over him. Amen. Sorry, that's all the words I know.

"Next we'll christen this inn. Just think, a double christening. A new son and a new inn. The finest son and the finest inn in the whole bloomin' valley. What do ya think of that, William?" John chuckled and swung the baby in his arm. "I rather like the sound of that name. Why with a name like that, you should grow up big and strong. *If* ya drink all your milk. Now drink up."

CHAPTER FOUR

The Ring

The ring—his noble mother's—or so said Sir Sedgemore with his dying breath. The delirious ramblings of a dying man, or a friendly warning? Such were John's thoughts as he sat up, late at night, pondering the mysterious ring he rolled between his forefinger and thumb. It was a simple band, crafted in gold with a single small stone, looking much like a dewdrop resting on a leaf. The strange stone's iridescent rainbow of hues blended and shifted randomly in the light, mesmerizing the viewer. Save for the gem, it appeared quite plain—nothing more than an ordinary ring. But appearances, as they say, can be most deceiving—deceiving in a way that John was just beginning to realize.

The ring had been in his possession since Sedgemore placed it in his hand. From that time, strange dreams and nightmares plagued his sleep—visions of creatures with dirty near-human faces, childlike grins, and large black eyes, like deer. Their grubby long-fingered hands would touch him, pinch him, cling to him, poke and prod him. They probed his flesh—his very essence—for something unknown, something alien. Some of the hands recoiled shyly when they touched him, others caressed him kindly, and still more went on probing, never seeming to find what they were looking for. This would go on and on until John's mind could not bear another second of the smothering hands on his flesh. He would bolt up-right and find himself alone in his bed. A lingering presence, like eyes upon him, was always there to greet him. Often he would panic and jump up to check on his son, sleeping in his crib across the room. At times he allowed himself to fall asleep in the rocking chair with the boy still in his arms. He would awaken and hold the baby close, looking into the dark corners of the room. He didn't know what he was looking for, but always he would find the ring nearby.

This night was such a night, and, as usual, John found himself alone in his kitchen with the ring. It seemed to him that the ring was somehow responsible for his nightmares, but he could not rid himself of it. He hid it away in his handkerchiefs, afraid to let anyone see it, only to find it, some days later, back in his purse or on the table. More disturbing than this was his son's dependence on the ring. Without the ring, John could not calm the boy when his crying fits came; however, with the ring, William would be calmed immediately, even if sick with fever. The ring worked like a charm—like magic! In fact John suspected it was magic, even though a traveling priest had told him not to believe in such "poppycock and superstition." Yet there was no denying the strange presence emanating from the ring. It was a strong presence, so strong in fact that John sometimes spoke aloud to the ring.

"What do you want of me?" he would ask the ring out of frustration. "I'm takin' good care of the boy, now leave me alone!"

Then he would put the ring back into its hiding place, and for several nights thereafter, perhaps a fortnight, he would sleep easy. No alien creatures invaded his sleep.

But on this night, John didn't ask the ring any questions or make any promises. He didn't speak to the ring at all. He only contemplated the ring. The stretches of peaceful rest had grown shorter and shorter, and now John's mind began to unravel. A thought formed in his head: the thought of ridding himself of the odious ring forever. He didn't care what magical powers it had. He wanted sleep.

John took the ring and, donning a hat and cloak, went out into the cold winter night. He trudged across the muddy snow to the stable and took a shovel and pick from the wall in the tool room. Without hesitation, he marched out into the woods, the snow crunching under his feet.

He walked into the white frosted forest until he lost sight of the inn. The wood looked very different wearing its winter cloak. The only familiar features were his own footprints in the snow.

He leaned the shovel against the trunk of an ancient yew and broke ground beneath the snow with his pick. He shoveled and picked at the nearly frozen ground until his hands were raw and a sizable hole was before him. He then took the ring from his purse and dropped it unceremoniously into its freshly dug grave.

"Good-bye! William won't be needin' ya any longer. I am his father, and mother now!" With that, he placed a large stone over the ring and covered up the hole, packing it firmly with his shovel.

John turned around, suddenly feeling as if he were being watched. A rocky outcropping protruded from the snowbank across from him. He stiffened when he recognized it as the grave of Sir Sedgemore.

"Sorry, old friend, but it's better this way."

John kicked snow over his recent excavation. Then he nodded to Sir Sedgemore and strolled towards home, feeling a great burden lifted from his shoulders.

Halfway home, he got the notion that he better hurry, as he'd been gone from the inn for quite a while, and William might need him. Besides, it was cold out, and he wanted to be in front of a warm fire.

John arrived home, shivering with cold, to find his baby boy sleeping as peacefully as he'd left him. Seeing that all was well, he went to the commons room of the inn and started a large fire. Warming himself before the blaze, he looked at the ceiling, above which his guests quietly slept; blissfully unaware of his troubles and dreaming pleasant dreams, no doubt. He smiled and stopped shivering. Taking a deep, relaxing breath, he began to make preparations for breakfast.

As John measured out flour for his famous biscuits, he heard William stir in their room. He put aside his cooking and went up to see what had caused his son to awaken.

William lay in the crib, blinking and rubbing his puffy little eyes and frowning as if he were about to cry. Swiftly, John went to the child and gathered him up in his arms.

"What is it, William?" He felt for wet diapers. "No. Not wet diapers. Humph? Are ya hungry, my boy? No? What is it then?"

Then John realized that the boy was at ease, and the fit had been averted. Perhaps his son had only wanted some attention. Joyfully, he gave his son a loving hug and placed him back in the crib.

"I've got to go downstairs. I'll be right back with some warm milk! Won't that be nice?"

Triumphantly, John left the boy and went back to the kitchen. He had quieted the boy, and he had done it without the ring! He was very pleased with himself and proud of his baby boy.

He still hadn't lit the stove for breakfast, as it was early yet. He needed a fire in the stove to warm his son's milk, so without any further delay he went to the stove and prepared kindling and wood to light. But where were the lighting splints? He looked around the kitchen and didn't see any. Out of habit, he reached into his belt pouch. A sudden chill went through his body. It started at his fingers and went up his arm, filling him up with bitter cold. His fingers fumbled around in his purse, feeling the object they had found there unexpectedly. It was round and hard and oh-so-very cold.

John reluctantly removed his clenched fist from the pouch and held it in front of his face. He opened his hand cautiously, as if opening a bear trap. In the center of his quivering palm sat the ring. John sank down into his frame, like a scarecrow.

The ring? Hadn't he buried it in the hole? Perhaps he had buried something else by mistake. John blinked very deliberately in an attempt to wipe away the image. The stone stared up at him like a small glaring eye. He felt its icy, disapproving stare and threw it into the stove with disgust. It rattled around and came to rest in the ash pit.

"Confound you!" He shouted into the stove and slammed its heavy iron door.

Suddenly he remembered where he had left the splints. With purpose he went into the commons room and over to the fireplace where a blaze was still burning brightly. He took a splint from the mantel, lit it in the fire, and marched back to the kitchen with the intention of melting down the cursed ring.

He found the ring in the ashes and lit the fire, making sure the ring would be in the hottest part. Surely fire would melt the soft gold band, or at least shatter the stone. He watched the fire swallow up the object of his fears before he closed the stove door with a sigh of relief.

For the second time that night, John felt as if a burden had been lifted. However, this time, he wasn't completely convinced that his troubles with the ring were over. He quickly opened the door of the stove and peered inside. He looked into the flames until his eyes verified that the ring lay just where he'd left it.

"I'll not be tricked by ya twice!" He watched for a moment more and then, satisfied, closed the stove and continued to prepare milk for his infant son.

* * *

When John had finished feeding William, he began tending to the breakfast needs of his guests, who would be rising very soon. Some eggs, a slab of bacon, dried fruit from the cellar, ale and water, and of course his valley-renowned breakfast biscuits. He hurried through most of it, spending a majority of his time to ensure the perfection of his biscuits. He had all but forgotten the night's occurrences by the time he was setting the banquet table in the commons room.

As he went to set a goblet at the last place on the table, he felt a small stab of pain in his chest. It intensified, instantly becoming a searing pain over his heart. He smelled his flesh burning. It was as if someone were branding him. Dropping the goblet, his hand went to his chest, and it too was burned. Instinct took over, and John tore open his tunic, baring his chest. He heard a tinkling sound on the floor and looked down. To his astonishment, he saw the ring, spinning there like a top. It seemed to be laughing at him, and then it rattled to a stop at his feet. John stepped back from the ring. He couldn't believe his eyes. His senses were numb. Even the pain in his chest stopped, and he shuffled, like an automaton, over to the copper mirror on the far side of the hall. He examined his reflection in the metal, as if he were a ghost looking at his former self. Surely this sort of thing didn't happen in the real world! Was he dreaming? Was the ring haunting his sleep again? Had the whole night's activities been nothing but shadows in his mind? And what of now? Was he still in the world of dreams?

Dazed, John let his eyes wander from his face. He looked at his bared chest and saw a small circle there. Instantly the pain returned. Realizing that he was not dreaming, he took a closer look. Over his heart, a small circular shape blistered up, split by the scar Sir Sedgemore's sword had given him nearly a year before.

"My oath."

He turned and walked back to where the ring lay on the floor. "So, we are to be bound together in this."

John stooped over and picked up the ring between his fingers. It felt warm to his touch, but it no longer burned him. "Very well, if it's for *his* good, I accept!"

John slipped the ring onto the leather thong where he kept the inn's master key and tucked it into his tattered shirt. The ring felt surprisingly good to John, hanging around his neck. He smiled and went about his business a new man.

CHAPTER FIVE

Growing Time

W illiam, drink your milk!"

It was a familiar statement, and one that John had made many times in the past ten years. Usually the boy complied without any argument, but today he looked earnestly at his father and asked, "Why?"

John, not noticing the look, answered traditionally. "Because, it'll help ya grow up, good and strong."

"Oh, I'm never gonna grow up!"

John, now aware that this was serious, looked at his son. "What is it, William?"

"Nathan said that when he grows up he's gonna go to the king's court in Nyraval, and be knighted. Well, I said that I wanted to be a knight too, just like the ones you tell me stories about at bedtime. He just laughed, and everyone else laughed too. He said that I was a runt, and they don't let runts become knights. And they all laughed again."

John was next to Billy now, and he put his arms around him. The boy turned a tearful face to his father's chest and sobbed.

"I'm not like them, Father. Somehow ... I don't belong here."

"Everyone grows up in his own time, William. You're just takin' your time in doin' it. 'sides, the best measure of a knight isn't the size of his armor, but the size of his heart. I'm sure our good King William knows that, and if someday ya go to his court, he'll see what a good boy you are and know you're worthy to be one of his noble knights."

"Just like Sir Sedgemore, Father?"

"Yes, like him."

John pondered over his decision to tell Billy about Sir Sedgemore. Perhaps that would not be such a good name to know, if the wrong ears happened to be listening.

There was a great deal of disturbing talk these days. The rumormongers insinuated that King William had lost his mind after the death of his queen, and now his health was failing. As the king had no children, there was no obvious heir to the throne. War was a palpable likelihood. Forces outside and within the kingdom shifted and stirred. And as if this wasn't enough, crops, which had always been plentiful in Lyonesse, were on a steady decline, while visits from tax collectors had become more frequent.

There were whispers of yet another war with Gwythia, of secret meetings in the forest, of goblins and boggles staring in the bedroom windows of children, and of the Night Queen—a mysterious lady in dark armor, who haunted the crossroads by night. People had become distrustful of strangers, believing the countryside to be filled with spies and malicious faeries. This once restful kingdom had changed.

A sudden panic erupted in John's stomach, like he hadn't felt in many years. His eyes became hazy as he focused on that earlier time. He wondered if there might still be enemies lurking about, waiting to take away his boy. He felt ashamed that he had been so careless.

"What is it, Father?"

"Oh, it's nothin'. I just remembered somethin'—something that I had forgotten to do."

"What is it, Father? Can I help?"

"No, Son. Have you finished with your chores?"

"Yes, Father."

"Then perhaps you should practice your readin'."

"But ..." Billy picked up the wooden sword he had set down under the table.

"But nothin'! A knight must know readin' as well as swordplay, Sir William. You don't want to grow up to be as ignorant as your old father, now do ya?"

"No, sir!"

John gave the boy a puckish "dark look," and Billy eyed him back. They stared at each other like two drunken sailors and wrinkled up their noses.

"Soooo," John said in his best pirate voice, "ye callin' yer old man ignorant now, air ye?"

"Welll," Billy, said imitating his father, "I – What ye gonna do about it?"

"I ought t' skewer ya alive, ye old sea dog."

"Go ahead and try it, ye old sea dog."

At this, John picked up a rolling pin from the table and playfully thrust it at Billy. "Prepare to meet yer doo-oo-oom, Cap'n Billy."

"Prepare to meet yer doo-oo-oom."

And the battle was on. The two laughed as they fenced their way through the kitchen and out into the yard. Finally, as was the usual outcome of such skirmishes, the younger stood triumphant over his father, foot atop chest, sword pointed downward towards his cowering foe.

John went into another of Billy's favorite spiels. "Oh please, brave and noble knight, spare me and I'll promise to be a good dragon from now on."

"Do ya promise to never burn down another village?"

"I do, I do!"

"Do ya promise to never eat any more children?"

"I do, I do!"

"An' no more princesses!"

"Well ... no."

"Then I slay you dragon, in the name of King William!"

With this, Sir William thrust at the dragon, who died a suitably melodramatic death, complete with stiff limbs and death rattle. However, unlike most fairy tales, the dragon got back up and requested that the noble knight go practice his reading skills. The knight heaved a sigh of disappointment and left the battlefield for his studies.

John watched his son walk into their inn through the kitchen door. A quiet evening breeze came up from behind him. He quickly looked over his shoulder towards the thickly wooded hollow and fingered the ring under his shirt. It was a warm summer night, but a strange chill went through him as he scanned the trees. Were there any eyes hidden amongst the peaceful yews? What of the guests who stayed at his inn? How many of them might be spies? Assassins?

John scurried back to the kitchen as the sun started its final act of the day. The curtain of night would soon fall upon the Valley of the Yew and while most of the simple folk found comfort after a long day's toil, John endured the return of his familiar disquiet. The lengthening shadows played nasty games with his imagination, turning even the familiar into dark, skulking fiends.

A Jester Borne

C*rash!*
The rafters of The Valley's Finest Inn resounded with laughter as the many guests looked up from their evening meal to behold their newly adopted mascot and waiter facedown in a pile of victuals and dirty dishes.

Billy, his face smeared with gravy, looked up at the unusually well-dressed mob of patrons. They pointed and jeered at him. Some of them spewed or sprayed food from their mouths uncontrollably. Still others covered their mouths to whisper with neighbors between laughs. Billy didn't have to guess at what they were saying to one another. He had been the butt of an endless stream of practical jokes since their arrival, and this latest tripping was only another prank. Billy, dazzled by all the fancy clothing and talk, took this behavior as just another eccentricity of court life and etiquette.

The Earl of Wyneddham's contingent of guests had been in residence at the inn for three days. They arrived in the late afternoon and demanded each and every room, vacant or not. Their intention was to "just stay the night," or so they said. This being the return trip from a May Day festival in Penwyth, they quickly became involved in their usual courtly excesses. Their capacities for food and drink were bottomless, and their vices innumerable. They were up at all hours playing various "parlor games," placating the earl and countess, gossiping about fellow courtiers, boasting, gambling, joking, lying, swearing, and scheming. Then, of course, there were the "three W's" without which no court is complete: Wooing Wanton Wenches.

At any rate, Billy found himself the focus of their fancy, and as usual he was facedown on the floor. As he picked himself up, the rabble started to applaud. Billy didn't know what to do. He stood uncomfortably with gravy dripping off his face, too stunned to move. Without knowing why, he bowed to the mob. They applauded louder still. Billy oddly enjoyed their perverse adoration, and to show his appreciation he made his bow deep and theatrical. But alas when he reached the bottom of his ridiculous bow, he slipped in the gravy and wound up on the floor again. The nobles laughed until many had tears. Billy hid behind his tray and scurried off to the kitchen amid the tumult, which had exploded in the commons room.

John was at the kitchen table, busily preparing pies, when Billy burst in. Billy's eyes and gravy-smeared face were red. He ran to the washbasin and fell over it with his tray. John watched him carefully. He couldn't see Billy's face, but he could see by his wincing shoulders that he was crying. It was the way he cried when he wanted to be left alone, after the other children had teased him. But it had been many years since children had teased him. In fact, even though he was small for his age, it had been a long time since anyone from the valley had mistaken him for a child.

Billy was now a young man; at least by village standards. Most often he showed the wisdom of his years and was even, from time to time, quite insightful. Just the same, there was something juvenile about him. His temperament and good humor seldom led anyone to believe that he had any worries, and he was always able to see things from a childlike point of view. Some claimed this was due to his diminutive height, while others said that "living alone, all those years, with *that father* of his" was the cause of his youthful nature. Amid all this speculation, none could deny that he was the most helpful and likable of fellows.

However, it's hard for a fellow not to take it personally when someone he's just met doesn't like him. Such was often the case with Billy. It seemed there was always some guest or another who would look down on Billy, simply because they could look down on him.

This latest string of practical jokes from the earl's party was no different. It was just that there was no end to them. Usually pranksters grew tired of the jokes after a short while, but these grand lords and ladies had equally grand appetites for cruelty.

John started to say something but bit back his angry tongue. He knew Billy's moods and knew that he could say nothing that would bring ease to his son's troubled mind. And so they worked in silence—Billy on his dirty dishes and John on his pies.

Suddenly Billy blurted out, "I thought lords and ladies were supposed to be …" He couldn't finish.

John just nodded in silent agreement.

"How long do you think they'll stay, Father?"

"I don't know, William. Perhaps when the ale runs dry. I thought they would have left days ago."

"We do need the business."

"Not as much as all that. In fact, I could use a rest from all this. But they seem to have found something about the inn which makes them want to stay."

"It is a fine inn, Father."

"Aye, but there are finer inns, as I've told you – nearer ya go to the cities."

John and Billy stood in the kitchen, both secretly wishing that their invaders would find the heart to move on, both wondering what could possibly be making them stay.

"Perhaps it's your cookin', Father."

John smiled, knowing that his cooking was little more than passable for these fine lords and ladies. "Perhaps you've got two new lumps on your head."

Billy, still working with the dishes, heard a peculiar sound from behind him. He wasn't sure, but it sounded like a muffled laugh—a snigger to be precise. He heard it again and turned to see what could be causing his father's mirth. With the face of the devil himself, John half danced to the cupboard and retrieved a small jar.

Billy watched curiously as his father liberally sprinkled the pies with the contents of the jar. He wondered what could have caused John to take on such a jocular disposition so suddenly. John circled the kitchen table in a sort of dance, which reminded Billy of the spring festival dances in the village. He turned and skipped and sprinkled some more on the pies, making sure not to miss a single one, all the time humming a simple tune that Billy couldn't quite place.

"Shall we serve the pies, now?" asked John, filled with exaggerated pomp. He then picked up one of the trays and proceeded to take it into the commons room. Billy, still stunned by his father's performance, picked up the other pie tray, put on a brave face, and followed his father.

The rabble had quieted down from their last outburst, and so when John announced, to the lords and ladies that the dessert was "served," an audible "ah" was all that was heard.

"What delicacy do you serve us this night, innkeeper?" the earl asked.

"It's an old family recipe, milord."

"What is it, man?"

"It's called strawberry surprise pie, milord."

Billy knit his eyebrows. *That's strange, I don't remember any "old family recipe" for "strawberry surprise pie." In fact, I don't remember Father baking any kind of strawberry pie before.*

The earl interrupted Billy's thought. "Well, serve it, lad!"

Billy began to serve the pies to the guests, giving each their generous helping and even managing to smile as they took it. John was busy doing the same; only Billy had never seen him serve food with such enthusiasm. John was really enjoying himself as he served them and asked each to "eat up in good health."

Finally, Billy came to the man who had previously tripped him. He stared the large man in the face as he took his pie and grunted his approval. The man never said anything, but Billy watched him and his long feet. The woman next to the man saw Billy's precautions and smiled. Billy saw her smile and returned it gladly. He offered her some pie, which she politely declined, but as he passed, she leaned out and whispered in his ear.

"Don't mind him. He's just drunk – again!"

Billy looked at her smooth fair face and saw that she spoke earnestly. Of course Billy had seen her face before, but he hadn't noticed how kind her eyes were.

"Yes, milady," he said with a grin.

Billy finished serving his pies with a newfound hope. At last he had met someone of this court whom he thought was worthy of being called a lady—the kind of fine lady his father had told him tales about.

When Billy got back to the kitchen, he found his father bubbling over with good humor. He hummed while cleaning the kitchen, occasionally taking a few dance steps. For a man of his years, he showed surprising energy.

While Billy didn't consider his father aged by any means, he did find this sudden outburst of energy out of character. It had been some time since he saw John act in such a manner. The last time was on the occasion of a surprise birthday celebration for Billy. His curiosity was growing, but rather than ask, he decided to let his father enjoy himself and wait until he said something.

They worked together in the kitchen for a long while: Billy quiet and somber, John humming and jaunty, neither saying anything to the other. Occasionally some of John's mirth rubbed off on Billy, and he joined in, but then he would stop and wonder why he had been humming.

Finally Billy's curiosity got the better of him, and he exploded. "Father?"

"Um-hum," John hummed in acknowledgment.

"Father?"

"Yes, what is it?" John answered half singing.

"That's what I was goin' to ask you."

"What do ya mean?"

"What's gotten into you?"

John stopped his humming and looked at Billy. Then he smiled. "I just had a premonition … that our glorious guests will be leavin' us soon."

"And that would please you, Father?"

"Well, let's just say that even a fine meal can get caught in one's bowels for too long. The trick is to flush it out." With that said, John let out a laugh.

Billy cocked his head to one side and looked up at his father. "And how do you know that they'll be leavin'?"

"Because …" John paused for a moment, searching for the right words. "Because I couldn't possible top my strawberry surprise pies."

Suddenly a spark of an idea went off in Billy's head. He held the spark for a moment, encouraging it to grow.

"What's the surprise, Father?"

"Ah, that comes in the mornin'." John grinned, broad and sharp as a butcher's knife.

Suddenly the spark Billy held in his mind ignited his thoughts, and he walked briskly to the cupboard for final enlightenment. There, amongst the numerous clay jars of handpicked herbs and spices, was the jar his father had used when he sprinkled the pies. It was an old jar, and one that was seldom used. Billy remembered that it was usually on the back of the shelf, but since his father had done most of the cooking all his life, he couldn't remember what was in it. He got a footstool and reached up to grab the jar from the shelf. He lowered the jar and read the hand-painted label. The name was familiar enough to him, but he still couldn't place it. He looked over to his father who was watching him with his arms crossed and the same knowing smile on his face. He lifted the lid and smelled the now-empty jar. The memory of the herb came flying back into his mind.

His face went white, and his eyes grew to the size of goose eggs. He looked up again at his father. Then his mouth opened as if to say something, but his jaw just kept on opening until it had dropped as far as it would go. He let out a gasp.

"Why, what is it, my son?"

Billy answered, still stupefied by his father. "Ya didn't."

"I did."

"You didn't!"

"You saw me."

"You did!" Billy put his hand over his eyes. Slowly he slid his hand down over his face, and a small, nearly undetectable grin peeked out around the corners of his mouth. He pursed his lips together to stop from smiling, but then his eyes darted about quickly, and John could see the fire sparkling bright within them. Suddenly Billy laughed through his nose, making grunting sounds like a pig. His lips quivered uncontrollably and then drew apart, the ends curving up in a fashion that would cause rocks to crack open in smiles. Then he looked again into the jar.

Billy remembered the last time his father had dipped into this jar. He was very deliberate with its contents, only using a tiny pinch to create his home remedy for constipation.

"A whole jar, Father?"

"Well, I ..." John finished his sentence with a shrug.

The two innkeepers laughed and then started into their chores, each of them smiling and humming. Before they knew it, the guests had finished their dinner, and all they had remaining were a few dirty dishes.

"I'll finish up, Father."

"That's fine, Son. I'll just see to any last requests from our guests."

"Have they all retired for the evening?"

"As much as this crowd ever does. Well, g'night, Son."

"G'night, Father."

Billy turned back around to his pail of dirty dishes and continued to clean. He couldn't help but hum to himself. As he finished the last of the dishes, he said, "It's amazing how fast the chores get done when one really enjoys one's work."

The next morning, there was a surprisingly small contingent in the commons room.

"It seems that the majority of the earl's entourage are not at all themselves this morning" was all that the earl's physician would say. Shortly thereafter, he too was not feeling at all himself and had to make a dash to the back of the inn.

Much to Billy's delight, the lady with the kind eyes was there and had more pleasant conversation for him. She told him many things about court life. She talked about grand feasts and elaborate celebrations in great old halls of stone. Within minutes, they were chatting and laughing like lifelong friends.

Billy hung on every word and learned many things about her. She was the Lady of Cyndyn Hall and a distant cousin of the king. The unpleasant man who had tripped Billy was, unfortunately, her husband.

"You should see him at home, away from this lot – when he's sober – he's much more courteous then."

"I'd like that, milady."

"Well, yes. I'd like to see it more often myself. Perhaps when you come to Dyven you can visit our home?"

The lady's statement took him by surprise. Had she really invited him to visit her? She had said it, but did she really mean it? He looked again into her kind eyes and knew that she had spoken earnestly, even if she had spoken lightly.

"What is it, William?"

"I – I don't think that will be possible, milady Cyndyn."

She laughed. "Oh please, call me Lady Myrredith. Lady Cyndyn is only a title, and Cyndyn Hall is a great distance from here."

"Yes, mi—Lady Myrredith. And won't you please call me Billy? Everyone else does."

"Oh no. As I said before, you look far too much like a William to me. Now, why don't you think it will be possible to visit me next time you go to Dyven?"

"Well, that's just it, mi—Lady Myrredith. I don't think I'll be goin' to the city."

"Why not?"

"Because, I've never gone."

"Never?"

"No—never, milady."

"My dear boy, whyever not? I should think a clever young man like yourself would do well to go to the city."

"But how would I go? What would I do? Where would I stay?"

"Don't be ridiculous, William. I've already invited you to stay with me. I would take care of everything."

"But how would I get there?"

"Well … You could leave with us."

"But, I—"

"Enough buts, William."

Billy stopped dead in his tracks. "I'm sorry, milady."

Lady Myrredith put her finger under his chin, raised his head, and looked him straight in the eyes. "I can't get over how familiar you look. Especially when you pout. Well, that's of no consequence. It's decided. You shall leave with us on the morrow and visit us at Cyndyn Hall."

Billy's head was spinning. At long last his childhood dream of going to the city and seeing all its wondrous spectacles was about to come true. And to be visiting a lady of the court in her home! Why, surely that was the most anyone could ever hope for.

"On the morrow?"

"Yes, William. We are planning to leave for home in the morning."

"I must tell my father!" Abruptly, Billy's beaming face fell into a look of defeat. "My father."

Lady Myrredith saw Billy's sudden disappointment and concern. "Your father can run things for a short time, while you're gone. Let me speak with him, William."

Billy looked at her and forced a smile. "No. Thank you, Lady Myrredith. I think I had better talk to him."

* * *

Once John made up his mind about something, he was a granite wall. So when Billy tried to convince him that the pretty courtier's intentions were honorable, it was not easy going. As Billy's enthusiasm chiseled away each of John's arguments, they became sharper, until all he was saying— or rather shouting—was "No, no, no!"

Billy couldn't understand his father's obstinacy. He only knew that in his heart he had always longed to go to the city.

"I'm never going to leave here. Am I, Father?"

"Is it so bad here?"

"No, Father." Billy shuffled toward the door.

"Wait," John said as Billy pushed on the door. "I don't think it'll do any good, but ... perhaps I should talk with this Lady Myrredith, before she tries to run off with the best dragon slayer in the realm."

"Father!"

"I'm not making any promises, mind you."

"Yes, Father."

"Well, where is she?"

"She's gone to the stables, Father."

John started for the back door with Billy following. John turned around and looked his son squarely in the eye. "You wait here." He then walked out the door and closed it behind him.

Billy peeked through the door as John walked to the stables and approached Lady Myrredith. She was riding a beautiful brown palfrey that pawed the ground eagerly. John gave her a curt bow, and she dismounted. They stood by the horse talking for what felt like hours. In fact it was only a few minutes, but Billy was still a child when it came to time.

Occasionally one of them would pet the magnificent mount, and at times they even seemed to be discussing it. John put his hand to his chest, a gesture Billy recognized as a sign that he was deliberating over something important. Lady Myrredith nodded and smiled.

Billy stayed at the door the entire time they talked. Lady Myrredith caught him watching them and gave him a reassuring smile before returning her attention to John. Oh how he wished he could hear what they were saying, but alas all he could do was watch and keep his fingers crossed.

Finally John gave Lady Myrredith a curt bow, excused himself, and walked back to the kitchen. Billy couldn't see her expression, so he studied his father intently as he approached. He could see that John was still fondling the front of his shirt, pondering something.

Quickly, Billy backed away from the door and busied himself with straightening the dishes. When his father walked through the door, Billy looked up nonchalantly. John's fingers tightly crimped his shirtfront; his eyes were focused on the floor, and his face was pale, but stern.

John saw Billy, and his expression became neutral. Billy recognized this as his gambling face—an expression no one in the valley could penetrate, not even Billy. Then John's expression settled into one of resignation.

"William, I've talked to Lady Myrredith and I've thought it over ... but I can't let you go."

"What? But why?"

"I can't explain right now. There are many things—"

"You never let me go anywhere." Billy was nearly in tears. "I've always had a longin' for the city! I get this one chance in a lifetime and you ... You've never understood!"

Tears started to flow down Billy's face, and he turned to run for the door. John futilely called after him. Billy rushed by all the startled guests in the commons room and didn't stop until he was in his room, lying on his bed.

By suppertime, Billy's pillow was soaked with tears, and he was all cried out. He got up lethargically and plodded downstairs to help his father with his usual chores.

Billy hardly gave his father a glance as they worked in silence. Conversely, John repeatedly had to drag his eyes away from his son in order to prepare the meal. Fortunately, there were few guests interested in an evening meal, and so there were relatively few chores to complete.

Billy retired to his room without a word to his father. The night passed slowly, as it will when one cannot sleep. Billy's mind still churned with thoughts of his depressingly boring future as an innkeeper, forever stuck in the Valley of the Yew.

He got up from his bed and went to the window. The moon shone brightly in the sky, painting the court between the inn and stables with blue light and purple shadows. He looked up and caught a falling star crossing the horizon.

"Star light, star bright, first star ere I see tonight ... Oh, what's the use. I've made that same wish every time, and nothin' ever happens."

At that moment, Billy heard the back door to the kitchen open and close and saw his father crossing to the stables. The yellow light from John's lantern surrounded him in a pale hallow, keeping the purple shadows at bay until the stable door had closed behind him.

Movement from the corner of the courtyard caught Billy's attention. He focused on it and saw the figure of a cloaked man skulking in the shadows on the stable wall. The man crept towards the large doors and stopped. He cast his eyes about the court suspiciously then slipped through the door like milk from a pitcher.

***

John was busy pitching hay into the stalls when the dark man entered the stable behind him. A sudden chill ran through him, and he straightened. John felt the ring go cold under his shirt and turned around as the man entered the light of his lantern.

From his high, soft boots to the hood on his cloak, the man was smothered in deep brown. He pushed back the hood and opened his cloak, revealing oily black and silver ringlets of curly hair that framed his long, angular face and the leather armor that sheathed his lean body. A bulge in the side of his cloak betrayed the presence of a weapon hanging on his hip. However, it was his bulging dark eyes that triggered John's memory and sent another chill through him.

John put on a smile. "What can I do for ya, sir?"

"You don't remember me, do you, John?"

"Aye, sir. You're here with the earl's party. Sir Banarel, isn't it?"

The man thoughtfully stroked the closely cropped mustache below his bony nose and the tiny triangle of beard that separated his thin lower lip and apple-like chin. He took another step closer. "I mean, you don't remember me from before."

"You were to the inn before, sir?"

"Aye, quite a number of years ago. Fifteen years to be exact."

"Please forgive me, sir, but my memory isn't what it used to be."

Sir Banarel took another step towards John. "I thought my visit would have left more of an impression on you. It was the day your inn burned down."

Banarel closed the gap between them. He thrust out his hand and shoved John back against the tack wall. He pinned him there with his left hand and instantly produced a dagger with his right. He then held the dagger to John's throat and leaned into him.

"No one called me sir in those days, only Banarel. Now tell me, John," he whispered, "I know that Sedgemore doubled back on us. Did he come back here?"

"I don't know who you're talk—"

Banarel thrust the tip of his dagger harder against John's throat. "I'd like to believe you, John. I really would, but the fact is, I'm still working for the same employer, and my employer told me not to believe you when you denied knowing Sedgemore. We know you knew him. When I killed

Lady Enaid and wounded him, he doubled back, didn't he? Now tell me, did Sedgemore come back here?"

John remembered the brave and beautiful Lady Enaid. The thought that the man before him had murdered her enraged him. "You know so much, how come you don't know—"

Again Banarel applied pressure to his dagger. John winced and stretched up on his tiptoes but couldn't escape its sharp point.

"You obviously don't know whom you're dealing with, John—the powers involved." Banarel looked around before continuing in a whisper. "His black magic works its way inside your head, calls on evil spirits, summons things a man can only wish were nightmares. He knows almost everything, sees almost everything. But you needn't be concerned with that. All you need know is that I have my blade to your throat, and I will kill you, if you don't help me."

John heard a hint of desperation in Banarel's voice when he said "help." He stared into the man's eyes, but the fleeting moment of weakness had been quickly erased by icy intent.

"This is your last chance, John. Did he come back here?"

John took a deep breath. "No."

Banarel went nose to nose with John and eyeballed him. "I'm sorry, John," he whispered, "but I think you're lying."

John felt the man lean into him and the dagger starting to cut. Suddenly Banarel cried out and jumped back. He examined his hand then quickly grabbed John's shirt again.

"What's that? What's in your shirt?"

John smelled burned flesh and looked down to see a faint glow from under his shirt. He couldn't help but smile.

"It's nothin'."

"Take it out!"

Reluctantly, John pulled on the thong around his neck. The master key to the inn and the ring appeared, and he let them drop to his chest.

"Ya see, it's nothin'."

Banarel's eyes widened and he gasped. "The ring!"

John said nothing but glanced around for a way out.

"You've had it all these years." Banarel lifted the leather strap with the tip of his dagger and examined the ring. "Then Sedgemore must be dead. And you … you know where the boy is!"

*

At that precise moment, Billy came through the stable door. He saw John pinned up against the wall by the cloaked man. "Father!"

A high-pitched hum emanated from the ring, and it began to glow. It shot towards Billy until it reached the end of the thong and vibrated there, tugging against its tether. A second later, the thin strap snapped, and the ring flew across the stable to Billy. Billy reached out to catch it, but instead of landing in his palm, it landed on his finger.

All three of them stared at the ring as it rested on Billy's finger, glowing and singing its shrill note. Billy examined it and recognized it as his mother's ring, but he had never seen it glow before! It frightened him.

"This must be my lucky day," Banarel said. "I get the ring, and the—"

Before Sir Banarel could finish, John stabbed the rogue's foot with his pitchfork. He followed this up with a swift kick to the groin and a shove, which sent him into the opposite wall.

Banarel gritted his teeth and glared at John. "You shouldn't have done that, old man." He leaned against the wall for support. "Now I'm really going to make you pay."

Just then, a horseshoe from the wall clunked down on Banarel's head, crossing his eyes. He wavered for a moment before the second shoe struck. Then he fell to his knees as the last two shoes hit the floor.

Banarel held his head and stared at them with one eye squeezed shut.

"Come on, Father." Billy grabbed John and pulled him towards the door.

Showing amazing fortitude, Banarel jumped to his feet and charged after them. John turned and held out his pitchfork. He caught the man square in the chest, but not before Banarel had thrown his dagger.

The weapon sliced through the air at Billy, who instinctively closed his eyes and held up his hand before his face. There was a sound, like the clank of a broken bell, as the dagger struck the ring on Billy's hand and fell harmlessly to the floor.

Billy opened his eyes and saw the dagger at his feet. He blinked twice then looked up as his father pushed Banarel back with the pitchfork.

Sir Banarel stumbled backward towards the nearest stall. His thighs caught the gate-rope and he flapped his arms for a moment, then flipped over the rope into the stall. A moment later, the horse inside whinnied, and Banarel sailed back over the rope, landing facedown on the floor.

Father and son started to make a run for it, however John looked back over his shoulder as he reached the door. Sir Banarel was not moving, and so John stopped. He watched a moment longer, then, sure that the man had been subdued, gave a quick, sharp whistle in Billy's direction.

Billy stopped halfway to the kitchen and spun to look at his father. "What?" he whispered.

John looked back into the stable, then back to Billy. "I think he's out."

Billy scanned around the courtyard then shrugged to his father. "Where is he?"

"No, not out-out; knocked out. He's just lying on the floor."

Billy and his father crept back into the stable and approached Banarel. The knight remained still—too still.

John finally bent down and placed his hand on the man's back. He shook him, then kneeled and placed his ear to the man's chest.

Billy watched his father and the door. Torn between staying and running, he settled for quaking with an occasional baby step towards the exit. His eye caught the dagger on the floor, and he picked it up. Now, a tiny bit braver, he stepped back towards his father.

John straightened suddenly, and Billy jumped back. "Come, Father!" He held out the dagger in front of him and waited for his father. John remained kneeling next to Banarel.

"What is it, Father? Has he got a weapon on you?"

"No. He hasn't even got a heartbeat."

Billy returned to his father's side. He dropped the dagger next to the body, and together they rolled Sir Banarel onto his back. Immediately they saw the U-shaped gash on his forehead and the pile of bloody straw where his head had been resting.

Billy stared at the body. "What's goin' on here, Father?"

"I'll explain later." John subconsciously reached for his shirtfront. He felt for the ring, then stared at Billy's hand.

Billy looked down at the ring. It appeared and felt the way it always had to him, except he had never dared to wear it before. Slowly he reached down, removed the ring from his finger, and held it out to his father.

John continued to stare at the ring, then reluctantly held out his hand. Billy placed the ring in his father's palm and gently closed his fingers around it. "What do we do now, Father?"

John looked back at Banarel. "I'm thinkin'." He put his hand over his heart. His thumb and first finger played with the front of his shirt while he squeezed the ring into his sweaty palm. He remained silent for a full minute, never budging. At last, John picked up the dagger and slid it back into the scabbard on Sir Banarel's belt.

"Go to your room, Son. Go to your room and I'll take care of this. And talk to no one!"

"But, Father—"

"No buts!"

Billy stepped back. He had never seen such intensity and anger in his father. He turned and walked towards the door.

John stepped away from the body. "Wait."

"Yes, Father."

John walked to Billy and placed a firm hand on his shoulder. Then he looked into his son's eyes. "You must never tell anyone about this. Never! It would be best if you forgot it altogether."

"But, Father—"

"I know, Son. I know. I raised ya to always tell the truth, but this will have to be our secret. If someone asks; you weren't here. Sir Banarel's death was an accident. That's all you have to say. Now off with ya."

* * *

Billy lay restlessly in his bed. He couldn't get the image of the dead man out of his mind, nor the rage in his father's face. John was acting so strange, as was Sir Banarel. *A knight shouldn't act like a common thief.* And what of the ring? Had it actually flown across the stable to land on his finger? *Surely it was an illusion.*

"It must have been flung by Banarel's dagger," Billy said absently. "When he threw that dagger at me ... he was so close! How did he miss?"

There came a soft knock upon the door. Then Billy heard, from beyond the door, the voice of his father.

"May I come in?" He seemed to know that Billy was still awake.

"Come in, Father."

This custom his father had, of knocking on his door before entering, was one that Billy found odd and unnecessary, but one his father had insisted on when Billy reached the age of manhood. In fact, Billy having his own room was a luxury his father had insisted on as well.

John opened the door and stood in the passageway, holding a lamp. The dim light made strange shadows on his face. Without a word, he entered and sat next to Billy on the bed, placing the lamp on the small table. He sat quietly for a moment, staring solemnly at his son.

"What is it, Father?"

John took the leather thong from around his neck. He removed something and offered it to Billy. A small gold object glimmered in his palm. It was the ring Billy knew had belonged to his mother. John showed the ring to him years earlier, and again when Billy asked to see it, but until that moment, Billy hadn't realized that John kept it around his neck.

No matter how many times he had gazed upon the ring or held it in his hand, Billy found it most exquisite and felt that his mother must have been equally beautiful. Just holding the ring, he felt closer to her, and even though he had no memory of her, she formed a very clear visage in his mind. Billy stared at the ring, marveling at its hypnotic beauty, and conjured up the beautiful image of his mother.

John spoke and brought Billy back from his dreaming. "This, ya know, was your mother's."

Billy nodded, and John took his hand. He placed the ring in his palm, and Billy felt its familiar, comforting warmth.

"Now it's yours to keep. Your time has come to go out and make your way in the world. Your mother wanted ya to have it. Perhaps it will guide you to your destiny."

These words sounded strange to Billy. Never before had his father talked of destinies. He looked at the ring and then back to John.

"Am I leavin', Father?"

"You're no longer safe here. I've already spoken with Lady Myrredith. It's all arranged. Ya leave with her on the morrow."

"But what of the inn, Father? Won't you need my help?"

John smiled with his eyes. "I'll manage somehow."

"Has this got somethin' to do with Sir Banarel?"

John hesitated then said, "Aye."

"Is he really dead, Father?"

John nodded. "The earl's physician confirmed he was killed by the horse. He'll inform the earl of the unfortunate accident after breakfast." Billy frowned and John added, "That's the way it must be remembered, Son. We can ill afford to explain it any other way."

"As you wish, Father."

They fell into a quiet spell, and then John spoke what was most on their hearts. "You haven't been farther from me than I could holler since … since you were christened. You haven't—I didn't—" John sighed. "Fifteen years, and I haven't prepared ya. I thought I'd have more time."

"Prepared me for what?"

"For anythin'—everythin'." John sighed again. "The worst part of it is, I already miss ya."

"I'm only goin' for a short while, Father!"

"That may be so, but it's the way of the world to make it hard for a man to return home." John paused. "Lady Myrredith is a kind and good woman. I trust her. But there are many you will meet who are not so kind—as you well know. Be careful of those other lords and ladies. They make games of other people's lives. Be 'specially wary of any stranger, and most important of all: don't show *anyone* that ring. Someday, someone who wants that ring very badly will try to hurt you to get it."

Billy sensed John's need for a confirmation. "Yes, Father."

The two of them stared into each other's eyes, and recognition passed over them that things would never be the same.

"Good. Good." John rose to his feet and crossed to the door, taking the lamp with him. "Now, try to get some sleep, my son."

"Yes, Father."

"I'll see you in the mornin'."

"Yes, Father. G'night!"

"G'night, William."

Then John was gone. The door closed behind him, leaving Billy alone to wrestle with his thoughts, as the darkness returned to his little room. Eventually, the long day's activities and the late hour caught up with Billy, and he nodded off.

The next morning the inn was thrown into utter chaos as the guests prepared to depart. Each spoiled member of the entourage wanted his or her things taken down "now" and not a minute later. Of course, there were more waiting for their things to be brought down than there were those who were doing the bringing. Added to this were the many trying to get in a last drink or bite to eat, and the earl settling up with John— making arrangements for Sir Banarel among other things. As all the guests mounted their horses and wagons, the commotion escalated, so much so that no one noticed a young man saying good-bye to his father for the first time.

CHAPTER SEVEN

An Unexpected Adventure

The wheels of the wagon squeaked to a stop. A muted groan was the only warning of the sudden halt that catapulted Billy head over heels into the muddy rut just behind the horse. Those witnessing this spectacle burst into laughter, and soon all in the vicinity were watching the scene with a great deal of interest. All laughed as the little man's muddied face came up, and he spat out a chunk of turf.

Billy crawled blindly out of the rut and found his hand on the hard, rough hoof of a horse. He blinked his eyes and looked up at the man mounted on the steed above him. The man leaned over in the saddle to have a better look at Billy. The shoulder guard of his bluish armor glinted as it dangled loosely on its straps.

"What's the matter, little man?" The guard gave Billy an ironic grin revealing a large gap in front where once there must have been two or three teeth. He backed up his horse a step and continued. "Don't you like the taste of the King's Road?"

"I've tasted worse," Billy quipped.

There was a moment of stunned silence before another guard spoke. "Aye, but where have you had better?"

The captain of the caravan guard snuffed out the following round of guffaws with one boom of his voice. "Hey!" he bellowed. "What's all this then? You two: quit gawkin' and give a hand with the earl's wagon!"

Billy, over his initial embarrassment, wiped his face off and then washed with water from one of the wagon's side barrels. Lady Myrredith handed him a cloth. He took it and bowed his head in thanks.

The slow-moving caravan had been traveling the King's Road for two days, having reached it shortly after leaving The Valley's Finest Inn. While it was one of the more rugged parts of the road, it had been uneventful, until now. So as soon as he dried his face, Billy's natural curiosity took over, and he ran ahead to see what had caused the caravan's most untimely stop.

As Billy approached the wagon belonging to the earl and countess, he saw that it was leaning over in back. It was about to tip over from the looks of it. Several men—primarily caravan guards—were working feverishly to right the heavy, ornate vehicle. Their ardent captain was yelling orders from horseback while his men, ankle-deep in muck, struggled with the broken wheel. Sir Aldrick, one of the courtiers, was gallantly aiding the frightened countess in her escape from the "horrible wreck."

The red-faced wagon master was desperately trying to placate the earl and remove any guilt as far from himself as possible. His head was bowed and he wrung his hat in his hands.

"Honestly, milord, I don't know what could have happened!"

"Um-humph," the earl replied.

"I—that is, my man—checked the wagons just this morning!"

"Um-humph."

"Your Lordship, this must be the work of-of-of... of *faeries!*" The large man flashed a sign of protection with his rough, thick fingers.

"Faeries, Master Finnian?"

"Aye!" The wagon master crossed himself for good measure. "What else could have caused such a dastardly trick, Your Worshipfulness?"

The earl cracked a crooked smile at Billy as he peeked from behind a wagon. "You don't think it could have been hobgoblins, or witches perhaps?"

"Oh no, my liege, it were faeries." He made yet another sign. "Undoubtedly!"

"Undoubtedly. Perhaps it was that little imp right over there." The earl pointed to Billy. "He seems to have a bit of the fay in him, wouldn't you say?"

The large teamster scratched his unshaven chin with the two fingers and thumb of his scarred right hand and measured the boy with his eyes. In his coat of mud, Billy's appearance was rather like some kindly wood sprite or brownie. He fidgeted uncomfortably under their scrutiny then ducked behind the wagon.

The earl stifled a laugh. "You see? Why he's disappeared just like that!" He snapped his fingers to punctuate.

Earl Cairmac, who had grinned throughout the conversation, was now laughing as he watched the husky teamster's face screw up into a scowl. Finnian glanced desperately to either side, sweating. He gave a curt bow to the earl, turned, and walked directly into the ankle-deep muddy water around the wagon.

Aber Finnian was a large man by anyone's account and many years as an ostler had made him strong as well. So when he put his back to the sideboards and heaved with the others, the wagon took a sudden lurch upwards. This was good for removing the broken wheel, however rather unfortunate for the earl's physician, who was, at that moment, debarking from the precarious wagon.

The old surgeon sat upright, having landed seat first in the same mire that was causing all the trouble of late. He sat motionless at first, shocked to find himself on the ground. There was light laughter as he gave a push to get up and discovered that the sticky mud around his bottom had him firmly in its gooey grasp.

"You oaf!" he shouted at the wagon master. "Don't think I don't know why you did that, Aber Finnian!"

The wagon master was mortified. He stood paralyzed. He didn't dare release the wagon until the new wheel was in place, but his face betrayed his desire to be somewhere else—anywhere else. He wrinkled up his face and closed his eyes tightly, as if somehow this might hide him from the irate physician.

The doctor continued to squawk and splash the muddy water at Finnian as his arms flailed wildly about him. Finally he stopped and looked around him. His little scene had the courtiers laughing uncontrollably, many holding their sides as if they would split. His bony mud-splattered face looked pitifully like a poor, lost mongrel instead of a refined court physician.

"Will someone kindly get me out of this muck?" He splashed both fists down into the water in frustration.

Without warning, two hands slipped under his arms and began lifting. He gave a push and was free from his sticky captor. Relieved, he turned around to see his savior, who was now helping him to his feet. There was Billy, grinning from ear to ear and covered from head to toe with mud, save for his face. The physician flinched with a gasp. Then he blinked his eyes and refocused on the little man's face.

"Oh, it's you!"

The physician pushed Billy aside and strode past him, seeking someplace to clean up and regain some of his dignity. All the while, he grumbled and mumbled and stomped.

"That some ragamuffin would come to my rescue, before a member of this court ..."

As he disappeared into the bushes, his grumbling became a full-blown rant. "Many of whom I personally delivered into this world!"

The earl, upon seeing what chaos this unscheduled stop had caused, informed the wagon master and the captain of the caravan guard, "You have the rest of the day to fix the wagon."

"But my lord—"

"Captain. We camp here tonight!"

That afternoon, Billy, the physician, and the others who had the misfortune of knowing the King's Road a bit too intimately found refuge in a nearby creek. Once clean and refreshed, they went about setting up the campsite for the night. Billy collected firewood and helped set up several tents before wandering off to find fresh game with a young guard named Duncan.

"The boy can be my packer," Duncan explained to Lady Myrredith.

"If he wants to go—"

"Oh yes, please!" Billy spouted.

"Very well then. Now don't get lost. I promised your father I'd look after you."

"Yes, milady!"

And they were off. Billy had never really been hunting before—not with anyone using a bow.

"Only squirrels," he explained to Duncan, "with the other boys of the valley. But that was a long time ago, and we only used slings."

The young guard smiled at this and recounted his own youth, hunting squirrels with his brothers, in the forests of Caithnessshire. "Now however, we're after more than squirrels, for we need somethin' fit for the earl's table."

Thus far all they had managed to find were apples. While they were a nice treat, they were not meat.

Duncan picked three of the apples and juggled them shortly before handing them to Billy. Billy, seeing the ease at which his companion accomplished this, tried to duplicate the feat, but to no avail, until the young man gave him a few pointers.

"Many of my clansmen are jugglers," he told Billy as he taught him the proper stance and basic technique. "Follow me. One, two, three!" Much to Duncan's surprise, Billy juggled the three apples—that is, as well as anyone who has just learned how to juggle.

"You're a natural!"

Then the young guard remembered his duty and cut the lesson short. They continued on their hunt, with the apples stored in Billy's pack.

Up ahead, there was a flash of grey-brown fur, and Duncan acted. The bowstring sung as he loosed an arrow after the fleeing doe. The arrow hit its target, but it wasn't enough. The deer only staggered sideways and continued to run into the trees. The guardsman tried to get off another shot, but it was too late. His prey was gone from sight.

"Quick," Duncan said, and he ran after it.

Billy joined in the chase. His blood was racing, his heart pounding. The excitement overwhelmed him, and he struggled to make his legs move faster.

When they arrived at the spot where the arrow had struck the deer, Duncan stopped and examined the ground. Fresh dark earth had been churned up under the feet of the frightened doe. Drops of blood were spattered on the rocky soil and in the tracks leading away into the thick woods ahead. Billy and the young hunter studied them for a moment and then continued the chase.

They ran by boulders and through bushes, under trees and over hills. They stopped shortly to check the tracks and to catch their breath, and then they were off again. Duncan marveled at Billy's ability to keep up. Despite his short legs, he did very well. Still, they ran on. The deer seemed tireless, and the two hunters, growing tired, were too busy giving chase to appreciate the change in the landscape.

They were now running down into a steep ravine, carved out of the rock by water and time. The mighty sculptor that had carved it away was no more. Now only a small stream babbled over the rocky bottom, like a spirit stumbling through its ancient bones.

Duncan stopped abruptly, and Billy pulled up behind him.

"What is it?"

The guardsman put a finger to his lips. He then pulled an arrow quietly from the quiver and placed it in his bow.

Billy held his breath as the archer slowly drew back his bow, sighting down the small ravine. The doe was only two hundred feet away. It seemed to be unaware of them as it bowed down to drink from the little stream, which bubbled along the rugged terrain of the bottom. The first arrow remained in its side. Its weary legs wobbled as it stepped across the irregular rocks.

Suddenly the doe's head popped up, and its nose twitched, sniffing the air. Then just as quickly, it darted a wild-eyed stare back over its shoulder. The guardsman loosed his arrow, but before it could strike home, a large blur of long greenish-gray fur shot in front of the deer. A creature, huge in stature, seemed to materialize out of the very rock itself. Instantly it was on the deer.

Then the arrow struck.

The creature howled in pain as the arrow lodged in its back. Its entire body shook, and its long, thick fur shivered as it moved over contorting muscles. One of its gory forepaws reached back over its shoulder and groped at the arrow, just out of its grasp. The long black claws, extending from the blood-matted fur of the paw, stretched in vain to get a hold on the cause of its pain. It let out another terrible cry of anguish and frustration. Then all movement stopped. The little valley fell silent, and Billy could hear the labored breathing of the great beast. His heart leapt to his throat, and he shot Duncan a glance, but the guard was still petrified, staring down the stream at the monstrous form before him.

Slowly the creature turned to face them. Its huge mass shambled around to expose the dreadful, hideous head. Its large golden eyes stared at them hungrily, and in its bloody jaws dangled the doe, hanging limply by its neck, like a field mouse caught by the farmer's cat. Indeed there was something faintly feline about the creature. Its short pointed ears stood near the top of its head, curving upwards, giving the impression of horns, with tufts of white fur protruding from them. Its nose was blunt, with long, white, catlike whiskers. But the eyes and the mouth, they were not familiar in the least. The eyes were large golden orbs, with two widening pupils—hungry, cunning, feral, evil—coolly calculating its next move. The maw, filled with long pointed teeth, cinched down on the deer's neck.

The men watched in horror as the deer fell to the ground in two pieces. The creature threw back its baleful head and shook it vigorously, swallowing a majority of the deer's neck whole. The creature slowly lowered its head until its eyes fell on the would-be hunters. They were now the prey.

The sudden realization that they were next on the creature's menu hammered terror into the very bones of the young men. The creature seemed to smile with pleasure as if imagining the taste of its new victims. Its yellow teeth were fully bared, framed by the red-stained face. A drool of saliva dripped from one corner of its terrible mouth, turning red before it dropped to the ground.

As if this was a signal, both creature and man moved. The man drew another arrow to his bow, and the creature sprung forward towards its new prey.

"Run, Billy, run!"

Billy didn't hesitate for an instant. He scrambled up the little bank of the streambed and ran away from the creature, up the deep ravine. He heard the twang of the bowstring and glanced back to see the arrow strike the creature near its shoulder. The beast didn't slow down, so neither did Billy. He ran faster than he had ever run before—his lungs snatching deep breaths and hastily exhaling, his heartbeat pounding in his ears. His whole body was shaking as he ran. He thought his legs would give out, but some-how they managed to stay under him, leaping over rocks and fallen trees, slicing through bushes and brambles.

Abruptly the ground under his feet slipped away, and he fell, skinning one knee and his hands. He stumbled up to his feet but was stopped dead in his tracks by a man's scream, which cried out and was quickly cut short.

Billy forced himself to take another step. He dared not look back. In the next step he was running. Again running like he'd never run before.

Blindly running from the monster behind him, not knowing where he was going or even what was just ahead.

He ran into a clump of trees and found himself on a narrow, overgrown path. Instantly he decided to take the path, hoping to find some kind of help or shelter. He was becoming tired but was spurred on when he heard his hunter behind him, crashing through the woods. Slowly he became aware of another sound—at first only a whisper. It grew louder as he ran up the path.

The woods ended abruptly, and Billy slid to a stop. He immediately felt vulnerable standing in the large clearing. Then his heart sank, for this clearing was the end of the ravine.

A small ribbon of water fell from above, sending a fine mist into the air, its sound echoing off the steep, rock walls surrounding him. He scanned the cliffs frantically for some means of escape: a ladder, stairs, a path, a rope, or even just a hole to hide in, but there was none to be found. He turned back to the dense wall of forest behind him with the thought of running back in, but at that moment another monstrous howl echoed through the trees, transforming the quiet wood into a menacing lair. Billy knew he was trapped and suddenly felt homesick for his father and the home he would never see again. He felt cold, lost, and very much alone.

Thirst abruptly gripped his throat, and he numbly went to the edge of the water. He leaned over and drank from the cool, clear water. He was reminded of the poor doe, as it drank from this same stream a short distance down the ravine. He pulled his head up, listening and looking for some sign of his pursuer, but all he perceived was the clatter of the waterfall and the waving of the trees in the breeze.

He reached down into the pouch his father had sewn into his breeches and pulled out the ring his mother had left him. It looked less grand, as he pondered its fate, and his own.

"Oh, Mother," he whimpered. "What am I to do?"

He squeezed the ring and once more wished his mother were alive. John, his father, was always first in his heart, but the mother he never knew also lived there. Her very absence had become a presence that shadowed Billy.

Again he felt this queer presence and tried to picture his mother the way he had always imagined her. As he did, he focused across the water to the waterfall. There was a darkness behind the base of the fall. Was something there? Billy got up and stepped back, feeling as if someone were watching him from behind the falling water. Warily, he crept around the pool at the bottom of the fall. Then he saw the darkness behind the fall for what it was: *a small cave!*

Billy leapt into the pool and swam across the water and through the fall. Shortly, he reached the place he hoped would be his sanctuary.

It was an agreeable little cave, as caves go—a bit dark and damp, with nothing to take the chill off him, but Billy didn't mind, considering the alternative of waiting for the beast in the clearing. The floor of the cave sloped gently down to the lapping water and was covered with a fine dark carpet of moss. The smooth walls and ceiling tapered back, meeting the floor about eight feet from the entrance.

The sky outside was slowly darkening as the sun entered its final hour. Billy turned away from the mouth of the cave to take another look around. As his eyes adjusted to the lack of light, he saw that the cave walls had some sort of pattern on them. Eventually his eyes made out lines and circles, then an entire picture. It was a mural that depicted men on a hunting party. Billy followed the drawing back and came to a most disturbing picture. It only took him a moment to recognize the large fangs and horrible eyes. Undoubtedly the person who drew these had also witnessed the horrible monster kill his friends and had run for refuge in this cave. Billy's foot tapped something on the floor and it rolled away. He watched it roll over, barely able to make it out. Then two dark holes stared up at him. His breath caught in his throat. The skull continued its blank stare. Billy then made out the remains of what must have been the cave's artist.

"You never escaped."

Billy turned and started for the mouth of the cave. Before he had taken his second step, he heard its chilling howl from somewhere beyond the waterfall. He looked through the scintillating curtain of water and pieced together the outline of the trees surrounding the clearing. All was still, and then a large grey shape emerged from the trees. Even with his distorted view of the outside, Billy could make out the horrible golden eyes searching about, the blunt nose sniffing the air, and then the slow, purposeful walk to the pool in front of the waterfall. As it got to the edge of the water it hunched down and drank. Without warning. it raised its head to let out a horrible, howling scream that descended into a deep grumbling noise like laughter—low, malevolent laughter.

The creature paced around the edge of the pool, sniffing and grunting. It circled around the water and back again, faster and faster, sniffing and snorting. The creature came to the side of the pond, and Billy could see it clearly. Its face and paws were still smeared with sticky red blood. Billy shivered at the thought of Duncan's fate. Then instantly he realized that if he could see the creature, then it might see him too. Carefully he picked up his foot and moved it back, looking to make sure he didn't step on something that would alert the monster to his presence. He looked up to see what the creature was doing, but it was too late. The beast's cold, golden eyes were locked on him. Billy held his breath and hoped that being still would hide him from its probing eyes. The creature stood perfectly still and stared – and stared – and stared. Slowly the hideous grin returned to its face, and Billy knew that the creature could see him. It ran its black tongue over the front of its sharp jagged teeth and stretched its jaw as if preparing to take a large bite out of something.

Billy's stomach knotted up. His throat tightened. His whole body shook and his legs gave out, dropping him to his knees on the cave floor. His already-skinned knee smarted as it contacted the mossy rock, but he ignored it – the pain overridden by fear. His eyes never left the horror outside, and its greedy eyes never left him.

The creature reached out one of its bloody paws, its sharp ebony claws scratching the rock a few feet from the cave. Then it put this paw down in the water with a splash. It quickly withdrew the wet extremity and disdainfully shook it, attempting to get rid of the cold water. It repeated this with the other paw. It tried again and again to get to Billy in the cave but couldn't come close without getting wet.

Billy was in hysterics. Each time the creature was repelled by the water, it would rearrange its stance and stretch out farther. In this way, it managed to inch closer and closer. Finally the large golden eyes narrowed, and it bounded into the water with a great splash, lashing out with one paw at the cave.

Billy fell back from the mouth of the cave just in time. The next raking attack came right behind and caught the side of the cave where Billy had been. The waterfall pounded on the creature's furry head, and it thrashed around in the water trying to bite and claw it. Then Billy's ears were filled with the horrid, sinister laughter of the creature as its face came into the cave opening. It snarled at Billy and snapped out another paw at him. One claw caught on Billy's breeches and pulled him to the floor. Billy felt the point of the claw bite into his ankle. He let out a yell and pulled away in reflex. The cloth of his breeches gave way with a loud rip, and Billy scrambled for the back of the cave as the creature attacked again.

This time Billy barely dodged the claws as they sliced through the air in front of his eyes and raked the side of the cave. Frightened beyond reason, Billy threw the first thing he could get his hands on. He watched in horror as the monster caught the skull in its teeth and shattered it, ejecting bits of bone into the air. Billy knew he was done for on the next attack.

The creature raised its claws for the final blow, and Billy's mind went spinning. Instinctively he drew his legs in and tucked himself into a tight ball. He closed his eyes as the deadly claws descended on him. There was a great howl from the creature, then – nothing.

Billy opened his eyes. The monster was still in the cave mouth, but its head was turned back towards the outside. Its claws were poised just inches from Billy, and then the great paw fell to the floor and was quickly withdrawn.

Billy heard something outside. The creature turned back to Billy, momentarily eyed him, and then darted from the cave.

Billy sat stupefied, completely bewildered at his continued existence. The monster's behavior was plainly baffling. Was this some kind of trick? Was it just toying with him? Billy remembered seeing a cat play with its prey before devouring it. On impulse Billy uncurled himself, got up, and went to the cave entrance. It was twilight, and clouds in the darkening sky glowed red like fire.

The monster was on the edge of the pool, shaking off its wet fur. Blood seeped from a deep wound to its hindquarter.

Across the clearing Billy saw a man riding a great grey horse with barding over its large, sturdy body. It pawed aggressively at the ground with its shaggy hooves and shook its armored head wrathfully at the monster. The man sat proudly upright on the horse, almost defiantly, with a long white lance in his right hand and a shield on his left. He wore pale leather armor and a shiny plumed helm upon his head. A light breeze moved through the ravine, bringing the white plume and ribbons of the lance to life. Billy saw a dark stain on the ribbons as they fluttered in the breeze, and deduced that the lance had inflicted the monster's wound.

The creature stalked left, then right—studying the mounted man. The horse countered, giving nothing away, showing no weakness to its enemy. In the dimming light, the two foes stared at each other across the small clearing. The man touched his spurs to the sides of the horse, and they broke into a gallop towards the creature. The creature sprung to the side, showing a great deal of agility for such a large animal. With thundering hooves, the horse turned to meet its objective, and the lance came down level with the creature.

There was a terrible thud and a loud crack as the lance found its mark deep in the beast's side and shattered, sending splinters into the air. An almost human scream escaped the throat of the wounded thing before it fell on its side, breathing coarsely. It wheezed, coughed once, and then lay still.

The man turned his mount around and moved closer to the fallen beast. He threw the broken lance to the ground and lifted his visor to better examine the body. Billy took this as a good sign and so started out of his little cave and across the pond.

The victorious warrior leaned over his horse and looked down at the fierce fangs protruding from the thing's mouth. The fallen monster's eyes snapped open, and the horse and rider both jolted back, but it was too late. The creature was on its feet. Its claws immediately flew to the horse's side and head, and its teeth sank into the armor on its neck. Billy could see the eyes of the horse grow large and feral with fear. The beast shook its head as the knight drew his sword from the scabbard. There was a loud snap, and the horse collapsed, throwing its rider to the ground with a crash. A loud grunt jumped from the man's mouth as the wind exploded from his lungs. His long sword flew through the air and stuck point down in the sand before Billy, who now stood knee deep in the pool, frozen by fear.

The knight slowly rolled up to his knees. He pulled off his helm and tossed it to the ground as he shook his head. His long brown hair swept around his head, and beads of sweat rolled down his furrowed brow. He blinked twice and then stood to face the beast that had just slaughtered his stallion. It was kneading its long, bloodied claws on the horse's corpse and staring coldly at the dazed human before him.

The knight's hand absently grasped at his side but only felt the empty scabbard there. Frantically he glanced around. His eyes stopped on his sword. He barely noticed the little man standing behind it as he focused on his distant weapon. His sword looked so far away, too far to reach quickly, and all his other weapons were on his dead mount. He looked back to the growling beast. It wiggled and shook in anticipation as it readied itself to pounce.

The man darted to the left and then ran directly at his sword. The strategy worked, for the beast sprang in the direction of the feint, missing his victim and almost going into the stream. The man ran as hard as he could, but it wasn't enough. The quick reflexes of the monster allowed it to turn and rejoin the chase with hardly a lost step. The man's face was red, and he panted forcefully as he strove to reach his sword. However, it was too late. The creature gained on him in a matter of a few steps and smashed him to the ground with a raking leap. This heavily battered the knight, but he managed to roll out of the way as the monster passed.

The creature stopped and turned around. The man came up weakly to his elbow and stared at the beast coming towards him—its large, wide eyes glaring at him, its mouth drooling thick red blood. The creature came to a stop, and its eyes strayed from the downed warrior. The man, by reflex, followed its gaze. Just a foot from his side he found the odd little man, pointing his lost sword at the monster with both hands.

The sword wavered as Billy struggled to hold out its heavy blade. He didn't know why he had drawn the sword from the sand or how he had gotten to where he was. He glanced down at the prone man. The back of his leather armor was shredded, and Billy saw blood. The man's face was curiously calm, but Billy looked into his green eyes and perceived turbulence.

All three of them acted at once. The creature started to charge, Billy stepped forward and thrust with the sword, and the knight pushed up from the ground and seized his sword from Billy's trembling hands. The creature was on them instantly. It swung at the armed man first, but he skillfully dodged. Unfortunately, fear overwhelmed Billy's untrained reflexes, and the attack struck him before he could flinch. He felt the claws slash across him as he was knocked back several feet into the stream.

Billy felt a pain like fire burning on his chest and the cold water around him. The pain faded, and he felt nothing but cold. By sheer will, he forced his head forward out of the water and stuck a hand out behind himself. Dazed, he looked through his knees at the two combatants just ten feet away.

The creature renewed its ferocious attack, but the knight countered with a quick step to his left and a slash of his sword across his foe's mighty paw. Once more, the monster cried out, but continued to press its attack. Again it lunged at the man, and again the man sidestepped, slashing this time to the creature's neck. It reeled back in pain, but then quickly turned and raised up on its rear legs. This maneuver surprised the warrior, and forced him to fall backwards as the monster brought down its weight on him.

In the blink of an eye the knight brought his sword up and planted its pommel firmly next to him. The creature clawed at his shoulders and fell upon him. It curled back its lips baring a maw full of snarling teeth.

"Die, dragon!" the man growled through his teeth, but the beast would not oblige. It gnashed its fangs and let out a spiteful roar that dwindled into a growl. Its entire frame quivered, and the growl gave way to gagging as it gasped for air. The knight turned from the hot, putrid breath of the monster as it hovered above him, panting in jagged breaths, its teeth mere inches from his face. The heavy brows over its eyes relaxed, and it collapsed on top of him.

Billy was barely conscious now, and a peculiar pain began to nag at him, throbbing in his chest. He looked down and saw blood pooling in long gashes running across it. Billy fought to stay awake, but alas it was too much for him. He fell back into the water. The last thing he saw, before blackness surrounded him, was the first evening star. He feebly made a wish, and fainted.

* * *

Billy awoke feeling something tugging on his leg. He inclined his head forward and saw the huge hairy beast's eyes glaring down at him, its mouth around his foot. Horrified, Billy tried to scramble out of its grip but found he had no strength. The creature hauled him roughly onto the bank of the stream and dropped his foot. It softly padded over to him until its face was just above him. Billy felt a deep revulsion, but still he was unable to move. The creature grinned, showing its great maw of teeth. It then licked Billy's chest, grinning even deeper as it savored the taste. Then with an amazing amount of gentleness, it rolled him over and picked him up by his tunic.

They were moving. In the dark, Billy perceived the blurred outline of trees and rocks rushing by, as the creature carried him deeper and deeper into the forest. Billy hung limp like a cloth doll in its mouth. The monster trotted along for hours, seemingly tireless. Billy realized the creature was taking him to its lair.

It seemed the creature's appetite had been quenched; its stomach bloated horribly—impossibly—by its previous gorging. And still they moved on through woods, across streams, and over hills, but why was the creature taking Billy back alive? The only answer caused Billy to cry out, but alas even this was too much for him. He was sure that he was to be a fresh, live dinner for the creature's mate, or hungry cubs, or maybe a snack for later when the creature's incredible hunger returned. Billy fell in and out of consciousness, always awakening to find himself held tight in the horrible thing's mouth, still moving.

At last, a huge cave—its mouth obscured by an even larger rock— loomed before them. *The lair!*

Billy's hope for escape faded as the monster entered the cave and plopped him down near the entrance on a large, flat stone, worn smooth by many footfalls. Billy looked beside him and gasped. In a corner of the cave's entrance lay a pile of well-gnawed bones, bleached white by the sun.

Billy's captor let out a terrible roar back into the cave. Much to his horror, there came a responding growl from the darkness. Then slowly, out of the deep shadows, another of its kind emerged. Several young, the size of large dogs, crowded in beside it. They glared at him with their yellow eyes and hungry mouths. With lips retracted, the large gnashing fangs and slobbering tongues moved closer to Billy. Then instantly they rushed him, their horrible mouths opening wide—

Billy sat up screaming. He looked about him and saw that he was no longer in the creature's lair, but in a big blue tent. He had been dreaming or rather "nightmaring" as his father called it. However, now he was awake. He was sure that he was truly awake, for the pain in his chest was far too real.

A man suddenly ducked in through the flap in the tent. He was tall and lean with broad shoulders and well-muscled arms and legs. His long brown hair was pulled back from his face, wrapped in a blue ribbon, so that it sprang out from the back of his head like the tail of a horse. As he entered, his face and body were tense, and his brow wrinkled with concern. He relaxed once he saw Billy was safe. He had a kind face, and his green eyes sparkled as he gave Billy a gentle smile.

"Lay still, my brave little friend. There are no dragons here."

The man's voice was soft and pleasant. Billy lay back down, but his mind was full of questions.

"That was a dragon? And you vanquished him? Where's Duncan? And—"

The man gently placed his hand over Billy's mouth. "I am sorry. Your friend, the Highlander, is dead. Now lay still and rest, for you need your strength."

Once the man was sure he had successfully quieted the boy, he continued. "Aye, that was a dragon, a forest dragon, and perhaps the last of its kind." He spoke the last with a strange sadness. He paused for a moment. "And I am Sir Hugh, son of Sir Sedgemore, knight-errant, and champion to the king."

Billy's eyes popped open. "Sir Sedgemore? The king?" Before he could say anything more, Sir Hugh had his fingers to Billy's lips.

"Shhh, my friend. There will be plenty of time to talk later. But now, sleep." The knight then narrowed his eyes and stared at Billy.

"What's the matter?"

"Have we met before?"

"No. I would remember you."

"Then it's nothing. Don't worry, my friend. Rest."

Billy closed his eyes. Weariness got the better of him, and he fell into a fitful sleep, dreaming of knights and dragons, which were all too well defined now for him to rest quietly.

The smell of breakfast awoke Billy. He breathed in the smells of the food cooking and savored them. It was a pleasant smell, and he half expected to hear his father's voice asking why he slept so late. But the bed was not right, and the light had a strange tint to it. He opened his eyes to discover he still lay in the blue tent. He felt the urge to stretch as he yawned, but the wound and the tight bandages around his chest made it most uncomfortable.

Billy painfully propped himself up on his elbows and looked around the tent. He lay on a bed made of leaves and pine needles and covered with a fine thick fur. In one corner there lay a cushion and a lantern. Next to the lantern lay a small open chest with papers and writing quill.

In the opposite corner was something that caught Billy's attention and fired his imagination. There was a tall wooden post with a full suit of armor hanging on it. From the magnificent white plumed helm to the silver filigree on the breastplate and greaves, it was beautiful. And from the armor-scarecrow's arm there hung the silver spurs of a knight. The armor's surface reflected the strange blue light, giving the suit a glow, as if the source of light were within it. Leaning up against the post was a beautiful shield of plain polished metal. It reminded Billy of a silver pot a peddler had once shown him. In front of the shield was a sword with an elegant white grip and silver hilt. A bright blue gemstone sparkled in the pommel. The scabbard was equally ornate, being covered with pebbled leather the color of bone and capped at either end with skillfully sculpted silver, which crept sparingly towards the middle like twisted vines of ivy. There was something familiar about the sword.

Billy painfully got up and crossed to the weapon. His fingers reached to touch the pale grip. Then his hand was upon it. He held it there for a moment and then recoiled. He shuddered at the memory of facing the dragon. Had he really stood before the fearsome monster with nothing but the heavy sword trembling in his unskilled hands? The memory was unnerving, unbelievable, unthinkable, and yet there he was, and so was the sword. An uneasy feeling came over him. He spun around to see the tall brawny knight standing at the tent's entrance. Billy had been in a trance and hadn't noticed him enter.

"I see you've recovered some of your strength. Good!" The knight held out a plate of food and a goblet. "Here are some victuals to help you along."

Billy stared at him as his mind flashed back to the first time he had seen the man's handsome face. The taut, blood-stained features of the warrior had changed, but it was the same man.

The man smiled. "I think you'll need to eat before taking on another dragon."

Billy blinked, and then something inside him growled. Until then, he hadn't taken stock of his stomach and was overcome by sudden, incredible hunger. He took the food from the knight with a bow and a "thank-you" and immediately began to cram it into his mouth without regard for common table manners.

The knight left but quickly returned with more food for himself and his ravenous little guest. They ate in silence. As Billy's stomach began to fill, his hunger lessened, and he began to remember his previous awakening. It felt like a dream now.

"Sir *Hugh?*"

"Aye."

Billy's mind was full of questions. He wasn't sure where to begin.

"The monster – the dragon?" The knight nodded and Billy continued. "It is … dead?"

"Aye. If not, I'm afraid he'll be very put out with me for stealing his warm coat." With this he gestured to Billy's bed.

Billy paled as he realized he'd been sleeping on the skin of a dragon. He stared back with wide eyes at the smiling knight.

"No wonder I had nightmares!" Billy brushed himself off, in an attempt to get rid of whatever unthinkable thing he might have picked up from the dragon's hide. He stopped his brushing and shuddered as he had done before with memories of the foul beast, which had come so close to devouring him.

Sir Hugh was hard put not to burst out laughing, but he remained politely subdued in his mirth.

"Say, I thought dragons had scales!" Billy said.

"They do."

Billy examined the dragon's hide more closely. Hesitantly he touched it and felt its long soft fur. Still curious about Sir Hugh's statement, he ran his fingers against the nap, and something tiny and sharp nicked his fingers. He looked at the place where he had pulled the hair back and could see hundreds of small green and black scales, each one with many gray and white hairs growing from it like the hair on an old pinecone.

Billy returned to his meal and finished his second helping. Then he handed his empty plate to the grinning knight.

"More?" the handsome warrior said, astonished at his guest's appetite.

"No." Billy patted his belly. "No. I don't think I could take another bite. Thank you."

"You are most welcome, my brave friend."

"I'm not brave."

"Well, it's not every man who would stand toe to toe with such a monster."

Billy could only shrug in answer.

The knight spoke half to himself, "Although why he was awakened from his deep slumber only the devil knows." He made eye contact with Billy. "Yes, I think you're very brave."

"But it was you who vanquished him."

"Maybe, but that does not diminish your bravery in the least, my humble young friend."

Hugh rose and started to stack his dishes.

"And you are the son of Sir Sedgemore?"

Hugh stopped and stared at Billy. "Aye."

"My father told me about him. He must be quite famous!"

The knight's face became grim and he looked away. "Some would say infamous."

Billy didn't understand, but he could see that Sir Hugh didn't wish to talk about his father. He took a deep breath and changed the subject. "Not to seem ungrateful, but how is it that ya came to the waterfall when ya did?"

The knight was still staring into the distance. "That is a story in itself, but I will spare you the details. I was returning from a mission for my lord, the king, when I happened along a village not far from here. The entire village had been destroyed and all the inhabitants were gone—their food still on their plates. Not even a dog or cat was there to be found. I admit I was confounded by it all. And then I saw the signs, and the tracks of the beast. I tracked him to the stream, and the rest... I think you know the rest."

The knight paused in contemplation before renewing the conversation. "And you, my fine young fellow, what on earth brought you to that ill-fated ravine?"

Billy looked at him and started to speak, but then his eyes opened wide, and all he could blurt out was "Lady Myrredith!"

"What?"

"Lady Myrredith!" Billy continued frantically. He began to gather what little belongings of his were there and preparing to leave. "Ouch!" He put a hand to his ribs. "I must go! I'm sorry. Thank ya for your hospitality, but if I don't get back soon, Lady Myrredith will be very worried!"

"Slow down, my little friend. Did you say Lady Myrredith?"

"Aye." Billy pulled on one of his shoes.

"Would that be Lady Myrredith of Cyndyn Hall?"

"Aye."

Sir Hugh's countenance was contemplative, as if remembering with fondness some long-forgotten friend.

Billy noticed the warrior's expression. "Do you know Her Ladyship?"

The knight nodded. "Aye." He was obviously still wading in memories.

"Well, I'll give her your best." Billy pulled on his other shoe.

"No! No. I'd like the honor myself. I'll accompany you back, to greet her personally."

Billy noticed that his newly found friend had a glimmer in his eye that had not been there before.

Sir Hugh grabbed up his dishes and left the tent. Before Billy could take breath, Hugh returned and handed him the dishes.

"Here. Would you please wash these for me? I'll pack up the rest of our little camp and then we'll be off."

Billy started out of the tent but was stopped by the warrior's gentle hand.

"My friend. I'm afraid I don't even know your name."

"Billy."

"William, is it?"

"No, only Father and Lady Myrredith call me William."

"I see."

"Billy is what my friends call me."

"Then Billy it is, and glad to make your acquaintance!"

The two shook hands and stared at each other for a moment, both secretly feeling that a bond had been forged between them, a bond that would link their future paths in some uncertain way.

CHAPTER EIGHT

The Journey Continues

Two weary travelers wandered into the firelight of the camp that
night. Though very different in build and attire, their faces were
the same: both drawn long with the fatigue that comes from a difficult
journey.

The first man was tall and well built, with long brown hair, which he
wore pulled back from his fine, firm features. He was dressed in quality
blue clothing and pale leather armor, the latter exhibiting signs of battle.
He carried a heavy war saddle flung over his shoulder and a long blade in
an elegant scabbard at his side.

The other man appeared to be little more than a boy, although his
weary countenance added many years to his visage. His breeches and
shoes were of a coarser material than his companion's and were obviously
well worn. His jerkin was the only thing that did not fit the rest of his
image. In fact, it didn't fit him at all and would have looked more natural
upon his friend's tall frame. It was smooth and white with a high collar
and extra-long flouncy sleeves. The bottom of the shirt was untidily
tucked into a wide belt.

Straggling behind the two dusty travelers came an equally dusty packhorse, carrying a larger load than would be normal for such a beast of
burden. It dragged tiredly along, the small man tugging on its lead.

Deep wagon ruts and trampled earth surrounded the camp—left behind by the large caravan that had been there. Now only one wagon, one tent, and a few horses remained. Several men slept around the dying fire, all having the rough appearance of mercenaries or caravan guards.

The smaller man's face showed relief as they entered into the dim light, but the tall man glared about and pursed his lips together.

Billy saw his companion's jaw tense. "What is it?"

Sir Hugh hissed through clenched teeth. "They sleep!"

He marched to a space between two of the sleeping men. He tapped both with a light kick and cleared his throat. Both men showed little sign of waking. One turned on to his side mumbling, the other did not budge. Hugh was fuming. He took a deep breath and let it out. In one move, he dropped his saddle on the man to his left and drew his sword with his right hand. Billy saw only a flash, as the dim firelight danced off the long silvery blade. The edge of the blade stopped sharply at the one man's throat, as the saddle thudded on top of his partner.

Instantly the men around the fire came to life. Those who were able, sat up grabbing at weapons and blinking their puffy eyes as they gaped nervously about the camp. Two of them, however, found this extremely difficult. One had the weight of a saddle on his head, the other, the cold steel of a blade at his gullet. The latter chose not to move at all.

"What is it?" one man exclaimed, facing out from the campfire into the darkness.

Sir Hugh released the man under his blade and tapped this bewildered bloke on the shoulder. The man turned to find that he now had a sword at his throat. He made a desperate move to bring his sword around, but the angry knight dashed the blade aside and riposted to bring his blade back under the man's chin.

"I should have slain you all where you lay, for such lazy foolishness! But dead, you would not learn your lesson, and would be of little use in Her Ladyship's defense."

The guard pinned by Hugh's saddle finally pushed it aside. "Who in the blazes are you?"

The man next to him answered. "It's Sir Hugh, the King's Champion."

Recognition and embarrassment flooded into the men's faces as they learned who had entered their camp as they slept. Each man grumbled some feeble excuse as well as a few curses under his breath.

One sour-faced guard spotted Billy. "Oh, so the young scalawag has finally returned!"

"We've been lookin' for ya for four lousy days!" another said.

"Where ya been?" a third asked.

"Where's Duncan?"

There was silence as they looked around the camp for their friend Duncan, who had disappeared with Billy earlier that week. Then they all stared at Billy.

The roughest of the guardsman approached Billy and went to one knee. He pushed back a stock of unkempt black hair from his face and restated the question. "Where's Duncan, lad? Where's my cousin?"

Billy looked at the man's face with cloudy eyes. Tears poured out of them, and he turned away from the man. Duncan's kinsman turned to fix his eyes on Sir Hugh, his face a perplexed frown.

"What does this mean?"

Sir Hugh's face was somber, but he had replaced the anger which had been there with sympathy. He looked directly into the kneeling man's eyes and spoke low. "I'm sorry. Your cousin is dead."

"What? But ..."

The man's expression slowly went from disbelief to one of somber acceptance. His eyes were downcast as he asked the inevitable question, which seldom has a satisfactory answer. His voice was flat and squeezed out in a half whisper.

"How did he die?"

The King's Champion widened his stance, as if the answer would sway him with its weight. He swallowed hard and looked about him at the faces of the men who had been companions of the deceased.

"He died well." Hugh cut himself short. The grieving relations might not want to know that their loved one had been digested by a monster.

Duncan's cousin raised his head again to look at the knight. His face was stern, and his eyes searched those of Sir Hugh.

"By what means was he killed? Who shall pay for Duncan's blood?"

Sir Hugh recognized the man as a member of the Highland clans and knew their penchant for reprisal. They feuded amongst themselves for generations, to the founding of tradition. This was a root of weakness and a source of strength.

At last Hugh sheathed his sword and answered the man's query. "He died ... fighting a dragon."

The man's face paled, as did all the others around the fire. Their eyes widened, some staring nervously into the darkness.

"But fear not, your cousin's blood is already avenged."

Hugh went to the packhorse and, with some effort, relieved a large bundle from its back. He paced back to the fireside with the dragon's hide. The men scrambled back as he unfurled it and revealed the hideous huge head. Its large, dead eyes stared at the men. Its face was frozen in a vicious, hateful snarl.

The monster lay still on the ground with its snout crinkled and lips curled back. Long, sharp teeth protruded from its powerful jaws while the tongue lolled to one side. Though it was clearly dead, its visage still made them shiver.

Duncan's cousin turned to the man next to him. "I thought Duncan would be safe, away from our feud. That's why I brung him here."

"What passes here at this late hour?" grumbled a voice from behind the men. It startled all those around the dying fire.

Each man turned to view the Lady of Cyndyn's husband coming from the wagon. In private, he was often referred to as "the Lady of Cyndyn's husband," as he was not considered the true Lord of Cyndyn by most. In truth, he wasn't a lord of any kind by birth. He had merely married into it. He won his noble wife's hand in a tourney held by her senile, widower father, the late Lord Cyndyn.

Sir Aonghas, as he was also known, grasped in his right hand a large mace, which he lifted and let drop into his left hand in a slow tempo. The repeated hefting of this heavy weapon would have been a rigorous chore for an average man, but he was not an average man.

Sir Aonghas was a lumbering, brutish hulk, with hair covering his body and face, the coarseness of which matched his drunken sense of humor and perpetuated his given epithet: Boar of Dyven. He looked like a giant as he approached the silent men at the fire's side. He wore a heavy, dark fur draped over his frame, the color of his thick beard. Underneath, he wore naught but a white night gown and a pair of ridiculous soft ankle boots of red velvet. His appearance would have been comic had he not been so menacing.

Sir Hugh gave him a curt bow. "Your Lordship."

The giant man nodded. "Sir Hugh, what a *pleasant* surprise." He gave the knight an ironic smile, which gave some inkling to the others that it was not so pleasant a surprise.

Both men were painfully aware that had Sir Hugh competed in a certain tourney years before, instead of stopping to thwart the invading army of Gwythia, *he* would be the Lord of Cyndyn Hall. What's more, both knew that this would have pleased the current Lady of Cyndyn Hall.

The large man spoke, again well-seasoned with irony. "Undoubtedly you've been out rescuing damsels and slaying dragons."

The King's Champion said nothing, but stepped aside to reveal the evidence of his latest victory.

Aonghas' eyes met the dragon's and popped open. He stepped back, shaken by the instantaneous fear that took hold of him. He almost dropped his mace but recovered just in time to save his foot and his dignity. His composure regained, he feigned a yawn in pretense of boredom, a poorly executed mimicry of the theatrics employed by the Earl of Wyneddham. As he finished this little spiel, his eyes fell upon Billy, who collapsed against a rock in exhaustion.

"Oh, I see our two lost sheep have returned home, *finally!*" Aonghas then started into Billy, attempting to leave the whole dragon issue behind. "Do you know that I had to apologize to the earl for your absence, and he left us behind anyhow? You're in a lot of trouble, little man."

One of the guardsmen interrupted him. "Not two, milord!"

Aonghas, not used to being interrupted, stopped, looked at the man angrily, and then lifted his mace to wag it at Billy. He pointed the weapon at him and took a deep breath to renew his pontificating. Abruptly his expression changed to a combination of curiosity and frustration, and he turned his attention back to the guard who had spoken.

"What do ya mean, 'not two'? Not two what?"

"Not two lost sheep, milord."

Sir Aonghas looked at this man and saw the sorrow and anger inscribed on his features.

Duncan's cousin spoke again. "Only one has come home. Duncan is dead—killed by that horrid monster." He pointed with disgust at the dragon's remains and spat.

Aonghas was speechless. He turned away from the fire and mumbled something to Sir Hugh.

Hugh tipped his head to him. "Thank you, milord."

Still mumbling, the Lady of Cyndyn's husband wandered back to his wagon, annoyed by the knowledge that he wouldn't be able to sleep for the rest of the night.

This however was not the case for Billy or Sir Hugh. After relieving the packhorse of its heavy load, they both found a place to lie down in some soft grass and quickly fell into a deep slumber, neither one dreaming about much of anything.

* * *

The next morning was full of activity as the camp was uprooted and packed away for travel. While the guards attended to most of the preparations, Lady Myrredith was busy fussing both over and at Billy. Hugh and Aonghas kept themselves active, staying out of each other's way. The only time the two of them spoke was in the customary courtesies exchanged when the King's Champion presented himself to Lady Myrredith. Billy witnessed their formal, but curt exchange, and Aonghas' failed attempts to usher his wife away from his old rival. Finally, Aonghas became impatient and left to take out his frustrations on the procrastinating guardsmen. Billy left too, sensing that the two nobles wished to be alone for a moment, perhaps to reminisce over old times.

At last, with the wagon packed and horses harnessed, they left. Lady Myrredith had decided, much to Billy's joy and her husband's grief, that Sir Hugh must accompany them, "at least until we reach Cyndyn Hall!"

All the travelers were of good spirit as they went along their journey to the great hall, which had been home to Cyndyn lords for generations. That is, all the travelers but three: Sir Aonghas, Llyren, and Billy.

Sir Aonghas stayed much to himself, grumbling and watching his wife as she enjoyed Sir Hugh's company. Llyren, Duncan's mourning cousin, was in a mood as dark as the black sash he wore draped over his shoulder.

Billy was something of an emotional chameleon. When with Llyren, he felt deeply saddened by Duncan's death, yet when he was with Lady Myrredith and Sir Hugh, he was happy and forgot his troubles. This was all very confusing to him, as he bobbed back and forth, caught in the tides of a rough emotional sea.

Hugh noticed Billy's perplexed expression. "You seem to be in a bit of a quandary, my friend. What is it?"

Billy shook his head. "I don't know! It's just that ... How can I feel so sad over the loss of Duncan and yet feel so happy with you and Lady Myrredith, all at the same time?"

"Ah. That is a puzzlement. You touch on the very essence of the human heart. I'm afraid if there is an answer to your question, I don't know it. Perhaps you should be thankful that your heart is big enough to contain two such warring emotions." With that, Hugh took three apples from a basket and tossed them to Billy.

"What are these for?"

Hugh grinned. "Well usually people eat them, but you told me your friend Duncan showed you another use for them."

Billy gave Sir Hugh a puzzled expression

Hugh's grin broadened. "I had it in mind that you should entertain us and lighten your own burden with a little juggling."

Billy remembered how Duncan had taught him to juggle the apples, and he realized he did have some good memories from his short friendship. He stood up, widening his legs into a good stance, and was just about to start when the wagon heaved to one side with a loud thud, forcing Billy to sit. Then the wagon continued to rumble down the King's Road.

"But the wagon is moving!"

Hugh winked at him. "All the more entertaining."

"And it will be great practice, my charming young friend," Lady Myrredith said.

Aonghas, who was driving the wagon, simply grunted his disapproval. His manner spoke volumes of his contempt for the lot of them and their "frivolous behavior."

Billy paid him no heed, preferring to believe that he was grunting at his team of horses. Billy carefully took his stance and began to juggle the apples slowly. Toss by toss, mile by mile, he gained confidence and skill in the topsy-turvy wagon until even the larger bumps and lurches were no more than minor inconveniences.

Finally, Billy had to stop. He sat down, exhausted, as his audience of two applauded his efforts. Aonghas grunted and urged on the horses.

That evening, Hugh began teaching Billy the basics of playing lute. They entertained Lady Myrredith and the guardsmen with juggling, singing, lute music, and even dancing at times. Even Aonghas and Llyren the Glum, as he was now called, were put at ease and smiled large toothy grins as they were caught up in the merriment and camaraderie the two amateur minstrels brought to the road-weary travelers.

They traveled on, and as they did, Billy took advantage of Hugh and Llyren's presence to learn; lute and singing from the knight and more juggling from the Highlander. Even in teaching him, they found joy. Billy learned quickly, gaining skill with the lute and expanding his already considerable skills at juggling. Llyren, an accomplished juggler, as were many of his clan, and Sir Hugh, equally well skilled in lute, soon found themselves challenged by Billy's aptitude and insatiable thirst for knowledge. He was truly gifted.

Billy's singing voice had a calming, birdlike quality, and when given a chance, the guests of his father's inn had frequently requested to hear it. He was even a favorite at the valley's festivals, but he was no longer in the company of such simple folk. It never occurred to him that nobles and men as worldly as caravan guards might have the same tastes. So, it was much to his delight when his singing was pleasing to his fellow travelers. What's more, he had never been able to accompany himself with an instrument before, and this gave him a marvelous feeling of freedom.

Although he only played what simple tunes he had learned on Sir Hugh's lute, his companions were impressed. Unfortunately, as hard as he tried to be a serious minstrel, Billy continually fell into antics that drew hysterical laughter from his audience. While this might have been a setback of sorts to another, Billy took it all in stride, smiling with great satisfaction when he relieved tensions, especially tensions between the two rival knights.

Thus it went for three more days, when the small retinue reached Plyth, a small village on the edge of Wyneddhamshire. Like most outlying villages it had little to offer the traveler, so they continued. They passed through rich farmland and by late afternoon came to the Canter River, which bordered the lands surrounding Cyndyn Hall. At this point Llyren asked to be released.

"But why?" Sir Aonghas asked. "We haven't reached Cyndyn Hall yet!"

"Well, I've a likin' to go straight to Dyven and take the first ship for Caithnessshire. There be kin there, in the Highlands, who'll need to be told of Duncan's daith. An' besides you're just out of sight from home as it is. Please dock me whatever ya think fittin'."

"Are you sure you wouldn't rather spend the night warming yourself by our hearth?" Lady Myrredith asked from behind her husband.

"Aye, milady. The sooner I unburden myself of this news, the better. It might even end a feud."

"Then here." Aonghas handed him a bag. "And good journey to ya."

Llyren took the bag and felt its weight. Then frowning, he peeked into it. His eyes grew large. "This is far more than our agreed price, sir."

Sir Aonghas looked sternly at him. "It is your and Duncan's entire pay. The rest is heriot, for his family."

"Aye, sir! Thank ya, sir!" Llyren then bid his farewells to the others.

When he came to Billy, he smiled broadly. "As for you, my wee friend. You'll be welcomed at my clan-fire anytime!"

Llyren slapped the rear of his horse and rode up the river, waving behind him. Before he was out of earshot, he shouted back. "And Billy, don't forget to practice that trick I showed ya!" Then he went out of sight around the bend.

Sir Hugh continued to watch Llyren as he disappeared. "What trick?"

Billy answered with a gleam in his eye. "I'll show ya tonight."

They moved across the river onto Cyndyn lands. The boards of the old bridge creaked their misery at the wagon's passing.

Billy was struck by a thought. "Say, what did he mean, I was welcome at his 'clan-fire'?"

One of the guards heard Billy and rode up next to the wagon. "He honors ya greatly, for amongst the Highland clans, only a member of the clan can attend the clan-fire."

Billy looked to Sir Hugh who nodded his concurrence.

"Tis true. You have a good friend in him, for he will not forget you. Such words are not spoken lightly by a Highlander."

As they traveled still closer to Cyndyn Hall, Billy was happy knowing he had made such a good friend as Llyren. However, as he was surrounded by so many friends of late, his greatest joy came from knowing that, for a short while, he had helped the proud Highlander to forget his woes.

Billy's excitement grew as he and his friends passed by fields and orchards bordered by endless rows of hedges and stone walls. Billy looked out into the passing greenery and saw the life that abounded there. Hundreds of tiny flower blossoms filled the air with their perfume. The insects, birds, and ground squirrels made the hedgerows their home. He even saw a small red fox trot out of the shrubbery with dinner in its mouth, then dart back into a hollow. Occasionally a farmer would look up from his work and wave or bow before resuming the final tasks of his day.

The sun was setting, and Sir Aonghas hurried the horses to get home before dark. At the next bend they entered a lane lined with great elm trees, carefully planted long ago and now reaching across the road far above their heads. The large branches were like beams in the arched ceiling of a gallery, and indeed it felt as if they had entered a great hall.

Aonghas called one of the guards up next to the wagon.

"Ride ahead and tell the chamberlain we come—with guests—and have the servants prepare a feast—and quarters for our guests. Well, what are ya waiting for? Do you want me to tell him myself?"

"No, milord." The man smiled and kicked the flanks of his horse. He rode swiftly down the road and out of sight to warn the Cyndyn household of their master's return.

The wagon creaked and rattled as Aonghas urged on the horses. The countryside was quiet and serene, with gently rolling hills and cottage farmhouses set back from the road behind fields and clumps of trees. Wisps of smoke escaped their chimneys and wafted over the trees into a darkening sky of red and violet streaked clouds. The common folk were in for the night, and small lights flickered in the windows of their homes.

The sun was all but gone as Billy looked away from the woods now lining the side of the road. He looked ahead and gasped. "What—I mean—

Is that ...?" He climbed to the front with his head between Sir Aonghas and Lady Myrredith.

"Aye, lad." Aonghas sat up tall and proud. "Cyndyn Hall!"

Lady Myrredith tugged on Billy's arm, inviting him to sit with them in the front of the wagon. Billy, entranced by what he saw, plopped down on the seat between them. His jaw dropped open, and his eyes attempted to match his mouth's widening size.

Before them, a mountain of squared rock and masonry approached. Its rugged form was silhouetted against the sky—a dark giant, abruptly jutting from the surrounding flatlands.

The last ray of sunlight faded. If not for a string of newly lit torches lining the last stretch of road, they would have been in darkness. Billy could hardly take his eyes off the huge form of the fortress, but light coming from over a distant hill caught his attention.

"Lady Myrredith? What's that glow, over yonder hill?"

"That's the city, William."

Billy's eyes gleamed with thoughts of exciting days ahead.

"But you will see that soon enough."

"Are we so close? When shall we go there?"

Lady Myrredith smiled. "Soon enough, my impatient friend. Tonight I think we should rest and recover from our long journey."

"I don't know if I can sleep. So much to see, so much to do! I don't know where to start!"

"A good meal perhaps," Sir Aonghas offered.

"Aye, and a night's rest on a real bed," Sir Hugh added.

"Yes indeed, sir. Yes indeed."

Seeing the two knights in such gentlemanly agreement made Billy feel wealthy, warm, and well fed. Indeed they had been acting more like old friends than old rivals for the past two days.

"Tomorrow," Lady Myrredith said, "I shall show you the dwelling my family has called home for ten generations!"

CHAPTER NINE

Cyndyn Hall

The huge fortress loomed over them, seeming to rise infinitely beyond the torchlight, becoming one with the nearly starless night sky. The wagon rumbled across the drawbridge and through its arched gateway, which looked to Billy more like the gaping mouth of a monster with its sharpened portcullis teeth than an entrance to someone's home.

They entered the main courtyard. Echoes of the horses' hooves clattering on the closely placed stones filled their ears as the dark rock of the great inner walls repelled volleys of sound.

Billy was firmly on the ground before the wagon came to a complete stop. With eyes as big as apples, he trotted past two rows of confused servants, up the large steps of the main hall, spouting "Good evenin'" to all. He arrested his charge in front of the thick, deeply-carved doors to survey the vast courtyard and wagon below.

Lady Myrredith was being helped down by a frail-looking, elderly servant, somberly dressed from head to toe in grey and black. Even his thinning hair followed suit. Around his neck he wore a dark chain, and from the chain hung a large silver key.

When Her Ladyship reached the ground, she took a wide stance with her hands on her hips and faced the great hall. The entire ward held its breath. Her eyes scanned the edifice, checking the placement of every well-remembered piece of masonry. Satisfied, she cast her eyes once more on the darkly dressed chamberlain and nodded.

The old man, bowing deeply. "Welcome home, milady."

"Welcome home, milady," the cheerful crowd of servants echoed, and then they likewise bowed.

Billy, being the only soul standing erect on the steps, stood out like a scarecrow in a winter field. Feeling aware of his prominence, he too bowed deeply – too deeply.

The ensuing spectacle might have been normal, even commonplace among a troupe of traveling acrobats, but to the assembled household staff and nobles, Billy's tumble down the steps was awe inspiring. For Billy, finding himself neatly kneeling before Lady Myrredith, so far from where he had started to bow, was simply mystifying.

Sir Hugh broke the stunned silence. "Well, that's certainly the most interesting bow ever visited on the masters of Cyndyn Hall."

With that, the chamberlain snapped his fingers and the entire court-yard exploded into action. Servants began unloading the wagon while others tended to the horses. Still more ran back into the hall or other parts of the castle on numerous duties—all orchestrated by the chamberlain's snapping fingers. It was all Billy could do to keep out from under foot. He couldn't even take a second to get onto his feet.

Amidst the bedlam, Lady Myrredith bent to help Billy back to his feet. "Are you hurt, my dear?"

Billy immediately took inventory of his body, patting himself all over for broken bones. Much to his surprise, he hadn't a scratch.

"I'm fine." He looked up at her kind eyes and gave her one of his rock-shattering, ear-to-ear smiles.

Lady Myrredith laughed and, taking Billy by the shoulder, walked him up the steps. Hugh and Aonghas followed. The caravan guards came a few steps behind them.

"William," Lady Myrredith said, as they reached the threshold, "I think you'll get along here just fine. I just have to keep the scullery maids from falling completely in love with you."

Aonghas frowned. "That's just what we need; another distraction for those already distracted rumormongers."

"Oh now, they're not all that bad!"

"Oh no?"

"They're like that everywhere. Remember what it was like in His Majesty's court?"

Sir Aonghas sighed. "Aye. That nest of vipers!" Immediately he remembered Sir Hugh at his side. "No offense intended, good sir."

Hugh chuckled. "None taken, sir. None taken. Who knows better than I, the bite of those venomous servants of my lord?"

Although the King's Champion made this statement with jocularity, he unintentionally bit off some words, telling those listening carefully that the subject was more sensitive to him than he was letting on. Sir Hugh caught Billy's concerned expression. He placed a hand on his shoulder and forced a smile. Billy returned the smile, and they entered the main hall.

The travelers shed some of their belongings and cloaks in the ante-chamber. Billy saw a large fire blazing in the next room and rushed ahead of the others.

The central chamber of Cyndyn Hall was immense. Billy thought of his father's inn and the simple, cozy commons room. If his father had a commons room this large, he could serve many times the customers he did presently. Then Billy laughed when he imagined the enormous stack of dishes that would be dirtied.

Lady Myrredith descended the steps to join him on the main floor. "What is it, William?"

"How many dishwashers do ya have?"

Her ladyship laughed. "What do you mean?"

"Well, it's so ... so big!"

"Oh that. Legend says that Cyndyn Hall was built by giants. It was known as Fomorllech-Dunom in those days."

Billy's eyes and mouth sprung open in astonishment. "Giants?" His eyes darted around expectantly, but the only creature that came close to meeting his expectations was Sir Aonghas.

Aonghas grinned. "No, little man. They're all gone now—slain by the first Rudthar."

Lady Myrredith placed her hand on Billy's shoulder. "My father—"

"God rest his soul," interjected a passing servant.

"My father, Rudthar the second, was named after him."

Billy absorbed Lady Myrredith's short history lesson as he drank in the sights, sounds, and smells of the busy hall, being readied for their homecoming feast. Servants rushed from place to place around the ·banquet table, setting down dishes and cups, trays of food, and pitchers of water, wine, and ale.

The service was all of copper, silver, and pewter, each reflecting its own rendition of the firelight—the main source of illumination. The fire pit, which was almost floor level, was located in the center of the room. The smoke and flames tasted a pig, spitted over the pit, before they journeyed up into the conical flue that rose like a huge column to the dimly lit arches of the distant ceiling. For a moment Billy thought he saw some movement in the dark recesses of the ceiling, but dismissed it as shadows dancing in counterstep to the firelight.

A slender, shadowy man with a lute slung around his neck leaned against one of the flume's supports. His inky clothes were cut unlike any Billy had seen before, with many ribbons and gobs of fancy stitchwork. A floppy feathered hat topped him off. He looked like a great stuffed raven. The stranger was talking quietly with the caravan guard who had ridden ahead. Both were drinking from pewter tankards and looking into the fire.

"Who's that?"

"Who, William?"

"That man with the lute!"

Lady Myrredith focused on the ebon man. "I don't know."

Sir Hugh stepped forward. "*That*, is the scalawag of all minstrels!"

The lute-toting man turned to see who was making such a fuss. His dark eyes fell on Sir Hugh and widened. Finally, his mouth opened into a smile too sweet to be honest, and he spoke.

"Sir Hugh! What an unexpected pleasure it is to see you again."

His speech was heavily accented and breathy—over emphasizing the *h* and *s* sounds—so that he sounded somewhat serpentine. He bowed deeply with a great deal of pomp and well-rehearsed swishing.

"And this beautiful creature must be Her Ladyship, Lady Myrredith," he hissed. Again he bowed over dramatically and grinned his saccharine smile.

Billy, who had never heard anyone speak in such an exotic manner, was fascinated. The dark man's tongue bespoke of faraway lands that he had only heard about in tales. His voice was low and melodic and had a subtle subduing quality, even though it was definitely alien.

Lady Myrredith was not in the least impressed. "And you are …?"

"Oh, I-I-I." The man stammered, thrown by his ineffectual flattery.

"Allow me," Sir Hugh said, pushing back protests by the dusky stranger. "This is Don Miguel Medina Scarosa."

With this the man gave his most outlandish bow yet.

While he was still bowing, Sir Hugh continued. "Troubadour extraordinaire, minstrel at arms, and unscrupulous scoundrel!"

Don Miguel Medina Scarosa straightened as if stabbed in his posterior. He looked Sir Hugh in the eye. "Sir! You-you insult to me."

"Only justly."

"Well, I demand … I demand—"

Hugh smiled. "Satisfaction?"

He was in fact asking the minstrel whether he would cross swords with him to regain his dignity. Scarosa understood the knight's inference and gawped at him, seemingly horrified by the thought.

"No!" he blurted. When he had taken a deep breath to collect himself, Don Miguel continued. "No, Sir Hugh. I would demand—no, no, is *request*, yes request—that you give to me another chance to-to-to prove to you that I am no such the rascal that you are thinking I am."

Sir Hugh, who was now smiling broadly at seeing the troubadour sweat, broke into a good-hearted laugh and slapped the man on the back.

"Very well. Let us hear some bright music to entertain us while we dine. And none of those dark tales of battle you are always tossing about."

Don Miguel bowed in agreement and strummed on his lute. He stroked his mustache thoughtfully and conjured up his first ballad from the cobwebs of his repertoire. As the company of nobles and guardsmen sat down to feast, he began a soothing song about the first flowers of spring.

The troubadour droned on through the meal, breaking occasionally to pull a drought from his tankard and snack on a bite of roast pig. While his singing voice lacked luster and his choice of ballads lacked culture, his playing was nimble and eloquent. Sir Hugh, in spite of his apprehensions, seemed to enjoy the music, giving Scarosa the full measure of his second chance.

Sir Hugh turned to Billy. "Now I think it is your turn. Give the troubadour a rest and let us sample some juggling."

Lady Myrredith nodded. "Yes. And perhaps a song!"

With more coaxing from the others, Billy was out in front of the table, his hands filled with apples. He tossed them up and began to juggle. One—two—three—four—five! The hall fell silent, except for the crackle of the flames and the pitter-patter of the apples in Billy's magical hands.

He crisscrossed their paths back and forth, changing rhythm as easily as anyone takes breath. His audience was mesmerized. Even Billy was susceptible to the spell. His mind hardly knew what his hands were doing as he went through the routine of tricks taught to him by Llyren, who admitted he could not perform them himself.

Finally, Billy began to tire and decided to stop before he dropped an apple. He let the apples fall into his hands for the last time, except for the last one, which he caught on his forehead.

The room erupted in applause. During Billy's exhibition, the entire kitchen and housekeeping staff had crept into the hall. The tremendous sound from their clapping and cheers shattered Billy's concentration. He turned to look around the room, and the apple fell from his head. In his struggle to catch the fallen apple, he forgot what he was doing and dropped the other four. The room exploded in laughter and more applause. Billy froze, half-bent to catch the one apple. Slowly he lowered his head and then his shoulders, turning his pose into a humble bow.

Billy glanced up and then meekly kneeled to pick up the fallen apples. One of the apples had rolled to the feet of Don Miguel, who stood passively watching Billy.

Sir Hugh cleared his throat. "Don Miguel, was that not a most spectacular display?"

Don Miguel looked up at Sir Hugh. "Oh, yes. I am in agree." He took a deep breath and continued. "Of course, I have seen better in the court of my king, in Hispania, but it was *most* surprising. I did not know I was in the company of such comedic talent." With that he scooped up the apple at his feet and tossed it at Billy.

Billy caught the apple. "Thank you. I could show you how to do those tricks, if ya like!"

"No. I do no *toss* apples."

"Oh. Well, maybe you could teach me some songs on the lute then."

"Perhaps."

Billy put the apples on the table and was about to sit down again when Lady Myrredith spoke.

"William, perhaps you would sing for us now? Don Miguel?"

"Yes, Your Ladyship?"

"Would you be so kind as to loan William your lute?"

"Well, I-I would be happy to accompany him."

"I would like to hear William play."

"Aye!" spouted the caravan guards in unison.

Hugh slapped the table. "Yes, indeed."

"Well ... it is no a toy for a-a-a juggler, Your Ladyship."

"Yes, I am aware of that, Don Miguel. I have all confidence in William's ability to play the lute."

"Well," Scarosa grumbled, "then of course."

Billy strode to the bowing troubadour and carefully arrested the lute from his hands. He took a false step as if to stumble into a pratfall but stopped abruptly and glanced back at Don Miguel's gaping expression.

Bill gave him an impish smile. "Don't worry, I won't break it."

Don Miguel Medina Scarosa was a dark man, and an even darker one as he blushed. He crossed his arms and turned away from the laughing crowd. There he pouted and stared into the fire pit. A moment later, he snapped his fingers at a servant who brought him a new tankard of ale. He snatched the drink from the tray and prodded the servant away.

A few moments lapsed before the snickers died down and the hall fell silent.

Lady Myrredith cleared her voice. "Well then, William, let us hear some light, happy music."

Billy began to strum a light, soothing melody on the lute. His style was not as refined or elaborate as Don Miguel's, but its light-handed simplicity appealed to all those who heard it, putting them at ease. It was at this point that Billy wove the pure, sweet sound of his voice into the song.

There was a wee lad from the Valley O' the Yew
He wished to be knightly with good deeds to do
Rescue a princess
Defend what is true
But what's a poor lad from the valley to do?
There was a wee lad from the Valley O' the Yew
He wished he could see how the courtly folk do

Dining with princes
With forks and knives too
But what's a poor lad from the valley to do?
He dreamt every day, by the light of the sun
He wished on the stars, when the day's work was done
There was a wee lad from the Valley O' the Yew
He met some new friends who were noble and true
They offered him friendship
And kindness beside
And as they were leaving, they offered a ride
So what was the lad from the valley to do?
Stay at home with the chickens, and not much to do?
There was a wee lad from the Valley O' the Yew
He met with a dragon and thought he was through
Along came a hero
A brave knight was he
And he saved the wee lad who now sings gleefully
And he'll sing gleefully, when his comrades feel poor
And he'll sing gleefully, till he can sing no more

Billy played late into the night to the delight of all but Don Miguel Medina Scarosa. The Spaniard brooded throughout the evening over the same bowl of soup and then skulked away to his chamber.

Billy, tired from the long journey and all the excitement, gave in to the demands of his body and asked if he might be shown to a bed. Lady Myrredith, Sir Aonghas, and their guests were likewise tired, and all decided to retire as well.

Lady Myrredith took Billy's hand. "Come. I'll show you to your room."

They followed the chamberlain as he picked up a lamp and led them up large, spiraling steps and into a long hallway with dark, vaulted ceilings. Tapestries adorned the walls between a dozen oak doors that lined either side. Their footsteps reverberated in the hallway as they walked towards the far end. At that end of the corridor stood a large double door lit by a torch on each side. The guard stationed beside the door came to attention as they approached.

Her Ladyship pointed to the double doors. "That, is where I sleep."

The gaunt chamberlain stopped at the door immediately to the right side of the passage. He faltered as he inserted a key in the lock and then looked to his mistress. His old eyes sparkled in the dim light, probing Lady Myrredith for assurance.

"What is it, Eadwig?"

"Well, Your Ladyship—"

"Is the room not ready?"

"No, Your Ladyship. It has been prepared as you requested."

"Then proceed."

The loyal retainer nodded and unlocked the door with a clank. He grunted, and the door creaked open. A sudden draft caused the lamp to sputter and go out.

Eadwig took a splint and lit it in the nearby torch. "Detestable, drafty halls," he mumbled as he lit the lamp.

Billy squinted his tired eyes and looked about as Eadwig brought the dim lamp into the room. Billy could make out a large room, about half the size of the commons room in his father's inn. There was a small fireplace in one wall and a huge bed in the middle of the opposite wall, with a bear-skin draped across it. Like in the great hall, the ceiling was high and dark, and each wall was draped with a tapestry, the pattern of which he couldn't discern. The air was thick and musty, reminding Billy of a cellar.

Lady Myrredith whispered. "This was once my brother's room,"

Billy looked at his host. Her face was grave as she stared at the bed. "Your brother?"

Lady Myrredith gazed at Billy and then blinked as if shaking off a spell. "Yes. This room hasn't been used since ... Well, for many years."

Billy spied Eadwig also staring sadly at the vacant bed. The old chamberlain suddenly sprang into action when he realized he was being watched. He lit some candles, then quickly turned down the bed.

"This room is all for me?"

"Yes, William. Have a good night. Sleep well. I'll see you on the morrow." With that, Lady Myrredith turned and went out the door, followed by Eadwig.

"G'night, milady. G'night, Eadwig."

Eadwig turned to Billy with his hand on the door. "Good night, young sir." He stared at Billy, then backed out of the room, gently closing the door behind him.

As the door closed, Billy felt the same inhospitable draft. It gave him a chill, so he promptly got into his nightshirt and then into bed. It felt good to lie down on the big, soft bed, under the thick covers. Billy felt very content, despite the unfamiliar surroundings. It had been a great day, and now he was ready for a good night's sleep. He closed his eyes and soon dreamt of castles with dragons, and maidens in need of rescue.

In the night, Billy woke with a chill. He opened his eyes to find the candles burned out and the room dark. He turned over and pulled the covers up under his chin, but the chill would not leave him. He felt for the covers. From his chin to his feet, all the bedclothes were in place.

At that moment, he saw two eyes staring out of the darkness. Billy sat up, rubbing and blinking his tired eyes. "Lady Myrredith?" He looked back to the foot of the bed, trying to focus, but the eyes were gone. He scanned the room. There was nothing out of place. Slowly he lay back on the bed. As his head hit the pillow, he heard a low thump. Instantly he sat up again, surveying all the corners of the room.

"Who's there?"

Billy was very still. He listened for a response—for a sound. He heard nothing.

"Who's there?"

There was no answer.

Billy sat in bed for a long while with his feet and covers gathered around him. Finally fatigue started to seduce him back to sleep.

"Ha!" he yawned. "Spooked by a shadow."

The chill had left Billy, so he fell back on the bed, pulled the covers up snugly, and went back to sleep.

The next morning Billy awoke to a light rapping sound. He opened his eyes. It was still dark in his room, and at first he did not remember where he was, but then the bearskin tickled his nose and it all came back.

The rapping sound came again.

"Hello, sir. Are you *up*, sir?"

Billy hopped out of bed and went across the cold stone floor to the door. He pulled it open with a squeak.

"Good morrow, sir." A serving girl stood at the door, twisting a braid of mousy brown hair. Her eyes were on the floor. "I was sent to fetch ya for the mornin' meal."

Billy, still in his nightshirt, rubbed his eyes and stretched. The girl's eyes came up to Billy's, and he smiled at her. Her bright eyes smiled back, and then she shyly turned her face away with a girlish giggle.

Billy, suddenly aware that he stood in front of a girl wearing nothing but his nightshirt, quickly hid behind the door. "I'll get dressed."

Billy quickly slipped into his clothes and out his door to join the serving girl in the hall. Without a word she turned and started to lead Billy away. Billy walked quickly to keep up, always just behind her shoulder. He watched her face for any sign that she was going to talk to him. Billy found her looks appealing and so took little notice of where she was taking him. After several turns and two short staircases, it became apparent that she was not going to speak on her own.

"What's your name?"

"Beth, sir."

They were silent for a few more steps.

"My name's Billy."

"Yes, I know, sir."

Silence again.

"Where's breakfast?"

"Her Ladyship has taken breakfast in the garden, sir."

"Please don't call me *sir*. It makes me … nervous."

"Yes. Good morrow, Lady Myrredith."

Billy looked up to see that they were entering a large courtyard with numerous fruit trees and flowers. Lady Myrredith sat at a table under the shade of a plum tree. There was a short, roly-poly woman serving her water.

Beth stepped aside for Billy to pass and started to leave.

"Thank you, Beth."

"You're welcome, sir." The girl blushed, gave him a quick curtsy and then quickly disappeared.

"Well, I see you're already breaking hearts, William."

Billy turned around to face Lady Myrredith. "What?"

The lady broke into the most delightful laughter. It sounded like birds singing and made him smile.

"What is it, milady?"

She gave him a broad smile. "Nothing, William. Come and eat your breakfast."

Lady Myrredith and William ate their breakfast in the quiet garden, stopping occasionally to comment on the beautiful morning. They were just finishing when Don Miguel entered.

Upon sighting the Spaniard, Lady Myrredith rolled her eyes and sighed. Don Miguel was not aware that Her Ladyship was watching him. He plucked a rose from the garden and sniffed it. A wide, sickening grin spread itself across his dark face as he sighted the breakfasting lady.

"I had hoped to avoid that pompous peacock this morning."

Billy looked over his shoulder to see this "peacock" of Lady Myrredith's. He spotted Scarosa, then looked back to whisper to his host. "What's a peacock?"

Lady Myrredith said nothing as the troubadour approached.

"Your Ladyship!" Scarosa made a grandiose, well-rehearsed bow. "What a pleasure it is to see you this fine morning."

He held out his hand and offered the rose to Lady Myrredith. She took the flower wearily, and Don Miguel snapped to an aloof, erect posture, looking much like a post.

"A rose for a rose," he hissed.

Lady Myrredith looked at the rose briefly and then tossed it aside on the table.

"Do you no care for the rose, milady?" Don Miguel sounded hurt.

"Quite the contrary. I care for my roses very much. In fact, I planted them in this garden just so I might enjoy them blooming *on* the bushes, while I eat my breakfast."

"I see." Don Miguel stroked his mustache. "Well, perhaps you would allow me to join you?"

"Of course. Have a seat, Don Miguel."

"You are most gracious, milady."

As he sat, Lady Myrredith rose. "William and I were just leaving."

Billy and Don Miguel both rose with her. She started for the door.

"Come along, William. We have a great deal of exploring to do today."

"Yes, milady!" Billy filed in behind her. Passing through the door into the castle, he looked back into the garden. "G'morrow, Don Miguel!" He waited for a response, but none was forthcoming.

Lady Myrredith stepped through a small wooden-framed door and down a narrow, curving corridor. Billy followed like a stray dog on the heels of a new master. She stopped in the middle of the hall and looked in both directions. Billy, without knowing why, also looked from side to side. There was no one and nothing in sight, except for the blank stone walls of the passageway.

She bent down and whispered in Billy's ear. "No one knows about this passage. Not even the servants or my husband!"

Billy looked around again. He was very puzzled. "What? This passage?"

Lady Myrredith smiled. "No, not this passage. *This* passage!"

She pushed on two small stones in the wall, and a passageway opened directly before them. Chill, dank-smelling air caressed Billy's face and tickled its way down his neck. His eyes and mouth popped open. Lady Myrredith placed a hand over his mouth and shushed him. There was a shuffling sound from down the corridor.

"Quickly!" whispered Billy's host. She grabbed him by the hand and pulled him into the secret passage.

The rock wall closed and darkness surrounded them. Billy stumbled several times, but the gentle grip of his guide never faltered as she led him further into the winding passageway and up a small spiraling staircase. After a moment his eyes adjusted, and he could make out the outline of Lady Myrredith in front of him.

Finally, they stopped climbing. There was a clank, and Billy saw a small sliver of light appear in the darkness. Its brightness nearly blinded him. He ducked his head and squinted, but in the growing light he could see Lady Myrredith's silhouette. The golden light adorned her angelic beauty and lit up her fiery hair like a halo.

Suddenly the light revealed a dark, demonic face just behind Billy's companion. It bared its horrible little fangs, as if to bite the lady. Billy screamed and, grabbing Lady Myrredith's hand, ran through the strip of light, which had widened into a door. Billy looked over his shoulder as they cleared the opening. He could see nothing following them.

"What is it, William?"

"A demon!"

Billy continued to pull her along. The Lady of Cyndyn Hall stopped running and started to laugh uncontrollably.

"Come, milady!" Billy frantically waved for her to follow.

Her Ladyship was beside herself. She tried to stop laughing, but every time she looked at Billy's face, she broke out in laughter again.

Billy looked again to the passage from which they had just escaped. There was still no sign of anything following. *Is this some kind of trick?* He looked back to Lady Myrredith, who was beginning to collect herself.

"What was it you saw, William?"

"A demon! I think."

Lady Myrredith giggled and motioned William to come to her. Cautiously, he approached. She gently took his hand and led him back to the doorway.

At first Billy resisted, but one reassuring smile from Her Ladyship and he went willingly. She pointed into the doorway.

"There is your demon, William."

Just inside the opening Billy could see what had frightened him so: a creature about his size, with wings and curved claws, carved out of stone. It was frightfully realistic, and even though Billy could now see that it was stonework, it made him uneasy.

"What's that?"

"*That*, is a gargoyle. It's supposed to frighten away evil spirits, not handsome young men!"

"Evil spirits? I think somebody must have got it wrong!"

"If only you could have seen the look on your face!" Lady Myrredith giggled again.

"It was the look on *its* face that worried me."

They both laughed. Each time they managed to stop, one or the other would start laughing, and they would start all over again. Billy laughed so hard that he fell down and rolled on the ground.

This put Lady Myrredith into stitches. She held her side and tried to regain some composure. Between laughter and breaths she tried to speak. Finally she managed to say something. "Oh stop it, Rory, you really are ... are ..."

The lady's laughter had stopped, and her voice fell silent. She reached out and leaned against a small dark stone that protruded from the nearby tower wall. The stone door began to close. Billy managed to sit up and watch as the door shut with a soft thud. Again, with the secret passage closed, Billy could not see where the stones of the door began and the wall ended. Billy had never in his whole life seen anything like it.

"How did you do that?"

There was only silence from the lady. Billy stopped his inspection of the wall and looked into her face. She held her eyes closed tight and her brow scrunched together. The tower seemed to be the only thing holding her up. Billy watched her, waiting for a sign. He was very close now and could see every detail, every line of her face. The lines made her look oddly old. Billy could tell that some of the lines were from happy times, but there were still many more sad and worrisome lines—each one with its story to tell. He wondered why he had never noticed them. Perhaps they had never been so deep as they were that moment.

"What's wrong?"

Lady Myrredith pursed her lips together and opened her eyes. Her face changed back to its usual calm beauty, with just a whisper of the storytelling lines. She smiled a half smile for Billy, but he felt strangely saddened. He knew that he would never look upon her kind, pretty face again without seeing something of those melancholy lines.

Lady Myrredith looking out over the wall. "Do not be concerned, my friend. It is just an old flower I carry around in my heart. It's old and faded. I should have found a way to lay it down by now. I suppose I just like holding on to it."

Billy watched her for a moment. Her eyes were wandering on some distant place. Shortly she turned and focused on Billy. Again she smiled, but this time it was a comforting, unforced smile.

"You remind me so much of him," she said at last.

"Of who?"

"My brother."

"Your brother?"

Lady Myrredith reached out a hand and helped Billy to his feet. She held his hand and walked to the edge of the great castle's wall. It was a glorious day. The sun shone warmly on their faces, and a soft wind flowed over the wall. It tugged at Lady Myrredith's long, wavy hair, forcing her to brush the locks from her face as she spoke.

"Yes. My brother and I used to do everything together. In fact the last time I used that secret passage, it was with him. I don't know why I decided to show it to you. I guess I ... Well, you're so much alike—always dreaming of rescuing damsels from dragons and other heroics. You even have his eyes."

The lady stared quizzically into Billy's eyes, and then suddenly her own were drawn away. She looked out over the ramparts and pointed into the wind. "Look. You can see the top of the cathedral from here!"

Billy hopped up on the crenel in the wall and scanned in the direction she indicated. Lady Myrredith looped her arm around him and pulled him close to her. He sighted down her arm to where she pointed. Just over the farthest hill he saw numerous threads of smoke, and in their midst, a steep, pointed roof with shiny dark tiles.

"Is that the city?"

"Yes, William. That is Dyven."

"When do we go there?"

"In time, William. In time."

"But when?"

"In a couple of days. I think it will still be there then."

Billy looked at his smiling hostess and smiled back at her. "Oh, very well. I guess I can wait. I still haven't seen all of your castle, *yet*."

"That's right. Now come down from the wall before you give my heart a fit."

"Oh, I'm not gonna fall. I've climbed on my father's stable gates hundreds of times, and they're ever so much narrower than this old wall."

Lady Myrredith took a wide stance with her hands on her hips. "Just the same, I'd feel much better if you were down here on this part of the *old wall* with me. If I had to tell your father that I let you fall from the top of my wall, well—"

"Where is your brother?"

Lady Myrredith froze, and her face lost its mirthful demeanor again. Billy sat on the crenel as she turned her back to him. He heard her take a deep breath and release it.

"My brother is no longer with us."

She glanced over her shoulder at Billy, who stared back.

"No. That's too easy," she said under her breath. "I mean ... he's dead."

Billy thought the wind must have taken a sudden chill. He wanted to say something to his friend, but could think of nothing worthy of the situation. After a pause, she spoke again.

"He was still just a boy. Father showed the secret passages to me first. I decided that I would in turn show Rory. After all, we had no secrets from each other. He was younger than me, by a few years, but he always insisted on going off on his own."

Lady Myrredith stiffened and stepped away from Billy. "One night, he went into one of the passages alone. He must have become confused, down there, in the dark. He didn't know the way as well as I. The servants looked everywhere for him. I was afraid Father would be angry with me for showing Rory the passages, so I didn't say anything. I went looking for him there by myself. If I had known, I-I finally told my Father, but by then it was too late. They found his little hat, at the edge of a bottomless pit, in the catacombs beneath Cyndyn Hall. If only I hadn't ..."

Billy came down from the wall and to the lady's side. He took her hand in his own and held it to his heart. Without another word she knelt down and embraced him. She held him tight. After several minutes, she sniffled and spoke into his ear.

"You are the only one I have ever talked to about this."

She pushed away from him and held him at arm's length. "William, you must be very careful in the secret passages. I don't want you going into any of them without me. Do you understand?"

Billy nodded.

Then Lady Myrredith smiled. "Do you still want to explore the rest of Cyndyn Hall?"

Billy returned her smile. "Yes, if you do."

"Me? There's nothing I'd like doing more."

Lady Myrredith wiped her puffy red eyes dry and, taking her young companion by the hand, continued their tour of Cyndyn Hall. They strolled along, Lady Myrredith pointing out interesting features and dropping in a history lesson or two, for good measure, which included plenty of knights, dragons, giants, and more secret passages.

"And here we are, back at your room!" The Lady of Cyndyn Hall opened the thick oak door.

Billy watched as Lady Myrredith entered the dark and gloomy room. Without hesitation she crossed to the far wall and fiddled with some long sashes that hung there. All at once, the dusty tapestry in front of her fell away, and bright light burst through the tall stained-glass window that stood behind it. Multicolored shafts of light poured into the room, pushing out all but the darkest of corner shadows. There were reds and blues, yellows and greens, all bright and cheerful. Billy, who still stood outside the door, looked in both directions.

Myrredith fanned at the dust raised by the fallen tapestry. "What is it, William?"

"Well, it's just that in the light it looks so different. I thought it might be the wrong room."

Lady Myrredith laughed. "Come in, William! This is your room." She paused and looked about the room for a moment. "You know, this room does look very different in the light. I had forgotten how beautiful it could be. My great-grandfather had originally thought to make this room a chapel."

"What happened?"

"A priest protested that putting the only real chapel in the shire so near to the lords' living quarters might scare off the common folk. That's why he built the chapel off the garden, and then later started the cathedral and abbey in town. He gave this room to his son, and it has since belonged to the heir of Cyndyn Hall."

"Then this was your room?"

"No. It was my brother's. After he *passed on*, my father ordered it sealed. It has remained so, all these years. I only opened it now, for you." Billy bit his lip. "I don't know what to say."

"It is only what you deserve, my friend, for you have lifted a burden from my heart and made me feel young again."

In the new lightness of the room, Billy could see everything that he had missed or had been too busy for. The room was not as colorless as he had originally thought. Many of the items that were black the night before were now deep brown or red. The light coming through the colored pieces of glass added color to everything. It made the pink in Lady Myrredith's cheeks glow soft and warm. It also painted a picture on the stone floor and rugs. In addition, it revealed furnishings that he had failed to see. A small writing table sat in one corner with a chair, and, to Billy's joy, a suit of armor stood guard just behind it.

"Wow!" He crossed the floor to examine the dark plate mail.

"It belonged to the first Rudthar."

Billy scrutinized. He took in each scar and scratch as if he were present at the battle that had put them there.

"Touch it, if you like," said his all-but-forgotten guide.

Billy reached out and touched the smooth, cold steel. He caressed it with delicate care, letting his fingers rest momentarily on a rough spot in the breastplate. The room may have come short of being a chapel, but Billy would have never noticed.

"Wow!" he said in a reverent whisper.

Billy let his hand slide back across the buckles and onto the back of the suit. His fingers found a large hole there with jagged edges. He instinctively retracted his hand and leaned to the side to see the gaping rent he had felt.

Lady Myrredith stepped closer. "He was betrayed by someone he trusted."

Billy's face came out from behind the armor abruptly and stared at her in shock.

Billy's host shrugged her shoulders. "My father said, 'one of the problems of being trustworthy is not always being able to tell who is worthy of trust.' Sometimes I think a person would be better off in a band of outlaws you know you cannot trust."

While the lady was talking, Billy's eyes strayed to the giant tapestry on the wall behind her. It was different from the others in that its primary color was green instead of red, and it had been woven in a very different style. It depicted a vast, lush valley with people and many strange creatures. The valley felt familiar to him, but he knew that he had never been anywhere like it. Billy felt drawn to the tapestry and temporarily forgot the suit of armor.

As he silently crossed the floor, Lady Myrredith noticed his gaping expression. "What is it, William?"

Billy pointed at the tapestry. "Where's that?"

Lady Myrredith turned around and stared at the tapestry until Billy was standing next to her. She stepped behind him and put her hands on his shoulders.

"This is a very special tapestry, William. I doubt there is another like it, anywhere in the kingdom. It was a wedding gift to one of my ancestors, who was reputed to have a bit of the fay in her blood. According to legend, her wee relatives were so pleased by her marriage that they wove this especially for her."

"You mean, faeries made this?"

She smiled. "It's supposed to depict the homeland of the little folk. Do you like it?"

"Oh yes!"

"It was Rory's and my favorite. I just forgot it was here."

It made Billy very happy to hear Lady Myrredith talk about her brother without the previous faltering.

"The little people have their own kingdom?"

"Why yes! Do you see the great feast over there, near the river?"

Billy looked at the middle of the valley, along the sky blue river, which flowed through its heart. There, on the green banks of the river, a large number of people and creatures gathered. They were celebrating together in a great feast, drinking and eating from a banquet table as large as a barn. All the people were small. Some of them were no larger than the birds they dined with. The detail was astounding. Even Lady Myrredith, who had seen many fine tapestries in her time, appeared amazed at its artistry.

"Yes, Lady Myrredith. I see it."

"Do you see who's at the end of the table?"

Billy looked closer and saw, at the head of the table, a jolly little fellow dressed in purple with a golden crown upon his head. He was drinking from a long, curved horn, and in his other hand he held a golden wand.

"*That*, is the King of all Faerie. The King of Tirn Aill."

"Is he magical?"

"Oh, most certainly, as are all the little people that live there."

"And the people of *Tirn Aill*... they're all little people?"

"I think so."

"Can the king grant wishes?"

"Well, I suppose he can."

"I wish I could go there."

Lady Myrredith rested her chin on Billy's head. "Me too, William."

The two of them gazed at the tapestry for a long while. They daydreamed, letting themselves wander the paths of Tirn Aill, a pair of pilgrims. They were abruptly brought back to their senses by a sharp knock at the door.

Sir Hugh entered. "My, this is quite a room!" They turned to face him, and he added, "So this is where you two have been hiding. It's nearly time for supper."

Both Billy and his guide felt a nudge from their stomachs. They had entirely forgotten about supping. Billy's innards gave an audible complaint about the poor service, but the sight of the King's Champion was so satisfying that they put aside their hunger to welcome him.

"Hugh! Is it really that late?"

Billy rushed the knight. "Sir Hugh! Lady Myrredith showed me all over the castle. Did ya know there were secret passages? Do ya wanna see one? Can I show him, Lady Myrredith?"

Hugh crossed his arms. "Now, Billy, I think that Lady Myrredith showed you those secret passages, because she knew you could keep them a secret. You better not tell me, just in case there are spies around."

Sir Hugh winked at Billy who returned the wink, pretending to lock his mouth with an imaginary key. Billy then handed the key to Lady Myrredith, who graciously accepted it.

"Why thank you, young sir." She then slipped the make-believe key away.

The three companions left the room and traveled down the corridor in the direction of the main hall. The two nobles led the way, walking side by side, with their young friend tagging along behind.

Sir Hugh turned his attention to the lady. "I missed your company terribly at dinner. Sir Aonghas and I had to share it alone with that vagabond singer."

She frowned at the mention of the Spaniard. "How is Don Miguel?"

"Oh, being his usual, tiresome self. Myrredith—I mean, milady—I know I said I would give him a second chance, but you don't have to put him up for me. I just don't want you to be taken in by him. He's not—"

The lady held up a hand. "Never fear, my father warned me, long ago, about traveling minstrels, alchemists, and their ilk."

"Did he also warn you about wayward knights?"

"Well, he did tell me that a knight's best friend was his horse. And that a knight who has recently lost his best friend might fall into the arms of a woman, if he wasn't careful."

"A woman?"

"A woman with long, straight hair, big brown eyes, and the snout of a horse!"

"What?"

"But fear not. I have a solution."

Hugh smiled and eyed her suspiciously. "Oh really?"

"Just follow me."

Hugh and Billy followed their hostess out of the main hall and across the large courtyard. As they approached the far side, a boy ran up to the mistress of Cyndyn Hall and bowed.

"Thomas, would you bring Pomponnel here, please?"

The boy stared at his mistress as if wanting confirmation of her request. Billy saw marked trepidation in his eyes.

Lady Myrredith also noticed the boy's hesitation and smiled. "What is it, Thomas?"

"Wouldn't you rather see Glynda, milady?"

"No, Thomas. Now run along."

Thomas bowed again and ran around the corner.

Hugh gave Lady Myrredith a quizzical look. "Pomponnel?"

"Aye."

"What manner of name is that?"

"A fitting one."

"Who is she?" Billy asked.

Lady Myrredith looked at him and laughed. "Oh, just someone I think Sir Hugh should meet."

"A lady friend?"

"Well, Pomponnel is hardly a lady, but a friend ... I do hope so!"

Hugh eyed the lady next to him suspiciously. Billy thought he detected some pain hiding under the knight's expression.

At that moment, Thomas reappeared leading—or rather struggling with—a beautiful silver-grey steed. Its mane and feathery fetlocks moved like glistening black flames over its muscular neck and licked at its thick ashen hooves. The spirited creature reared up and tossed its majestic head, as if the bridle were scornful.

Billy backed up a step and watched Hugh who stood completely motionless before the magnificent, feral beast. The jaw of the King's Champion hung loosely on its hinges, while his eyes stared on in childlike adoration.

The horse's tantrum became more violent, and Thomas fell to the ground, unable to hold on to the reins. Without hesitation Hugh moved between the steed and Lady Myrredith and caught the reins. As if by magic, the animal became calm. Thomas, frozen with fear, stared blankly at the beast, half expecting to be trounced. The others likewise gawked at the subdued creature.

The lingering silence was broken by a nicker from the horse. As if awakening from a trance, Billy and the others blinked their eyes and glanced at one another.

Lady Myrredith stepped forward. "Well, allow me to introduce you. Sir Hugh, this is Splendore Pomponnel. Splendore Pomponnel, this is Sir Hugh."

Hugh turned his head to the side. "Splendore Pomponnel?"

Before Lady Myrredith could answer, the horse nickered again and stepped towards Sir Hugh. Hugh stood still, waiting for the beast to reach him. Without warning the horse gently pushed Hugh with its nose.

Lady Myrredith laughed.

Hugh grinned. "What is it?"

"That horse has been waiting for you for a long time."

"What?"

"No one, but no one has been able to break that ornery beast, much less get near it!"

Hugh looked appreciatively at the beautiful animal before him. The creature stared back at him. Each one, man and horse, sized up the other. The horse nodded, and Hugh reached up to run his hand through its thick, dark mane. Splendore Pomponnel moved in closer, and Hugh's hand glided along his sleek neck, down to his meaty chest.

The knight continued down the horse, letting his hand slide over the silky grey and silver coat. Then without a word he grabbed a handful of mane and leapt onto its back. Hugh sat still for a moment, holding tightly to Splendore's mane. The horse remained docile. Hugh urged his mount forward, and it obediently complied. Hugh slowly rode the horse across the courtyard then returned to his astonished friends with a smile plastered across his face.

"Well it seems that you have a new companion," Lady Myrredith said.

"Aye, I think Splendore Pomponnel and I are going to be good friends. There's just one thing I'd like to know."

"What's that, Hugh?"

"Why give a horse two names?"

Don Miguel suddenly appeared beside Billy. "A horse with two names?"

Lady Myrredith turned to face the troubadour. "Yes, Don Miguel. This horse has two names."

"But why?" The curious Spaniard walked towards Sir Hugh and Splendore. "Was one not enough?"

"No," answered the Lady of Cyndyn Hall. "As a matter of fact, one was not enough."

Don Miguel continued to walk closer to the horse. "It appears to be a fine animal, but two names, milady? I think perhaps you give too much respect to this horse." With that said, he started to walk behind Splendore.

"Don't …!" shouted Hugh and Lady Myrredith in unison.

In a flash, Splendore Pomponnel lashed out with his hindquarter at the disrespectful minstrel. The attack came precisely at eye level, but incredibly Don Miguel avoided it. The deadly hooves slashed through the air miraculously missing the Spaniard's vulnerable head by mere inches. Miguel fell to the ground and rolled out of the way, coming up on his feet two yards away from the cantankerous beast.

Lady Myrredith watched the troubadour dust himself off and check for broken bones before she spoke to him. "It appears that it is you, Don Miguel, who does not know how much respect to give a horse."

Don Miguel looked at her. His voice trembled. "Perhaps you are right, Your Ladyship. Now, if you will excuse me, I think I should go inside."

Lady Myrredith smiled. "But of course."

Splendore Pomponnel neighed and took a step back. Don Miguel's shoulders jumped in response. Swiftly the Spaniard circled around the horse in a wide arc, keeping a wary eye on him until he was out of sight.

All those present in the courtyard laughed as Miguel disappeared into the main keep. Hugh was nearly beside himself.

"Yes, I think Splendore Pomponnel and I are going to be great friends!"

With that, the King's Champion nudged his new mount in the flanks, and they sped towards the gatehouse.

Lady Myrredith cried after him. "Hugh! Hugh! What about supper?"

Sir Hugh stopped the splendid steed and turned to face his hostess. "Don't worry! I haven't got a saddle. I'll be right back!"

Lady Myrredith, Billy, and Thomas watched the exuberant knight sally forth through the gate of Cyndyn Hall. He looked more like a twelve-year-old boy than the King's Champion.

"We might not see him till bedtime," Lady Myrredith said with a smile. "As a youth he loved nothing better than to ride bareback through the woods."

"How well did ya know Sir Banarel?" Billy asked.

Lady Myrredith turned from the gate. "The man killed at your father's inn?"

Billy nodded.

"Not well. Our journey to Penwyth was the first time I had seen the man."

Billy nodded. "Oh. Do ya think he was a good knight?"

"Why do you ask, William?"

"Nothin'. I just wondered what he did, before ..."

"Still dreaming of becoming a knight?"

Billy answered with a grin.

"Well, Sir Banarel was a foreigner by birth, but I'm told he earned his spurs performing some 'secret service' for the king. I don't know when he was assigned to the earl."

"Assigned?"

"Yes. It's a privilege given to the lords of the realm. They can request one of His Majesty's knights as a protector, although some lords request one just for the social status, but only the king has the authority to make such assignments."

"Is one of His Majesty's knights assigned to *you?*"

Lady Myrredith smiled and shook her head. "No, William. I have no need for a protector, or a trophy warrior. Besides, I have my husband, don't I?"

Billy nodded, and Hugh trotted through the gate.

"Back so soon?"

Hugh smiled at Myrredith and brought his mount to a stop. "Well, to be honest, another few steps and I might not have come back till bedtime."

Lady Myrredith and Billy laughed as Hugh dismounted and handed the reins to Thomas, who reluctantly accepted them.

Hugh patted the boy on the back. "Everything's fine, Thomas. I don't think he'll trouble you too much anymore." Then he turned to the horse. "Behave yourself, my friend. We'll go riding again in the morning!"

Lady Myrredith and Billy eyed their companion as he watched after Splendore Pomponnel. When he realized he was under their scrutiny, he turned to his friends and smiled.

Lady Myrredith spoke first. "Hugh, Splendore Pomponnel is yours."

"Milady, I ... How can I ever repay you for such a treasure?"

Lady Myrredith placed her hands on Billy's shoulders. "You already have."

As they entered the great hall, Billy saw Scarosa, in what appeared to be his favorite spot: leaning up against a chimney support. His lute hung around his neck, and in one hand he held a well-heaped plate, while the other pushed food into his thin-lipped mouth. His near-fatal introduction to Splendore Pomponnel hadn't dented his appetite one bit.

When Scarosa spotted his host, he set down the plate. Then he scanned the area while he wiped his greasy hands on a passing servant. Finally, he found his tankard and washed down the mouthful of food. Sir Hugh and Lady Myrredith didn't seem to notice the troubadour's gluttonous behavior as they crossed the hall and sat at the dining table, but Billy watched him in fascination. He remembered what Lady Myrredith had said that morning in the garden and turned to Sir Hugh.

"Is a peacock a kind of pig?"

Hugh shot him a quizzical expression. "No. Why?"

Billy leaned over and whispered. "Lady Myrredith said something about a 'pompous peacock' this morning—"

"She said what?"

"She said she had hoped to avoid the pompous peacock this morning, when we were at breakfast in the garden."

"Who else was there?"

"Don Miguel—"

Upon the utterance of the Spaniard's name, Sir Hugh broke into uncontrolled laughter. Most everyone in the hall took notice of his guffaw, including Don Miguel, who tucked his lute under his arm and strutted over to the table.

While Don Miguel approached, Sir Hugh regained his composure and leaned over to whisper to Billy. "Now that," he said, indicating the troubadour, "is a peacock."

Again Sir Hugh laughed.

"Lady and gentle sirs." Scarosa gave them a superfluous bow. "What wondrous entertainment can I bring you tonight?"

"Let us hear soft music, which might help *pheasant* go down easy."

Lady Myrredith touched Hugh's elbow. "I'm sorry, Sir Hugh, but I don't believe we have any pheasant tonight."

"Oh? My mistake."

The Spaniard leaned forward. "Perhaps, Sir Hugh, it is a love song you wish to hear?"

Sir Aonghas appeared at the main entrance and shouted to Don Miguel. "No more love songs! I wish to hear songs of glory and battle!"

Upon hearing this, the entertainer bowed his acquiescence and strummed the first notes of a very popular and traditional warrior's song. Don Miguel sang the first verse alone, but then Sir Aonghas, with tankard in hand, joined him on the chorus. What Sir Aonghas lacked in talent he made up for in enthusiasm. His gusto for singing was only matched by the displeasure it seemed to bring the other half of the duet. Don Miguel squinted one eye and tried vainly to harmonize with his partner.

Billy smiled broadly at Sir Aonghas, remembering fondly the men who got a belly full of ale in his father's inn and abruptly broke into song. He was more than content to sit and listen to the duo, as even a small taste of home, no matter how sour, helped in his stand against homesickness.

At his first chance, Don Miguel slipped into several unfamiliar ballads, and Sir Aonghas was forced to sit them out. The troubadour sang of stormy battles and conquest on distant shores, of the glory, fame, and riches of the victorious. At first his songs were acceptable, even warmly received, but the small successes went to his head, and, in this cocky state, he decided to sing an especially unsavory song. To say that its gory lyrics hedged on the unappetizing would have been overly kind.

Lady Myrredith slammed her cup down on the table. "Please!"

This so startled Don Miguel that he stopped singing, in order to catch his lute. The hall reverberated with the sound of its mistress' voice, and then everything was quiet. All eyes were on Lady Myrredith.

"Please, Don Miguel, we are trying to eat. Play for us some traditional ballads."

Don Miguel opened his mouth to argue the point but stopped. He closed his mouth and stood red faced at the center of the room. He looked first to Sir Aonghas, then slowly a satisfied, serpent-like smile spread across his thin lips. He stroked his mustache and focused his eyes on Sir Aonghas' wife and the King's Champion. "Ah, I see that the lady has been put in the mood for a love song."

"No! Just something less bloody, and more ... palatable."

Don Miguel's eyes shifted back and forth. Then he turned away for a moment and strummed his lute, tuning it. When he turned back around, he was strumming contemplatively.

"Ah! I've got it. A song of romance from my homeland."

"Is that all you know; love ballads and battle hymns?"

"Well, Sir Hugh, they are most popular these days."

With that, Miguel sang a song of two lovers, forbidden to love. It ended in tragedy as only such love songs can and left the audience flat.

Myrredith looked down the table. "William? Are you finished dining?"

"Yes, milady."

"I think it's time Don Miguel had a rest. Will you please entertain us?"

"That is no necessary, Your Ladyship!" Scarosa argued. "I am no tired."

"Yes, but I am."

Don Miguel Medina Scarosa was stunned. His jaw went slack, and he stood frozen. Billy came to his side and held out a hand for the Spaniard's lute. He loosed it and handed it over as if surrendering a sword. Then with a "humph," he held his head aloof and strutted out of the hall.

"A temperamental peacock at that," Hugh said under his breath.

Lady Myrredith laughed. "You've been talking to William."

Billy started to sing before the King's Champion could answer. He began with a well-known song and invited everyone to join in. Before long, even the servants were singing. They spent the rest of the evening laughing, singing, and just enjoying the camaraderie.

Just before the company retired for the night, Sir Hugh and Sir Aonghas sang a song together for Lady Myrredith. Billy's effort to mend the gap between them was paying off. He went to his room very weary, but with a feeling of accomplishment.

CHAPTER TEN

The Spirit of Cyndyn Hall

That night Billy went to bed and dreamt of faerie kings and feasts. Just as the night before, he awoke with a chill. He found the candles burned out and a pair of eyes staring at him from the darkness. Billy threw up the covers and hid underneath them. He waited there, curled up like a hibernating squirrel. He listened, but all he could hear was his own breathing. Then he heard a low thud, the same as the previous night.

"Who's there?"

There was no answer.

Now, turtlelike, Billy slowly poked his head out from the covers and peeked at the foot of his bed. There was only darkness.

* * *

The next two days went slow for Billy, as everyone was too busy to spend much time with him. Lady Myrredith was busy with the affairs of her holdings, while Sir Hugh and Sir Aonghas had business of their own. At dinner, Sir Aonghas was agitated and started to quarrel with Sir Hugh more than once. Each time, Billy quickly came to the rescue with a song.

Billy was aware of the tension building, and it made him restless. He wanted to go to town, but had to settle for exploring the castle on his own. And while Cyndyn Hall, with all its secret passageways and giant walls was interesting, he longed for something new.

Looking for company, Billy tried to approach Don Miguel on several occasions. At first Scarosa simply ignored him, but later became irritated and shooed Billy away, accompanied by a few select expletives.

Not being one to give up easily, Billy decided to ask Scarosa for a lute lesson. Don Miguel was in the kitchen when Billy found him. The troubadour had waylaid Sir Aonghas there and was talking to him in hushed tones.

As Billy approached, Aonghas grabbed the thin Spaniard by the front of his blouse and lifted him to his face. "What? Where did you see them?"

Don Miguel held out his hand and pointed in the direction of the gardens. The giant of a man dropped him and marched out the door, knocking over vases and pots full of food as he departed.

Don Miguel looked around at the kitchen staff and sighed as he brushed off his clothes. He stopped abruptly when he spotted Billy.

"What do *you* want?"

"I was gonna ask you to give me a lesson."

Suddenly Scarosa snapped. "I give you a lesson, you little pipsqueak!" With that he picked up a clay pot and hurled it at Billy.

Billy ducked the pot, and it splattered against the door jam. Ale splashed in all directions, but Don Miguel wasn't through. He picked up a cup and likewise threw it at his would-be student. Without thinking, Billy reached up and grabbed the cup out of the air. It startled him, almost as much as his attacker, but still Don Miguel was not finished. He became enraged and hurled another cup at Billy, and then another. Don Miguel's face reddened with each projectile Billy caught.

Billy had no intention of aggravating the troubadour further, but something instinctive took over, and he started to juggle the cups.

Don Miguel began throwing random items at the young juggler: pots, pans, dishes, food, whatever was handy, but still his efforts were fruitless. His target simple stepped aside and kept juggling.

Billy caught a plate and began to juggle it with the cups. After a couple of items went by, Billy set down a cup and reached out again to add a large spoon to his collection of dancing utensils.

Scarosa shouted, in frustration, and produced a dagger. One of the cook-women saw the blood in his eyes and smacked the weapon from his grip with her rolling pin. Miguel scrambled for his lost blade, but his opponent deftly stepped on it. He attempted to budge the beefy woman and found this problematic. With his hand still on her foot, he glared at her. The cook kept her weight on the dagger and glared back, hefting her rolling pin in the manner of Sir Aonghas with his mace.

Don Miguel Medina Scarosa was shaking furiously. He whipped around and charged directly at Billy, forcing him back to the doorway. Without hesitation, Miguel overtook Billy and literally ran him down. The young juggler and his impromptu act were scattered across the floor.

Scarosa rushed through the door to exit the kitchen. "Stupido!" he shouted over and over as he disappeared down the corridor.

Billy sat up on the floor of the hallway, just outside the kitchen. Still stunned, he considered the mess surrounding him. Far down the hall he heard a crash and the voice of his attacker shouting in his foreign tongue.

As Don Miguel's voice faded into the distance, laughter and applause filled Billy's ears. Don Miguel had caused an unprecedented mess for the servants to clean up, but the entertainment must have been worth the few broken dishes. The kitchen staff stood Billy up and patted him on the back, laughing and congratulating him on his "victory." He felt like a hero for a moment, until he remembered the mess he and Don Miguel had created.

Billy started to clean up the mess, but all the servants insisted that he leave the cleaning to them. All that is, except Beth. She handed him a tray and placed broken pottery on it. It reminded him of the time his father's inn had been the site of what was commonly called "the valley's finest brawl."

Billy and Beth worked well together, and she seemed to enjoy his company. Frankly, Billy found her company equally welcome. There, in the kitchen, in the midst of common folk, he felt truly at home for the first time since his arrival.

Even after the mess was cleaned up, Billy stayed to help in the kitchen. He fit in so well that the staff forgot he was a guest. When things quieted down, the servants fell into their usual habits, chatting the scuttlebutt that castle servants do.

Meggy, the burly cook who saved Billy from Scarosa's dagger, spoke first. "Gawd help us, but Her Ladyship's man lit out o' here in a fume, now didn't he?"

"Oh, the temper on that man!" said another servant.

"I'll say!" said yet another.

"I wonder where he was goin'," Billy said.

"I heard that snake, what was just in here, whisperin' somethin' about Her Ladyship and Sir Hugh bein' together in the garden."

"Aw, now that's been long dead and buried," an elderly cook-woman said, "ere since *he* come to live here!"

"Now what's he gone and dug up old bones like that for?"

"He's after somethin'."

Billy looked up from his chores. "What?"

"Who knows?" the old woman answered.

"But whatever it is, *he's* in it now, and ya know what that means."

"Well," Meggy said, "the first Rudthar may have kicked all the ill-tempered giants out of Cyndyn Hall, but the last Rudthar—"

"God rest his soul!" all the servants piped in unison.

"The last one went an' let 'em back in!"

The servants laughed.

One of the girls held her side and slapped the table. "That's a good'n, Meggy!"

"I don't understand."

Meggy stopped giggling and looked at Billy. "Oh, it's nothin' my boy, just a bunch of old hens, havin' a chuckle. Say, Beth, why don't ya take the young master here an' fetch us some water?"

"Yes, Mum. Will you follow me, sir?"

Billy nodded, and they left the kitchen. Beth led the way to the well at her usual pace. Billy lengthened his stride to catch up with her, and she quickened her own to stay ahead. Before they knew it, they were running across a large stone courtyard.

In the middle of the yard there was a small well with a bucket on a rope. They arrived at the well simultaneously and stared across at each other, panting. Billy took the bucket and dropped it into the well. He tried to catch his breath as he hauled the full bucket back up the deep well.

Still winded, Billy looked to Beth. "What were they talking about?"

"Who?"

"The cooks."

"When?"

"Just now. Don't ya want to talk about it?"

"No. Not really."

"Oh! Why not?"

"I don't wanna catch trouble."

"Trouble? With who?"

"*Him!* Sir Aonghas!"

"You wouldn't get into trouble with him."

"Oh, ya don't know."

"What?"

"Well, ya promise not to repeat a single word of this?"

Billy ceremoniously crossed his heart.

"*He*, Sir Aonghas, isn't usually as he's been of late. He's usually not so nice to us. When he's drunk—which is nearly all the time—he beats the servants, but since you've been here he's changed. My mum says it's on account of you. Well that is until a day ago. He's been spending a lot of time with Don Miguel. My mum says he's a bad one, that he's just an idle troublemaker an' a worthless smell-feast! Well, you know. Ya saw him today. An' he's nothin' compared to Sir Aonghas on a jag."

"Yes. I think I know what you mean. We've just got to keep him from drinking so much."

"Aye, but how?"

"I don't know."

Billy filled two large jugs by the well and picked them up to carry back to the kitchen. Beth tried to carry them for him, but he wouldn't hear of it.

"I'm not useless ya know!" Billy started back towards the kitchen.

Beth snuck under his arm and hoisted a jug from his grip with a giggle. "I'm not useless either."

"Yes, I know. Say, what was that business about Lady Myrredith and Sir Hugh?"

"Well, since you'll probably find out about that anyway."

She set down her jug, and Billy did likewise.

"Long ago, Sir Hugh and Her Ladyship were very close. Everyone thought they would marry. And so they would have, if her father hadn't given her to *him*."

"Sir Hugh and Lady Myrredith?"

"Aye."

"I think I finally understand."

The two of them stood for a moment, each contemplating their situation. After a sigh from both, they picked up the water and silently carried it to the kitchen.

* * *

At the evening meal, Billy did his best to keep Sir Aonghas in good spirits and yet keep him away from the alcoholic kind. It wasn't easy, for each time Sir Aonghas finished a drink, Don Miguel snapped his fingers, and the servants filled the empty cup. The only course for Billy was to start singing early and get Scarosa out of the picture.

As before, Billy started with songs that everyone could sing along with him. All those years he had spent listening to drunken singers in his father's inn were finally paying off. He knew many popular songs, and soon everyone was singing, laughing, and having a good time.

The only ones who didn't join in were Sir Aonghas and Don Miguel, who sat together brooding and drinking far too much ale. Billy made several attempts to get Lady Myrredith's husband away from the Spaniard, only to be pushed away by the latter. Billy became very concerned when he saw Scarosa whisper into the brutish knight's ear.

Aonghas looked over his tankard at his wife and her former suitor, as they laughed and enjoyed each other's company. His eyes seethed and he slammed his drink down on the table. All eyes focused on him as he stood and kicked his chair away. Finally he leaned on the table and scowled at his wife and Sir Hugh.

A servant approached him from behind. "Is there something I can fetch for milord?"

Aonghas turned and grabbed the servant by the neck, sending the serving tray of spiced meats flying. He growled at the servant through clenched teeth then threw him to the floor. Lastly, he shot a dark look at Billy and stormed from the dining hall.

Lady Myrredith stood up. "Where are you going?"

"Out, woman!"

"Where?"

Lady Myrredith's husband stopped in midstride and turned halfway round to face his wife. He looked down his shoulder at her, with one corner of his lip curled. "I'm going to town," he said, biting off each syllable. With that, he turned and exited.

The hall was still silent when Don Miguel attempted to slip away from the table and head after Aonghas.

Lady Myrredith raised her voice in a commanding tone. "Don Miguel."

"Yes, Your Ladyship," the Spaniard said sheepishly.

"Don't come back."

"I beg Your Ladyship's pardon?"

"Do not come back. I do not want to see you or even hear of your presence on Cyndyn lands ever again. If I do, I can assure you that you will not be pleased with my solution. Now, good-bye!"

"But my things—"

"Eadwig, see to it that this vagabond and his belongings are off Cyndyn lands within the hour."

Eadwig stood behind her chair. "A pleasure, milady."

Don Miguel bowed his head and took his lute from Billy. Eadwig snapped his fingers twice, and Don Miguel followed the chamberlain out of the great hall.

Lady Myrredith watched the troubadour leave and then turned to Billy. "I should have done that days ago. William, please sing for us a happy song, so that we can forget this unsavory business."

* * *

Before he went to bed, Billy got a lamp from Eadwig and reexamined the faerie tapestry. Every night since seeing it, he had dreamt of going to Tirn Aill, and now, even in the day, he was dreaming about it.

That night, as Billy dreamt, he saw himself, Sir Hugh, and Lady Myrredith all running off to Faerieland. Suddenly his dream shattered, and he sat upright in the bed. He felt the same familiar chill as he looked into the darkness at the eyes that were staring back at him from across the room. He reached back to the bedside table and flung the shutter off the lamp. Instantly the room was light.

Billy's eyes popped open in astonishment. A young boy stood across the room where the eyes had been. He was dressed in fine pale clothing and high soft boots of grey leather. The boy shaded his pale eyes and shrunk away from the light. He stared at the faerie tapestry for a moment and then silently turned and walked to the corner behind the armor. Billy watched as he disappeared into the shadows.

Billy jumped out of bed and scurried to the corner. As he neared the armor, the lamplight spread around the corner, illuminating the area.

Billy looked left and right, but no one was there. He leapt back and spun around to scrutinize the room behind him. He was alone.

Just to be sure, Billy covered every corner in the room, searching all the nooks and crannies large enough to hide a boy. He began to think he'd seen an apparition.

Billy went back to where he last saw the boy. He examined the empty corner, then shrugged and turned to go back to bed. At that moment he felt a chill run up his spine, and he scampered back to bed as quickly as his feet would carry him.

No sooner had he covered the lamp and lay down, than he was sitting up again. He lifted the hood of the lamp and sat on the edge of the bed, staring at the corner. Something gnawed at his mind.

"A secret passage!"

Billy slipped on his shoes and shuffled back to the corner to reexamine it. He spent the next few minutes looking for his secret door, scouring the corner for a clue, for even a hint of a clue, but he really didn't know what he was looking for. The other secret doors Lady Myrredith had shown him were crafted so well that he hadn't been able to detect them until they were opened. So he searched for a hidden lever or trigger stone. He found nothing.

He'd been so terribly restless the past two days, for lack of something to do, and now he had something truly interesting. He wondered if this new intrigue might be a product of his imagination or simply a case of wishful thinking.

Billy leaned back against the suit of armor and rested his hand on the sword. The sword shifted with a soft click and immediately the wall in front of him opened. He shivered, not sure if it was due to the icy draft which came from the newly opened portal, or the excitement of finding it.

"Well at least it's not my imagination."

Billy flew to his bed and donned his clothes, stuffing several candles into his special pocket. Then he rushed back to his new discovery and stood staring into its gaping blackness.

What about Lady Myrredith's warning? Surely I won't get lost! I'll only go a little ways, then I'll come back the exact same way.

Armed only with the light from his lamp, he took a deep breath and stepped through the opening.

Billy found himself in a small, bare, circular room with a domed ceiling and a narrow passage leading off to the right. There was a soft, low moan coming from the passage. Billy surmised that it was caused by the cold draft coming through it. He took the passage, which almost immediately turned into an even narrower stairway. The small stone steps wound their way, like a snake, down into the darkness, turning too sharply to see more than a few feet at a time. There was an unexpected sound from down below. Billy stopped.

"Who's there?"

Billy's voice echoed in the stairwell, coming back to his ears like bubbling water. As the sound faded, it changed. It seemed to be laughing at him. He held his breath and listened again. It was quiet. Then he heard a sound coming from further down the stairs – footsteps running on a stone floor, and laughter. Billy swallowed, tightened his grip on the lamp, and continued down the steps.

The snaking steps became tightly coiled, descending round and round until Billy felt dizzy and out of breath. He went faster and faster, feeling strongly drawn to whatever was waiting for him at the end of the passage. He knew that he must be under the ground by now, and still it continued to go deeper and deeper into the earth. The air smelled of moist soil. Slick patches of slimy black fungus grew between the stones of the dark passage, which glistened with moisture. The farther he went, the harder it was to maintain his footing, and he became frantic.

All of a sudden, Billy's feet slipped out from under him, and he went sliding and tumbling down the steps. He rolled uncontrollably down the passage, not missing a single painful step, his lamp clattering down behind him. Without warning, the steps ended, and Billy was hurled into the darkness.

* * *

Billy's head pounded like an empty keg rolling down a cobblestone road. He opened his eyes. He had been unconscious for a while—for how long, he couldn't tell.

Once he regained the focus of his eyes, Billy saw that he sat on a stone floor, near the center of a large circular chamber with several dark narrow doorways. His lamp was resting on the floor, just a few feet away. Like the first room of the secret passage, this chamber was topped with a high domed ceiling. Around the room he could see several large rectangular pedestals of stone, one of which supported his back. Each pedestal was approximately seven or eight feet long and carved with intricate patterns and the images of dancing skeletons. There were statues of people atop many of them. Billy thought it odd that the statues were lying on their backs.

Billy's attention returned to the lamp. It was sitting upright, glowing with its usual dim, quivering light. It seemed strange that it would still be lit.

Billy felt the hair on the back of his neck stand on end. He spun and looked to the top of the pedestal behind him. The mysterious boy he had seen in his room was there, staring down at him. Billy fell back to the floor in surprise. The boy smiled and jumped agilely to the floor at Billy's feet. He stood towering over Billy, pointing and laughing. Then just as quickly, he turned and ran down one of the corridors leading from the chamber. Billy got up, grabbed his lamp, and gave chase.

"Wait!"

Billy followed the boy for several minutes, often losing sight of him. He chased the sound of his laughter, catching a glimpse of him as he turned a corner into another tunnel. The boy led him down several corridors, through a number of small rooms and a half-dozen intersections before Billy realized he didn't know where he was going, where he was, or even which way he had come.

Billy stood in the middle of a four-way intersection. He looked down the corridor behind him. Its smooth floor, steeply angled walls, and arched ceiling looked exactly like those of the other three tunnels. Far off to his right, laughter echoed in the corridors.

"Blast!" He looked again down the corridors, searching for something that might look familiar. Not seeing anything uniquely recognizable, he shouted after his prey. "Boy! Boy! Come back!"

Laughter from some far-off tunnel was his only reply.

"I should have listened to Lady Myrredith."

At that moment, the boy appeared before him. The youth smiled at Billy and shrugged apologetically. Then he turned and motioned for Billy to follow. Billy eyed the intersection and the corridors, pondering whether he should trust the boy or his instincts, which were confused.

"Oh well." He moved to follow the boy.

The mysterious boy never looked back at Billy, and as with Beth on Billy's first morning in Cyndyn Hall, the boy never allowed Billy to come along beside him.

Billy didn't know why he continued to chase the boy, when he didn't know where they were going. Something was pulling him forward, drawing him closer. The boy laughed. If only Billy could catch the elusive child, he could put an end to this silly game and go home, but each time he started to catch up, the boy increased the pace. They were now sprinting down the corridors. The strange boy's laughter increased in proportion to their speed.

Billy was starting to tire. He knew he would have to stop soon, but he was too out of breath to say anything.

At that moment Billy's lamp sputtered and went out. Enveloped in darkness, Billy stopped running and knelt on the floor to catch his breath. The mysterious boy's laughter continued down the corridor.

"Stop," Billy gasped. "Stop!"

He fumbled with the lamp as he recovered his wind. The sounds of his mysterious guide grew distant and faded away, replaced by the reverberation of his own labored breathing. Billy located the tiny tinderbox in the lamp's base and removed it. The flint and steel slipped from his grasp and fell to the floor. Billy panicked. His heart began to race as he groped the cold floor in the darkness. At last he found the tools and after considerable effort managed to light the lamp.

Billy looked ahead as the lamp's glow brightened. The fluttering light illuminated the face of the boy just two feet away and Billy fell over from fright. The boy again laughed at Billy and motioned for him to come forward.

Billy stood and dusted himself off. He picked up the lamp and started to step forward. A chill ran up his spine as he looked down and saw that his foot hovered over a dark area in the floor. He retrieved his foot and lowered the lamp to have a better look. A cavernous black hole, as dark as the pit of Hell, stared back at him. Billy sharply inhaled and stepped back from the abyss. With apprehension he tore his eyes away from the chasm as his mind fumbled with a startling notion. He focused on the strangely familiar boy ahead of him, who continued to grin and motion for Billy to come forward.

The cheerful boy stepped forward, stretching out an open hand. Billy stared at it and stumbled back. As Billy retreated, the boy advanced, until he was standing, in midair, over the yawning black pit. He held out both hands to Billy, his glad expression supplanted by haunted, pleading eyes. In that moment, Billy realized the boy had the same eyes as Lady Myrredith.

Billy stepped up his retreat, backpedaling away from the apparition. As he backed into the next intersection, the phantom boy lowered his arms and sank into the abyss, disappearing beneath the floor.

Billy, deciding that he would much rather be in his bed at that moment, turned and sprinted back up the hall he had just traversed. He retraced his steps, trying to find his way back to the large round room, but remembering which turns he had taken proved more difficult than he imagined. He paused in the middle of several intersections and frantically looked in all four directions, before deciding which way to go. This went on for about an hour. Despite feeling panicky, he stopped and rested, trying to calm down before continuing.

He tried to reassure himself. "You'll be fine." He repeated this as he absently rubbed his finger in the groove between two stones. Some of the rough cement crumbled and fell to the floor. "Just have to stay calm."

He got up and restarted his search. He found it impossible to remember which corridors he had traveled. He walked on and on, his hope of finding the circular chamber diminishing with each step. He was about to give up when he came to a passage that felt very familiar. He rushed down the corridor hoping to see something he could definitely recognize. As he got to the next intersection, he saw something on the floor. Cautiously he approached the item to examine it. His excitement dissipated into thin air. The object was a candle, and just across from it was a small pile of cement dust.

"No!" He clenched his eyes shut. "I'm goin' round in circles. Oh, why didn't I listen to Lady Myrredith?"

Billy felt tired and frustrated and most definitely lost. He flopped down on the floor of the passage and sobbed. He grabbed the candle and stared at it through his tears. Then he placed it in his pocket. His fingers ran across the smooth, warm metal of his mother's ring. Billy had almost forgotten it was there. He let his fingers caress its curved surface. Just feeling the ring in his pocket gave him some comfort. Somehow it connected him to the world and made him feel safe. He slipped the tip of his finger into the ring and fetched it out. The warm gold loop shone in the dim lamplight, and Billy slipped it all the way onto his finger.

"Mother, what should I do? What should I do?"

He repeated the question several times, letting the sound of the words fill his ears until they formed an answer in his head. *Rest now,* they said. *Rest, and when you awake you'll walk out of here.*

Billy curled up against a corner and gradually drifted to sleep.

* * *

Billy found himself on the road to the kingdom of the little people. He was alone, being pursued by something. He tried to run faster, but whatever was following only gained on him. Billy could feel it coming closer and closer.

A soft, sweet voice whispered in his ear. "William."

Billy tried hard to ignore it.

"William."

Billy opened his eyes. The voice was his mother's. The mother he had always imagined. She was a beautiful lady, wearing a long flowing dress of white and pink. She smiled at him and spoke in the same elegant manner as Lady Myrredith.

"William, you *will* come to Tirn Aill, but first you must leave this place. Come. Follow me."

Without a word, Billy got up and followed his mother. She took his hand, and they seemed to float through the twisting, turning corridors. Finally she stopped and turned to him.

"Here, William. Rest here, and when you awake, follow this passage. It will lead you out into the world you know."

Billy sat where she had indicated. He was very tired but wanted to talk with his mother—to ask her questions. She turned and started to walk away.

"Mother? Mother, wait!" But it was too late. Her image melted into the darkness and vanished.

"No! Wait, Mother!"

Billy was awake. His own shouting had woken him. His lamp had burned out, and it was dark, except for a thin shaft of light coming from the ceiling up ahead.

Billy brushed himself off and went to the source of light. There was a small round chamber at the end of the passage with a partially collapsed roof. Sunlight streamed into the room, filtered only by some shrubbery that grew around the rim of the hole. Billy stacked some of the broken ceiling stones together in a large pile and climbed up the rubble to the light. He peered through the hole and could see that he was now at ground level. Quickly, he crawled out through the hole and started pushing his way through the bushes. The plants were terribly entangled, overgrown, and thorny, so it was slow going at first, but he kept his head down and kept crawling.

At last, Billy broke through to a place where the weeds were pushed back, just enough to form a trail of sorts. The path was too small for Billy to do anything but continue crawling. From this tiny tunnel in the weeds, he could see that he was about to clear the bramble.

All of a sudden, a hare came scrambling into the hole. It shot down Billy's collar and into his shirt. It's hard to say which was the more frightened by the unexpected close proximity of the other, but before you could count to one, Billy sprung to his feet and expelled the hare from his clothing and into the waist-high brush.

As the dust settled, Billy became aware of a shadow hanging over him. Slowly he lifted his eyes. A husky man in a brown wool robe stood directly in front of him. He held a heavy stick poised above his head in both hands. The man stared at Billy, his jaw gone completely slack. Billy, unsure of the man's intentions, stared back, watching the formidable club out of the corner of his eye. The man's stunned expression told Billy that he was harmless, so he smiled and took a step forward to introduce himself. Before Billy could say "hello," the man screamed, dropped his stick, and ran in the opposite direction.

"God save us from diabolical brownie magic!" the man spouted as he ran away.

Billy shouted, "But ... Wait!" and gave chase.

The robed man gained a good head start, as Billy had a spot of trouble getting out of the bramble. The man never looked back. He only ran away, holding up a cross behind himself and babbling in Latin. As they came through a small group of trees, Billy saw a high wall up ahead. The man made a sharp right turn and went through a wooden gate, slamming it behind him. As Billy approached, he heard the bolt slide home on the other side. Then the gate rattled as the man fell against it with his back.

Billy listened to the man's labored breathing. "Hello?"

The man let out another scream. Then Billy heard his quickened footsteps receding into the distance.

Billy waited, then pounded on the gate, but no one came to let him in. He looked around and found that he was in a large, walled orchard. Billy decided that he would try to climb the wall and follow the man.

The wall was covered with ivy, so the climbing was fairly easy. It reminded Billy of all the times he spent at home in the woods, climbing trees. Billy got to the top of the wall and nearly fell off. He had expected to maybe see a small garden or courtyard, but instead, directly in front of him, filling his entire view, was the largest single building he had ever seen. The massive structure towered over him. He gazed up to the top and saw the striking arches and tall roof he had seen with Lady Myrredith from the wall of Cyndyn Hall. Somehow he had managed to get all the way to the cathedral, in Dyven! Billy had no idea that it would be so large, so tall, or so beautiful. Still, while it intrigued him, something about it also frightened him.

Billy heard a ruckus building inside the grand edifice. It was coming closer and closer. He had an uneasy feeling, the kind he got when he was about to be caught doing something he wasn't supposed to do, being somewhere he wasn't supposed to be. Billy stood on top of the wall and looked out over the orchard. He saw the outer wall, just beyond the third row of trees to his left, and quickly scaled down the wall into the orchard.

Billy ran across the orchard with as much speed as he could muster. Just before he reached the wall, he heard some men coming through the gate behind him. He stopped for a moment to survey his next obstacle.

The outer wall of the orchard was nearly as formidable as the wall he had just come from, but did not have an abundance of vines growing on it. He started to panic, and then he saw the means to his escape. A thick old tree, heavily burdened by its fruit, had extended its branches to rest on the wall.

Billy ran to the tree and glanced back towards the cathedral. He could still hear the men coming into the orchard, but the trees blocked his view. He squatted and jumped as high as he could. His hands just missed the lowest branch. His noisy pursuers were now coming in his direction. Fighting back panic, Billy took a step back and tried to reach the branch again. This time his fingers scraped the bark, but he couldn't get a grip on it. Now his heart pounded, and his breathing became rushed.

He looked around the tree and spied several darkly robed men, led by the first man he had seen. They were in jocular spirits, laughing at their guide, who was waving his arms about in wild gesticulations. Even so, they made Billy fearful.

Billy knew they would find him if he didn't get out of the orchard immediately. Once more, he stepped back from the tree and eyed the elusive branch. He took two additional steps back and charged. He stretched out his hands as he leapt and caught the bough. Quickly he swung his feet up and straddled the branch. Without another thought, he ascended the trunk and ran out on a limb that offered its fruit to people on the other side of the wall. As he broke through the branches atop the wall, he saw, for the first time, the city stretching out before him.

CHAPTER ELEVEN

The City

Billy had long dreamt of visiting Dyven. Since he was a boy, he had heard guests at his father's inn boast of the wonders they had seen there. They swore there were pastry shops as big as houses; giant taverns as long as a street; and streets lined with nothing but silversmiths or clothiers or potters. Soldier, sailor, beggar, merchant, wizard, and priest—all brushed elbows and butted heads in its busy thoroughfares. From the most common man to the richest prince, the city drew them in. And now Billy, son of an innkeeper, had been drawn there too.

It was still early morning, and few people were up and about. Billy wasn't sure if he really wanted to be seen just yet, so he tried avoiding the main streets, choosing instead to walk down the alleys.

An aged peddler walked by, pushing his cart and singing an ancient barter song. The sounds of his wares accompanied him, rattling, banging, and clanging against one another and the cart. Billy listened to the odd music he made and remembered the first time he had heard the song sung. In the Valley of the Yew, the only peddler had been trading cloth, and his song was of cloth. This city peddler's song mostly repeated the line, "Your old iron for new."

The old man stopped for a moment to rest his hands. He stretched and rubbed his tired appendages, looking around the narrow cobblestone street. His eyes stopped when they came across Billy's dirty face in the alley. The peddler smiled at Billy, then picked up his cart and went on his way. Billy watched him until he disappeared around the corner.

Billy listened to the music of the iron peddler fade into the distance as he ventured out into the vacant street. At that moment, he heard jingling and looked up to see a woman coming out from a tall, narrow stone house on the opposite side of the street. As she closed the door behind her, the bronze shoe hanging above the door swung, and a small brass bell announced the door's closure. The woman was wearing an apron and carrying a large basket of laundry. She looked up at the swinging shoe for a moment before spotting Billy.

"You! Boy!" she squawked.

Billy jumped back into the shadow of the alley. He looked around, hoping that she might be talking to some other boy, but then she looked directly at him and beckoned with her head for him to come closer. Billy reluctantly stepped into the sunlight.

"Boy!" the woman repeated. "Copper in it, if'n ya run down to the pub an' fetch my mister!"

"Where?"

"The pub. On the square, boy! Well don't ya know anythin'?"

Billy shrugged.

The woman put down her basket. "Say, do ya want the bloomin' coin or not?"

Billy shrugged again.

Out of thin air, a boy appeared next to Billy, dressed from head to ankle in faded clothes. His face and hands were dirty, but it was his odious odor that first caught Billy's attention.

The boy rushed past Billy. "I'll fetch 'im, mum!"

Billy watched from the mouth of the alley as the barefoot boy talked to the woman. A few seconds later, he held out his hand. The woman raised her left eyebrow and crossed her arms. The boy smiled, turned, and ran back to the alley.

"Come on then." He tilted his head to indicate that he and Billy should head down the street.

Billy stared at him.

"Well let's go! Don't wanna keep the missus waitin', do we?"

The smiling boy winked and then tugged Billy down the street by his arm. Billy was confused but decided to go along with his newfound partner, until something better came along.

As they trotted down the street, the boy yelled back to the woman, "We'll be back wif 'im in a jiffy, mum!"

Rounding the corner, the boy turned to Billy. "You're new at this, ain't ya? I can't imagine anyone turnin' down an honest coin for anythin'! Name's Stitch. What's yours?"

"Billy."

"Well Billy, what were you doin' sneakin' round the cathedral?"

Billy stopped cold in his tracks. "What do you mean?"

Stitch stopped to face Billy. "I saw ya. I saw ya sneakin' over the orchard wall. Were ya stealin' apples?"

"No! I wasn't stea—!"

"Oh it's fine wif me, chum. You don't have to lie. Why we're practically brothers, you an' me."

"What?"

"I've been on me own for a long time now. I know what it's like to be hungry."

Billy's stomach growled in answer, and he realized that he was indeed very hungry. "Yes. Hungry. I am hungry."

"What? After stuffin' yourself on sacred apples?"

"Well, I didn't get to eat any apples."

"In the orchard and didn't get any? What kind of thief are you?"

"There were some men that came while I was—"

"Ya got caught then?"

"No."

"Oh. But no apples."

"No apples," Billy mumbled, feeling ravenous. "And I'm no thief!"

"I agree. Now come on. The pub is just a bit from here."

"What's a pub?"

"You really are new."

Stitch grabbed Billy by the wrist and hauled him down the street again. They passed through several narrow alleys that Stitch called shortcuts, but Billy's nose and stomach called revolting. Billy could hear a noise rising somewhere in front of them. The sound frightened him as it grew louder and louder. They turned a corner, and the noise filled his ears.

They stood on the edge of a large square, which was packed full with people. Everywhere Billy looked, people, people, people, like bees around a hive. There were more people than Billy had ever seen together in one place. *So this is the city.* The air buzzed with sound. Voices rose and fell in constant competition with the overwhelming ruckus. As one voice faded from prominence, another would take its place. Above this riotous chorus were the ancient songs of the merchants. Each proclaimed that their particular wares were unequivocally the best available under the sun.

Billy gawked at the constantly dancing colors, as people pushed, slid, and bumped their way through the throng. Those who weren't trying to get somewhere were busy poking, smelling, fondling, sampling, or looking at the cornucopia of items for sale. Often he saw the dull shine of tarnished copper coins in the morning sun. Then a flash of silver or the rare glimmer of gold would catch Billy's eye. Money was changing hands at an alarming rate. A tug on his arm roused Billy from his daze.

"Come on!" Stitch shouted.

Billy followed his guide. "Is it always like this?"

"Like what?"

"Like this!"

Stitch looked back at his wide-eyed companion and continued to push through the crowd. "Where ya from, Billy?"

"The Valley of the Yew."

"Don't you have a market there?"

"No, not like this!"

"Stitch!" someone shouted from their left.

Both boys stopped and looked in the direction of the voice. All Billy could see were bodies weaving in and out, like a great school of fish. Suddenly, a boy dressed very much like Stitch—only shabbier—popped out of the crowd.

The boy waved at them. "Hey, Stitch!"

"Pinch!" Stitch shouted in return.

The boy smiled as he approached. He nodded at Billy. "Who's he?"

"Billy," Stitch answered.

"New boy?"

"Yup."

Pinch looked at Billy. "How long you been on your own?"

"I left home a couple weeks ago."

"He's green to the city today," Stitch added.

The boy frowned at Billy and shook his head. "Green today."

"He's fine, Pinch. I'll show him the ropes."

"Then he's all yours. Just keep him out of my way. Got it?"

"Got it, Pinch. Say, you're awful jumpy today."

Pinch eyed the crowd suspiciously then pulled Stitch over to the edge of the mob. Billy followed.

"Any action?" Stitch asked.

"Some." Pinch gave him a big smile. He pulled a small, well-rounded pouch out of his shirt. He eyed the crowd as he replaced the pouch and continued. "Many fat today, but be very careful."

"I always am."

"I seen Derian's men in the street."

Stitch stiffened. He nonchalantly inspected the square. "How many?"

"Two of the no good backbiters!" Pinch then he spat angrily. "Nothin' worse than a thief gone moral."

"Don't worry, Pinch. We always out fox 'em."

"Yeah, but somethin's different today."

Stitch patted Pinch on the belly where he had put away the pouch. "You're just jumpy, with a purse full of coin. Don't worry."

Pinch leaned in and spoke out the side of his mouth. "I'm workin' wifout a bump,"

"I always do."

"Yeah, but you're the Stitch!"

Stitch smiled broadly. "Listen, Pinch, if it don't feel right, go home. You'll just make the rest of us jumpy."

"Maybe I will."

Stitch turned and walked away. "Come on, Billy. We've got to take care of your errand."

Billy pushed his way past a man with a basket of fruit on his shoulder, to follow Stitch. "What was that all about?"

"Never ya mind that now. I'll explain it later."

Stitch pulled Billy through the swarm of people across the square. As they approached the center of the square, Billy saw a small grey statue of a fish with water bubbling from its mouth. It arched its back, riding atop a small wave of the same grey stone. The water ran down the statue into a circular raised pool. Several pottery merchants were sitting on the ledge of the pool, tending their wares.

Billy marveled at the never-ending flow of water from the fish's mouth. "What's that?"

Stitch rolled his eyes. "That's a fountain! I suppose you've never seen one of those either."

Billy shrugged. "Well, I haven't."

"Look, I don't care if ya get your measly one copper, but it is honest, easy money, an' it'll put some bread in your hole. Now come on!"

Billy didn't hear Stitch. He just stood, gawking at the fountain. He was brought to his senses by Stitch jerking his arm nearly out of the socket. Billy fought to keep his balance as he was dragged back into the crowd.

"Come on! We're almost there. I'll show ya round, after we've fetched the cobbler."

Billy filed in behind Stitch and headed around the many pottery vendors. As they got to the opposite side of the fountain, there was a small crowd gathered in a circle around a man in colorful garb. Stitch ignored the spectacle, but Billy's curiosity urged him to investigate. He pushed his way past all the elbows and hips until he was at the edge of the circle.

The man in the center of the crowd was dressed entirely in yellow and red silk. Even his shoes and ridiculous, three-cornered hat were of the same loud, checkered material, with tiny silver bells attached at each point. Billy had never, in all his life, seen anyone dressed so foolishly.

The colorful performer walked around the circle in a well-rehearsed drunken stupor, contorting his face into silly, jeering expressions and pretending to drink out of a dark red bottle. Then, when he was directly in front of one of his audience, he would explode into hideous cackles or fall down. When he came to Billy, the actor stopped and took a double take. He then looked incredulously at his bottle and tossed it over his shoulder. This action brought a great deal of laughter from the crowd as well as a great deal of attention to Billy. Everyone was looking and laughing at Billy as much as they were the entertainer. Just as the bottle was about to come crashing to the ground, the clown turned and made a diving catch. The crowd gasped and then applauded his feat. As the crowd quieted, the man made two more bottles appear. Billy had no idea where they had come from. *Surely that was magic!*

The man bowed his head and then, much to Billy's delight, started to juggle the three bottles. He worked the bottles round and round, then crisscross. Yellow and red flashed in the sun as he passed by. Billy watched, admiring the man's skill and listening to the familiar pitter-patter of the bottles in his magical hands. The man was good—very good—maybe even better than Llyren the Glum, Billy's friend and teacher. Billy remembered how he and Llyren had practiced tossing the apples back and forth, forming complex patterns, which alone neither of them could do. He wished there was some way he could join in and juggle with the clown.

Suddenly, without thought, Billy's hands reached out and plucked the bottles out of the air: one, two, three. The foolish juggler's jaw fell open in dumbfounded amazement, and the crowd laughed at his astonished expression. The bottles continued to make the juggler's pattern in Billy's hands. The crowd buzzed with excitement.

Billy, realizing what he had done and not wanting to steal the show, decided to toss the bottles back to their owner.

"Follow me!" he said. "One, two, three." Then he sent the three bottles, in sequence, to the man before him.

With a great effort and jingling of tiny silver bells, the dazed performer pulled himself together and caught the bottles. He tried, comically, to settle them into a pattern and managed to get the bottles aloft again without breaking them or the rhythm. The crowd applauded appreciatively. When he was sure of his control, the clown eyed his unexpected juggling partner, who stood grinning at him from ear to ear.

Billy bowed to the man, mimicking Don Miguel as well as he could. Then he took a step backwards and beckoned for the bottles with his outstretched hands.

The street performer tipped his head. "Very well. Let's see what you've got! Four, five, six, you're in a fix."

Again the bottles flew the gap between them, and again they were caught and sent aloft.

"Seven, eight, nine, I feel fine," Billy answered, as he continued the poem taught to him by Llyren and Duncan of the Highlands.

Several of the pottery merchants around the fountain stopped their usual activities and turned their attentions to the jugglers. Billy started the juggler's rhyme over and stepped up onto the first step of the fountain as he let loose the last of the bottles.

Again and again the bottles were tossed. The crowd swelled as more merchants and their customers suspended their activities to be entertained. While it was not particularly uncommon to see a single traveling entertainer in Dyven, seeing two seemed to most as if the circus had come to town. Billy felt that everyone in the market must be focused on them. As the street clown was showing off his skills, a fat drunk stumbled out from the mob and handed Billy three more bottles with a grin. Billy smiled and bowed to the man in thanks. Upon seeing that his small partner was also equipped, the clown's smile broadened. He gave Billy a nod.

"Follow me!" they shouted in unison. A murmur ran through the throng and then hushed as the jugglers filled the air with bottles. Sunlight sprang from the dancing bottles as they traveled from hand to hand to hand.

Billy stepped up one more step to place himself at a height equal to his partner and widen the gap between them. He was completely unaware that he stood on the fountain's lip.

The whole crowd was cheering and chanting the little rhyme louder and louder. Just when Billy thought that the cheering had reached its peak, his partner would take one big step back and shout, "One more time!"

The crowd roared, and the juggling would continue. Billy admired the great skill with which the man controlled his audience. *They follow him like sheep.* Billy felt the pulse of the crowd too but did not know how to act on what he felt.

Billy was sure now that their audience had had enough, but the man across from him simply looked inquisitively at the people, and they cheered, "One more time!" Billy's partner took one more step backwards and nodded to him. Billy watched every move carefully.

When they reached the last line of the rhyme, the two jugglers gave each other a nod and increased their speed. The mob was mesmerized. They swooned under their entertainers' power. Billy felt infused with energy from the cheering people. Never before had he felt so invigorated. He could hardly contain himself. For a moment he felt unassailable and forgot what he was doing. Then he saw that his partner had stopped juggling, and the last of the bottles were speeding at him.

Billy was already juggling three bottles, and here were three more. Billy's mind froze. His hands reached out to catch the incoming bottles and insert them into the pattern, but he was off balance, and he threw the last bottle over his head. By reflex he stepped back to catch it. His foot found nothing to stand on.

The next thing Billy knew, he was sitting in the fountain, spitting out a stream of water, like the grey stone fish just behind him. The entire throng broke into uncontrollable laughter. Many of them fell to the ground and rolled around, holding their sides. The water in the fountain was cool, but Billy felt warm as the blush of embarrassment rushed to his face and ears. Then the nature of his predicament settled on him, and he too found he could not control his laughter. He tried to get out of the fountain but slipped and fell back in. He rolled around in the pool, squirting water out of his mouth and laughing. It felt as if the entire city was laughing.

Over the laughter, Billy heard a faint cry. It was the cry of a lone man. Billy couldn't make out what he was screaming. Then like ripples on a pond, the crowd surrounding the man quieted and turned to face him. Finally the entire market was quiet, except for the one man.

"Thief! Thief!" he yelled.

The crowd backed away, and Billy could see a man in a yellow shirt and brown trousers searching himself and the faces around him. "I've been robbed!"

Just then another voice came from deep within the crowd.

"Thief! Thief! My purse has been cut!"

Just as the crowd turned its attention to the last voice, another rang out in the same cry from another location, then another and another and another. A low hum began to buzz through the crowd. It grew until all the people in the market square were shouting and yelling at one another.

Billy listened to them for a moment, before his ears caught another sound. A clattering sound was building underneath the angry voices and drawing nearer. Half a dozen horsemen with long spears entered the square. They were dressed all in brown leather, with yellow ribbons trailing from their spear tips. Behind them rode two striking men.

The first was a lean man with a greying black beard. He rode on a highly spirited charger the color of melting snow. He wore a long sword on his left side and a dagger on the other. Around his neck he wore a bronze chain of office, similar to the one Billy had seen worn by Earl Cairmac. This man surveyed the market with cold grey eyes and slowly entered the square, followed by his companion. The noisy crowd became still. All eyes were upon this commanding figure as he advanced wordlessly towards the fountain.

The second man looked out of place amongst all the soldiers. He was not at all warriorlike in his manner or dress and was exceptionally overweight and sloppy. He had no armor or weapons that Billy could see and rode a ragged black cob that was straining just to carry its load. Billy noticed that many of the people glared at him contemptuously as he rushed up beside his companion.

The fat man leaned over to whisper to his companion as they rode farther into the crowd. Both men focused on Billy. The lean man studied him with a steely, disquieting glare. Then the warrior and the fat man halted. The latter, having finished whispering, slouched back into his saddle and eyed Billy with an expression reminiscent of a snake.

The only sound Billy could hear was the water bubbling from the fountain.

Then the man on the pale horse spoke. "What is going on here?" His voice was bitingly clear.

No one said anything. Then the man in the yellow shirt took off his hat. He spoke cautiously, his voice trembling with the sound of uncertainty. "Captain, I've been robbed."

"And me too!" a second man said.

"And I as well!" a woman from behind him shouted.

Several more people piped in to report their losses, and the crowd began to buzz.

"Silence!" the captain shouted. His eyes remained glued to Billy. When the square was quiet again, he indicated the dripping juggler with a nod. "And this is the thief?"

Billy didn't move. He felt as if he were nailed in place by the captain's stare.

The man in yellow clinched his hat. "Oh no, Captain. That isn't possible."

"Not possible, eh?"

"Oh no, sir."

"Then what did this thief of yours look like?"

The captain's question was answered by silence.

"Well? ... " The captain held up his hands and addressed the entire market square. "Did *anyone* see the thief?"

Again there was silence.

The captain dropped his hands. "I see. And I suppose you saw nothing as well, my little fish?"

Billy just shrugged and sheepishly shook his head as two of the mounted guards rode up to the fountain. Billy looked at them and saw that they were glaring at him.

A woman from the crowd stepped forward and curtsied. "He was entertaining us, Captain."

"Yeah," another said. "That's why we didn't see anythin'. We was watchin' 'im!"

"That's right. We was all watchin' 'im. An' the other one too."

The captain raised his hand. "What other one?"

Someone shoved Billy's juggling partner forward. "Him!"

The clown stumbled with a loud jingle of silver bells and caught himself on the lip of the fountain. He looked up from the water at Billy. Hurt and disbelief filled his eyes.

There was another long silence. Then all at once the whole crowd started to mumble.

The captain as he crossed his arms. "I see." He raised an eyebrow, and a tiny smile crossed his lips as he looked over the ridiculous pair. "Arrest them."

The mumble from the mob became a rumble, as the two guards reached down and plucked Billy out of the fountain by his arms. He was stunned as one of them roughly hoisted him over his horse like a deer carcass. He craned his neck and saw two more guards tie the hands of the foolish juggler behind his back. Then Billy's keeper smacked him in the ear with his boot.

"Take them to the tower," the captain commanded.

The guards had just started to move, when the mob quieted, and Billy heard a familiar voice.

"I said, what passes here, Captain?"

Billy was still dazed from the kick to his ear and, hanging upside down, like a piece of meat, had all the blood rushing to his head. He strained to hear the man speak over the sound of his own pulse. He turned his head but could not see him.

"Well ... sir ..." the captain stuttered.

"Speak up, man!" the voice grumbled.

"Well ... Sir Aonghas, we have just arrested these thieves—"

"Thieves?"

"Yes, Sir Aonghas. I believe these two distracted the crowd while their accomplices were cutting purses."

"You believe?"

"Yes, sir."

"Well, I know the small one's been mistaken for a faerie, but since he's been a friend to my wife and a guest in our home, I don't believe anyone's ever mistaken him for a thief."

"A ... friend?"

"Yes."

"Oh. Well ... perhaps we were ... mistaken?"

"Yes, Captain."

Billy found himself upright and being lowered to the ground. The trip down was much gentler than the one that brought him over the horse's back.

"Come along, William," Aonghas said. "We ought to be going home."

Billy rubbed his ear and looked up at his former captor. The man smiled apologetically as Billy went to the side of his rescuer.

"What of the other one, milord?"

"Oh, you mean Malcolm the Magnificent?"

"That's Malcolm the Magnificent?" Billy said in open amazement.

The remaining prisoner nodded. "At your service."

"Gosh! Llyren told me about him!" Billy told Aonghas. Then he turned to Malcolm. "You're the best!"

Malcolm the Magnificent snickered and smiled. "Not with my hands tied behind my back." He then gave a meaningful look to the captain of the guard, who cleared his throat and nodded for one of his men to cut the juggler free.

Malcolm bowed to Sir Aonghas. "Thank you, milord."

"You're welcome, Malcolm. It's been a long time since you've been to Dyven, and I'd hate to think of you wasting your talents on dungeon rats when ya could be entertaining Lady Myrredith and myself tonight."

"I'll be there … with bells on, milord!" Malcolm bowed again.

Aonghas turned to leave the square with Billy. "So what are you doing in town? Did ya come looking for me?"

"Sir Aonghas?" interrupted the captain. "What should I do?"

Aonghas slowly turned around to face him. "I suppose ya should do what you're paid to do, and catch the thief!"

"Yes, milord."

"Look, Oswyn … you are the captain of the city guard. I know ya didn't get there overnight. You ought to pay less attention to your pet thief, Derian, and more attention to your own innards."

With that, the captain bowed to Aonghas and went back into the crowd. Billy and Lady Myrredith's husband left the square and started back to Cyndyn Hall.

"Where's Lady Myrredith?" Aonghas asked, as he mounted his horse.

"I guess she's at home, sir."

The knight scowled at his diminutive friend. "What do you mean?"

"Sir?"

"You *guess* she's at home?"

"Aye, sir."

"Then ya didn't come to the city with her?"

"Well ... no, sir."

Sir Aonghas pulled Billy up behind him. "Does my wife know you're in town?"

"No, sir."

Sir Aonghas grunted and urged his horse forward. Billy wasn't sure if the grunt was for him or the horse.

As they rode, Billy briefly relayed what had happened to him the night before, leaving out any mention of ghosts and such. He was afraid that such talk would only upset Lady Myrredith if she ever heard. *And besides,* Billy told himself, *it sounds too much like a tall tale.*

When Billy finished, Sir Aonghas grunted. "I guess we're both in for it now!"

Billy nodded.

Out of the blue, Aonghas asked, "Did ya see him?"

Billy knitted his eyebrows. "See who, sir?"

"The boy ... the one that haunts the catacombs under Cyndyn."

Billy flinched and was suddenly struggling to remain on the horse. He flapped his arms in circles and finally grabbed hold of Aonghas' arm as the beefy knight reached back to steady him.

"Thank you."

After a spell, Aonghas said, "So I take it you've seen him."

"I ... I didn't want to say anythin' in case Lady Myrredith were to hear of it."

"Aye. Tis a tragedy that wounds her heart enough without that. She won't hear of it from me."

They rode in silence for a while. Billy, not having seen the road into the city, was content to be quiet and take in the sights. He, like Sir Aonghas, worried about what Lady Myrredith would have to say to them. They came to a small creek that crossed the road, and Sir Aonghas stopped to let his horse have a drink.

"You know my wife, she's very ... special. I wish more than anything I could tell her how much she means to me."

Billy nodded in silent agreement.

"Sometimes I think she deserves better than the likes of me. I'm too rough. She's a real lady. She only married me out of duty to her father. She'd be better off with someone who understands her better ... like Hugh. Did ya know she was going to marry him, before ...?"

"But that was a long time ago."

"She's in love with him."

Again Billy found himself saying nothing. The two of them sat and listened to the babbling water of the creek. Billy was the first to break the silence. "I think she loves you too, sir."

Aonghas looked back at his young companion and made eye contact. He narrowed his eyes, attempting to discern Billy's intention. Billy could see that the large man was truly in pain.

"I really do, sir."

Billy couldn't tell what was going on in Aonghas' mind, for the rugged knight only turned around and coaxed his horse down the road. The remainder of the trip was an eternity for Billy. Aonghas didn't say anything more, nor could Billy think of a single word to say. The passing scenery, while new to him, went by unnoted.

CHAPTER TWELVE

Glad Tidings

As Sir Aonghas and Billy approached Cyndyn Hall, Billy noticed there was only one guard on duty. Upon spotting them, the guard left his post and ran back into the castle.

The main courtyard was still, except for the clatter of Sir Aonghas' mount. Billy peered under the knight's arm and saw the lone figure of Lady Myrredith standing atop the main steps to the great hall. She stood in a wide stance with her hands on her hips, her long red hair and dark green dress flowing with the afternoon breeze. Even from a distance, any fool could see that she was in no mood to be trifled with. Billy ducked back behind Sir Aonghas.

"So there you are," she declared, "at last!"

Billy waited for Sir Aonghas to respond, but he didn't even grunt.

"While you've been off drinking with that confounded Spaniard—"

"I haven't seen Don Miguel!" Aonghas shouted back.

"I don't care who you were with, we needed your help. I have the entire castle split up in search parties looking everywhere for—"

At that moment, Billy came into sight of Lady Myrredith, and she stopped. Immediately, she ran down the great steps to the courtyard. "William!"

Billy slid off the horse with Sir Aonghas' help and stood on the cobblestones at the foot of the steps.

Lady Myrredith reached the bottom of the steps and scooped Billy up into her arms. "Oh, William," she said holding him tightly, "thank God, you're safe! Thank God! I thought you ... like my brother ... Oh, William!"

She released Billy and pulled away to look him in the face. She was smiling with tears running down her cheeks. She quickly pulled him to her again and hugged him even more tightly. Billy thought she would squeeze the stuffing out of him. Suddenly she pushed him away. Her eyebrows were closely knit and her eyes strong. Billy braced himself to receive a blow, but she only shook him by the arms.

"William!" Her voice quacked. "Don't ever do that again! Promise me you won't wander off again. You scared the life out of me. Promise!"

Billy lowered his head. "I promise."

"Cross your heart?"

"Hope to die." Billy crossed his chest with his hand and nodded.

Lady Myrredith put her hand under Billy's chin and lifted his face. She smiled at him and then kissed him on the forehead. Then she stood up and looked in her husband's direction. "Thank—"

Sir Aonghas was already out of earshot, turning the corner in the direction of the stables. She and William hadn't noticed him turn his horse and quietly ride away.

"Thank you," she whispered.

Billy looked up at her face. She had an unhappy expression again, and Billy could see that she already regretted her harsh words to her husband. He took her hand, and they entered the great hall to call off the search parties.

Everyone in the castle showed great joy at Billy's return—everyone, that is, but Eadwig. The chamberlain was the last to return to the great hall, having searched for Billy in the deepest parts of the castle. He appeared in the great hall, wiping the dirt and cobwebs from his face and clothes with great disdain. Upon spotting the newly returned lad, he stared at Billy down the long line of his blackened nose and grunted in much the same manner as was Sir Aonghas' fashion.

Eadwig straightened his tunic in a taut manner. "Might I be excused, milady? It seems that many places in the lower parts of this great castle are in need of tidying."

"Yes, Eadwig," his mistress said mirthfully, "but perhaps they could wait until after you've had a chance to tidy yourself?"

The chamberlain opened his mouth to address Lady Myrredith, but that was as far as he got. He stood motionless, his old eyes staring blankly.

"Yes, milady." Eadwig bowed, turned sharply, and left in the direction of his quarters, mumbling to himself. "Blasted Cyndyn sense of humor," the old man said as he turned the corner.

"I think he's a bit put out," Lady Myrredith said with a laugh.

"Put out?" Billy said. "I think he'd like to put me out."

Sir Hugh appeared behind Lady Myrredith. "He'll get over it. He always does."

His hostess smiled. "Aye. I do believe he wanted to put you out more than a few times."

"Eadwig wanted to put Sir Hugh out?"

"Yes, Billy. Before I earned my spurs, I don't think that Eadwig had much use for me."

"You knew Eadwig before you were a knight?"

Sir Hugh nodded. "I was a squire here in those days."

"And my father thought the world of you."

Billy watched as Sir Hugh and Lady Myrredith exchanged a volley of glances. They said nothing, but he sensed something pass between them in the silence.

Finally, Lady Myrredith turned to Billy. "Well, William, you still haven't told us what happened to you."

Billy began his tale with the discovery of the secret passage in his room. Again, as with Sir Aonghas, he was very careful not to make mention of any ghosts. By the time he got to his juggling act in the market square, it was time for dinner. Malcolm the Magnificent had arrived just in time to repeat their performance.

"Then I stepped back onto the fountain ..." Billy said, juggling from atop the table.

"No laddie," his partner corrected, "you stepped *in-to* the fountain."

Billy laughed and stepped back. Again, as earlier that day, his foot found only air. Billy had hoped to skip over this last part of his repeat performance, but alas, his usual run of luck prevailed.

Billy had managed to hold on to two of the bottles, and he swung them around in circles, desperately trying to right himself. However, it wasn't enough, and he went down like a windmill toppled by a storm. Everyone gasped, sure that the fall would break Billy's head, but Sir Hugh appeared and caught him. Billy looked up at the king's champion, surprised to see him. At that moment he remembered the third bottle.

SMASH! The bottle exploded on the back of Sir Hugh's head. The handsome nobleman blinked twice and then slowly crumpled to the floor, taking Billy, two astonished servants, and two trays of food with him.

The entire commons room was awash with a mixture of laughter and gasps. Lady Myrredith, Eadwig, and Beth rushed to aid the fallen. Eadwig slipped on some spilled soup and collided with the circuslike spectacle. Aonghas, Malcolm, and many others held their sides against the laughter that threatened to split them. The tangled figures on the floor held everyone's attention, and so no one, not even the guard, was aware that a lone figure had entered the hall.

The cloaked figure stood at the top of the steps with arms crossed, tapping one foot impatiently. Gloved hands irritably pushed back the forest green hood of the cloak, revealing a young man with well-groomed reddish hair and an impertinent frown. He attempted to call attention to himself by clearing his throat, but the din was simply too loud.

Angrily he unfastened his cloak and tossed it to the floor. Beneath the dark cloak he wore fine clothes, all of sky blue with silver thread trimming and a white lion emblazoned across the chest. At his waist he wore an ornate dagger and pouch, and strapped across his chest a small silver huntsman's horn.

Again he stood and tapped his foot, awaiting some attention. At last, when it appeared that no one was going to acknowledge his presence, he grabbed the horn and put it to his lips.

The sound of the horn snapped everyone's head around, and the hall became hushed. Eadwig regained his footing and sprang out of the crowd in the direction of the new arrival. The young man dropped the horn and surveyed the room with one eyebrow cocked high on his forehead.

Billy scrambled up to see what had caused the sudden uneasy silence. Climbing onto the table, he saw the striking figure in blue.

"Who is tha—?"

"Shhh," hissed several servants around him.

Billy looked back at them. They stood with their heads bowed. The only people whose heads remained up were the nobles. All were very still, with the exception of Hugh, who squinted one eye and rubbed the back of his head. Billy returned his gaze to the young man. They made eye contact, before Billy bowed his head to avert his eyes. In his peripheral he watched Eadwig move up the steps to the stranger and bow deeply.

"Forgive our lack of formality. I assure you there was no insult intended to our liege or his honored servant. Please enter the hall of the Cyndyns and share with us what news our Sire deems us worthy to hear."

Billy listened intently to Eadwig's words. They sounded different from the manner in which he usually spoke—more practiced.

The young man answered in a sweet, clear voice. "Well … as it is tidings of such gladness I carry …"

Eadwig swooped down to pick up the youth's cloak. "Please, come refresh yourself." Eadwig snapped his fingers in rapid succession.

Suddenly the hall was bustling. The servants rushed around, busying themselves with dinner duties. Billy looked up and saw them setting a place for the young man next to Sir Hugh's seat.

Billy peeked again at the stranger and noticed that his cool, hard face now wore a warm smile and glad eyes. He bowed to Lady Myrredith and the two knights. Billy jumped down from the table and hastily helped Beth clean up the pottery and food he had inadvertently broken and scattered.

"Who is that?" he whispered to her.

"He's the King's Herald," she whispered.

"The king?" Billy exclaimed, much louder than he had intended.

"Yes, the king." The youth was now standing directly in front of him.

Billy looked up. The herald was little more than a boy with a soft, almost-feminine face. However, he was no mere boy, for all present showed fear or, at the least, respect to his person. Billy once again made contact with the youth's piercing blue eyes. A sharp, albeit condescending intellect stared back. Billy pursed his lips and fought back an urge to run all the way home to his father. Instead, he simply bowed out of the messenger's way and scooted back behind a column.

The King's Herald laughed and sat down. It was a friendly laugh—not at all malicious—and very much like Lady Myrredith's bird laugh.

Billy peered out from the shadows and observed the youth eat a small bite of food and drink from a goblet. The hall was gravely quiet as everyone anxiously watched the king's messenger consume a full goblet of wine. When he had finished, he placed the cup on the table and stood. He faced Lady Myrredith, bowed, and spoke in a loud, clear voice.

"His Majesty, William, King of Lyonesse, announces the marriage of his niece Princess Kathryn to Prince Gaelyn of Gwythia. Further, he wishes it to be known that, from the day on which she weds, Princess Kathryn is to be heir to His Majesty's throne and kingdom entire. You are therefore requested to be in attendance in His Majesty's court on the last day of this month to witness the holy vows and coronation of his heir. Long live the king!"

"Long live King William!" shouted the ensemble.

The messenger then picked up his goblet and held it out to a servant, who filled it. "And now if you will join me in a toast ..."

Lady Myrredith, her husband, and Sir Hugh raised their cups.

"To Princess Kathryn," the herald said.

"Much health and happiness," Lady Myrredith added.

The messenger drank the toast with the nobles and then bowed. "I must take my leave, Lady Cyndyn. There are many in the kingdom that do not yet know of this joyous news."

Lady Myrredith bowed her head. "Yes, of course."

The young messenger bowed again. He took two steps toward the exit, then stopped. He turned to look at Billy, then back to Her Ladyship.

"As you know, milady, Princess Kathryn is most fond of light entertainment. Perhaps you could ask Malcolm the Magnificent to come along with you ... and his, uhm ... assistant as well?"

"Yes, thank you." Lady Myrredith nodded again, and gave a smile to Billy whose eyes popped open.

As the herald left the hall, Billy jumped to his feet. "May I be excused?"

"What is it, William?"

Billy, bounced from side to side. "I just want to get another look at the King's Herald."

Myrredith smiled. "Hurry up, William, or you'll miss him."

"Thank you, Lady Myrredith!" Billy bowed and ran from the hall.

The herald was mounting a black horse with blue and silver tack as Billy exited the main keep. The youth wheeled his mount around and trotted out of the inner ward with Billy in pursuit.

Billy stopped at the gatehouse and watched as the young messenger passed by the torches on the far side of the drawbridge. The King's Herald turned and caught Billy gawking beside the gate. He smiled and, showing tremendous control, reined the majestic black steed up on its rear legs. Once in the air, he saluted by raising one hand above his head. The instant its hooves touched ground, he spurred his mount into a gallop and charged down the dark, elm-lined road away from Cyndyn Hall.

Billy was still watching the herald when another rider emerged from the trees on the side of the road. This second rider sat upon a pale horse with long, flowing fetlocks. Both rider and mount were encased in strange armor fashioned in black metallic plates with silver filigree. The stranger rode into the middle of the road and stopped to watch the herald disappear into the night.

Slowly the rider's head turned until the owl-like face of the helmet stared directly at the gatehouse of Cyndyn Hall. Immediately Billy felt tingly and uncomfortable under the dark warrior's gaze. He looked to his left and then his right. Billy stood in front—or more importantly, outside—of the castle's defenses alone. He remembered that the few guards Lady Myrredith kept during these times of peace were inside the castle.

Billy took a step back, and the pale horse turned towards him. He took another step, and another. Each time, the rider matched his steps with an advance. Billy leaned into the shadows of the gate and then sprinted into the gatehouse.

"Syrail, Syrail!" Billy shouted to the guard who sat eating his dinner in the gatehouse.

"Wha—?" the large man said, his mouth wrapped around a trencher.

"Raise the bridge! Lower the gate!"

Syrail, confused by Billy's excited state, dropped his food and stood up, looking back and forth between the lever for the portcullis and the wheel for the drawbridge.

Finally Billy leapt to the portcullis lever and released it. A loud, rumbling, clattering, clanking sound filled their ears as the massive wooden structure came down across the gateway and slammed into its home. All this commotion was punctuated by the whinny of a horse from around the corner.

Billy waited a moment before peeking out of the gatehouse. The inner ward was quiet. Syrail appeared behind Billy. The guard's towering frame blocked out the light from within.

"What's this all about?" Syrail whispered.

"Someone's out there."

"Who?"

"I don't know, but I didn't like the looks of him."

Syrail drew his sword as Billy crept out of the gatehouse. Together, they peered around the corner at the dark gateway and portcullis at the far end. The dark rider was just beyond the gate, studying the castle's defenses as the horse strutted in tight arcs on the drawbridge.

Syrail stepped in front of Billy. "Who goes there?"

Horse and rider immediately froze and focused on the gateway. Slowly the animal approached the portcullis until the warrior was inches away, staring between the thick wooden beams.

"Who goes there? Identify yourself, sir!"

The black-clad warrior regarded the bellowing man with indifference but shifted forward when Billy stepped out from behind him. Without a word, the warrior reached up and slipped off the ornate helmet. Pointed ears peeked through short flaxen hair as it spilled out around a beautiful feminine face. Her eyes, like large almond-shaped amethyst, sparkled and scrutinized Billy with cold, feline reserve.

"Zounds, it's the Night Queen!" Syrail said under his breath. He hastily crossed himself and shepherded Billy to the rear, before backing up.

Billy knew well the legend of the mysterious woman some called the Night Queen. He heard guests at his father's inn speak of her turning young boys into feeble old men, men into stone, and making the best milk cows go dry all with a glance, but, of course, none of them had seen her with their own eyes. It was usually some friend of a distant cousin-in-law or some such tenuous connection, and so Billy had always considered her the sort of myth told to naughty children to make them behave. Now, myth or not, the exotic visage terrified him.

The armored woman extended her hand quite naturally and Syrail halted. Billy glanced at Syrail. His expression was strangely dull. When Billy reestablished eye contact with the strange lady, the hint of a smile crept on to her alien features.

178 | K. C. HERBEL

Billy, though frozen with fear, perceived her hand reaching for the dagger at her waist. He broke free of his fear and stepped behind Syrail. He tugged on the big man, trying to pull him back to cover, but he would not budge.

At that moment, there was a clamor from behind, and Billy turned to see a dozen guards spill out from the main keep. They charged across the inner ward, some of them going to the gatehouse while the others ran up the steps to the battlements. Billy looked to the portcullis again, but the woman was gone.

"What's goin' on here?" Garth asked.

Billy looked at the sergeant of Lady Myrredith's guards and said, "The Night Queen is outside! She's coming after us—"

"Whoa right there, laddie. Syrail, what happened?"

Syrail turned around, blinking his eyes. "What happened where?"

"What happened here, you lout! Why have ya dropped the portcullis?"

Syrail looked over his shoulder at the gateway. "I don't know, Garth, it was Billy here what done it."

Garth turned his attention back to Billy. He crossed his arms and stared down his nose at the little juggler. Billy swallowed hard.

At that moment, one of the men who had gone to the top of the wall hollered down. "There's no one out there, Garth!"

"Well ...?" Garth pinned Billy in place with his eyes.

Billy fidgeted. "There was a woman in black armor, and Syrail said it was the Night Queen, and she would have attacked us if we hadn't dropped the gate, and—"

"Syrail?" The sergeant's sharp tone cut Billy off like a sword.

Syrail swallowed and looked back and forth at Billy and Garth. Just then, he noticed the sword in his hand and sheathed it. Finally the lumbering guard shrugged. "I don't know, Garth. I only just got here myself."

"But you saw her!" Billy said. "And you said she was the Night Queen!"

Garth glared at Syrail. "The Night Queen?"

Syrail shrugged, then Garth turned to Billy.

"The Night Queen is a faerie tale, told to children to keep them in line."

"That's right," Syrail said.

"You just let your imagination get the better of ya, lad. Shadows dancin' round in the torchlight, that's all." The sergeant then shouted to his men on the wall to come down and raise the portcullis.

Billy protested and continued to fuss until Garth agreed to post more guards at the gatehouse, "just to be safe." Then together, the two of them returned to the main keep.

"You gonna tell Lady Myrredith about this?" Billy asked.

"Naw. She's got enough worries, what with the weddin' an' all."

"Oh, right. I almost forgot!"

Long after the King's Herald left, Billy forgot about the Night Queen and was squirming in his skin for another reason altogether. He had often dared to visit the king and his court in dreams, but dreams were not as scary as reality.

"Am I really going to see the king?"

Myrredith smiled. "Yes, William. How many times must I tell you?"

"I don't know. How many is that?"

"At least twenty!" Hugh said with a laugh.

"I just can't believe it. Pinch me again. I must be dreamin'."

Sir Hugh obligingly pinched Billy on the arm.

"Owww! I guess it must be true. I'm goin' to see King William. I'm goin' to see King William! I'm goin' to see King William?"

Billy examined himself. He just couldn't believe this was really happening to him, a common lad from the Valley of the Yew! He looked down at his hand. The ring his mother had left him was still on his finger. Since he slipped it on, the previous night, he had all but forgotten it. Now he was strangely aware of it on his finger. It was tingling, as if it were too tight. He twisted it off his finger and placed it back into his pocket.

Lady Myrredith called to him. "William, that boy you told me about—the one you were with in town ...?"

"Stitch?"

"Yes, Stitch. Did he show you where he lived?"

"No, milady. I don't think he has a home like you or me."

Lady Myrredith exchanged somber glances with Sir Hugh and Eadwig. "These feral boys ... there seem to be more of them each year. I don't recall seeing any as a girl. Eadwig, was I somehow sheltered from this problem?"

"No, milady. There just weren't any in those days—not in Lyonesse."

"Where are they all coming from?"

"I can't say, milady, but I have noted their ranks swelling over the past five years or so."

"Indeed. Captain Oswyn would agree with you. They're 'all orphans,' he says. Was it ever like this before?"

"Before we made William our king, he battled King Marcus of Gwythia at Maedwedun. Dyven saw scores of orphans after that day ... but that was long ago."

"Say, that reminds me," Billy said. "Isn't Gwythia our enemy?"

Hugh nodded. "Aye, they have been."

"Then why is Princess Kathryn marrying some Gwythie prince?"

Again Hugh answered Billy. "With a Gwythian prince in the royal family they're not likely to start another war, now are they?"

"No. I guess not. I just don't see why they have to attack us. There are kingdoms on Albion so much closer. Don't they have to sail past Damnonia to get here?"

"The lords of Gwythia have long coveted our lands."

"Aye, milady. The Gwythians have crossed the Irish Sea, to invade Lyonesse, since before the coming of Caesar."

Billy shook his head. "So long? Ya think they'd have given up by now."

* * *

That night, Lady Myrredith began making arrangements for the trip to the king's court. She and Eadwig were hard at work in her study until late and hadn't noticed that Billy was still awake.

"Why are you in such a hurry to get everything ready now? The end of the month is nearly three weeks away."

"It will take us nearly a fortnight to get there, William, and I would like to arrive a few days early."

"Oh. Is there anything I can do to help?"

"I think perhaps you should be sleeping now."

"But I'm not tired."

"You will be tomorrow if you don't get some sleep now."

"But I—"

"And tomorrow we may be leaving."

"Tomorrow?"

"Yes, tomorrow."

"Can't I stay here with you tonight? My room is …"

"What is it, William? Is there something the matter with your room?"

"No, it's just … I don't want to be alone."

"Feeling homesick?"

Billy nodded.

Lady Myrredith turned to Eadwig. "Well fine, I suppose you are old enough, but please don't disturb us."

"Thank you, Lady Myrredith. Thank you, Eadwig."

Several hours later, Lady Myrredith and Eadwig doused the lamps and called it a night. Billy was asleep on a bearskin rug near the fireplace, a quill in one hand and a partial letter to his father beside him.

Eadwig gently took the quill from Billy's hand and placed a quilted cover over him. He picked up the letter and scanned it in the dim firelight. A smile ran across his face, and he placed the letter on a tray with the quill.

"What is it, Eadwig?"

"Pardon me, milady?"

"Why are you smiling?"

Eadwig quietly closed the door as they left the room. "I seem to recall, oh … many years ago, a certain young lady fell asleep on that very rug while her father worked by candlelight."

Lady Myrredith smiled.

"He's such a fine lad, writing his father and all. It's just odd."

"What, Eadwig?"

"Well it struck me as peculiar that he would even know his letters."

"That's because you've never met his father."

"Most boys coming from the countryside can't spell their own name, nor do they have a need to. Is the father a scholar?"

"No. I think he's barely literate. He might even need help in reading that letter, but I'm sure it's his doing. Lord only knows how William learned, though he is very special."

"Yes, milady."

"Eadwig?"

"Yes, milady."

"Am I wrong to feel ... proud of William?"

"I don't believe I've ever told any Cyndyn that they were wrong, milady. I don't believe I've ever needed to."

Lady Myrredith smiled at the elderly chamberlain. She placed her hand on his arm. "Do you ever miss Rory?"

Eadwig stared at his mistress. His jaw dropped open as if to say something, but the words escaped him.

"Sorry, Eadwig."

"No, milady. It's just ... I didn't think you wished to speak of him."

Lady Myrredith bowed her head in contemplation. "I didn't."

Eadwig regarded the woman whom he had watched grow from a timid girl into a formidable ruling lady. With fatherly affection, he lifted her chin. Her face was that of a child, as she looked into his eyes.

"Yes, milady. We all miss Master Rory."

She grabbed his hand and gave it a squeeze. They stood in the hallway for a time, each of them focused beyond the world around them.

Eadwig snapped out of his daze and gave her hand another squeeze. "Yes, well ... good night, milady."

Lady Myrredith held on to his hand for a moment before releasing him. "Good night, Eadwig." Then she ambled silently to her room, still lost in her memories.

CHAPTER THIRTEEN

Wedding Pilgrimage

The next day, the wedding party left Cyndyn Hall: two horse-drawn wagons, fifteen guards, two servants, three nobles, one professional entertainer, and a tired, but excited innkeeper's son.

"How long will it take us to get there?"

Lady Myrredith grinned. "I told you, William. It should take us nearly a fortnight to get there, so you might as well relax. We've got many days of travel ahead of us."

Billy groaned and lay down in the back of the wagon. He tried to get some sleep, but his mind was still racing with images of beautiful courtiers and hundreds of knights in bright, shiny armor; of feasts in giant, luxuriant banquet halls; and of entertainment by the best troubadours and circus troops the kingdom had to offer. However, the best daydreams of all were of the royal wedding and coronation. Billy wondered what these grand events would be like. He tried to imagine them in every detail.

After Billy had exhausted his imagination on the coronation and cloud watching, he practiced his lute playing and juggling, both of which impressed Malcolm the Magnificent. By the time the party came to a stop for the day, Billy was tired.

Lady Myrredith had decided to take a respite in a place where the road crossed through a large heath. A violet blanket of heather stretched out around them in all directions, broken only by a winding brown ribbon of road and bordered by low-growing evergreens. A quiet breeze, fathered in distant mountains, rolled across the heath, gently caressing the blossoms and transforming the road into a fanciful beach. The sun was still high in the afternoon sky, but once the mistress of Cyndyn Hall had breathed in the locale's perfume, it was impossible to convince her that there might be a better spot farther down the road. It wasn't that she wouldn't hear any objections, but rather that she didn't hear them. Her mind was wandering elsewhere.

"We'll camp here" was all she said as she waded into the fragrant heather.

Sir Aonghas, after a few terse words, threw up his hands, repeated his wife's words, and started to unhitch the team. Billy, curious as ever, climbed down from the wagon and trotted after his patron lady.

When Billy caught up with Lady Myrredith, her eyes were damp and misty. She stood with her arms crossed, staring over the heather to the horizon. At last she looked down to her unusually quiet companion. His eternally quizzical eyes stared into hers, and as always, she couldn't resist smiling.

"William, have you ever picked wild blueberries?"

"Of course, milady. I *am* from the Valley of the Yew."

Lady Myrredith returned a quizzical expression of her own. "Are there many berries there?"

"Oh, only the best, milady. But especially blueberries. My father makes the best blueberry pie."

"I hope it's nothing like his strawberry surprise!"

"Strawberry surprise, milady?"

Billy looked earnestly at Lady Myrredith, then suddenly blushed when he saw her knowing grin. He averted his eyes and tried to stifle a giggle.

"Did you think I hadn't figured it out?"

Billy laughed. "Well, I just hadn't thought much about it."

"The earl's physician was quite impressed!"

They laughed and would have laughed much longer if Lady Myrredith hadn't put an end to it.

"William," she said, attempting to be solemn, "I will simply burst if I don't stop laughing. Please go to the wagon and fetch us each a basket, so we may collect a few berries."

"Yes, Lady Myrredith."

Billy quickly did as she had bid him and returned. "Tonight, I will bake you blueberry pie."

"Oh?"

Billy saw her surprise. "My father didn't do *all* the cookin', ya know?"

"But how will you bake a pie, out here?"

"It's not exactly pie, but my father taught me a little something that should do the trick."

"Very well. I'll gather berries over there."

Billy looked at the hollow pointed out by his patron. It was a low corner of the heath, where the heather ran into the trees. A densely wooded thicket formed what appeared to be a small dark cave.

"There's nothin' in there but old spiders, I'll wager."

"I'll take that wager, young sir."

"What wager?"

"That I can find more berries in there, than you can out here."

Billy surveyed the heath with a discerning eye. "Done!" Then he ran to the nearest blueberry bush and began to pick the fruit.

Lady Myrredith laughed and strolled off to her hollow, the basket swinging from her arm. "Remember, William ... we're only counting the berries in your basket, not the ones in your belly!"

Billy looked over his shoulder at her and licked his blue-stained lips. "But eating them is half the fun!"

"Yes, but we can't count what we can't see."

"Wait! Lady Myrredith?"

She stopped and turned to face him.

"What do I get when I win the wager?" he asked.

"Well, when *I* win the wager, young man, you will owe me a song – and *I* choose the song."

"But what if *I* win?"

"Then, I suppose … *you* get to choose the song!"

Without giving Billy a chance to say another word, Lady Myrredith turned and went on her way, laughing delightfully. Billy stood open-mouthed and speechless. He opened his mouth to argue for a different prize but then realized that the only thing he would get was further behind on the wager.

Billy went from point to point like a bee, hovering at each blueberry bush just long enough to collect their bounty. He expertly picked them, choosing only the ripe berries and placing them in his basket. Of course some few did manage to escape the basket and find their way mysteriously to his mouth.

Billy picked blueberries until he noticed that his shadow had grown considerably long. He looked at the half-full basket in his indigo hands, then back the way he had come. He had walked a long distance from the spot where he and Lady Myrredith made their wager. The land sloped gently down away from him, and now he could see over a large portion of the heath. Looking down to the road, Billy saw a wisp of smoke rising up between the seemingly tiny wagons, a sure sign that the others had finished setting up camp.

Billy started to run back to the wagons, allowing the incline to move him along faster and faster. As he cut his way through the heather, he caught a glimpse of Sir Hugh entering the hollow his competitor had chosen for berry picking. Billy nimbly changed his direction and headed straight for the little grove. His new course brought him to a small log, which he jumped over, startling a hare from its hiding place. It raced along with him momentarily, then ducked into a hole and disappeared.

Winded but cheerful, Billy came to the edge of the woods. He kneeled to catch his breath. Between the branches and vines, Billy again caught sight of Hugh. He stood up and started to wave to his noble friend but then decided it would be much more fun to sneak up on the King's Champion and surprise him.

Carefully, step by step, Billy stalked his prey. He had always liked to sneak around in the woods near his home. He was good at it, much to the chagrin of the Valley of the Yew's inhabitants—the usual target of his impish disposition. He had hounded hunters, shadowed trackers, and even snared a few trappers in his youth, not to mention the dozen or so farmer's wives he scared half out of their wits. In the woods Billy felt at home, never nervous or clumsy.

Sneaking up on Sir Hugh should be easy.

Billy snaked his way through the woods. He thought he heard birds chirping up ahead but then realized it was Lady Myrredith's laugh. *Good, I'll sneak up on both of them!*

Billy's heart raced as he imagined the faces of Lady Myrredith and Sir Hugh when he jumped out to scare them. He followed their voices as he crept through the dim light of the underbrush. He stopped abruptly when he spied an opening just beyond the trees in front of him. Shafts of sunlight shone through the tree limbs and ivy onto a small patch of heather no larger than his room at home. Sir Hugh and Lady Myrredith stood on opposite sides.

Sir Hugh spoke in a low voice. "He's not with you?"

"No, I suppose he's off picking blueberries."

Hugh smiled. "I thought I might find you here."

The two nobles stood with their eyes locked on each other. Neither one moved or said a word for several heartbeats. Billy was about to pounce, when Lady Myrredith spoke.

"It's been a long time, Hugh."

"Aye, Myrredith."

They were quiet again. Both Lady Myrredith and Hugh took a step towards each other. Billy was too caught up in watching them to initiate his plan.

"Do you remember?" she asked, moving closer.

"Aye." He nodded.

"Do you?" she whispered.

They were very close now, and Hugh answered her by slipping his arm around her waist and suddenly lifting her up into his arms. "I was going to carry you away, like this!" He laughed and then spun around several times.

"Put me down!" she protested. "What are you doing?"

"I thought I was carrying you away." Hugh stopped turning and stood, holding Lady Myrredith in his arms. "I couldn't then …"

"Oh? Couldn't you?" she said, no longer resisting.

"I wasn't strong enough yet."

Myrredith played the damsel in distress. "But you saved me from the terrible dragon …"

"He wasn't so terrible."

"And you were going to take me home, to your castle."

Sir Hugh's demeanor took a sudden turn. The smile left his face, and he slowly lowered Lady Myrredith to the ground.

"What is it, Hugh?"

He turned away. "It's nothing."

"No." She grabbed his hand and moved in front of Hugh, clasping his hand between both of hers. "It's me … Myrredith. The one you could always talk to. Remember?"

He shook his head. "I'm sorry. I've spoiled the moment."

"There will be other moments, Hugh."

He reached out and gently stroked her hair with the back of his fingers. "Not like this one."

Hugh looked away from her again, and Billy saw the anguish etched on his face. It was like seeing all the woes in Lady Myrredith's eyes for the first time. Since that moment, he couldn't help but see them. Now he felt as if Sir Hugh's face would never seem the same either.

Lady Myrredith placed her hand on Hugh's shoulder. He struck the trunk of a tree with his fist.

"Confound him!" he whispered.

Hugh inhaled deeply and let out a heavy sigh. He rubbed his eyebrow with his index finger and took another deep breath before beginning.

"When you mentioned taking you home, I thought about the home of my childhood—Castle Gallugarth. Home of my father, and his father, and his father … My mother's home, until Ergyfel came and took it."

Billy could taste the bitterness on Hugh's tongue as he spoke.

"I'm sorry, Hugh," Myrredith said.

"And my father … declared a traitor by that snake! That coward … It destroyed my mother. After …" Hugh took in a breath that caught in his chest. "She wasn't able to take care of me. And me, the son of a 'traitor' … What future did I have? I would be lost if not for your father."

Billy scowled. *Sir Sedgemore—a traitor? Not possible!*

Hugh looked down at himself and frowned. "The devil took every-thing. My mother's home, my father's honor … All that I have left," he said stretching out his arms, "my entire domain, stretches from here to here."

"Some might envy the simplicity of your situation. No taxes, no servants, no household worries—"

"No legacy, nothing to inherit. Even if I had a son, he'd get nothing of value."

"Oh yes he would!" Myrredith said.

Billy nodded his head. His wondered what it might be like to be the son of Sir Hugh, the King's Champion. *What a fantastic father he would make.*

"Once again, I'm sorry, Myrredith. Confound this self-pity!"

"It's only natural, Hugh. You're entitled."

"Entitled?" Hugh raised his voice. "I am entitled to nothing! I am the King's Champion!"

"Even the King's Champion must have feelings."

"Feelings, or weakness?"

"Hugh—"

"Myrredith, I don't think that even you can understand. I can allow myself no weakness. I must be as straight and constant as my sword. Not just because I am the King's Champion, but because of who I am – who my father was. That will never change."

"Is that why you didn't come?"

Hugh straightened and stepped back. "I was in battle! The army of Gwythia was invading, and I—"

"No. Not that." Myrredith took a step towards him.

Hugh continued, driven by feelings long caged. "I left as soon as the battle was won. If only I had ..."

Lady Myrredith opened her mouth but paused before speaking.

"What would you have done, Hugh? What would you change?"

"I would have come for you."

"And what of your duty—your honor?"

Hugh turned away from her. "Damn duty, damn honor," he whispered. "I was in love with you. I was a fool!"

"And the kingdom?"

"Yes, yes," Hugh hissed, "even the kingdom. I would have left it all for you."

Billy could see Hugh's body shake as a single tear slipped from his eye and fell to the ground.

"So that's why I haven't seen you for so long."

"Cyndyn Hall was the nearest thing to home I knew, but when your father gave your hand to Aonghas ..."

"I didn't realize that you still felt so deeply. And you never fell in love?"

"I have given my heart but to one lady."

Myrredith placed her trembling hand on Hugh's shoulder. He glanced at it, then strode away through the thicket and vanished. The one love of his life remained behind, staring after him with tears rolling down her cheeks.

"Oh, Hugh," she whispered. "That wound was to both our hearts." She closed her eyes and fell to her knees sobbing. "We just weren't meant to be."

Billy lay still on the ground, stunned. He was vaguely aware of a salty taste on his tongue, and his vision becoming blurry. He wanted to run to his friend, hold her hand, and reassure her, but he dared not. If she knew that he had been there, it would only make things worse. Billy desperately wanted to be anywhere else but was afraid to move. He closed his eyes so he wouldn't have to look at Lady Myrredith and wished that he were home.

Billy waited for a long while, wondering how he was going to get out of his predicament. There was a rustle of leaves, and he opened his eyes to see Lady Myrredith walking away through the trees. He got to his feet and ran to the open heath. As he broke into the clearing he saw his patron emerging from the evergreens. He froze where he stood, not sure what approach to take with her. Then she saw him.

"Over here, William!"

Billy waved to her and reluctantly took his first step towards her. With each step his pace increased, until his feet were racing as fast as his thoughts. Soon he was by her side.

"Well, William. How well did you do?"

Billy suddenly had trouble getting his feet and tongue to work at the same time. "Um, um," he stammered, losing step with her. "Well—fairly well—and you?"

Lady Myrredith looked down into her nearly empty basket. She held it out to show Billy. "You were right. Nothing but old spiders in there."

Billy just nodded, wondering what he should say.

"That's fine," he said at last. "I've still got enough to make pies."

"Are you well, William?"

"What do you mean?"

"Your eyes."

"What about them?"

"They're a little red."

"Oh." Billy froze again, his mind whizzing into high speed.

Lady Myrredith stopped as well and waited for his explanation.

"Well, um, my eyes always get red when I run through the heather." Billy braved a look at his patron, hoping that, just this once, she wouldn't realize he was lying. Fortunately she just smiled and nodded.

"Me too," she said.

"Yes. I see that," Billy said as they continued their walk back to the wagons.

While the last details of setting up camp were finished, Megan and Rhianna began to make the evening meal. Billy, after insisting that he was no stranger to pots and pans, was allowed to help. Megan and Rhianna were horrified when Billy started to place the ingredients for his "blueberry pie" into small pans and cover them with clay.

"You are not making mud pies in my pots!" Megan bellowed.

Billy shoved one into the fire. "It's not a mud pie!"

"But that's dirty!" Rhianna exclaimed. "Her ladyship won't—"

"Be patient. All will be revealed."

Megan shook her head. "I don't know..."

Billy looked up at her from the fire. His hands and smiling face were smeared with mud. He winked and said two words: "Trust me."

The meal served by Megan and Rhianna was well received by all, as both were excellent cooks, on or off the road. All eyes were on Billy as he removed his strange concoctions from the fire and allowed them to cool. When Billy saw that Lady Myrredith was finished with the main course, he took one of his creations and placed it in front of her.

Lady Myrredith raised one eyebrow and looked askance at the dubious object before her. "What should I do with it?"

"Break it," Billy said. "Here, use this mallet."

Billy handed Lady Myrredith a small wooden mallet. She took the mallet and tapped the top of the hardened dark clay. Her first few strikes did nothing.

"Perhaps his lordship's mace will do the trick," Garth said.

Everyone laughed but Billy, who was nervously watching his patron. She glanced over to him, and he nodded for her to continue.

Lady Myrredith smacked the top of the small earthen dome, and it cracked. A small trace of steam escaped through the cracks and wafted in front of Sir Aonghas, who was still rolling with laughter. Suddenly he stopped and sniffed. Then he pulled the pan from in front of his wife and leaned over it.

"It smells good!"

Sir Aonghas broke away the rest of the clay to reveal a golden brown pie. Without hesitation, he cut out a large piece and took a bite from the steaming morsel. Everyone held their breath and watched as Lady Cyndyn's husband attempted to cool his mouth.

"It's hot! It's hot!" he said taking a gulp of wine. Then finally he added, "Say, this is good!" Then just as quickly as he had taken the first bite, he took another. Although he had a problem with the temperature, it was obvious from the way he crammed the pie into his mouth that he was enjoying it immensely.

Quickly the other pies were dispensed and cracked open. There was enough for everyone to have one piece and for a couple to have two. Much to Billy's credit and amusement, there were no leftovers.

When dinner was finished, and the last pot clean, Billy and Malcolm entertained around the campfire. After they juggled together, Malcolm juggled knives while Billy sang. The men who weren't on watch added their own small talents to the merriment by singing and dancing. Syrail, the largest guard, tossed around two smaller men, Terry and Tom Fox, in an impromptu tumbling routine that had most everyone roaring with laughter. However, it was the unwitting sergeant of the guard, Garth, who really brought the assembly to their knees. The well-liked, but completely tone-deaf, old campaigner struggled at length to teach Billy a battle hymn he said he had "sung with the late Lord Cyndyn, God rest his soul," when they fought side by side against the King of Gwythia. Finally

Albyn and Fercus, two old campaigners in their own right, came to Billy's rescue by singing the actual tune. Others then joined in and would have liked to continue singing into the night, but it was time to turn in. By the time Sir Hugh and the rest of the first watch were turning in, Billy was soundly asleep.

The next day, they traveled until late afternoon. Apart from this, the small entourage proceeded down the rugged road in much the same manner. The days dragged on, each one much like the one before, the scenery subtly changing as they pressed deeper into the heart of the kingdom. Hugh spoke very little during this time, and Billy's enthusiasm for the trip was starting to fade.

"Oh, we're never gonna get to the king's court," he mumbled.

Sir Hugh, riding next to the wagon, overheard him and replied, "We are almost there now, my friend."

Billy snapped out of his moping mood. "We are?"

"Yes. Only three more days."

"Oh," Billy mouthed, sinking back into boredom. "I thought you meant we were close."

Lady Myrredith turned to Billy. "Well, we are much closer than before."

Billy sighed. "I suppose. It's just that I hate waiting. And nothin' exciting has happened in ... well in days."

At that very moment there came a loud *thunk* from the barrel beside Billy. It startled him, and he looked over to see an arrow stuck in the barrel exactly where his hand had been a moment before.

"Yeow!" Billy shouted and ducked behind a large bag of grain.

As he peered out from behind the bag, Billy saw several more arrows whiz past his view. He heard one of the guards cry out as an arrow struck him and took him to the ground. Someone outside shouted, "Brigands!" Another arrow came into the wagon past Sir Aonghas and buried itself in Billy's grain bag. Billy jumped back, and Sir Aonghas snapped the reins of the horses.

"Hya! Hya!" he shouted, lashing the horses into a gallop.

Billy, having just leapt to his feet, was off balanced by the wagon's sudden acceleration. He tried to catch himself on the large water barrel at the back of the wagon but instead found himself flying out the back of the wagon with only the wooden lid in hand.

Billy let out an explosive grunt as he hit the ground. With the wind knocked out of him, he gasped for breath. Then suddenly he was surrounded by a flurry of thundering hooves. He squeezed his eyes shut and lay very still, trying desperately to catch his wind. He remained there until he was sure that the second wagon had passed completely over him.

Shortly, Billy's breathing returned to normal. He coughed, spit the dust from his mouth, and pushed himself up to his elbows. There was a great deal of shouting and confusion from the road in front of him. He looked through the dusty haze between his knees to see the wagons and guards fleeing down the road, pursued by a score of bandits. Dazed and panting, he watched them turn and pass out of sight behind a copse of trees.

Billy sat up and stared in disbelief down the road. The weight of his situation began to settle on him. Just moments before, he had been safe and sound, in the company of lords and ladies, on his way to see the king! Now he was alone, left behind by his friends, far from home, without food or money, on a stretch of road he had never seen before in his entire life.

They probably haven't even noticed I'm gone. Not that I really blame them. They've got plenty to worry about right now, like staying alive!

Just then the sound of battle arose from down the road.

"Drat! They must have caught up with the wagons."

Billy listened carefully and heard the clash of steel on steel and cries of pain. He also heard Sir Hugh yelling orders and Sir Aonghas bellowing underneath the racket.

Billy bit his lip and whispered a plea heavenward. "Please let them get away."

Billy jumped to his feet and surveyed the area, to determine which way to run. It was a narrow stretch of road, lined by tall evergreen trees. The road was empty, except for himself and Syrail—the unfortunate guard, whose body lay sprawled across the road, struck through the heart by a cursed arrow. The big man's eyes stared blankly up at Billy, a look of surprise frozen on his face. Billy turned away so he wouldn't have to look at the corpse.

What else could go wrong?

As if in answer to Billy's thoughts, several men emerged from the woods on either side of the road. They were a ragged lot, dressed in bits of mismatched armor and animal skins. Each one wore a dagger or knife by his side, and many carried a bow and clutch of arrows. They began to draw together, closing the distance between them and Billy.

"Well, well, well," mouthed one of the thugs, scratching his broad, stubbly chin.

Billy took a couple of steps back.

"Well, well, well," repeated another man from behind him.

Billy flinched and spun around at the sound. There was a bandit, one or two steps away, and still others just beyond that. Billy glanced to either side. He was completely surrounded. Like a scared rabbit, Billy made a break for a gap between two of the highwaymen.

"Get 'im!" one shouted, and the two men dove for Billy, striking their heads together.

Billy slipped in between them and raced to the trees. He cleared the first row of trees and glanced over his shoulder. His pursuers were scrambling to catch him. At that moment, Billy felt a large hand on his back and saw the ground moving away as he was hoisted into the air.

A low, gravelly voice said, "Where you go, little man?"

Billy squirmed and kicked, trying to break free from his captor. It was no use. He was hauled up about four feet off the ground, like a kitten by its mother. Another hand grabbed Billy and wheeled him around.

"You flop like fish, little man." A gigantic man held Billy up to his face. Then he burst out laughing. "Yes, like fish!"

Billy stopped struggling and stared in awe at the mountainous form in front of him. Until now, the biggest man he had ever seen was Sir Aonghas. However, next to this brute, even Lady Myrredith's husband would look like a boy. From the hamlike fist, which held him up, to the chiseled face, the behemoth figure looked to Billy exactly like a ...

"Giant!" Billy screamed, flailing about and beating on the towering man.

His captor held him out at arm's length. "Giant?" he exclaimed, casting about. "Where?"

Then the giant looked back at Billy and let out a great guffaw. Throwing back his head, he shook with laughter and pointed at Billy with his free hand. His booming voice echoed through the woods. Then, as if displaying a trophy, he held his quarry up and strutted towards the road.

"Look. Redgnaw catch the fish," the laughing giant proclaimed.

All the highwaymen gathered around and began to laugh at Billy flapping on the end of the giant's arm. Then they walked out of the woods and onto the road.

"What ya gonna do wif 'im, Redgnaw?" one of the men shouted.

"Yeah!" another said. "How ya gonna cook the little bugger up?"

Redgnaw examined Billy. "I don't know."

Again Billy stopped his struggle and gawked at the giant. Redgnaw stroked his chin and stared at his catch. Then he scratched his head and spun Billy around for a better look.

"Please don't eat me, Mister Giant, sir."

The bandits plunged into another round of laughs and jeers. At end, the giant looked at Billy's gloomy face. "Well, I need pet too. You be Redgnaw's pet."

"What goes on here?" shouted a man from deep within the trees.

At once the men became quiet.

"We just have fun, Sygeon," Redgnaw said.

"You stupid oaf!" the man yelled, betraying his accent. "You are not being paid to have fun!"

Billy tried to see who was speaking, but the man stayed behind the trees. Billy could only make out his thin build and dark clothing.

"You always too bossy, Sygeon," the giant grumbled.

"That is because I am the boss! Remember?"

"Yeah. You boss now, but when we get back ..."

The man struck his cane against the trunk of a tree. "Shut up, you fool! Now go! The others may need your help. And when you are done ... kill the boy! Remember, my brother wants no survivors."

With little hesitation, the band of brigands started down the road. The giant fell in, toting Billy along with him. Billy struggled against the giant's grip, but to no avail. At first they trotted, but then broke into a sprint as the sounds of battle grew near.

When they made the bend in the road, Billy saw that a tree felled across the road had stopped the wagons. Sir Aonghas and Sir Hugh were all that remained of the fighting men. The field was littered with the bodies of bandits and Lady Myrredith's honor guard. Beyond them, Megan was pulling Rhianna up onto Sir Hugh's horse. Her Ladyship was trying to mount a horse, which kicked and spun erratically. The frightened beast smacked a brigand off his feet before she managed to climb onto its back.

Lady Myrredith held back her feral-eyed mount. "Aonghas! Hugh!"

Both Lady Myrredith's husband and the King's Champion glanced back. Sir Aonghas' opponent thrust with his sword. Aonghas turned back just in time to turn the blow aside and riposted by smashing the man's hand.

"Go!" Hugh and Aonghas shouted.

An arrow flew inches from Myrredith's face, and another stuck in her saddle. She could barely control her horse. "Come with us!" she shouted back.

"Now, woman!" Sir Aonghas shouted to his wife.

"No! I'm not leaving you!"

Sir Aonghas turned and smacked the horse's rear with his hand. The horse bucked and immediately lunged forward, taking its teary-eyed rider up the road and over the downed tree. Rhianna and Megan followed close behind on the surprisingly well-behaved Splendore.

With his back still turned, Aonghas could not defend himself. One of the brigands took advantage of the situation and struck him, opening up a gash on his right arm. He let loose an unintelligible war cry and spun around. As he did, he swung the massive hunk of metal he called a mace and flattened two of his foes. Then Hugh downed another with a deadly swing of his sword. The two knights gritted their teeth as they struck down one bandit after another. They moved like wild men through the ranks of their enemy, whose blood spattered their fine clothing. They had each been wounded, but seemed oblivious to everything but parry and attack. Two more brigands fell.

When the outlaws started the attack, they outnumbered the travelers by more than two to one. Now it was eight against two, and the two knights were on the attack. Upon seeing their reinforcements, the eight remaining bandits beat a hasty retreat, with the noblemen giving chase.

Aonghas and Hugh looked up as they charged. Their eyes widened when they spotted Billy in the grasp of a giant.

"Billy!" Hugh shouted.

At that moment, the reinforcement party pulled back on their bows. "No!" Billy cried.

The archers let go a flight of arrows, but in their haste only two hit their intended targets. The first pierced Sir Hugh's right thigh, the other Sir Aonghas' chest. In addition, two of the retreating bandits were unfortunate enough to be struck down.

All four men fell to the ground. Sir Aonghas lay in the road and clutched the offending arrow. Sir Hugh, who had fallen to his knees, broke off the arrow in his leg and stumbled over to help his companion. The bandits regrouped and slowly moved in on their prey.

Hugh helped his friend to sit up. Aonghas' breathing was shallow, and he coughed painfully. Then his eyes came up on the approaching men. He gritted his teeth and snapped the shaft of the arrow in his chest. Billy could see the big man's eyes widen in pain. He growled like a great bear and rolled up to his knees. The bandits, though they now outnumbered the wounded knights sixteen to two, stopped their advance.

For a long moment, no one on the road moved. The two noble knights rested on their weapons and glared across the narrow gap at the ragged highwaymen. The air was still. Billy thought he heard the sweat drip from the tired combatants to the dusty road. His mind raced. *What are they waiting for?*

Without warning, both sides sprang into action. Billy's compatriots got to their feet as the bowmen desperately struggled to get arrows notched, but it was too late. The bandits had let down their guard. They had advanced much too close for their bows to be useful. The two mighty warriors swung and disarmed four of their assailants at once. Pieces of their smashed bows flew into the air with a hundred splinters. The other archers immediately dropped their bows to draw more useful weapons.

Hugh and Aonghas shrieked bloodcurdling wails and waded into the fray. Redgnaw was in the back of the pack and slowly backed away when he saw the mayhem that the two bloody fighters visited on his allies. Strike after mighty strike, Sir Hugh and Sir Aonghas smote the brigands. They looked more like farmers harvesting hay than knights doing battle. They no longer bothered to block the feeble blows of their enemies, and soon there was no need. The miserable remaining highwaymen cowered before the crazed warriors. They vainly tried to escape the terrible onslaught, but before they could run, all the would-be bandits lay at the blood-splattered boots of the knights.

Hugh and Aonghas stumbled forward over the bodies, preparing to attack the giant. They breathed heavily through clinched teeth and hefted their weapons up to strike.

Redgnaw quickly pulled out a long black dagger and pointed it at them. While it was little more than a knife to the giant, it was easily long enough to pass through either man's body.

"Let the boy go!" Sir Hugh said between breaths.

"Now!" Aonghas demanded. "Now, or so help me, I'll tear out your—"

Redgnaw suddenly pulled Billy in close to his chest and held the sharp dark blade under his chin. Billy could hardly breathe.

"Go away!" Billy's captor bellowed.

Hugh took a step. "Give us the boy, and you can go."

"No!"

The two knights each took another step forward, and Redgnaw started to draw his dagger across Billy's throat. Billy squeezed his eyes shut as the blade painfully cut into his flesh. A small trickle of blood ran down the young juggler's neck.

"Stop!" Hugh yelled.

The giant backed away. "Come close, I kill little friend."

There was a short, choppy sound, like a bird flapping its wings, and suddenly a dagger appeared in Redgnaw's forehead. His eyes crossed as he stared at the weapon protruding just above them. A puzzled expression flashed across his face, and he relaxed his grip. Billy fell to the ground and rolled out of the way just in time to see the colossus collapse in a heap on the road.

Billy looked away from the giant's body, into the trees near the side of the road. Malcolm the Magnificent stepped out from behind a bush with one dagger still in hand. Billy stared incredulously at him as he cleaned some blood off the blade.

Malcolm noticed the stare of his young protégé. "What? You think juggling is the only thing I can do with them?"

At that moment, there was a loud thump. Billy spun around to see Aonghas and Hugh lying in the road beside the recently slain Redgnaw. Billy and Malcolm ran to them.

Hugh lifted up his sweat-soaked head and pointed to the larger man. "I'll be fine. Just help Aonghas."

Aonghas lay facedown, his great mace beside him. Malcolm and Billy carefully rolled him over and leaned the unconscious warrior up against the dead giant. There was a large red stain on the road where the knight had been lying, and soon there was a growing pool of blood on Aonghas' chest around the broken arrow shaft.

Malcolm gripped the protruding shaft and gently tugged on it. Without warning, the broken shaft slid out in his hand. Malcolm stared at the bloody stick. "Good God!"

"What is it?" Billy asked.

"There's no head."

"What?"

Malcolm handed what was left of the arrow to Billy. The deadly missile had broken on both ends.

Malcolm frowned. "There's no head! The blasted thing must have come off inside him."

"Is that bad?"

Malcolm ripped his patient's shirt open. "Well, I had a kinsman, lived most of his long life with a piece o' spear floatin' around in him, but it was just in his leg. After a score o' years the spear tip worked its way out. But in a man's chest ... I don't know."

"What do we do?"

"Quick, tear me off some of that cloth and bring me some strong drink from of the wagon."

Billy shot Malcolm a puzzled look.

"It's not for me! It's for them! Now hurry, lad!"

Billy and Malcolm tended to Aonghas' wounds for a long while. When at last he was stabilized, they assisted Sir Hugh. He had already bound most of his injuries, but the arrow still remained in his leg. Malcolm cut away Hugh's leggings around the thigh.

"Here." Malcolm handed the noble knight a jug of spirits.

"I shouldn't—"

"Shut up and drink. You're gonna need it."

"But—"

"But nothin'! You're in no condition to be doin' anythin' but restin'! Now drink up and lie down."

Hugh stared hard at his new doctor and then his leg. He then took the jug and started to drink.

"I'll be fine," he told Billy, and then laid back.

Malcolm nudged Billy. "Do you see this?"

Billy looked as Malcolm gently moved the shaft of the arrow. His patient stiffened and shot upright. Malcolm placed his hand on Hugh's shoulder and calmly pushed him back. Hugh immediately started to drink more from the jug.

"Did ya see it, laddie?"

"Yeah. I think so. It looked like there was a small bump, on the side of Sir Hugh's leg. It sort of moved when you wiggled the arrow."

"That's right, laddie. That is the arrowhead. And do ya know what we have to do with that arrowhead?"

"Pull it out?"

"Not exactly. We're gonna have to push it through, but at least it won't be stuck in there like His Lordship's."

"Won't that hurt?"

"Yes," answered the reclining knight.

"But not as much as pulling it back out!" scolded Malcolm. "Besides, I have the notion to wait until you aren't feelin' much of anythin'."

"And when will that be?" Billy asked.

"Oh, I'd say about the time he finishes that jug. Now come along, my young apprentice. We have some cleanin' up to do."

Billy and Malcolm left Sir Hugh to his drinking and, after checking on Sir Aonghas, started to clean up the carnage that covered the road. First they collected Syrail and the other bodies of the caravan guard and reverently laid them on the side of the road. Billy had not seen that many bodies before and most certainly had not handled any. It was a task that Billy abhorred but knew that he must do.

After the last guard had been tended to, Billy went to the wagon to get a drink of water and rest for a minute. As he reached for the drinking cup, he noticed that his hands and arms were smeared with blood. He opened the spigot and washed off the gore as quickly as he could. The cool water turned red as it took the blood from his hands. He watched the stained water run to the side of the road, to the feet of his fallen friends.

Garth, Darryl, Albyn and Fercus, Llechvein, and both Fox brothers lay among those on the side of the road—all friends, all dead. He looked at their still, pale faces and remembered his words just prior to the attack.

"Excitement," he mumbled to himself. "I could do without it."

"What was that?"

Billy turned to face his new mentor. "What?"

"I couldn't hear what ya said, laddie."

"Oh ... nothin'."

Billy watched, in shock, as Malcolm searched one of the corpses still in the road and took a small pouch from the dead man's belt. "What are ya doin'?"

Malcolm squatted near another dead bandit, picking through his belongings. He looked up at his protégé's open mouth and round eyes. "What?"

"You-you're ..."

"I'm what? Robbin' them? You're bloody right I'm robbin' them."

"Well—"

"Well nothin'! If things were reversed, and it were me that was layin' here instead of this unfortunate lout, do ya think he'd be havin' any second thoughts about it? No! Of course not! And that's the way of it. He's dead, and got no use for his things anymore! I've got no means or intentions of trackin' down his kinsmen and disgracin' their name, by returnin' his things. What do ya think his family would say, hmm? 'Oh, thank ye sir.

We sure are glad knowin' that our boy was a no-good, lousy thief? No, it's better this way."

Billy felt short of breath as if he'd been the one pontificating and not Malcolm. During the entire speech, he had held his breath, afraid to breathe. Malcolm finally lowered his gaze and Billy breathed. He watched from a distance as Malcolm continued to comb the bodies. At last he seemed satisfied and called for Billy.

"Come on, laddie. We still need to take care of this lot."

The two jugglers picked up the bodies of the dead highwaymen and unceremoniously stacked them on the side of the road, opposite the fallen guards. As they laid down the last brigand, Billy looked at Redgnaw. The giant's body lay in the middle of the road.

"Now how are we gonna move him?"

Malcolm studied the body and the road. "If we had a horse ..."

Billy scanned the woods. "I bet we could find one."

"I don't know. This bunch of outlaws scared them off. They could be halfway to Dyven by now. Besides, it's starting to get dark, neither of us knows our way around here, and we've still got one more patient to tend to."

Billy looked at Sir Hugh, who was approaching the uncustomary condition of slobbering drunk.

"Can you do it without me?"

"It won't be all that bad. Come on. I think he's numb enough."

Billy and Malcolm knelt on either side of their patient and examined the wound. Malcolm tore away more of Hugh's leggings.

"You were right!" Sir Hugh declared. "I didn't feel a thing."

Malcolm leaned close to Hugh. "I haven't pushed the arrow out yet."

"Oh."

Malcolm finished the preparations for binding the wound. He looked at Hugh and placed his hand on his shoulder, then indicated the jug in the knight's hand. "Is there any of that left?"

"I think so." Hugh shook the jug.

The last few swallows sloshed in the jug, and Malcolm snatched it from his patient's grip. He put the vessel to his lips, tipped back his head, and drained the jug.

"Hey!" Hugh protested.

Malcolm raised an eyebrow at the man lying beside him. "I think you've had enough, Sir Knight. And now, on the count of three, we push the arrow through. Ready?"

Billy nodded.

"One..."

"On three, you say?" sputtered the inebriated knight.

"Yes. On three! Ready?"

"Ready."

"One..."

"You're not going to push it on two are you?"

"No, Sir Hugh. I'm not gonna push it on two."

"Because I've seen that trick before."

"Yes, Sir Hugh. We'll all count to three and I'll push the arrow out. Ready?"

"Ready. Just don't push on two."

"Look, what would be the point in countin' all the way to three, if I we're just gonna push the bloody thing out on two?"

"Well—"

"Don't worry! I've done this before."

"That's what worries me."

Malcolm glared at the King's Champion until he was sure that he would be quiet. Then he looked at his assistant. "Are ya ready, laddie?"

"Ready, Malcolm."

"Now then," Malcolm said with some finality. "We all count together. Follow me..."

They all spoke in unison. "One... two..."

When they reached two, Malcolm the Magnificent pushed the arrow through the thigh and pulled it the rest of the way out in one swift movement. Hugh's face went white, and he sat up, grabbing Billy's arm.

"Three ..." Hugh mouthed. "I thought you were going to three."

"I lied," Malcolm said.

Sir Hugh stared at him. At last his eyes rolled back, and he fainted. Billy caught Hugh and gently laid him back on the ground.

"He should sleep now, laddie. Here, help me with this bandage."

It was nearly dark by the time they finished binding Hugh's injuries. Billy quickly collected firewood. Then he and Malcolm cooked up a light supper and retired. There was no entertainment around the campfire that night—no singing of songs or telling of tales, no juggling or joke telling, just two tired men who silently ate their food and stared into the hypnotizing firelight, until sleep overtook them.

* * *

The morning came far too early for the four men who had spent the night literally *on* the road. Sir Aonghas faded in and out of consciousness several times. When Billy and Malcolm went to put him in one of the wagons, Sir Aonghas suddenly came to and grabbed Billy by his shirt.

"Tell her," he wheezed.

"Tell who, what?" Malcolm asked.

"What?"

"Tell who, what?" Malcolm shook him gently.

Aonghas blinked and looked back at Billy. "Billy ... you will tell her for me, won't you?"

"You're not gonna die."

"Promise me!" Aonghas insisted. "Promise me."

"Yes, Sir Aonghas. I will tell her. I promise."

Aonghas smiled at Billy, then his head nodded forward, and he was out again. Sir Hugh limped over and helped Malcolm and Billy put the large man in the wagon. It took more out of him than he had expected, so he had to rest. He was a long way from recovery, and the alcohol he had consumed the night before was taking its revenge. He held his pounding head as he sat on a stump just off the road.

Billy approached him. "Are you well?"

The knight squinted up at his little friend with one bloodshot eye. "I didn't realize I had been shot in the head."

"We took the arrow out of your leg."

"But you left the one in my head!"

Billy laughed at his heroic companion. Sir Hugh wasn't the type to complain about pain. After his battle with the dragon, he never said a word about his injuries. Now, for his head to hurt more than his leg, and enough for him to say so, Billy knew he must be feeling really lousy.

"That must be some hangover."

"Billy?"

"Yes, Sir Hugh."

"If I ever get shot again, be sure to keep the alcohol on the outside."

Malcolm stuck his head out from the supply wagon, with a piece of jerky in his lips and a jug in his hand. "Breakfast is served! Look what I found! I think the cook was holdin' out on us." He came down from the wagon, then handed Billy a yank of jerky and stuck the jug in front of Sir Hugh. "Hair o' the dog, sir?"

Sir Hugh got a whiff of the bottle and immediately turned a pale green. He clamped a hand over his mouth, spun around on the stump, and leaned over its edge. His body convulsed, and his two companions turned and walked over to the wagon.

"Some people just don't know what's good for 'em," Malcolm said.

"Yeah. I think Sir Hugh was just trying to tell me that."

Malcolm held the jug out to Billy. "Have a snort?"

"No. I think I'm with Sir Hugh. It's much too early in the mornin' to be bitin' into anythin' that bites back!"

Suddenly there came a rumbling sound and the clip-clop of horses charging up the road. Billy saw a wagon through the trees. He glanced back to Malcolm, but Malcolm was gone. Billy scanned the woods and found his mentor behind a tree with a pair of daggers in hand.

"Get out of the road!" Malcolm hissed.

Billy stared at him. "What?"

Malcolm peered down the road and then wildly waved a dagger at Billy. "Get out of the road."

At that moment, a horse-drawn wagon, with soldiers on either side, turned the bend in the road and came in their direction, or more precisely in Billy's direction. He was still in the middle of the road, a bite of jerky hanging from his lips and one hand in his belt. He stared at the wagon as it came thundering up the road. The driver spotted Billy and the body of Redgnaw in the road. He pulled back on the reins until he was standing up with the reins above his head.

"Whooa! Whooa!!"

Billy turned to run up the road away from the wagon but tripped and fell. Billy's memory flashed to the day before, when he had fallen off the first wagon. Again he lay very still and hid his face in the dirt. There was a great deal of noise from the horses and wagon as the driver desperately tried to bring them to a stop. Billy could hear the stretch of leather and the creak of wood as the rumble of hooves subsided.

Billy looked up through the dust cloud and saw the front leg of a dark horse, just inches away. His eyes followed the leg up to the horse's head, which stared down at him with its big brown eyes. It snorted at Billy, and he flinched. This spooked the horse, and it jumped back.

"Whooa there, Abigail. Whooa!" the driver of the wagon shouted.

Billy scooted away and got to his feet. He felt something sharp in his back and looked over his shoulder. There he saw a well-armored warrior, mounted on an equally well-barded horse. The sharp object in his back was a long spear with a red and gold streamer. Behind this warrior, there was another, wearing identical armor and colors.

"Stay right where you are," the warrior ordered.

As the dust settled, Billy saw a familiar figure emerge from the back of the wagon. "Lady Myrredith!"

"William!"

The soldier lowered his lance, and Billy ran to Lady Myrredith. They embraced like lifelong friends who hadn't seen each other in many years.

Her Ladyship sniffed. "I thought we had lost you."

"Only for a moment. You can't get rid of me that easy."

Lady Myrredith laughed. "I should have known you'd show up. I'm so glad you're safe, William." Then she hugged him again. "Is-Where are Sir Hugh and my husband? Are they—?"

"Alive, milady?" Malcolm came out of the woods. "Aye, they're still with us."

The two warriors turned their horses to face him. Malcolm held out his hands and bowed to them. Billy noticed that the daggers were nowhere to be seen.

"Malcolm the Magnificent, at your service, gentlemen."

One of the warriors looked at Lady Myrredith, who simply nodded to his silent question. Both men raised their lances and moved up the road.

Malcolm continued. "And as I was sayin', milady, they are still with us—at least for the present."

"What do you mean?"

Malcolm held out his hand and led Lady Myrredith towards the wagon where Sir Aonghas lay. Hugh limped over to greet her.

"Hugh! Thank God!" Lady Myrredith looked over the King's Champion. She could see from his torn, bloodstained clothes and manner that the battle had been hard won.

Hugh gave her a stiff bow. "Milady."

Lady Myrredith rushed forward and took his hand. Billy looked away as the two nobles exchanged "courtesies."

"Sit down, Hugh. You need to rest."

As the knight sat back down on the old stump, Lady Myrredith noticed the bodies of the caravan guard laid out beside him. Her eyes went from corpse to corpse. These were all men that she had known for years and had handpicked for this journey. Each man had served her family well and deserved the honor of escorting her on such a trip.

"All dead," she muttered. "All dead."

Malcolm came up beside her. "They fought well, milady, but alas there were just too many of the bastards! Oh, beggin' Your Ladyship's pardon."

"No apologies necessary, Malcolm."

"He's right, milady. These men did the Cyndyns honor."

Lady Myrredith nodded to Hugh and then bowed her head to the deceased. "May they be rewarded in Heaven."

Malcolm took Lady Myrredith by the elbow. "Your Ladyship's husband lies in yonder wagon."

Lady Myrredith allowed Malcolm and Billy to escort her to the wagon. Malcolm helped her into the wagon and left. Lady Myrredith found her husband unconscious. She knelt and took his hand.

"What happened, William?"

Billy climbed up into the wagon. "He was shot in the chest. We couldn't get all of the arrow. The tip … It's still in there."

"Has he been like this the whole time?"

"No, milady. He's come around a couple of times now."

"What did Malcolm say? What are his chances?"

"I don't know. He didn't say, exactly. Perhaps you should ask him."

Lady Myrredith reached out and brushed a shock of dark hair from her husband's face, then she and Billy sat in silence.

Billy heard Malcolm talking to the wagon driver and looked up. The two armored warriors were now six. They were analyzing the battlefield with Sir Hugh. When Billy looked again to Lady Myrredith, there were wet streaks running down her cheeks. How beautiful she looked to him, even in her grief.

"He wanted me to tell ya somethin'. He made me promise."

Lady Myrredith sniffed. "What was it, William?"

"He wanted me to tell you that … that he loved you."

Lady Myrredith closed her eyes and sobbed. Billy could see her hand tighten around Aonghas' fingers.

"I'm sure he'll be all right, Lady Myrredith."

"No. No. He's dying."

"Please, don't say that."

"He's a good man, but he wouldn't have told you to say that if he were going to be fine."

One of the armored warriors walked up to the wagon. "We should be leaving, milady. Your husband and Sir Hugh finished this lot of villains, but there may be more lurking about."

"Yes, quite, Sir Ewen. We need to get my husband back to the earl's castle immediately."

The knight bowed curtly, turned, and signaled his counterparts. Two of them rushed to the wagon and hitched up their horses. In short order, they had Lady Myrredith, her husband, Sir Hugh, and Billy on their way. Malcolm and four knights remained behind to take care of the bodies.

* * *

The next day, they buried the dead. Lady Myrredith asked the earl to preside over the ceremony to honor the brave men who had died protecting her. It was a dark, rainy day, which ended having never seen the sun.

The following days at Hillshire passed very slowly for Billy. While he was a guest in Waru-Dunom, the earl's fine home, and free to go where he chose, he did not care to explore it. He was too worried about Lady Myrredith and her husband.

Aonghas, despite the efforts of the earl's doctor, showed no sign of recovery. Her Ladyship was almost constantly by his side. When she wasn't, she moped around the castle. At the few meals she attended, she ate very little and talked even less. Billy, Sir Hugh, and Malcolm did their best to cheer her up, but even their best tricks and ballads failed to lift her spirits. The earl, being a compassionate man and an old friend of the Cyndyns, forewent the customary formalities in order to ease her discomfort.

One night, Billy went to Aonghas' room. He watched from the doorway as the earl wrapped a quilt around Lady Myrredith. She had fallen asleep at her husband's side. The old nobleman leaned over and kissed her gently on the forehead. It reminded Billy of the way his father had tucked him in at night. He missed his home and his father and his own little bed.

Late on the third day, Billy and Hugh were talking with the earl about continuing their journey to the wedding. Lady Myrredith burst into the room. She was practically skipping.

"How's Sir Aonghas?" Billy inquired. It was the first time since their arrival that he dared ask. Until that moment he was sure the question would bring her to tears.

She smiled. "Oh, much better! He woke up and we talked for a while. He's sleeping now."

The earl stretched out his hands. "And how are you, my dear?"

"Oh, I'm much better now!" Lady Myrredith put her hands in those of the fatherly old man. "Thank you ever so much. I don't know how I will ever be able to repay you for everything you've done."

"It's nothing, my dear."

"But the doctor, the medicines—"

"It is my pleasure. I knew your father well—God rest his soul. I owe a great deal to him, including my life. Now there's a story." The old man's eyes seem to focus on some distant point, then he smiled at Lady Myrredith. "A story that I'm sure you've heard too many times already. The point is, if I could come to the aid of Rudthar's daughter and didn't ..."

"But you did, Finney. Thank you!"

The earl grinned. "It's been a long time since anyone called me that. You must do it more often. Tell me, my dear, would you do me the honor and accompany me to the wedding?"

"Well, I don't think Aonghas will be well enough to travel."

"Sir Aonghas can stay here and rest. My doctor will watch over him."

"I don't know if I should leave him. When do you expect to leave?"

"Day after tomorrow. If we leave any later, we'll miss the wedding."

"And if we leave sooner?" Billy prompted, his spirits climbing higher than they had been since he arrived.

"Then, my dear boy, well then we'd just be bored to death."

"Oh, not me, milord! Not me!"

The earl peered down at Billy with his bright grey eyes and chuckled. "No, I suppose not." Then he patted Billy on the back. "He reminds me of another young lad, eh Myrredith?"

Lady Myrredith looked at him, and a smile slowly spread across her face. "Yes, very much so. Please allow me to think over your offer. I will give you my answer in the morning."

"Very well, child. But for tonight, allow me to properly welcome you to Hillshire with a feast."

That night Waru-Dunom was alive with festivities. There was a feast in the great hall and entertainment. A small troupe of thespians, on its way to the royal wedding, had stopped for the night. They gave a short performance to repay the earl's hospitality.

When the actors had finished, Lady Myrredith turned to Malcolm. "Perhaps Malcolm the Magnificent and his exceptionally talented assistant will dazzle us with their skills?"

"Yes, of course, milady," he replied.

"Yes, of course, milady," echoed his impish assistant.

Malcolm and Billy stood in front of the head table and bowed. For the occasion, Malcolm had donned his gold and scarlet costume with the silver bells. He had also given Billy a small red cap, which tapered to a single point with a silver bell dangling on the end. When they arose from their bow, Malcolm put on his comedic three-cornered hat and winked at Billy. Then Billy put on his hat and winked back.

"Tonight, my assistant and I would like to juggle ... six wine casks!"

A murmur went through the room.

Malcolm held up his hands for quiet. "But ... neither one of us was thirsty enough to empty that many."

Laughter shook dust from the rafters.

"So, we're goin' to use eight bottles instead!"

The crowd cheered.

Billy and Malcolm each gathered four empty bottles. They then went to the center of the hall, faced each other, and bowed.

"One, two, three," Billy said.

"Follow me," the master answered.

Years after that night, those present would rave about the incredible feats of juggling they had witnessed in Hillshire. Some would say it was only by magic that the two jugglers kept so many bottles aloft. For many, it was the best they would ever see.

When Malcolm and Billy concluded their act, Sir Hugh handed Billy his lute and whispered in his ear. The knight then strode across to Lady Myrredith and bowed. "Would Her Ladyship care to dance?"

Lady Myrredith smiled broadly. "But what of your leg, Sir Hugh?"

Sir Hugh waved her concerns aside and escorted her to the center of the hall. He nodded to Billy, who grinned and strummed the first chords of a pleasant, traditional dance song.

Myrredith smiled at Hugh. "Do you remember—?"

"The first time we danced?"

"Yes," she said with a curtsey.

"In Cyndyn Hall," he responded with a bow, "to this song."

Myrredith appeared bemused. "Yes."

The remainder of the earl's guests stood back, and the noble couple began the dance alone. It was a popular dance learned by all young people, from the lowliest farmer's son to the noblest lord's daughter. So by the second verse, the floor was full of dancers. On the third verse, Billy picked up the tempo. Faster and faster he played, until on the seventh verse the dancers were laughing and whirling around at dizzying speeds.

Suddenly Sir Hugh fell, grasping his thigh, and Billy stopped playing. The remaining dancers collapsed to the floor as well.

Breathless and giddy, the dancers sat on the large flat stones of the great hall's floor. Occasionally a couple would break out in laughter, and others would follow. Even the earl, who had only watched his guests, was caught up in the laughter.

"Very good, young man! Well done!"

"Thank you, milord." Billy looked back to Hugh, who waved for him to continue. "Would you like to hear another, milord?"

"Yes, yes, yes! And why not? We haven't had this kind of lively spirit here since my dear wife passed away."

Billy struck up a tune for the tired dancers as they rested. He sang in his usual clear, sweet voice, and soon it was the only sound to echo through the large chamber. Many of the revelers remained on the floor and quietly gathered around the young balladeer. Billy's audience fell under the spell of his intoxicating voice.

The final reverberations of the last note faded away, leaving the hall in utter silence. Billy looked around uncomfortably. He wasn't sure what to think. Were they silent because they hated his singing? Then, just when he was about to spring up and run away, the assembled guests broke into resounding applause and cheered for more.

"Lady Myrredith! Lady Myrredith!" Billy cried over the hubbub.

Myrredith emerged from the crowd, leading Sir Hugh. She came over to Billy and patted him on the shoulder.

"What is it, William?"

"What song would ya like to hear next?"

"I'm sorry, William. I think I should tend to Sir Aonghas. He may have need of me."

"Oh," Billy said dolefully.

"Now, William, don't stop on my behalf. You have a room full of eager listeners."

"May I play a song for ya, as ya leave then?"

A man shouted from the audience. "Let him sing you a song, milady."

"Sing us another ballad!" said a young lady.

The Earl waved his hands. "How about another dance?"

The crowd began to buzz. Billy heard some of them shouting requests over the others. Finally, Lady Myrredith leaned down and whispered in his ear. Billy bowed to her and strummed the lute. The mob quieted.

Lady Myrredith turned to face Hugh and held out her hand. Hugh took her hand on his arm and escorted her from the hall.

"G'night, Lady Myrredith! G'night, Sir Hugh!" Billy said.

"Good night, Lady Myrredith! Good night, Sir Hugh!" his enthusiastic following echoed.

Billy laid into the next song with a vengeance. It was a lively dance number, which required the dancers to shout back responses to Billy's lyrics. They responded to it with even more enthusiasm than the first dance tune, with all present joining in the dance.

After that song, Billy sang another and another and another. Just when he was ready to take a break, someone would step up and request yet another tune. It was long into the wee hours before Billy was able to convince his newly acquired devotees that he had to stop and go to bed.

As he made his way upstairs, a voice called after him. "William!"

Billy turned and saw the earl following him up the corridor, a servant by his side.

"William, my young friend, how can I thank you? You have brought a great deal of joy into my home tonight, the likes of which I've not seen in years. I only wish my son were here to see it, and to meet you! You must consider yourself welcome to visit me anytime you will."

"Uh-h-h, well ... Thank you, Your Lordship."

"Oh, poo! I know what you mean to little Myrredith." He quickly glanced at his servant. "That is, Lady Myrredith."

The elderly earl leaned in close to Billy, nudged him with a friendly elbow, and whispered. "You can call me 'Finney' too."

The servant, who had until that moment remained facing forward, flinched. The earl gave him a sideways glance, then winked at Billy. Before the servant knew what was happening, the earl straightened and strutted down the hallway. The servant had to jump just to catch up with the old man. At odd intervals, the servant would turn back to gawk at Billy and then stumble as he tried to keep up with his master's quick steps. Billy watched them go out of sight and then went up the stairs to his room.

The next day was utter chaos in that castle of Hillshire. The night before saw a light drizzle, which steadily built until the rain was coming down in buckets. Those who were not leaving were in preparation to do so, and many were the times that those coming were in the way of those going and vice versa. Billy began to feel like a rat underfoot as he dodged his way from place to place. A thrown horseshoe, a small kitchen fire, a dropped sack of flour, and a broken axle added to the confusion.

Billy was looking for refuge from the downpour when he finally ran into Sir Hugh, or rather, into two young ladies who were admiring Sir Hugh from the stables. Billy found their behavior intriguing.

One would whisper in the other's ear, then they would point and giggle. A girl, younger than the others, came into the stables and joined them. Billy backed into the shadows to study the trio unobserved and let his eyes stray to the blacksmith shed where they focused their attentions.

The shed was vacant, except for Hugh. The King's Champion was stripped to the waist. His lean, muscular body was wet with sweat as he labored over the bent axle. Billy marked that his friend was the only knight bending his back to help. Billy watched as the noble warrior pitted his strength against that of the red-hot axle. Again and again he smote the glowing iron with heavy blows of his hammer. It sang out its agony with bell like cries. In the end, the metal would prove no match for the man. With each clank of the hammer, the axle became subject to his will.

A woman in a dark cloak walked in between Billy and his view of the smithy. She stopped and stood outside the stables, with the rain beating off the broad hood of her cloak. Hugh continued to work on the axle, unaware of his swelling audience. A flash of red hair fluttered from the woman's hood. A slender pale hand reached up to retrieve the troublesome lock, and the hood of the woman's costume drew back. It was just enough for Billy to make out the familiar profile of Lady Myrredith.

The girls, just a few feet away, giggled, and she spun to stare at them. Billy could see that she had not been aware of their presence. Without a word, she pulled the cloak around her and crossed into the main keep.

Billy decided that the shed where Hugh was working looked less crowded than the stable. He made a dash across the courtyard, but as he approached the blacksmith's shed, a serving girl appeared in his path. One foot went left, the other right, as Billy attempted to avoid her. He soon learned that when the forces of nature conspire against you, it is useless to resist. The innocent girl and the clay pot she had been carrying went crashing to the cobblestones before she knew who, or even what, had hit her. Hugh looked up from the anvil to see Billy and the girl sprawled amongst potsherds, in a puddle. Billy caught his eye and shrugged as Hugh grinned and shook his head from side to side.

When Billy had picked up himself and the girl, he entered the shed. He shook himself off like a dog and started to wring out his clothes.

"Have ya ever seen anything like this, Sir Hugh?"

"What, the rain?"

"No. All this ... confusion."

Hugh chuckled and put the axle back into the fire. Billy followed him back to the forge and noticed that Hugh's wounds from the forest dragon were still red. He thought back to that fateful day, which had somehow bound them together forever.

Billy absently reached out and touched one of the angry scars. Hugh jumped at the feel of his friend's cold, wet hand.

"Hey!"

Billy traced one of the jagged scars with his finger.

"What is it, Billy?"

"Thank you."

Hugh looked down at the line Billy followed. "I told you before, my friend, it is you who is owed thanks. What I did for you, was the merest ... gesture of kindness."

"But I would have died without your help!"

"As would I have, without yours."

The two friends stared silently at each other for a moment, and then in unison they laughed. They didn't understand why, but it felt good.

Billy looked in the direction Lady Myrredith had gone. "Sir Aonghas seems to be doing well."

"Aye. If not for his stubborn insistence, Lady Myrredith wouldn't be going on to the wedding."

"He was shouting so loud! I thought he must be well enough to travel with us."

"Not yet. That was mostly a show for his wife."

"Aye."

"Say, would you pump on that bellows for me?"

"What, this?"

"Aye."

Billy pumped the bellows and felt the heat of the forge on his face. He looked away from the fire to the courtyard where the exodus comedy continued. "Well, *have* ya ever seen anything like this?"

Hugh looked out at the anarchy and shrugged.

"It's just that—they've been planning this trip for days, and well...look at 'em!"

Hugh brought the hammer up on the anvil and rested his hand and chin on the handle. He surveyed the courtyard and shrugged again. "As the saying goes, no matter how well you place the cornerstone, a castle in a swamp will not stand."

Billy held his hand out into the torrential rain. "Or in a river."

Hugh and Billy laughed and then began to work on the axle again. By the time they had it fixed and back on the wagon, suppertime was upon them. They cleaned up and ate a hearty meal with Lady Myrredith and the earl before retiring to their well-deserved beds.

CHAPTER FOURTEEN

The Guests Are Welcomed

The trip from Hillshire to Nyraval went very quickly for Billy, as he was in the company of many interesting people from the earl's court. Malcolm the Magnificent was also enjoying his newfound friends, among them Sir Ewen and several other knights. Billy treasured listening to their stories and entertaining them with juggling and song. Of course he was also with Lady Myrredith and Sir Hugh, who had become something like a family to him. Aside from the death of the caravan guards, and having to leave Sir Aonghas at Waru-Dunom, the trip would have been just grand. If anything, now the trip was coming to an end too quickly. The only interest to revoke this feeling came from the knowledge that the king waited at the end of their journey.

As they traveled closer to King William's court, other caravans joined them. The number of wagons and people grew until their procession was like an army. Proudly they marched on, with banners flying and voices raised in joy. The rainbow of colors swirling before his eyes awed Billy. The glisten of silver and gold, the sheen and brilliant hues of silken clothes, and the sparkle of precious stones threatened to blind him.

With less than a day's travel between them and Nyraval, the host stopped to rest for the night and ready themselves for their arrival in the king's court. While many would not actually be presented before their sovereign, they would be in his presence, and all wished to look their best. Armor and weapons were polished, while wagons and horses were scrubbed. Clothing and footwear, both old and new, were cleaned and shined. There were even some who bathed.

After he had collected firewood, fed the horses, and eaten dinner, Billy offered to help Sir Hugh polish his armor. The patient warrior gave his new squire a brief lecture on how a helmet was "definitely not a bean pot" then let Billy alone and returned to oiling his sword. At this time, several knights and their squires came around to greet the King's Champion. They looked very pleased to see him, and Billy noticed how all of them openly admired this noble servant of the king. Before he knew it, every knight in the caravan had flocked to Sir Hugh. Each one asked him to recall the tale of his battle with the forest dragon, and to show them the monster's remains. To end the bombardment, Hugh gave in to their requests. Billy listened from atop the wagon as the humble knight told of his adventure. Every so often, Billy felt eyes upon him and turned to see the young squires and knights staring at him in genuine amazement. Under such close scrutiny, Billy became embarrassed and quickly returned to polishing Hugh's helmet. Hugh soon tired of telling his tale. He picked up his lute and, with Billy's help, incited the gathered fighting men into singing a patriotic hymn. As they sang the last verse, the men dispersed and went back to their camps.

Billy and Hugh continued to shine the armor. Billy feverishly polished until it sparkled in the dim firelight. He looked at his reflection in the shield and saw the stars twinkling above his head. He turned to show Sir Hugh and found him leaning against the wagon with a gauntlet on one hand and a polishing cloth on the other. Hugh absently rubbed the smooth, bright metal and stared off into the distance.

"What is it, Sir Hugh?"

Sir Hugh did not respond.

"Sir Hugh. Sir Hugh?"

Billy started to tug on Hugh's elbow but stopped when he saw his silent friend's troubled countenance. A complex web of concern and pain had fallen over his face. Billy followed his steady gaze to the outskirts of camp. There, under the canopy of stars, he saw a woman kneeling with her head bowed and her hands clasped together in front of her. She looked very humble and small, alone in the dark. Without warning, she stood and instantly transformed into Lady Myrredith. He looked to his companion, whose eyes loyally followed the lady.

"Sir Hugh?"

"Yes, William."

"Um." Billy held out the shield. "This good enough?"

Hugh looked down at Billy's handiwork. His eyes popped open when he saw his reflection. Hugh reached out and took the shield from Billy. He smiled as he saw the halo of stars that surrounded his head.

"Now that's what I call a shine! We might make a squire of you yet."

"Well, if you could do it, I'm sure William can."

Lady Myrredith's appearance caught both Billy and Hugh off guard. The two of them snapped around to face her.

"Milady," they said in unison.

"I think it's time for you to be in bed, young man."

Billy grinned up at her and rolled his eyes in protest. "Yes, Lady Myrredith."

Billy watched the fire as he went to bed in the wagon. In the soft red glow, he could see the faces of his two best friends, the two people he loved best in the world, after his father. He watched them, as they sat in silence, staring into the dying embers, neither one looking at the other.

"G'night, Lady Myrredith."

"Good night, William."

"G'night, Sir Hugh."

"Good night, William."

Billy closed his eyes and listened to the silence. It said more to him than most people can say in a lifetime.

224 | K. C. HERBEL

Most of the camp was up long before the sun. The king's court beckoned to them, and all were eager to be there. Billy watched in amazement as many of the wagons were uncovered to reveal bright pastel colors. He climbed atop Lady Myrredith's wagon to get a better look at the spectacle. In the night, while he slept, many more wagons and caravans had arrived. In every flat area of the meadow, as far as he could see, there were beautiful wagons filled with wedding gifts of every description.

In a fanfare of trumpets and dancing colors, the likes of which has rarely been seen, the army of revelers hit the road. The earl's entourage took the lead, followed by Lady Myrredith and her escort. Behind them came another wagon and another and another, until all had fallen in line. There were thirty-seven wagons in all: thirty-seven wagons, several hundred horses, and easily more people than horses.

The morning air was cool and clean with the scent of blooming vines and flowers awakened by the recent rains. Billy closed his eyes and inhaled deeply. The sweet smell combined with the warm morning sun was intoxicating. He leaned back in the wagon and gazed at the long line of wagons behind them. Mounted warriors lined either side of the grand parade, each one with armor and weapons glistening in the sun.

"William?"

"Yes, Lady Myrredith."

"Wouldn't you like to sit up here in front, with me? I think you'll have a much better view of Nyraval, and Castle Orgulous!"

"Castle Orgulous! I don't know what's wrong with me."

Hugh rode up beside them. "What do you mean, William?"

Billy looked to the side of the wagon at the King's Champion. Sir Hugh's armor was so radiant that Billy had to squint to look at him.

"Everything is so beautiful! I nearly forgot where we were going!"

Billy stood in the front of the wagon next to Lady Myrredith. He stretched up on his tiptoes and scoured the countryside. "Where's Orgulous?"

Myrredith chuckled. "Be patient, William. The king's castle is only a short distance ahead of us."

Billy collapsed in the seat and put on a pouty face.

"Oh come now, William. Sing for us!"

"Well…" Billy groaned.

"Yes, sing for us," Hugh said.

"Well…" Slowly, one corner of Billy's mouth curled up and then the other. In his very impish manner, he turned to them and flashed a devilish grin. "What would ya hear?"

"How about—"

"Oh! I know. I'll play ya a little tune I've been workin' on."

Billy reached back into the wagon and pulled out Hugh's lute. As he tuned the instrument, Lady Myrredith turned to Hugh with a puzzled expression. Hugh simply smiled and shrugged.

Billy strummed the first cord of his tune. "I call this one 'Sir Hugh and the Dragon'."

Lady Myrredith returned her gaze to Hugh, who blushed and shrugged again.

Billy began to sing the heroic tale of Sir Hugh single-handedly taking on the fierce forest dragon. All those in earshot stopped talking to listen. Many also turned their eyes to look upon the subject of the song. One verse of such praise and appraisal was all that Hugh could stand. He spurred Splendore into a gallop and rode to the head of the huge caravan. Billy finished the second verse, then stopped.

"Why are you stopping?"

"That's all I have finished. Besides, I wrote it for Sir Hugh and he isn't even gonna listen!"

"Well, Sir Hugh isn't the kind of man who feels comfortable telling or hearing about his own exploits, even if they are quite heroic."

"Humility?"

"Yes, William. Among the best of knights, it is a valued virtue."

"I think that it's even more with Sir Hugh."

"What do you mean, William?"

"It's just that there seems to be something more. He is the noblest of knights, the King's Champion, the best, and still he seems to feel as if he's got to be even better."

"Yes. That's what it means to be the King's Champion: always under scrutiny, doing what is expected of you by others, showing no weakness or flaw. It seldom leaves room for a man to do what he desires in his deepest heart."

"Like you?"

Lady Myrredith looked at Billy with a furrowed brow. "What do you mean by that?"

Billy wanted to bite off his tongue. He hadn't meant to say it like that. He didn't want her to know that he knew about her and Hugh. He shied away from her penetrating eyes. Billy glanced nervously around, trying to think of anything that might save him.

A cry rang out from the front of their column. "Orgulous! Orgulous!" The cry echoed through the caravan. "Orgulous! Orgulous! Hurrah!"

Billy felt a rush of excitement like he'd never felt before. He was just minutes away from seeing the king's court, in Castle Orgulous! His lifelong dream had been to see the king and all his most splendid courtiers, and now it was about to come true. Billy remembered the day he left the Valley of the Yew with Lady Myrredith. Only a few short weeks had passed, and nearly every day since had felt more miraculous than the one before. He wondered if the news had reached his father that he was visiting the king. Most likely everyone would think him a terrible liar; after all, who was he? He was only the son of a poor innkeeper, from a remote part of the kingdom.

Billy once again stood up on his tiptoes in an attempt to see the king's castle sooner. The earl's wagons were turning a corner around the steep hill to their left. Billy could see Sir Hugh sitting, like a magnificent silver statue, at the turn. The knight's noble face was beaming as he gazed down the road. Billy strained to see what Hugh saw.

As the wagon cleared the hill, Castle Orgulous came into view. First one slender white tower peeked over the crest of the hill, then another and another. The elegant silver-roofed spindles stretched upward, like a snow-covered forest, a full dozen stone giants in all, with an apron of the same pale rock joining them together. Each step of the horses brought more of the grand edifice into view, until—at last—Billy could see the whole of Castle Orgulous. The splendid walled city of Nyraval snugly wrapped around its foot, and Loch Nyraval shimmered in the distance.

Billy struggled to catch his breath as a chill went up his spine. The beauty that lay before him was all he had dreamt it would be and more. Best of all, it was real. Billy felt something wet on his cheeks. He reached up with a shaky hand and wiped the tears away.

"What is it, William?"

"It's just so beautiful, Lady Myrredith!"

Sir Hugh was once again riding beside them. He smiled at Billy. "It was the same for me the first time I lay my eyes on Orgulous."

Billy returned his smile.

The King's Champion and the innkeeper's son laughed in unison. Lately, their laughter had become as familiar as rain in spring. It seemed to be the only way to express the pleasure they felt when they were together. The two friends' laughter was contagious. Soon it had infected Lady Myrredith and all those who heard it.

In the midst of their laughter, Billy started to play another of his own tunes. When he caught his breath, he started to sing. The melody was light and the lyrics simple.

I have a song upon my lips on this enchanted day
And if dark clouds come o'er my head I'll laugh those clouds away
With a ha ha ha ha ha tra-la tra-la
I'll laugh those dark clouds away

With a ha ha ha ha ha ha tra-la tra-la

And I'll be on my way.

Billy invited the revelers to join in, and they did. Other wagons in the caravan quickly picked up the song, until the entire army of wedding guests was singing. The sound of his music filled the countryside. Billy felt like a victorious general returning home.

As the caravan approached the gates of Nyraval, they met another, even larger caravan. Lords and ladies waved and shouted greetings to old friends and acquaintances long missed as the two columns of wedding guests merged. All the while, Billy's song continued. The new recruits to the merry army joined their voices gleefully to the chorus.

In this manner, the joyous revelers made their exuberant entrance into the city. As they passed through the neat, wide streets of Nyraval, its handsomely dressed people met them. Most of the citizens wore pale garments of fine muslin. Young and old alike waved flags and banners of blue, yellow, and white as the lengthy procession passed. They cheered and danced in windows and side streets, welcoming their special guests. Many of them, especially the children and young women, hailed Sir Hugh by name. Billy continued to sing his song and watch his humble friend. As with the second caravan, the people of Nyraval soon found themselves singing Billy's simple laughing tune.

The company of roisterers was nearing the great castle of their king. Billy peered up at the beautiful and imposing towers of Castle Orgulous.

From this angle, the immense pale fortress seemed to reach to the sky. Long blue and gold flags fluttered from the tops of the towers. Billy could see scores of people in bright costumes upon the curtain wall, waving and tossing flower petals down on them. Among their numbers he saw the Earl and Countess of Wyneddham, their physician, and others who had been in his entourage at The Valley's Finest Inn. Also, he recognized a few of the lords and ladies he had seen in Hillshire. Everyone was cheering and singing and dancing.

An unexpected patch of black drew Billy's eyes. He squinted up through the fragrant blizzard. Two men dressed in the darkest sable looked down on the festivities from a parapet above the huge, sculpted gateway. One wore an odd, tall hat and the other a gold chain of office around his neck. Neither one looked at all excited about the celebration that surrounded them. They coolly watched as the parade of nobles entered the castle. For a moment, it looked like they were watching Sir Hugh and Billy. The hat-wearing man whispered in the ear of his brooding comrade. They nodded in agreement, then turned and disappeared from view.

The next thing Billy knew, he was entering Castle Orgulous. It was a trifle dark as they passed into the gatehouse, but Billy could still make out the large gilded doors that were pulled back to allow them entrance. Each of the doors was decorated with exquisitely crafted gold panels depicting different events in the history of Lyonesse.

As they broke back into sunlight, Billy couldn't believe his eyes. The outer ward they entered was incredibly huge. There were stables and storehouses, a large smithy, and even a kennel. All were made of the same beautiful white stone as the outer walls, and the ground was covered with smooth pale cobblestones. Not one patch of earth showed through anywhere. It was all so perfect! The only thing that wasn't absolutely in order was a small section of wall near the back of the ward, which was under repair. There were some missing stones here, and several scaffolds and ladders had been erected around it.

The other incredible thing in the outer ward was the number of people rushing to and fro. There were servants and soldiers, lords and ladies, musicians and actors, laborers and craftsmen. Every profession seemed to be represented. It reminded Billy of Dyven's market square.

As soon as Lady Myrredith's wagon came to a stop, a servant and a young stable boy appeared and helped the women down from the wagon.

"Lady Cyndyn," the servant said, "what a pleasure it is to have you with us again!"

"Thank you ... um ..."

"Gullinburst, milady."

"Yes. Thank you, Gullinburst."

"Everything has been prepared for you, milady. We've had to make arrangements in town for many guests, but I took the liberty of readying the same rooms you had on your last visit. Is that acceptable, milady?"

Lady Myrredith scanned the busy ward. "Quite."

The other wagons were likewise being unloaded. A servant or two and a stable boy met each wagon. Again, as in the castle at Hillshire, what Billy saw could only be described as chaos. Sir Hugh waded through the mob on Splendore.

Gullinburst stepped forward to greet him. "Sir Hugh, what an honor to see you again!"

Hugh rolled his eyes. "Hello, Gullinburst."

"What a beautiful horse!" the chatty servant said. "Your quarters in the east tower are ready, as always, Sir Hugh. Will you be staying long?"

"Till after the coronation of our new heir."

Gullinburst reached out to pet Splendore Pomponnel on the nose. The snobbish steed snapped at his fingers. The pretentious servant snatched back his hand, just in time to avoid the bite.

"What an ornery beast!" Gullinburst exclaimed, counting his fingers.

Hugh patted his mount's neck. "On the contrary, I find Splendore an excellent judge of character."

The servant nervously eyed the horse and then muttered. "Uhmm ... Will you be with us long, Sir Hugh?"

"Yes, Gullinburst." Hugh grinned and then turned to Lady Myrredith. "Milady, it was indeed a pleasure to have escorted you once more."

"Yes, Hugh, a pleasure for me as well. Thank you."

"Perhaps, milady, I may have the honor again?"

Billy listened to the two nobles chitchat as if they were merely acquaintances. They sounded very distant and correct. He wondered if this was part of the expected behavior of which Lady Myrredith had spoken. It seemed tragically misguided somehow.

"Yes. I will need …" Lady Myrredith suddenly stopped.

"What is it, milady?"

"Nothing."

"Well, if ever you are in need …"

"Thank you, Sir Hugh."

Hugh bowed, turned Splendore in the direction of the stables, and rode away. Lady Myrredith watched as he disappeared into the farthest part of the huge stables reserved for the king's knights.

"And Sir Aonghas …?" Gullinburst nervously scanned the area. "Is he with you, milady?"

"No."

Gullinburst made no attempt to hide his relief. "I remember the last time Sir Aonghas was—"

"My husband, Lord Cyndyn," Her Ladyship scolded, "was wounded in battle near Hillshire and we were forced to leave him behind."

"I see," the cowed servant muttered.

Billy watched Gullinburst's face. Suddenly his eyes sparkled, and he smiled smugly at Lady Myrredith.

Gullinburst leaned over and spoke softly out the side of his mouth. "I could arrange for you to have rooms near the east tower, milady."

Lady Myrredith speared the servant with eyes of sharpened steel. Gullinburst immediately backed away from her. He pursed his lips and swallowed, as if his throat were very dry.

"But if you prefer your usual rooms … Shall I show you to your quarters now?"

"Yes. That would be fine, and once we are settled, I would like you to send word to Princess Kathryn that I wish to speak with her."

"Oh, I don't think Her Highness will—"

"Just send the message, Gullinburst!"

"Yes, milady."

Gullinburst turned and quickly walked across the outer ward. Lady Myrredith, Megan and Rhianna, several royal servants, and lastly Billy followed him. Billy had trouble keeping up with the group, as he was distracted by all the sights, smells and sounds, and constantly had to push through people crisscrossing his path. Again, this reminded him of his day in Dyven.

As Lady Myrredith's party approached the gate to the inner ward, Billy heard a woman's scream, and then four ladies wearing tall pointed hats rushed away from the entrance. They screamed and looked over their shoulders as they retreated from the dark archway. It took a few breaths for them to calm down, and then all at once they started to chatter. It sounded to Billy more like the clucking of excited hens than ladies from a royal court.

As they passed by, one of the tall-hatted ladies, still looking over her shoulder, ran directly into Billy and knocked him to the ground. She glanced down at him, before continuing to jabber with her companions.

"They're awful, terrible beasts!" the lady said.

"They ought to be destroyed!" said another.

"My Bruce says the king would never have allowed them here before Magister Ergyfel," the third said.

"That awful, terrible man!"

"That's what my husband says!"

"Did you see? That horrible beast tore my dress!"

"Well my husband says that the whole kingdom would be better off without that wicked man."

"Oh, he's really not so wicked."

"Maeven! Have you an eye for the magister?"

They blabbered and giggled their way across the crowded outer ward. The lady with the torn dress occasionally glanced back at the gate.

Billy dusted himself off and ran to catch Lady Myrredith. He was curious to see what "beast" could have the ladies so agitated.

Lady Myrredith, her maids, and Gullinburst were passing into the shadow of the gateway when Billy caught up with them. As Billy drew near, the pit of his stomach snarled. His legs froze, and the hair on the back of his neck stood on end. He didn't know why, but he felt distinctly in danger.

"Lady Myrredith! Stop!"

At that moment, an eerie howl arose from the darkened gatehouse. Billy reached into his pocket and touched his mother's ring. He did not feel the warm, smooth comfort he had expected; instead, it felt oddly cold and sharp. He wanted to climb inside of something and hide. Then the ring was on his finger. A shiver inched its way up his already tingling spine as another woeful howl bellowed forth from the darkness.

The beastly sound filled the air and slowly replaced the buzz of the outer ward as people stopped what they were doing to listen. Billy saw Lady Myrredith enter the sunlight on the other end of the gatehouse with Gullinburst. She and all the other people on that side were staring into the gateway. Billy looked around him. Everyone in the ward appeared to be staring at him, and then he realized he was standing directly in front of the gate. Two guards backed away from their posts by the gate, and Billy took this as his cue to do the same.

He took one step back, then another. Just when he was about to take a third, something moved in the shadows. Billy froze once again when a large wrinkled hand with long black claws fell into the light. Slowly, with calculated motion, the creature dragged the remainder of its sizable body from the murk. It was roughly humanoid in shape and largely covered with dull, scraggly brown hair and warts. Sickly bald spots of splotchy grey skin showed through the hair around the creature's joints, hands, and head.

Billy's eyes followed the muscular front limb up to the oddly misshapen shoulder and then to the gruesome face. The creature's physiognomy horrified Billy. He felt his heart skip and his mouth go dry as the miscreated visage confronted him. It raised its filthy snout and sniffed the air, at first carefully, almost cautiously, and then it breathed more deeply. The elongated lower jaw eased open, and the beast's lips peeled back to reveal rows of sharp yellow teeth. Its deep-set crimson eyes scrutinized Billy, dissecting his every pore. Its breathing increased until its ugly great body heaved with the inflation and deflation of its lungs. The raspy sound filled the outer ward.

The same fear Billy felt when he was face to face with the dragon enveloped him. The monster, now just ten feet away, squinted its sanguineous eyes and flattened its ears back. Billy spun around to make a dash for it, but before he could take a single step, he was downed.

As Billy lifted his face off the cobblestones, he felt the firm grip that had enveloped his ankle release. He scrambled to his knees and was knocked down again from behind. At once, an irresistible strength dragged him backwards and tossed him over onto his back. Billy felt like a stuffed doll. He lifted his head, and immediately a huge, coarse hand circled his throat. The ugly beast's face came down to Billy's and inspected him like a nearsighted carpenter looking for a splinter in his palm. Its nose twitched and sniffed. Its fetid breath struck his nose, and he tried desperately to pull away. Suddenly its eyes widened, and the corners of its long mouth broadened into a smile of malefic pleasure. Slobber drooled from its maw as it snickered and hissed.

Billy's tormentor raised its second horrible hand and pointed the long, black claw of the index finger at Billy's left eye. It then moved it back and forth with a twisting motion. Billy felt sure that the creature meant to take his eye, if not his life. He cried out, and the creature silenced him by tightening its grip around his neck.

There was a hissing sound and the smell of burnt flesh as Billy grabbed at its thick wrist with both hands. His captor cried out in pain and pushed him away. The monstrous beast grabbed its wrist and raised its face to the sky. The anguished howl, which issued forth from its misshapen lips, caused both commoner and noble to shudder.

Billy rubbed his throat and swallowed painfully. As he regained his wits, he felt a strange tingling in his right arm. It burned and intensified in his hand and fingers. He looked down at his hand, and for just a moment, he saw a faint blue glow from his mother's ring. Forthwith, the burning retreated down his arm and disappeared, until all that remained was a tingle in his ring finger.

Billy sat up as if someone had pricked him with a needle. The creature squatted back on its hind legs, holding its wrist and glowering at Billy. It snarled at him and lunged for his ankle. There was a bright flash of steel, and a long blade struck the stones between the horrible, long fingers of the beast's hand.

Billy and the monster looked up to find a warrior standing beside them. The sun's rays sprayed off his well-polished armor, obscuring his countenance, except for his clear green eyes that glared down at the beast with contempt. The beast growled at the man and recoiled from the sword that impeded its attack. The staunch knight remained unmoved, until the hideous monster began to slink away. Billy, no longer in fear for his life, noticed that the beast was tethered by a long chain attached to an iron collar around its neck.

Billy's savior leaned over and offered his free hand. "I can't leave you alone for a minute."

"Sir Hugh! I'm sure glad to see you."

Billy reached up to take the knight's hand, and suddenly the creature turned and sprung at Hugh.

"Sir Hugh!"

With an arrow's speed, Hugh moved aside and kicked the beast in the ribs. Immediately he followed with a slash of his sword. The creature fell to the ground, howling and holding its right ear. As Sir Hugh approached, it balled up and cowered from him. The noble knight gave the loathsome wretch a kick to its foul behind. It whined, much like a dog, and then wormed its way back to the darkness of the gateway, keeping an eye on its subduer.

Sir Hugh sheathed his sword and helped Billy to his feet.

"Are you well?"

Billy patted himself. "Aye, I think so."

"Hurry along now. Lady Myrredith is waiting for you." Hugh patted Billy on the back and sent him through the gate.

Billy edged his way to the gateway. As he started into the shadows, he heard the heavy breathing of the beast and froze.

"He won't bother you now."

Billy looked back to Hugh for reassurance. The handsome knight nodded. Billy took one well-measured step into the gateway and then broke into a sprint.

Billy flew into the sunlight of the inner ward and ran directly into Lady Myrredith's arms. Her arms surrounded him protectively and squeezed. All of a sudden, a hand on Billy's shoulder tore him away from his patron's embrace.

"Get away, you little ragamuffin! This is the Lady of Cyndyn, and you are not allowed in the inner ward until the feast!"

Billy stared up at Gullinburst, bewildered. The puffed up servant mistook his expression for one of mocking and drew back his hand to strike. Billy watched in openmouthed amazement as Lady Myrredith smacked the obtuse servant with a resounding slap across the face. The blow rocked Gullinburst back on his heels. The inner ward fell abruptly quiet again. Everyone was staring at them. Billy glanced around him, then eased closer to Lady Myrredith.

"What do you think you are doing?"

Gullinburst rubbed the cheek of his puzzled face. "I-I don't know what you mean, Your Ladyship."

"You were about to strike him, weren't you?" Lady Myrredith placed her hands on Billy's shoulders.

Billy recognized the commanding tone of her voice. It made him shiver uncomfortably inside, even though he was not the one she was roasting on a spit.

"I-I-I thought he was one of the entertainers—"

"William is not one of your cheap jongleur. Any fool can see that!" Lady Myrredith then turned to Billy. "Are you hurt, William?"

"No, milady."

"That awful troghoul didn't hurt you?"

"No, milady."

The stupefied servant cast his eyes on Billy. "I take it that he is … with you, milady?"

"However you take it, Gullinburst, you needn't bother showing us to our chambers. I know the way." With that, the Lady of Cyndyn Hall turned and started to escort her young friend away. "William? What did you do, to cause that beast—?"

"But, Your Ladyship—" Gullinburst spouted.

Lady Myrredith spun and glared at him. Immediately he became silent.

"Consider yourself lucky, Gullinburst. With the princess' wedding, I'm in a generous mood."

"But—"

"Don't press your luck."

Gullinburst lowered his eyes and bowed apologetically. "Yes, milady."

Lady Myrredith and company made their way around the huge two-storey barracks adjoining the wall near the inner gatehouse. Billy walked, wide-eyed, past the king's guards and knights who were in abundance here. Every bit of metal was polished and every strap buckled in place. He had never seen a finer, more complete display of armaments.

As they neared the smoky kitchen, at the end of the barracks, Billy looked back and saw Sir Hugh enter the courtyard area. First one knight shouted his name, then another. Without delay, nearly all the warriors turned and moved to greet their king's champion. The men cheered him, and Billy could see the genuine joy they showed at his arrival. To them, Hugh was more than their best warrior; he was the exemplar of all knightly virtues. Billy wondered if they would feel any different if they knew about Hugh's occasional bouts of "weakness" or his forbidden feelings for a certain lady. Billy shrugged these thoughts off as nonsense. After all, Hugh was still Hugh, no matter what his feelings. He smiled and watched with unbridled adoration as Hugh laughed and disappeared into a swarm of his clamoring cohorts.

When Billy turned back around, he couldn't believe his eyes. Across the huge inner ward stood the most spectacular keep he had ever seen. Not that he had seen that many, but this one put to shame anything he could have imagined. This grand edifice—the donjon—was the heart of Castle Orgulous and housed the rulers of Lyonesse.

Billy could remember hiding at the foot of the stairs in his father's inn at night, listening to weary travelers talk of the world's wonders. He especially loved hearing tales of the king and his splendid court. Every time he had heard the name Orgulous, he would practically jump out of his skin. His head would swim with images of himself standing before the king, being rewarded for some heroic deed. Then, before his father could discover him, he would rush back to his bed and dream.

Now, all the images created in Billy's mind were like dust before a sudden zephyr. From the pristine white marble steps to the blue and silver spires crowning the half-dozen towers, it was nothing short of *magnificent*.

Lady Myrredith dragged Billy along as he gawked at the splendor of the inner ward. As they approached the grand front steps, Billy stared up at the keep. He placed one foot on the first step and came to an abrupt halt. Despite its grandeur, the donjon gave Billy a strong feeling of foreboding. He took his foot off the bottom step and turned around, pretending to be more interested in the inner ward.

Lady Myrredith reached the head of the broad stairs and turned to see Billy at the bottom. "What is it, William?"

Billy spun around. "Um, what do you mean?"

"Is there something the matter?"

"Oh … no. No. Nothing."

Lady Myrredith observed Billy for a moment. He held his hands behind his back and rolled up on the balls of his feet, trying to appear relaxed.

"It's all right, William. Don't be frightened."

Billy saw a number of people staring at him from the top of the steps. He folded his arms. "Frightened? I'm not frightened."

Lady Myrredith raised an eyebrow, and Billy could see that she knew better. He took a deep breath and reluctantly placed his foot back on the lowest step. With a sudden burst of courage, he bounded up the steps, skipping every other one.

When he reached the top, Lady Myrredith smiled and placed her hand on his shoulder. "Well, I was frightened the first time I came to the king's home, but I suppose, you being a boy and all ... No, a boy like you wouldn't be afraid or even a little bit nervous."

Billy was unaccustomed to the ironic manner in which Lady Myrredith often chose to prod him. The simple folk in the Valley of the Yew were not so subtle when it came to jokes or teasing. He looked up at her, crinkled his nose, and shrugged. Lady Myrredith laughed and took his hand.

Lady Myrredith led her young companion through the extensive passages of the beautiful donjon. Everywhere he cast his eye, Billy saw intricate carvings in stone and tapestries of the finest quality. There were flags and weapons along some walls as well, which according to his guide, were trophies from defeated enemies of Lyonesse.

As in Waru-Dunom, the donjon of Castle Orgulous was bustling with servants, guards, and visiting nobles, only more so. It was slow going as they made their way up the keep. In the corridors and even in the stairwells, lords and ladies stopped them to greet Lady Myrredith and wish her well.

When finally they arrived at their quarters, Lady Myrredith asked the servants to unpack and went with Billy to explore the other rooms. They were spacious compartments, each with a different view of the inner ward. They could also see over the outer bailey walls of the castle to the surrounding hills. There was a large marble balcony off the central room. Billy went on to it and looked down at the people far below.

"They look so small from here!" He climbed onto the balcony rail and gazed out over the walls. "Are we in the sky?"

"No, William." Lady Myrredith gave a nervous laugh. "But we are rather high, so please come down from there."

"Very well."

Billy came down, with Lady Myrredith's help, and stood next to her. Together they watched the comings and goings of the tiny people below.

"Say, there's Sir Hugh." Billy pointed, then gave a yell. "Sir Hugh! Hello-o-o! I guess he can't hear me from here."

"Probably not. The ward is quite noisy today."

Billy was quiet for a moment, then regarded his lovely patron. "That monster that attacked me ..."

"The troghoul."

"That was a troghoul?"

"Yes. They're foul, dirty creatures. Ergyfel is the only person vile enough to exploit them. King William would never have allowed them before. I fear the magister's hold on the king is strengthening."

"Who's Ergyfel?"

"William, I'm sorry, but please don't say that name! He's the king's cousin."

"The king has a cousin?"

"Yes, William. Even the king has cousins."

"Oh yeah, you're his cousin too!"

"Only distantly."

"Can he become king?"

"Well, not now, thank goodness! Now that Kathryn is to be crowned heir, her lineage becomes all important and his claim becomes worthless as dust."

Billy noticed a smile slip cross Lady Myrredith's lips. "How come he has such a hold on King William?"

"Many years ago, when the magister first came to Orgulous, the king unwisely appointed him as his first counselor. After the queen died, the king's health began to fail. Since then, his dreadful influence has grown, both in the king and the kingdom."

"Where did he come from?"

"Across the Eastern Sea. It seems an ancestor of the king was careless there. Now we have to deal with their mistake."

Billy looked deeply into Lady Myrredith's eyes. She appeared to be in a trance. He could see the hatred for Ergyfel welling up in her. He had never seen her so angry. His instincts were screaming at him to change the subject, but his curiosity got the better of him.

"Why do you hate him so?"

Lady Myrredith blinked away her trance and glanced at her observant friend. "I don't hate—"

She made eye contact with Billy, cleared her throat, and restarted. "No, that's not true. I do hate the caitiff. He's a backstabbing, power-hungry snake! What's more, he brought evil sorcery to Lyonesse."

"He's a sorcerer?"

"Of the darkest kind. That's why you should be cautious when you say his name. It's difficult at times, but you must be careful."

"But if he uses witchcraft, why don't they—?"

"He would deny it."

"But if he practices the black arts—"

"A very hard thing to prove. And he *is* the king's cousin."

Billy sighed. "There must be a way. Has he ever turned someone into a toad … or a bird?"

"I think you've heard too many faerie tales, William. As with many things in the king's court, this snake moves with great care and subtlety."

"So he's never done anything that he can be blamed for?"

"Although he denies any wrongdoing ..." Lady Myrredith stopped and surveyed the area before continuing in a whisper. "And no one dares speak of it, there are those who believe that he is somehow responsible for the queen's death."

"Has he cast a spell on the king?"

Lady Myrredith looked away from Billy, over the walls of Castle Orgulous. She took a deep breath, then let it out. "I wish I knew. You are too young to remember, but there was a time when Lyonesse was ... a better place to live. There was no hunger, no crime, and no sorcery. King William defended the land from any evil. I barely remember it myself. However, since Ergyfel's arrival a great many things are not right."

"Like the troghouls?"

"As you discovered today, they're too unpredictable and dangerous!"

"Where do they come from? I've heard guests at the inn talk about them, but I always thought they were just spinning yarns."

"They didn't exist on Lyonesse before the magister came. Lord knows where he finds the awful brutes."

"Are they magical?"

"One of Rory's favorite tales told how the little people put a curse on them, because they stole something. But it's just a tale."

The two friends fell silent, as even the best of friends will do from time to time, and continued to observe the people below. Just then, Billy caught sight of Sir Hugh on the wall separating the inner and outer wards. What actually caught Billy's eye, was the appearance of the two gentlemen he had seen above the main gatehouse. They had their backs to him now, but Billy was sure it was them, as no one else in the entire castle wore such raven-like garments. They were conversing with Sir Hugh, who was fuming.

"Who is that with Sir Hugh?"

"Where?"

"Over there on that wall, near the barracks." Billy pulled himself up onto the balustrade and pointed to Sir Hugh.

Lady Myrredith grabbed on to Billy and sighted down his arm. Her eyes narrowed as she scanned the wall, then she straightened and pulled away from Billy.

"That's him," she said under her breath.

"Who?"

"Him!"

Billy focused on the inter-bailey wall. Hugh was becoming enraged.

Lady Myrredith paced into the central chamber.

"William, come away from the balcony."

Billy didn't move. His curiosity was piqued, and he wasn't going to leave empty-handed.

Lady Myrredith stood in the middle of the room, with her hands on her hips. "William! Come here!"

Billy was still trying to get a glimpse of the man's face. "I only want to know who he is."

"It's Ergyfel!"

At that moment, the man wearing the gold chain of office slowly turned and looked directly at the balcony. Billy's heart raced as he felt the eyes of the man in black upon him. It was as if he were being drawn towards the man, and for an instant he saw with perfect clarity every detail of his face—the thin lips, high cheekbones, aquiline nose, and fine crow's-feet all appeared to be just inches away. Billy looked into the deep-set onyx eyes as cold and black as a moonless winter night—eyes that stared back at him, taking in everything.

Suddenly Billy twitched, as if he'd been shaken from a nap. He had to grab the balustrade to keep from falling to the cobblestones far below. His right hand and arm throbbed fiercely as he gripped the finely carved stonework.

"Now come away from there!"

Billy's heart was pounding in his ears as he rolled over onto the balcony and dashed into the room. He shook his arm, and the pain became localized in his hand. He held it up to inspect it, and a small trickle of blood ran into his palm from around the ring.

Lady Myrredith stepped towards him. "Let me see that."

"It's nothing."

"But you're bleeding, William."

"No, it's fine. Really."

Lady Myrredith placed her hands on her hips. She wasn't about to take no for an answer. Reluctantly, he held his hand out. She inspected it and then started to take the ring off his finger.

"No!" Billy, pulling back his hand. "I'll get it!"

"What is it, William? Did I hurt you?"

"No. It's just … This ring belonged to my mother. It's all I have of her."

"I understand."

Billy took off the ring and was about to clean it off on his tunic.

"Ah-ah-ah! Stop that!" Lady Myrredith wagged a finger at him, then reached into a fold in her dress and handed him a handkerchief.

He bashfully took it. "Thank you."

Lady Myrredith took his right hand and washed it off in a nearby basin. Again she inspected it closely.

"You have such beautiful hands, William. Huh? The bleeding seems to have stopped!"

Billy retrieved his hand, then took his mother's ring and started to slip it back into his pocket.

"May I see it?"

Even though Lady Myrredith had shown nothing but kindness to him, and he trusted her completely, Billy just couldn't let the ring out of his possession. It hadn't left his person since his father had given it to him. John's words echoed in his head: *Don't show anyone the ring.* Billy's mind and hand vacillated.

"That's not necessary, William. You don't have to show it to me."

Billy felt almost ill in not trusting Lady Myrredith. Again his father's words came to him. *Lady Myrredith is a kind and good woman. Trust her.* He felt the familiar warmth of his mother's ring in his hand, and instantly his mind was clear.

"Here." He held out the ring in his palm.

"Are you sure?"

"Yes."

Lady Myrredith smiled and took the ring. She held it into the light and examined its smooth red-gold surface and tiny stone.

"I see why you were reluctant to show it to me."

"Oh?"

"Oh, yes. It's very beautiful." Lady Myrredith breathed on the ring and gave it a quick polishing on her dress. "I think it's the most beautiful ring I've ever seen."

"What? That ring? It's nothing compared to your ring!"

Lady Myrredith eyed the ring on her own hand. She wore an old Cyndyn heirloom, bearing the family crest and a large blood ruby.

"All that ring does is show off an expensive gem. But this ring ..." She held up Billy's ring. "This ring is perfect."

"Perfect?"

"Yes, William. It's perfect. Like you."

Billy held out his limbs and looked down at himself. He had a sturdy body that functioned well enough, but it seemed obvious to him that no one would find his body beautiful or well developed, much less perfect. Except for his hands, it wasn't formed very well at all and was, of course, much too small for someone his age.

Billy presented himself to Lady Myrredith with his arms out. "Perfect?"

Lady Myrredith smiled at Billy and shook her head. She kneeled before him and took his hands in hers. "Not here," she said, holding out his arms, "but here." She gently placed her hand over his heart. "Deep inside, where it really counts."

Billy regarded Lady Myrredith with a smile. She in turn smiled and placed the ring back into his hand. On impulse, Billy reached out and embraced her. She put her arms around him and squeezed.

"Thank you, Lady Myrredith."

"Thank you for letting me see it, William."

At that moment, while they still embraced, the large double doors to the room burst open. A beautiful fair-haired lady wearing an iridescent pink dress with blue ribbons entered. Lady Myrredith and Billy cast their eyes on her at the same time she saw them. The woman froze and gaped at them. She opened her mouth to say something, but no words escaped. Her eyes locked on Billy.

"Kathryn!" Lady Myrredith jumped to her feet.

The lady and Billy continued to stare at each other, and then she turned to Lady Myrredith, held out her arms. "Myrredith!"

"How wonderful it is to see you again!"

"And you. It's been much too long."

Billy noticed a lightness in the way Lady Myrredith ran across the room to greet her friend—as if the weight of her troubles had been lifted. Just seeing her in such a sprightly mood made Billy forget his troubles as well. The two ladies embraced and then separated to gaze at one another at arms' length. They held hands and smiled silently.

"Come," Myrredith said. "There's someone I want you to meet."

The lady followed her to where Billy waited anxiously.

"William. I have the honor of introducing to you Lady Kathryn, Princess of Lyonesse and heir apparent to King William."

Billy's mouth dropped open. He stood motionless and openly gawked at the princess.

"William…?"

Billy recovered his wits and bowed to the princess in the manner which Malcolm the Magnificent had taught him.

The princess acknowledged him with a stately nod.

"Your Highness, may I introduce to you my very good friend, William?"

"I am pleased to make your acquaintance, William. It isn't often that I get to meet another of Lady Myrredith's very good friends."

Princess Kathryn gave Billy another curt nod and turned to Lady Myrredith. She stared at her with an expression that asked for an explanation. "Well … is this why you wanted to see me?"

"No. Not exactly. I wasn't sure you would come to me, especially with the wedding—"

"Oh, don't be ridiculous! I came the minute Gullinburst told me you were here. I simply couldn't wait any longer. I had hoped you would come sooner."

"Yes. Well, we ran into some trouble on our journey here."

"We've heard. Something about Sir Aonghas being wounded?"

"By brigands!" Billy said.

Both Lady Myrredith and the princess had almost forgotten that Billy was there. They regarded him silently.

"Near Hillshire! And we—" At that moment, Billy pursed his lips and started to shy away from them.

Kathryn bent at the waist. "Brigands? That must have been very exciting!"

Billy, seeing that the heir apparent of Lyonesse was addressing him, picked at his breeches. "Well … yes, Your Highness."

"William?"

"Yes, Lady Myrredith?"

"Would you mind leaving us alone for a while? I need to discuss something with Kathryn—that is—Princess Kathryn."

Billy bowed to them and smiled. "Of course, milady. I understand."

Billy exited and closed the great wooden doors behind him. He was about to walk away when he decided he should tell Lady Myrredith where he was going. She had already begun to speak when Billy stuck his head back through the doors.

"Kathryn, I have a boon to ask of you—"

Lady Myrredith stopped when she saw Billy's smiling face protruding into the room. "What is it, William?"

"Well, I thought I should tell you, that if you need me, I'll be exploring the donjon – or the inner ward – or the curtain wall, or—" Billy stopped short when Princess Kathryn started to giggle. "Maybe I'll just explore the hallway, right out here."

The princess smiled. "I think you forgot to mention a good portion of Nyraval."

Lady Myrredith and her guest both laughed at seeing Billy's face turn such a deep shade of red. He quickly bowed and closed the door.

Billy roamed the hallway outside their quarters for nearly half an hour. During this time, he examined an old suit of armor and several weapons displayed on the wall. A young warrior, wearing chain mail and a tabard with the king's coat of arms, noticed Billy's interest in the weapons and engaged him in a very knowledgeable discussion of their history.

"And this is the sword of Cuchuramgar, the giant, whom King William defeated on a quest to Erin."

Billy ogled the seven-foot weapon. "Wow. It's so big!"

"Aye," his tutor said with a laugh, "but then Cuchuramgar was a giant. Well, I must be on my way."

"So soon?"

"Aye, laddie. I have duties elsewhere."

"Oh. Thank you."

The young man turned back as he was leaving and bowed his head. "It was my pleasure."

Billy watched his newest acquaintance go around the corner. As the warrior disappeared, the dark form of Don Miguel Scarosa appeared.

Billy hailed the approaching troubadour. "Don Miguel! Don Miguel!"

The Spaniard's eyes narrowed as they focused on Billy. His shoulders stiffened, and he turned his face away from his energetic rival.

"Don Miguel!" Billy moved to intercept him.

Scarosa, seeing that Billy was not to be put off by aloof manners, stopped in his tracks and glared at the young juggler. "What do you want?"

"I only wanted to say hello."

The Spaniard thrust his face down at Billy. "Well, I no want to say hello to you!"

Billy took a step back, feeling threatened by Miguel's aggressive posture. The troubadour took another step towards Billy and quickly glanced to either end of the hallway. Billy retreated again and felt the cool, smooth surface of the wall at his back. Then he too looked up and down the corridor. They were alone.

Don Miguel's hand was suddenly on Billy's chest holding him in place. "In fact," the Spaniard said, "I no want to say any words to you again! Except this..."

Without warning, Billy felt something sharp under the chin. He was quickly reminded of the time Redgnaw, the giant, held him captive on the King's Road. He peeked down at the dagger Don Miguel held to his throat.

The Spaniard jabbed Billy lightly and whispered into his ear. "You ruin my chance at the Cyndyn Hall. You will no embarrass me here."

"But—"

Miguel's blade sharply reminded him that he was not leading the conversation.

"You had best stay out of my way, or you will no like it!"

At that moment, the door behind Scarosa opened. Lady Myrredith appeared in the doorway and Billy looked at his assailant. Don Miguel leaned nonchalantly on the wall, his hand just above Billy's head, his weapon neatly put away, as if it had never been drawn.

The guileful troubadour examined his fingernails. "Well, it has been interesting, as always. Billy, you know I will be around... should you need my attention."

Miguel then bowed curtly to Lady Myrredith. "Milady." Without waiting for a reply, he spun and walked down the hallway.

Lady Myrredith watched the cocky Spaniard leave and then motioned for Billy to come. Billy ran to her and took her hand before entering the room.

"What did that wanton snake say to you, William?"

"Nothing. But I thought he was a peacock."

The Lady of Cyndyn Hall snickered softly. "Well ..." she said with a knowing grin. Then she put a finger to her lips to shush him.

Princess Kathryn was on the balcony, staring into the distance. She remained motionless as Billy and Lady Myrredith approached.

"Myrredith, you may leave us alone with him."

"Yes, Your Highness." Lady Myrredith bowed her head.

Billy was confused. He didn't have any idea why the princess would want to be left alone with him, or why the two ladies were talking so *formally*. Lady Myrredith gave his hand a squeeze, and he watched her leave the room.

"Lady Cyndyn has told us a great deal about you, William. I don't know whether to believe her or not."

"Oh?"

"Yes." Princess Kathryn turned to face him. She made eye contact for only an instant before he looked away. "She tells us—"

The princess stopped to reflect for a moment. "Did you know that she and I were friends from the first time her father brought her to Castle Orgulous?"

"No, Your Highness."

"She and I, and little Rory."

The princess moved behind Billy and paced over to a large high-backed armchair. Billy turned to face her. She stood for a moment in front of the chair and then sat. Billy couldn't help noticing how beautiful and regal she looked, enthroned on the chair. He could see that she was going to make a very impressive queen.

"Come, William. Sit here, next to me."

"Yes, Your Highness."

"William, it pleases us – that is – I am very pleased to see that Myrredith is in such high spirits. It's been a long while since I've seen her so, and with her husband lying wounded in Waru-Dunom ... Well, it's a wonder she even came. After hearing her talk about you, I can only believe that it is you that has somehow brought her this courage and happiness."

Billy smiled broadly and sat on the floor, looking up at the princess. *Yes, a very formidable queen.*

"What is it, William?"

"Oh – Um. If you'll forgive my sayin' so, Your Highness, ya look very …"

Billy didn't want to say "formidable," for he had last heard the term used by Sir Aonghas, when he described a particularly nasty encounter with a wild boar. After all, he didn't want the princess to think he didn't like her. If the truth be known, he found her beautiful and had liked her from the minute he heard her girlish giggle.

"Yes …?" the princess prompted.

Billy measured his words very carefully. "Well, I think you look very … beautiful."

"She said you were a charmer."

"Lady Myrredith?"

"Yes."

The princess leaned forward and touched Billy under the chin. She held his face up and stared into his eyes. Normally Billy wouldn't have stood still while a strange woman touched him, but her hand was so soft and gentle, and her eyes such a pretty blue, that he didn't mind.

The princess sat back in the chair. "And I'm inclined to agree with her. However, your charm is not what concerns me."

"What is it that concerns Your Highness? Can I do somethin' for ya?"

"William?"

"Yes, Your Highness?"

"What do you plan to do with your life?"

Billy was stumped. At no time, in all his days, had anyone seriously asked him this question. For a simple innkeeper's son, from an isolated valley, there weren't any choices. Everyone expected him to eventually take over running the inn for his father. He would probably find a wife, have children of his own, and die in the valley, which had always been his home. There wasn't much more a common fellow could ask from life. However, he had now come all the way to Castle Orgulous, and somehow that made all the difference in the world.

"I don't know, Your Highness."

"I see. So what were you thinking about?"

"Just now?"

"Yes."

"Well, it's just that until I met Lady Myrredith my life was practically written."

"What do you mean?"

"My father is an innkeeper. I am his only son, his only family."

"And so you too will become an innkeeper."

"Exactly, Your Highness."

"Please, William. Do you think you could call me Lady Kathryn? I'm not fully heir until I've been crowned."

"I think you'll make a wonderful queen! Don't you want to be queen, Your-Lady Kathryn?"

She stared across the room vacantly. Billy noticed sadness in her eyes. "I wish I knew," she whispered.

"Then we are in the same boat."

The princess regarded Billy with a queer expression. "Why do you say that?"

"Because, you were born to be queen, and I to be an innkeeper."

"I would wager you make a pretty good innkeeper already."

"And I think you'll make a great queen, but—"

Billy paused, and she made eye contact with him again. He could still see behind her lovely, smiling eyes a hidden sadness – a secret regret, an unfulfilled dream. This time, it was Kathryn who looked away.

Billy continued with caution. "But, I can see from your eyes … that you do not desire to be queen."

Lady Kathryn turned and gave him a cold, hard stare. For a moment, Billy thought she would strike him. He lowered his face submissively.

"How dare you! Desire has nothing to do with it!"

"I beg Your Highness' forgiveness. I am only a churl. I had no right to say—"

"No!" The princess cut him short. She paused for a moment. "You had every right – no, obligation – to say it."

Billy looked up at her. "Then you're not angry?"

Lady Kathryn shook her head and smiled. Billy, relieved to see he wasn't going to be cuffed, smiled from ear to ear. His companion laughed.

"No, William. I don't see how anyone could stay angry with you. I begin to see why Myrredith is so taken with you."

Kathryn got up from her chair and extended her right hand to Billy. He was caught off guard. Did she want him to take her hand? Maybe he was supposed to kiss it. She saw his hesitation and reached down and took his hand.

Lady Kathryn led Billy out on the balcony. A warm breeze brushed against their cheeks as they emerged through the archway. They stood quietly, hand in hand, looking over the surrounding countryside.

"Someday I will be queen. I wish I could have a good, honest, perceptive man like you by my side. Someone I know I can trust. Someone to keep my feet to the earth, make me laugh, and keep me from lying to myself."

"What of your fiancé, the prince?"

"A spoiled, arrogant foreigner."

Neither the princess nor the innkeeper's son could think of anything that would change all that, and so they fell silent again.

"William?"

"Yes, Lady Kathryn?"

"If you could, would you choose not to be an innkeeper?"

Billy considered the question a moment. "But what else is there?"

"Well, if you could …"

"Lady Kathryn, I love my father, and I will be happy running the inn, but it's just not ..."

"Not what?"

"I have experienced more in the last few weeks than I had in all my life before that. My dreams seem to be coming true before my eyes. I wish it could just go on forever, but sooner or later, I've got to wake up."

"This isn't a dream, William."

"But I *am* an innkeeper's son."

A bitterness in his voice surprised Billy. He never thought he would ever want to be anything but Billy, son of John, the innkeeper. He never thought he could be anything else.

The new acquaintances remained silent, contemplating their personal regrets, but Billy was not one to stay contemplative for long, especially when it came to unhappy thoughts. He wanted to laugh and see Lady Kathryn laugh as well.

Just then he had an inspiration. He ran to the next room and grabbed Sir Hugh's lute. Before Kathryn realized Billy was gone, he had returned. He emerged onto the balcony, singing his laughing song. His magical voice quickly dissolved her melancholy mood, and she began to laugh and sing along with him. Soon he was juggling and telling jokes for an amazed, happy princess.

They were having so much fun that they nearly forgot Lady Myrredith waiting outside in the hallway. Laughing, they both ran to the doors and flung them open. Lady Myrredith sat across the hall in a stone niche. When she saw her two friends enjoying each other's company so, she rushed over to greet them.

"Kathryn!"

"Myrredith! You said he was a charmer, but you didn't tell me what an absolute treasure he is."

Lady Myrredith laughed and placed her hand on Billy's shoulder. "I see you have another convert."

Billy shrugged and answered her with a sheepish smile.

THE INNKEEPER'S SON | 255

Kathryn looked to both of them. "Well, I really must get back."

"So soon?" they complained in unison.

Their princess smiled, then reached out to Lady Myrredith and embraced her. Next, she crouched so she was face to face with Billy. "I am so happy to have met you, William."

"Will I see you again?"

Kathryn reached out and mussed his hair. "Of course. You will be at my wedding, won't you?"

Billy nodded enthusiastically.

"Then I will see you there."

The princess started to rise but stopped to look him in the eye. "And, if you are here any time after that, I would welcome your company."

"Thank you, Lady Kathryn."

The princess rose and started down the passageway. Lady Myrredith and Billy stood and watched her leave.

Billy's companion put her hand on his shoulder. "Wait here," she said to him. Then she went after the princess. "Kathryn!"

Lady Kathryn turned. "What is it, Myrredith?"

Lady Myrredith looked up and down the hallway. "Kathryn. My boon? Will you grant it?"

There's that word again. What does she mean by a boon? Billy watched the two great ladies, his curiosity growing.

Lady Kathryn looked over her friend's shoulder at Billy. He could only see her eyes, but it was enough to tell that she was smiling. She returned her attention to Lady Myrredith.

"When I am queen," she said with a nod.

Lady Myrredith bowed deeply to the princess, and when she arose, the heir apparent turned and left the corridor. Lady Myrredith turned and beamed brightly at Billy.

"What is it?"

"A surprise for you, William."

"What?"

"William, it wouldn't be a surprise if I told you."

"Yes, but—" William was nearly beside himself with curiosity. He took a deep breath to get control of his excitement. "Oh, very well. I guess I can wait."

That evening, a host of nobles crowded the great hall of Castle Orgulous. Billy was disappointed when he saw that the king and other members of the royal family were not present. There was a great deal of noise and confusion as the wedding guests feasted in celebration of the coming nuptials and coronation. In fact, there were so many people and so much chaos that no one seemed to notice when Billy's usual luck with servants carrying large trays of food took its usual messy turn. Lady Myrredith and Billy decided that it was simply too much for them, and they hastily retreated to their apartment, asking the unfortunate servant to bring up their dinner later.

Lady Myrredith had given her servants permission to feast with the common folk in the outer ward, knowing that it would be a celebration they shouldn't miss. Therefore, she and Billy were feasting in seclusion when a knock came upon the door.

Billy arose from his dinner and answered the door. Much to his surprise, Sir Hugh was standing in the hallway.

"Sir Hugh!"

"Come in, Hugh!" Lady Myrredith said from the dining table.

Sir Hugh glanced in both directions of the corridor before entering. He was no longer in his beautiful armor; instead, he wore a handsome, quilted tunic of white with blue hose. An ornate bone-handled dagger dangled on a leather thong at his waist, and his long brown hair was tied back neatly with a blue ribbon. The entire image reminded Billy of the first time he had seen the noble warrior's face.

Lady Myrredith rose to greet him.

"Please, milady." Hugh indicated that she should remain seated. "I'm sorry to interrupt your supper, but I felt I should talk to you. Both of you."

"Please, join us, Hugh."

"No, thank you, milady. I only came to warn you."

"Warn us?"

"Yes, milady. Earlier today, I had an intriguing confrontation with the magister."

"Ergyfel?"

Both Sir Hugh and Lady Myrredith stared at Billy.

"What? What did I say?"

"Not what, but who, William. Remember?"

"You shouldn't pronounce that name, unless you really want his attention."

Billy considered this for a moment. "Because he's a—"

Billy covered his mouth with his hand. Immediately his eyes shifted from right to left, scanning the room.

Lady Myrredith reached over Billy and placed her hand on Hugh's. He slowly pulled his hand away from her touch and rubbed his forehead.

Lady Myrredith withdrew her hand. "What has that snake done now?"

Hugh leaned forward and spoke softly to his friends. "This afternoon, while I was on the wall near the barracks, he approached me. Before he could say anything, I accused him of recklessly endangering His Majesty's guests by bringing those confounded troghouls here! He said that there was no danger to any of the king's guests. I told him that he was wrong, and that one of the king's guests had already been attacked!"

"What did he say?" Billy asked.

"He wanted to know who it was that had been attacked."

"So he could apologize?"

Hugh raised his left eyebrow, giving Billy an incredulous look. "Hardly. In all the time I've known that vulture, he has never proven to have any care for the well-being of anyone other than himself. And he's never – never apologized."

"You think he's up to something, Hugh?"

"Undoubtedly, milady."

"But what?"

258 | K. C. HERBEL

"I wish I knew. Unfortunately he caught me off guard, when he asked me who it was, and I told him." Hugh looked out towards the balcony and stroked his eyebrow.

Lady Myrredith quickly shifted her focus to Billy. She put her hand on his and gave it a squeeze.

Hugh continued. "He kept after me – probing me about Billy."

"What could he want with William?"

"Aye. What could he want with me?"

"I don't know, but he was far too curious. Despite what he'd have me believe, his interest was not casual."

"But I've never met him."

"I wish I could say the same," Hugh said. "Say, maybe we can keep it that way."

"Impossible," Myrredith muttered.

"Well ... I suppose not, but I urge you to avoid him, William. He's evil."

"So I've been told."

"No!" Sir Hugh seized Billy's arm and locked eyes with Billy. "I mean it, William. That one is the devil's own. He will find a way to use you, or hurt you. Never doubt that."

The three friends fell silent. Then Hugh rose and headed for the door. "Where ya goin'?"

"Whenever I'm away, you-know-who goes unchecked. I've much to catch up on."

Sir Hugh turned and left the room, leaving Lady Myrredith and her companion feeling very uneasy. They spent the remainder of the evening in quiet, distracted conversation, shying away from the subject that was most on their minds. There were none of Billy's usual juggling tricks or songs that night. At last, Lady Myrredith retired, and Billy, without his usual arguments, did the same.

CHAPTER FIFTEEN

The Wedding

The wedding was scheduled for early morning, giving just enough time for the sun to peek into the inner ward of Castle Orgulous and shoo the dewdrops away. It was also just late enough for the previous night's revelers to overcome their soggy wits in order to attend the blessed event.

As was his usual habit, Billy rose with the sun. This wedding was *the* event of the decade, if not the century, and he wasn't going to miss a moment. No one in the Valley of the Yew had ever attended the wedding of a noble, much less the wedding of royalty. Before his feet hit the floor, his mind was made up to remember everything he saw and heard that day. To the people back home, Billy would be their eyes, ears, and heart.

He crossed the room to the water basin and splashed the frigid water on his face. As he dried himself, he looked out the small arched window. Streaks of yellow sunlight in the eastern sky forecast a beautiful day. He heard scuffling below and saw dozens of servants quietly crossing the inner ward in every direction—many of them placing decorations.

There were white poles spread about the ward, wrapped with blue ribbons. Miniature flags dangled from thin blue ropes draping between the poles, while flowers grew in pots around their bases. The crisp air bore a hint of roasted meats and freshly baked bread.

Billy dashed to his bedside. He stopped dead in his tracks when he saw that his clothes were gone. In their place lay another set of clothes: fine garments, fashioned in Cyndyn green and red, tied with a black hair ribbon, a note resting on top.

Billy snatched the note and opened it. The message simply read, "For William."

"For William?"

Billy warily picked up the colorful hat, not wholly convinced that the clothes were meant for him. Its color matched the scarlet hose that lay underneath it. While Billy didn't wear hose—or want to wear them—the hat was another story. It was something he might have picked out himself. The hat was large and floppy, with a number of black strips showing through slits in the red. Topping it off was a long greenish pheasant feather that swept over one side and back.

Billy put down the note and hat to untie the ribbon. Once untied, he tossed it aside with the hose and lifted the forest green tunic up to his body. It looked like a perfect fit. There were red ties down the entirety of each sleeve and in the middle to hold the front closed. Each tie was tipped with a tiny silver ball inscribed with a leaf. In addition there was a wide black belt and two large pockets in the front. Billy had never owned fine clothes such as these, nor had anyone from the Valley of the Yew. It was obvious, from the fit and special pockets that Lady Myrredith had ordered them made especially for him, but such extravagance was beyond belief. It was the greatest gift he had ever received.

Billy hastily slipped on the tunic. It was remarkable how well it fit. His clothes were usually hand-me-downs from his father, which even after alterations were too big and baggy, or they were gifts from neighbors with growing children, which usually meant they were snug where his body was imperfectly proportioned. As he admired his new clothes, Billy noticed a bit of green showing from under the bed. He reached down and pulled out a beautiful pair of soft suede boots to match the tunic. Without hesitation, Billy tried on the boots. They fit like bark on a tree.

Billy put on the hat and rushed through his door to the central chamber of their suite. Megan, Lady Myrredith's maid, was busy unwrapping the silvered mirror that her mistress had brought from Dyven as a wedding gift.

Billy burst into the room. "Megan! What do ya think?"

Megan spun around and regarded the young man in his new garb. Her eyes smiled as Billy turned around, modeling his gifts.

"About what?" she asked coyly.

"About what? Why my new clothes of course!"

"Oh, I suppose they're nice."

"Nice? Nice? Is that all – nice? Nice is when ya get your favorite pie on your birthday. These are fantastic!"

"Well—"

"They're practically the best gift ever!"

Billy stopped and felt for the pocket of his trousers, which of course was not there. His eyes widened and searched the room. His stomach tightened as panic began to rise in his chest. "Where are my clothes?"

"Your old clothes?"

"Yes!"

"I gave them to Rhianna. Why?"

"My mother's ring was in the pocket!"

Megan gasped and placed her hand on her lips. "Oh, my goodness!"

"What?"

"She's takin' them to the kitchen!"

"She's gonna wash them?"

"No! Burn them!"

Billy's face blanched, and instantly he began to sweat. He felt his heart pounding in his neck and ears. He threw his hat to a nearby chair and sped like a crossbow bolt out the door.

Billy cleared the main entrance to the donjon and leapt down the great steps three at a time. As he sprinted and dodged his way between the busy servants, his mind raced ahead. In his mind's eye he saw Rhianna tossing his clothes into a fire and the clothes going up in smoke along with his mother's ring. He cursed himself for his carelessness.

John had always sewn in pockets at Billy's request. It was a good idea for carrying valuables like feathers, pretty rocks, bugs, and frogs. However, at the moment, it was very clear that his pocket was not a safe place at all.

Panting, Billy rounded the corner of the barracks just as Rhianna came out of the kitchen. She was carrying a large platter of food and a pitcher, but no clothes.

"Rhianna!"

The servant girl looked up to see Billy rushing towards her. Her eyes widened, and she quickly backed away, turning to put herself between Billy and the platter.

"Keep away, Billy!"

Billy continued to advance, and so she took another step back. Unfortunately, in her attempt to avoid Billy's curse, she brought it upon herself. Forthwith, she tripped over a kitchen dog and went tail first to the ground, with Billy still a good ten feet away.

Billy leaned over her. "Where are my clothes?"

Rhianna, still dazed from her fall, stared blankly at her inquisitor as the dog licked breakfast from her cheek.

"Where are my clothes?"

When Lady Myrredith's maid still failed to respond, Billy dashed for the door she had just exited. As he reached the entrance, he saw that the kitchen was packed with servants, down to get their lords and ladies breakfast. Billy squeezed his way into the room and pushed through a dozen grumbling servants, trying to reach the large cooking fire.

At last he reached the fire and looked into the blaze. He watched in horror as the flames consumed the last remnant of his trousers. Impulsively, he reached into the fire, but the searing heat forced him back. He frantically searched for a tool. He spotted a small shovel hanging on the wall, then pushed through the crowd, snatched the shovel, and returned to the fire.

"Ow!" a servant shouted as Billy shoveled hot ash onto his foot. "You idiot!"

Billy never looked back but spouted a hasty apology and continued to drag ashes from the fire. The waiting servants backed away from the rising charcoal dust and yelled at Billy to stop. A moment later, a well-rounded woman hoisted him painfully upwards by his ear, and Billy dropped the shovel.

"Get out o' me fire, ya wee wart!"

"But my ring!" Billy pointed at the fire.

The woman shook a wooden spoon at Billy and continued to tow him away. "None o' your dribble! Now out o' me kitchen!"

The servants crowding the kitchen erupted in laughter as the cook released Billy's ear and sent him out the door with a swift boot to the rear. Billy rubbed his ear and glared at his expeller. The large woman snorted disdainfully, turned, and bowed deeply to her applauding peers. Without warning, Billy came catapulting over her back leapfrog style.

Rather than booing Billy, the servants laughed and cheered. Billy turned and bowed to his adversary.

"My apologies ma'am, but I really must get to that fire."

The cook-woman straightened and glowered at Billy with a grunt. He flinched in response, then quickly turned and ducked behind the first row of amused servants.

"Come out now, my wee ruffian, or I'll—"

"Now, Dana," said a man from the crowd, "don't let that Irish temper get the better of ya."

The cook turned in the direction of the voice and, putting her hands on her broad hips, gave the speaker a dark look that could wilt an evergreen. "Don't go tellin' me about me Irish temper, mister temper of Saxony at the drop of a kettle!"

"Now, woman," the man countered, "ya didn't seem to mind my Saxon heritage when ya married me."

Dana brandished the spoon at her husband and shook it. Her face was red as she slowly marched towards him.

"Because I married ya before I knew of your Saxon blood, ya oaf!" She lowered her voice to a threatening tone. "If I'da known … I should've married Stephan. He was a liar, but at least I wouldn't have to put up with a stubborn, ill-tempered, know-it-all husband who loves nothin' better than tormentin' his poor, hard-workin' wife every time he—"

Dana stopped abruptly. The kitchen was quiet, except for the sound of water boiling and a few scattered snickers. Her red face became crimson when she realized the roomful of amused servants hung on her every word.

"What are ya gawkin' at?" she grumbled.

The servants all laughed.

"Aw bother, the lot o'ya! Enough lallygaggin'!" Dana then turned back to her grinning husband and smacked him across the chest with the spoon. "We've got breakfast to serve and hungry lards and ladies awaitin'!"

The man took the utensil from her and spooned mutton hotchpotch onto the platter of a waiting servant. Dana turned and calmly strolled over to Billy.

Billy started to back away, fearing that now he would really catch hell from the large fiery cook.

"All's well, boy. I'm not gonna hurt ya."

Billy watched her cautiously as she approached. He kept his eyes peeled for an escape route should flight be necessary.

"Now laddie, what's all this about?"

"My ring."

"Yes, what about it?"

"I left it in my trousers." Billy was near to tears. "The ones my father sewed the pocket into, and Rhianna just burned them in that fire."

Dana smiled. "Oh, I see. Say, aren't you the boy that caused Danny to drop his tray last night?"

Billy looked at her nervously and shrugged.

"Yeah, that was you. Thought nobody saw ya, eh boy?"

Again Billy could only shrug.

"I tell ya what, I'll help ya find your ring, if ..." She paused until Billy looked up at her. "If you promise not to make any more messes."

"I didn't mean to make all those messes."

"All what messes?"

"He's really quite famous for them," said Rhianna from behind the robust cook.

Billy and Dana turned to see her standing in line with her tray.

"That is, at Cyndyn Hall he's famous."

"Didn't ya already take a platter of food, lass?" Dana asked.

Rhianna nodded and lowered her tray to reveal the food on her blouse. Then Dana looked at Billy with raised eyebrows. Billy answered her silent question with a simple nod.

"I see. Well, just promise me that you'll try."

"I promise."

"Where's that shovel?"

The large cook-woman and Billy went to the fire and carefully searched through the ashes. They searched until long after all the servants had left with their masters' breakfasts. Dana's husband and a young serving girl also offered to help.

"We'll never find it," Billy muttered.

"Yes we will," Dana said. "We just gotta keep lookin'. Gryff, you and Mary come over here. Sift through this pile."

Dana's husband nodded. "Yes, my love. We'll find it. Don't you worry, lad."

Billy was again near tears. "That ring is all I have left of my mother.

Dana touched Billy's arm. "Then we'll find it."

They searched and searched until they were all sure that the ring couldn't be found. At that moment Rhianna appeared at the door.

"Did ya find it?"

Billy looked up at her. "No."

"Not yet," Gryff added.

Rhianna crossed to where Billy was kneeling. "Megan told me what happened, Billy. I'm sorry. I didn't mean to lose your mother's ring. I didn't know…"

"I know. It's really my fault. I should never have taken it off my hand."

Reluctantly Billy got up and went to the door. "Thank you, Dana. Thank you, Gryff – Mary. Thank you all for looking."

Billy left with Rhianna following behind him. They walked silently back to the donjon with their eyes scouring the ground. When Billy finally arrived at their quarters, Lady Myrredith was waiting for him.

She came in from the balcony. "William, where have you—Oh no! What has happened to your clothes?"

Billy remembered, for the first time since he had left the room that morning that he was wearing his new clothes. He looked down at the black and grey smudges covering the front of his beautiful green tunic. He noticed too that his sleeves were dirtied, growing darker towards the cuff. He held up his hands and looked at the blackened palms. He felt hopelessly defeated.

Lady Myrredith shook her head. "Come here, William."

"I'm sorry, Lady Myrredith. I didn't mean to—"

"I know, William."

Billy clenched his fists. "Oh! I never do anythin' right!"

"Shhh, William. Rhianna, go find some soap and water to clean this."

"Yes, milady."

"Megan, ready a bath for William."

"Milady, that may be difficult, what with the weddin' an' all."

Lady Myrredith placed her hands on her hips. "He needs a bath!"

"Yes, milady." Megan hurried out the door.

"William, go to your room. Get out of that tunic. I want you ready to take that bath."

"Yes, milady."

Billy marveled at how, with such commanding speed, Lady Myrredith was able to take control of any situation. He hoped that he hadn't angered her too much by his little indiscretion.

Within the hour, Billy and tunic were scrubbed clean. This time, when he appeared in his new clothes, Lady Myrredith insisted that Billy put on the scarlet hose. After all, she couldn't have him "looking like some churlish barnyard oaf."

"But hose itch me!"

Lady Myrredith said nothing. She simply put her hands on her hips and stared at him. Without another word, Billy returned to his room and emerged once he had donned the red hose.

"That's better." Lady Myrredith smiled, then turned Billy around and started to tie his hair with the black ribbon.

"This tunic's still wet, Lady Myrredith."

"Well, it will just have to do."

At that moment, the sound of bells rang out from the inner ward. Lady Myrredith shot a glance towards the balcony.

"Quickly, William!" She held out her hand. "We haven't a moment to waste."

Billy put his hand in hers, and they were off; Lady Myrredith half-dragging him down the corridors and stairways of the keep. They saw only a few others, who were likewise rushing downwards.

"What is it?"

"The wedding bells, William!"

"Has it started?"

"No."

"What's the hurry?"

"Before the ceremony can begin they will close the chapel."

"But surely Lady Kathryn won't let them start without you!"

"I don't want to put that to the test. She might not notice."

Lady Myrredith and her damp companion reached the main entrance hall of the keep out of breath. She squeezed his hand tightly and pulled him through a doorway into a small courtyard garden. Billy was amazed at the energy and speed of his patron when she really needed it. All of a sudden they were in front of a large iron-bound door. A guard stood in front of this door with a large poleaxe at his side. To his right and left stood several fully armored warriors, their weapons at the ready.

"Please let us pass!" Lady Myrredith pleaded breathlessly.

"No, milady," the guard said. "I cannot."

Lady Myrredith looked quickly around at the faces of the warriors on either side. They only bowed apologetically.

"Blast," she whispered.

A young warrior who had been hidden behind the others, stepped forward. "I'm sorry, Lady Cyndyn, but our duty will not allow you to enter this way. I believe, if you hurry, you can still make it to the front door of the chapel."

"Thank you, Sir Owein."

Instantly they were off again. Lady Myrredith went even faster than before as she and Billy ran through the donjon. They leapt down the front steps of the great keep and sprinted around one side. As they turned the corner, Billy saw a large group of lords and ladies gathered around that end of the keep. It suddenly dawned on him that the entire wing of the donjon was in fact a grand chapel. He thought it was odd that he hadn't noticed it before. Lady Myrredith and Billy fell in behind the lords and ladies crowding through the large double doors of the chapel.

"We made it," Billy said.

Myrredith held her side. "I'll feel much better once we are inside."

Several other latecomers arrived and crowded in behind them. Slowly, they made their way toward the entrance. As more and more people crowded in around them, Billy began to feel uncomfortable. He felt as if he were being suffocated. *Must be these darn hose.*

He looked ahead at the chapel entrance, and the feeling turned from discomfort to fear. The same fear he felt upon seeing the cathedral in Dyven. He had already recovered his wind from their run, but suddenly it was difficult to breathe, and his heart started to race. Lady Myrredith looked down at him with an expression of concern. Perhaps she could sense his anxiety, or maybe it was his sweaty, trembling hand.

"What's the matter, William?"

Billy shrugged nervously. He didn't know what to say. He didn't know what to do, except maybe run away. In his heart, he really wanted to see the royal wedding, but he also knew that he did not want to go into the chapel for any reason.

They began to climb the many squat steps to the chapel entrance, Billy delaying at each step. Then they were at the top. Billy could hardly contain himself. *What must I do?* He looked away from the chapel, towards the inner ward. Something on the ground caught his eye.

Lady Myrredith stood at the chapel threshold. "Come along, William."

Billy ignored her and stared at the object that winked with a golden light from the cobblestones not so far away.

"My ring!" Billy dropped Lady Myrredith's hand. He pushed his way down the steps through the lords and ladies behind him.

"William! William! Come back!"

Billy reached the bottom of the steps and never looked back. He pressed his way through the remaining nobles and broke into a run. His eyes scanned the ground ahead for his ring. He reached the site where he thought he had seen it. There was nothing there. He looked in all directions. There was no sign of the ring, or for that matter anything else which could be mistaken for a ring.

"William!"

Billy turned to look at Lady Myrredith. She stood in the doorway of the chapel. Nearly all the lords and ladies were inside now, and the guards were preparing to close the doors.

"Hurry, William! Come quickly!"

Billy took a few steps towards her and then started to run. Almost halfway there, he looked back over his shoulder. Again he saw the sparkle of gold on the cobblestones. He stopped abruptly. Billy eyed the spot a moment, trying to focus on it. *It could be a ring.*

"Come, William! Hurry!"

He desperately wanted his ring back. Billy had to be sure that he wasn't just leaving it on the ground for someone else to find. Again he ignored Lady Myrredith's cries and ran farther into the inner ward. He kept his eyes on the spot where he had seen the golden glimmer. It continued to wink at him as he approached. When he was just a few feet away, it winked out. He scanned the area desperately. Then his eye picked up another shiny object a little farther away. He ran to the spot, and again he found nothing. Twice more he thought he saw his mother's ring glinting in the morning sun, and twice more his search came up empty.

Billy turned around. He was now in the middle of the inner ward, far from the chapel and Lady Myrredith. He felt ashamed that he had run away from her, and foolish for imagining that the sparkle of sunlight off a dirty old cobblestone could be his mother's ring.

At that moment, the bells rang out again. Billy spun around to see the mirthless face of Lady Myrredith disappear behind the closing doors of the chapel. He took in a breath to call for the guards to stop, but it was too late. The doors came to, and the guards lined up in front of the entrance.

Billy dropped his head and sighed. All his good intentions to represent the people of the Valley of the Yew were in that moment dashed aside. He would not be able to tell his father about all the splendid lords and ladies, or his boyhood friends about all the knights arrayed in their shining armor, or tell the hopeful young girls how beautiful the princess' wedding gown was. For that matter, he wouldn't be able to tell anyone anything they might wish to know about this once-in-a-lifetime event. He sighed again, and it caught in his chest. His sigh turned into a sob as tears welled up in his eyes.

Billy blinked, and a tear ran onto his cheek. He sniffed and watched, with cloudy eyes, as it fell silently to the ground. It struck a pink flower petal, strangely turning its surface blood red. Billy bent down to pick up the marvelous petal. As he lifted it from the cobblestones, his breath caught in his throat. Directly beneath the petal lay his mother's ring. The simple gold loop stared up at him. The sunlight winked off its smooth surface in greeting. Billy's legs buckled, sitting him on the stone pavement with a grunt. He stared dumbly at the ring. He reached for it but then pulled away.

He pointed an accusing finger at the ring. "It's all your fault."

The ring continued to stare at him – to mock him.

"I'd be at that wedding if it weren't for you!"

Impulsively, Billy snatched up the ring and ran across the ward to the castle's curtain wall. He drew back his arm to throw the ring over the wall, closed his eyes, and squeezed the ring in his hand. It felt soft and warm, as it always had. He imagined his mother giving the ring to his father for safekeeping. Her image grew stronger, and instantly his anger left him. He lowered his arm and considered the ring in his palm. He found nothing hateful there. In fact, the simple loop was a symbol of his mother's never-ending love. It was the only bond he had with her.

"Sorry, Mother," he whispered, "I'll never take it off again."

Billy slipped the ring on his finger and turned away from the wall. As he started across the inner ward, he felt unusually confident and complete. He inhaled deeply, and his nose filled with the scent of slowly roasted beef.

"Aw, who needs an old wedding anyhow? The feast is what's really important."

Billy renewed his vow to memorize everything that happened that day as he skipped a serpentine path through the brightly decorated white and blue poles. He headed towards the chapel side of the donjon, contemplating what he should tell Lady Myrredith but could think of nothing that made sense. Finally he decided not to make excuses. He would simply apologize, and that would be that.

Billy swung around the last of the fanciful flagpoles and into the vacant area of the ward. He straightened his new tunic and was halfway to the chapel before he realized there was someone directly in front of him. He stopped abruptly when the sun was suddenly eclipsed. He looked up to see the silhouette of a man. A bright halo surrounded the shadowy figure. Billy squinted and stepped to the side. The hue of the shadow hardly changed as it took on substance, but in transforming, it became a thin, darkly dressed man standing with his arms crossed. The veil of shadows lifted from his face, revealing his jet black eyes.

"Ergyfe—!"

The magister smiled and spoke in a deep, tranquil voice. "You have me at a disadvantage, my boy."

Billy felt as if he were in the wrong place at the wrong time—a feeling he had heard his father describe many times, but had not fully experienced, until that moment. He remembered Hugh's words of warning about the King's First Counselor. He glanced around but saw no way to avoid this contact.

"As you know," the magister continued, "I am Ergyfel, First Counselor to King William, and you are …?"

"I'm … Billy."

"Just Billy?"

"Um … well, I'm called William, by some."

"I see."

"It's nice to meet you." Billy then turned and marched away.

"Wait!"

Billy stopped. Too frightened to turn around, he stood with his back to Ergyfel. His entire body stiffened and he squeezed his eyes closed, waiting to be turned into a toad—*or worse: food for a toad!*

"I think I owe you an apology."

Billy's eyes snapped open, and he turned around. "Oh?"

"Aren't you the one – the one attacked by the troghoul yesterday?"

"Um, yes."

"Then you have my apologies." The magister bowed his head.

"I do?"

"Yes. It is by my order that they are present."

"Oh?"

"Yes. I find they make marvelous guards." Ergyfel paused, seeming to wait for a response from Billy. "You see, the king has enemies. I must protect him. If that means using troghouls, then so be it. Unfortunately they can be a little – shall we say – unpredictable at times."

"Yes," Billy whispered.

"I'm curious, my little friend. Do you know the old story of the troghouls and the little people?"

Billy shook his head.

"The troghouls were once a proud and beautiful race, but the loathsome faeries grew jealous and cursed them with ugliness. Since then, the troghouls have feuded with the little devils."

Billy remembered what Lady Myrredith told him about the troghouls and faeries. This was, at the least, a very different interpretation.

"They cursed them for no reason?"

"None, save their petty jealousy."

Billy chanced a glimpse of the counselor's face and found Ergyfel's eyes staring back at him with an expression that begged a response. Instantly Billy felt uncomfortable and looked away. "Say, why aren't you at the wedding?"

"I have my reasons."

Billy looked again at the imposing nobleman. The magister gazed across the ward. Billy held his tongue, waiting to hear Ergyfel's reasons.

"Even if I had the inclination," the magister said under his breath, "I wouldn't be welcomed."

"But you're her cousin."

Ergyfel only smiled, his eyes moving back and forth in thought—as if reading some invisible script. At last the magister spoke. "And why is it that you are not at the joyous event?"

Just speaking the words "joyous event" seemed loathsome to Ergyfel. Billy watched as his cool facade shifted to smother what smoldered under the surface.

"I ... I meant to be there, I just—"

"Don't like churches?"

Billy felt Ergyfel leaning towards him. He looked up and saw the dark eyes burrowing down on him.

Billy was completely caught off guard. "What?"

The magister removed his glare. "I said, I thought you mightn't like churches."

Billy mulled this over a moment. It was true that he felt uneasy near Orgulous' chapel and the cathedral in Dyven, but after all he had never really been in a church. At last he answered. "Naw, churches are fine, I guess."

"You guess?"

Billy only shrugged. The Valley of the Yew was too small to have its own Bible, much less a church, and while most of the inhabitants professed the new religion and called themselves "good Christians," they had never built one. It never occurred to him before to like or dislike churches.

Billy abruptly realized he was feeling at ease with the king's counselor, and his ease was replaced by trepidation. *Is there some magic at work here?* He consciously made a check of his entire body. There was no tingling or itching or anything else. *Oh, you're just being silly. Maybe Sir Hugh and Lady Myrredith just don't understand Ergyfel. After all, the rumors say that he's a sorcerer, and who wants to get to know a sorcerer? But then again...* Billy smiled to himself and shook his head.

At that very moment, Billy felt a shadow fall over him. He turned and saw Ergyfel's face just inches away. The strange sensation that had overcome him on the balcony returned. Billy was drawn to the magister's dark eyes. He couldn't bring himself to look away. He felt light-headed, and his thoughts began to drift.

"Why are you here?" Billy heard Ergyfel say. The words floated around in his head like warm milk. Then suddenly they turned and bored into his mind, and all Billy could see was the black wells of Ergyfel's eyes, which grew darker and deeper, blotting out the light and surrounding him. The words resounded in his ears as they wove themselves into his thoughts. *Why are you here?*

Without warning, the light returned, and the words were expelled from Billy's mind. His head stopped floating, and he found himself staring at Ergyfel's face. There was a tingling in his hand, a ringing in his ears, and he felt sure that Ergyfel had asked a question, but he must have been daydreaming, for he couldn't remember what it was.

"I beg your pardon?" Billy said.

Ergyfel blinked, and for a moment confusion passed over his cool visage. He straightened and looked across the ward. "Nothing," he said through his teeth. Then he fell into a contemplative silence.

The ringing in Billy's ears became more defined, and he realized it came from the bells of the chapel. He turned to the chapel and saw the guards opening the doors.

"They're done with—" Billy turned back to Ergyfel, but he was gone.

Billy quickly scanned the area around him. He was the only person in the entire ward, save the few cooks and servants who were still busy with their preparations for the wedding feast.

A loud cheer went up from behind Billy, and he turned to see the newly married couple exit the chapel atop the shoulders of a half-dozen knights. Princess Kathryn was the perfect image of beauty. This was the first time Billy had ever seen her new husband, the third Prince of Gwythia. The would-be sire of the kingdom's heirs was a handsome, youthful man who looked over the crowd with an aloof stare. However, Billy saw this as an act, for when the prince gazed at his new bride, his face took on an expression of boyish adoration. Once his eyes were upon the radiant Kathryn, he could not move them. She too stared at her husband—with an expression Billy took to be hope. They were, as is often said, "a lovely couple." Seeing the two young rulers so enthralled put Billy's heart at ease. It was a sign of hope and peace for their homelands. Billy memorized every detail so that in the years to come, he could tell everyone back in the Valley of the Yew what a splendid sight they made.

As the newlyweds hit the bottom steps, the cheering from within the chapel redoubled. Billy could hardly bring himself to look away from the glory of the prince and princess, but the boisterous clamor grew so loud that he was forced to retrain his eyes on the crowd inside the ornate entry. He found another group of jolly nobles making their way from the hall of worship. He was about to dismiss the whole vociferous lot of revelers and return his attentions to the royal couple when the glint of bright metal caught his eyes from within the dark chapel—just beyond the crowd. Billy decided to move closer to get a better look.

When Billy was a few steps from the mob, it momentarily parted, and he caught sight of a man wearing a gem-encrusted crown of gold, slowly moving through the crowd. Billy's heart skipped a beat. Thinking quickly, he jumped up onto the stone baluster, frantically trying to see over the nobles who suddenly seemed ever so much taller than they needed to be.

As the king appeared from Castle Orgulous' chapel, hungrily rubbing his middle and complaining about the "rather miserly" breakfast he had been served that morning, Billy thought it strange that the king should look so *ordinary*. That is, aside from his royal trappings, the king looked very much like an ordinary man in the twilight years of his life. He was slightly stooped over and had a long beard of white.

Billy took a closer look at the king, and the ordinary qualities began to slide away. A glimpse of the great leader King William had once been poked through the seemingly ancient facade. His warrior's spirit, though long faded, still lived deep behind his bright blue eyes. His purposeful actions bespoke of the virtues that had made him great, and Billy was reminded of heroic tales he had heard many times as a boy. The bandy legs, which had once propelled a proud warrior into battle in defense of the kingdom, now moved unsteadily, and the once-potent body had been worn down and scarred by hard years of campaigning and illness. However, there could never again be any doubt in Billy's heart that the man he saw before him was King William of Lyonesse.

Billy forgot himself in his observations and admiration of the king and suddenly found himself being pushed off the balustrade by the surrounding nobility. He hit the ground with a thud that knocked the wind out of him. As he struggled for breath, his deposers advanced on him, unaware of his presence. He was swallowed up into their midst as he scrambled to his feet. He gasped for air as he was whisked away in front of the throng like a leaf before the wind. Unable to catch his breath, or to escape the forward inertia of those around him, Billy was dragged across the inner ward.

"Stop!" Billy gasped as he was jostled back and forth. Knees and elbows struck him on all sides. "Let me ... Ouch!"

At that moment, the pressure of bodies against him ceased, and he was spun around. His breathing was still difficult and his chest hurt, but all these concerns vanished as he came face to face with King William.

The king stopped and scrutinized Billy, as did the crowd of nobles and guards around him. There was a moment of uncomfortable silence as Billy's eyes flashed around him, looking for a friendly face. Billy noticed a guard smoothly place his hand on the hilt of his sword, and panic gripped his mind. The king was just inches away! Billy froze, afraid to move even the slightest bit. However, he was still out of breath, and he was forced to gasp for air. Billy reached up and tugged on his collar, and the guards moved forward. Billy heard the sound of sliding steel and immediately went to his knees, bowing before his king. The king raised his hand to stay his guards. It was deathly quiet, and Billy held his position. A low, rolling growl from the king's belly broke the silence.

Billy cocked his head in surprise. From the corner of his eye he could see the king still staring down at him. Billy felt terribly embarrassed for hearing his king's stomach make such a noise. He quickly looked away, not wanting anyone to know that he had heard. The aroma of roasting meat and fresh-baked pies suddenly entered Billy's nostrils. *Goodness, but I'm hungry.* Down deep within him, Billy felt a rumble building. *Oh no! Please! Not now!* Billy wished he could stop it, just as he held his position, or the king could stay his men with the wave of a hand, but nature is not a mistress easily stayed, and Billy's stomach voiced its own discontent.

Billy wished he could curl up and hide under one of the flower petals beneath his knees. *Should I say something?* As if to sympathize, the king's innards again expressed their resentment at being ignored—this time much louder than before. Billy was sure that he could not have been alone in perceiving the sound. Billy risked another look at the king.

King William smiled at Billy. "I suppose that even the king needs nourishment from time to time, eh boy?"

Billy grinned back. "Yes, Your Majesty."

"Then let's get on with it." The king coughed to clear his throat, then in a lusty voice announced, "Let the feasting begin!"

The celebrations weren't officially to begin until the sun had reached its zenith, but Billy noticed that when King William made his announcement, no one seemed interested in arguing with the famished monarch.

The king winked at Billy, and then he and his courtiers were on the move. Their abrupt migration left Billy in shock. Speechless, he turned on his knees to watch them leave.

As the parade of nobles followed the king and newlywed royals to the keep, Lady Myrredith appeared next to Billy. He felt her hand upon his head and looked up to see the wetness of tears on her cheeks. Her eyes followed her childhood friend, the princess, with great devotion. Billy rose to his feet to get a better look.

Billy watched the royal couple move up the stairs of the donjon. "Ya think everything will work out?"

"Yes, I think so. I really think it will."

Lady Myrredith stepped in front of Billy and placed her hands on her hips. Billy readied himself, trying to think of something to tell her.

"William, why did you run away from me like that? Are you ill?"

Billy was surprised. Lady Myrredith wasn't angry with him. She was only concerned. Billy felt ashamed.

"I'm fine, milady. Lady Myrredith?"

"Yes, William."

"I'm sorry I-I-didn't go to the wedding with you."

"Don't worry yourself, William. I'm just sorry that you missed it. It was a beautiful ceremony. Oh, all the lords and ladies, the best knights of the realm, the royal couple, the king …! Every noble in the kingdom was there!"

"Not every noble."

"Well, everyone save Aonghas."

"No—" Billy pursed his lips when he realized that he had opened his mouth when he shouldn't have. He didn't dare tell Lady Myrredith that he talked with Ergyfel. *She'd have a fit.*

"What do you mean, William?"

"I … It's nothin'. Tell me about the ceremony."

"Now William, you must have meant something." She widened her stance and crossed her arms. "Was there someone out here with you that I should know about?"

Billy hid his face by pretending to look across the ward. "Naw."

"William, you are a terrible liar. Who was it?"

Billy looked at her and started to deny her accusation but found he couldn't do it.

"Were you out here with a girl, William?"

"No." Billy rolled his eyes. He leaned close to Lady Myrredith, put his hand over his mouth, and mumbled.

"Who?" she asked.

Billy mumbled into his hand again.

"William, I can't understand what you're saying with your hand in front of your mouth!"

"You told me to be careful when I said his name."

Lady Myrredith looked thoughtful for a moment and then suddenly blanched. "*He* was here?"

Billy nodded.

"Did he see you?"

Billy nodded.

"Did he say anything to you?"

"Yes. We ... talked for a while."

Lady Myrredith's eyes widened. "You talked with the magister?"

Billy swallowed. "Aye."

Lady Myrredith closed her eyes. She straightened and pursed her lips, tilting her head back.

"He even apologized for the troghouls."

Lady Myrredith's eyes popped open, and she stared at him.

"It's true! Honest! He apologized to me standing right there."

Lady Myrredith grabbed Billy's hand and led him to the donjon. She said nothing until they were in their quarters.

Finally, after a barrage of questions, Billy yielded to Lady Myrredith and relayed the entire conversation between himself and Ergyfel, to the best of his memory. Lady Myrredith paced the room, anxiously listening to Billy and biting her thumbnail.

"And then I think he asked why I was here."

"Why you were outside the church?"

"No. I think he was asking why I came to Castle Orgulous."

"What did you tell him?"

"I didn't tell him anything. The bells of the chapel rang, and when I turned back around he was gone."

Lady Myrredith's brow was tightly knit as she turned away from Billy. She bit on her thumbnail again as she stared out the window to the inner ward.

At that moment, there came a knock at the door.

"Who is it?"

"It's Hugh, milady."

"Come in."

Sir Hugh opened the door and entered. "Where have you two been? I've been looking for you everywhere!"

"Here," Billy answered.

"Well, come along. King William has declared that the festivities are to begin now! I know you don't want to miss any of ..." Hugh trailed off when he noticed Lady Myrredith's demeanor. "What is it?"

Lady Myrredith crossed to Hugh and looked into the hallway before shutting the door. With her back against the door, she began.

"Our William had a very interesting conversation with the magister."

"What?"

"Yes."

"When?"

"While the rest of us were in church."

Hugh shot a glance at Billy and then back to Lady Myrredith. "I thought he was with you!" Then he quickly turned and addressed Billy. "I thought you were with her!"

"No." Lady Myrredith crossed her arms.

"What happened?"

Billy shrugged. "Nothing. We simply ... talked."

"I don't understand why, but he's somehow interested in William."

The King's Champion furrowed his brows and shook his head from side to side. "What could he possibly ...? What could Billy ...?"

"Don't you think, maybe you two are overreacting a little? I only—"

Myrredith and Hugh stared incredulously at Billy.

Billy retreated a step. "Fine, fine, so maybe you're not."

"No, wait." Hugh caressed his eyebrow. "You may be right."

Lady Myrredith kicked his foot. "What?"

Sir Hugh raised an eyebrow. "Maybe we're meant to overreact. But whatever the case, if we don't get to the feast soon we are going to be missed, and I'm sure the magister will not overlook the opportunity to make something of it."

"And maybe we can keep an eye on him too."

Hugh nodded to Myrredith. "Come then."

He opened the door and she placed her hand on his arm.

"Stay here, William."

Hugh turned to her. "No. Billy is safer coming with us."

Lady Myrredith stared at Sir Hugh and then nodded. "Come along, William, but stay close."

Billy took Lady Myrredith's outstretched hand, and the three of them left for the feast. As they emerged from the great donjon, Hugh looked to the grim-faced lady on his arm.

"Remember," he whispered, "this is a wedding celebration you attend today, not a funeral." With that he gave her a smile for encouragement and patted her forearm.

Lady Myrredith put on a smile and took a deep breath in preparation for meeting the day's challenges.

CHAPTER SIXTEEN

The Wedding Feast

The feast was already underway when Lady Myrredith arrived at the inner ward, escorted by Sir Hugh and Billy. As they descended from the donjon, Billy took in the entire banquet. The food and revelers were arrayed in front of him like some beautiful painting. It reminded him of the faerie tapestry hanging in his room at Cyndyn Hall. The king, the newlyweds, the ambassador from Gwythia, and several nobles sat upon a dais at one end of the ward. Below them, across the cobblestone yard, musicians played, jugglers juggled, servants served, and people laughed between bites of food or speech. The air was abuzz with the noises of merriment. While the guests of Orgulous were not fanciful faeries or unicorns, they all looked just as joyous as the faerie king's court—all, that is, but one: Ergyfel.

Upon noticing their party approach, Ergyfel's counterfeit smile melted to a contemptuous scowl. He was standing on the dais, near the king, talking into the ear of a courtier whose mouth was full of mutton. His smile returned and he spread his arms wide in a mock emotional greeting. "Ah, at last! Nothing to worry about. Just as I predicted—they would be along any moment—and here they are!"

Being the only one with the gall to wear black to the princess' wedding, his actions caught the attention of most everyone. Billy felt uncomfortable as the feasters shifted their focus to him.

Billy noticed Hugh tense, and his hand wander casually over the bone handle of his dagger, but he never missed a step. He proudly escorted Lady Myrredith to the front of the dais, indifferent to all the attention.

"Your Majesty." Hugh bowed to his king.

Lady Myrredith and Billy likewise bowed.

King William had a short coughing fit and then recognized the new arrivals, gesturing with his right hand. "Sir Hugh, Lady Myrredith ... boy."

Billy wondered if that counted as being introduced to the king. He hoped there might be more to it than a simple, dangling "boy." Perhaps he could say a word or two or just tell the king his name, but he didn't feel like this was a good time to question Lady Myrredith on court etiquette.

Sir Hugh rose and escorted them across the front of the long dais. Billy was looking for a spot for them to sit down in the crowd when Lady Myrredith tugged on his hand, and he found himself being dragged up to the dais. His stomach sank as he realized Sir Hugh was leading them to three empty chairs to the right of Princess Kathryn—not far from the king himself.

No, this can't be!

Billy looked back over his shoulder. His eyes scanned the throng for a cozy, empty, anonymous spot that he could just slip into. There wasn't a single vacant seat in the ward. Up on the dais everyone could see him, and while he didn't mind attracting attention when he was juggling or singing, he abhorred the thought of having this huge audience watch him eat. At that moment, his considerable appetite vanished.

"William?"

Billy turned. Lady Myrredith waited at the end of the table. "What is it, William?"

Billy didn't know what to say, so he just shook his head.

"Come along then. We're sitting next to Princess Kathryn!"

Billy numbly nodded and followed her. If he were to tell anyone from the Valley of the Yew that he sat with the princess and king in Castle Orgulous, they would call him the biggest liar since the Devil himself.

A servant seated Billy with Lady Myrredith on his left and Sir Hugh on his right. Once again he scanned the enormous crowd that filled the inner ward. Everywhere he looked, shiny silks and rare gems dangling from elaborate jewelry greeted his eyes. Nobles, nobles, nobles, as far as the eye could see, still arrayed in their best wedding clothes, being waited upon hand and foot by pampering, attentive servants and entertained by a dozen performers. Billy spotted Don Miguel among the performers and made eye contact before the Spaniard disappeared into a band of dancing acrobats. All was a dazzling swirl of color and light. Billy began to relax when he saw that the revelers were far too busy feasting and otherwise celebrating to be concerned with his insignificant part in these events.

Billy's appetite returned the instant a servant placed a thick slice of lamb next to some vegetables on his plate. The smell entered his nose, and his grumbling stomach reminded him just how hungry he was. It felt like years since he had eaten. He became so excited that he grabbed the meat with his hand. Before he could take a bite, a pain shot up his left leg, from the shin. He looked to his left and saw Lady Myrredith take a bite of carrot very deliberately from her fork. Billy froze for a moment, watching his patron slowly spear her ham and cut off a tiny, bite-size piece with her knife. He then sheepishly put the ham back on his plate.

"Sorry," he muttered.

Billy didn't know what had gotten into him. Even before Lady Myrredith had taken the time to teach him proper eating etiquette, his father had shown him basic knife and fork manners—garnered from noble guests at his inn. So while most of Lyonesse and indeed the known world ate from trenchers with their fingers, Billy had to practice the strange customs of the local nobility.

At first it seemed like a waste of time, but good manners were important to his father. After all, their little corner of Lyonesse wasn't completely isolated, and The Valley's Finest Inn was, in John's words, "no Irish cave!" In the end, it had been the "way knights eat" argument that won him over.

Billy picked up his utensils and started to eat in proper Cyndyn style. As the first savory bites of lamb reached his mouth, he wondered if the prince from Gwythia used a fork and knife the same way that he was taught. He cautiously leaned forward and looked down the table. Next to Lady Myrredith was Princess Kathryn and beyond that, her new husband. Billy quietly observed as the sire of his nation's future rulers worked his utensils. Shortly, Billy concluded that while the young royal appeared familiar with the knife, the fork must have been of relatively new acquaint. Billy smiled to himself and dug into his dinner, comforted by the idea that he was no worse off than the future king, at least when it came to manipulating food on his plate.

After a few more bites, Billy decided to get another look at the foreign prince. Again he was cautious as he leaned forward, taking some small sugar-candies from a plate across the table. He turned his head to face down the table to his left and came eye to eye with King William. Instantly Billy sat up straight in his chair and hid behind Lady Myrredith. He shoved the candy into one of his front pockets then waited for a moment before risking another look. As before, he found the king looking his way. He threw himself back in his chair and sat at attention.

Why is the king looking at me? Did I do something wrong? Were those candies the king's? Maybe I shouldn't have used my hand again.

Billy looked down at his hand. It was clean. He took stock of his whole person. Nothing was out of place. His clothes were on straight. Neither hands nor face were smeared with food. Billy was stumped. His curiosity mounted, until he had to take another look at the king.

Billy found that when he looked again, the dark figure of Ergyfel was leaning over King William. The king said something to Ergyfel that caused the sorcerer to cock an eyebrow and look in Billy's direction. Again, as during the wedding, when they made eye contact, Billy felt strangely uncomfortable. The magister bowed his head to King William and turned away from the table. Billy watched him as he walked to the side of the dais and motioned to a darkly dressed man with a tall hat. Billy recognized him as the same man he had observed with Ergyfel on their arrival at Castle Orgulous.

"I wonder what they're up to."

Billy looked at Hugh, who was staring over Billy's shoulder. Billy followed his gaze to Ergyfel.

Billy turned back to Hugh. "The magister?"

Hugh nodded. "Aye, and his wretched brother."

At that moment it dawned on Billy that Sir Hugh had probably been watching the suspicious vizier the entire time.

"His brother?"

"Half-brother. He has no claim to the throne, but he's no less dangerous."

"Dangerous?" Billy observed the targets of Hugh's intense stare.

"Aye, and I can't keep an eye on Sygeon if I'm watching you-know-who."

"Sygeon?" Billy whispered the name to himself. *Why does that name sound familiar?* Billy scratched his head and looked at the two men, dressed dark as crows. *I know I've heard that name before, but where?*

Abruptly the two half-brothers turned and walked in opposite directions— Sygeon away from the dais, and Ergyfel directly back to the king's table. The magister stopped to whisper in the king's ear and then continued. Billy and Hugh turned back to face the table.

"Well, I'd like to know—" Billy said.

"What would you like to know?" a low, sonorous voice asked from behind him.

Billy froze as a long thin hand snaked down onto his shoulder. Its touch was icy, even through Billy's new clothes. Billy turned his eyes to the pale fingers. It was a well-manicured hand with a stunning gold ring on the middle finger, much like the one Lady Myrredith wore, only much larger. Around the long fingernails, Billy detected traces of yellow and purple stains. He followed the hand until his eyes fell on the midnight black of the owner's sleeve. Billy swallowed hard.

"Well, my young friend ...?" Ergyfel prompted.

Billy didn't remember the question. "I don't know, Magister."

"What do you want, Ergyfel?" Lady Myrredith asked.

"I thought perhaps the boy would like to know that King William has asked me to introduce him."

Billy spun around in his seat. "He did?"

"Why yes, but before I can properly perform my duty ..." Ergyfel glanced at Lady Myrredith and cleared his throat. "I must know something more about you."

Hugh placed his hand on Billy and squeezed to get his attention. Billy looked away from Ergyfel to Hugh. Hugh was silent, but the message in his eyes was loud and clear: *Be wary!*

"Your name is William?" Ergyfel asked.

"Yes," Lady Myrredith answered.

"Thank you. I will accept answers from the boy himself, Your Ladyship."

King William's First Counselor was speaking most politely, but even Billy could sense the threatening undertone to his words. He looked up and saw the magister was still waiting for his answer.

"Yes, but I've already met the king, ya know."

The magister raised an eyebrow. "You did?"

"Aye. Right after the wedding, I sort of fell down and—"

"Oh yes ... that. That was not a proper introduction for a wedding guest seated at this table. Now, your name is William, nothing more?"

"No, just William, but mostly I'm called Billy."

"Yes, I remember. And your father ...?"

"Just John."

"Your father is John the Just?"

Billy and Hugh laughed, and then Billy said, "No, just John, the inn-keeper."

"An *innkeeper*. Your father is an innkeeper?"

"Yes."

Ergyfel rolled his eyes and glanced at Lady Myrredith and Hugh disparagingly.

Billy felt that he should add something to his father's description. "My father owns The Valley's Finest Inn."

"Yes, yes. I'm sure it's very nice."

Hugh laughed again. Billy and his inquisitor looked at him.

"Well, is there something wrong with this inn?" Ergyfel asked.

"No, you pompous … That's the *name* of the inn, Ergyfel—*The Valley's Finest!*"

"Oh, I see. How quaint. And just where is The Valley's Finest Inn?"

"In the Valley of the Yew."

"Valley of the Yew?" Ergyfel's face slackened.

Billy watched the dark eyes of the King's First Counselor widen and then narrow again as he focused on Sir Hugh.

"The Valley of the Yew," Ergyfel mouthed. He was silent for a moment, then straightened. "Well then. Can you vouch for the boy, Sir Hugh?"

"Lady Myrredith is the boy's patron, but I will gladly vouch for him."

The lady spoke up. "Yes, of course we—"

Ergyfel held up his hands to the two nobles, signaling his acquiescence. "Yes, yes, yes. That should be more than enough, Lady Cyndyn. Are you ready to meet your sovereign in earnest, William?"

Billy swallowed and nodded.

"Come with me."

Billy stood. Lady Myrredith and Sir Hugh each took one of his hands.

"I'll be fine," he said. "I've dreamt of this moment all my life. What could go wrong?" Billy thought for a moment. "Don't answer that."

Billy's friends released his hands, and he followed Ergyfel. As they rounded the table and came out front, Billy felt his heartbeat increase. He felt as if every eye was upon him as they crossed the long dais to the king. Each step was an eternity.

At last, Billy, son of John the Innkeeper, stood where he had wanted to stand for as long as he could remember. It was the culmination of an extraordinary journey and the pinnacle of all his dreams, but as much as he wanted to, Billy couldn't bring his eyes up from the wooden planks of the dais. His stomach bunched from side to side as he waited. He began to think that it would have been better not to eat at all. Billy was snapped out of his trance by the sound of Ergyfel's voice.

"Your Majesty, I have the pleasure of introducing to you William, son of John ... the Innkeeper."

Billy felt himself bow, as if he were a puppet with someone else controlling his movements. His supporting knee began to wobble. *I must not fall!* It seemed strange to him that the formal circumstances should make such a difference between this and the first time he ever met his king. The first sudden encounter hadn't given him any time to think, but now, the waiting allowed his mind to breed a whole new strain of fear that wrenched his guts and rattled his bones.

"Rise, boy," the king commanded.

Billy willed himself to stand. He slowly brought his eyes up to look upon King William. The king likewise was taking good measure of Billy. His blue eyes sparkled with recognition.

"Son of an innkeep—Why, I know you. William, is it?"

"Yes, Sire."

"Of course. You're the boy with the very sensible, if somewhat boisterous stomach."

Billy grinned as he felt the blood rush to his face. "Yes, Sire."

Ergyfel bowed. "Your Majesty, I have some rather pressing duties to attend to."

"Quite so. You are excused." The king returned his gaze to Billy. "You say your name is William?"

Ergyfel let out a low grunt. Billy saw the magister's hand clench into a tight fist. The king coughed shortly, then Ergyfel turned and left the dais. Billy could see that he didn't like to be brushed off in this manner. When the First Counselor turned to bow to the king, he glanced in Billy's direction, his dark eyes seething.

Billy turned his full attention back to the king. "Yes, Sire."

The king cleared his throat. "How came you by that name, William?"

"My father says that he named me after Your Majesty."

"Is that so?" The king grinned.

"Yes, Sire, although most of the time I'm just called Billy."

"Billy? Seems a bit disrespectful, I should say. After all, you were named after me."

"Oh no, Your Highness! It's quite the opposite."

"How's that?"

"Well, Your Majesty ... As I said, my father named me after you, but most everyone in the valley says that I ought not be called anything save Billy, as it is the name that fits me best."

"Fits you best, does it?"

"Yes, Your Majesty."

"Perhaps for now, but when you've finished growing ..."

"Sire, I'm full grown now."

"What? How old are you, boy?"

"Near fifteen winters, Sire."

The king paused to contemplate what Billy had told him. "Well, perhaps you'll still grow a little more yet."

Princess Kathryn leaned towards the king. "Regardless of his size, he's very talented, Your Majesty."

"Talented? And how is it that you know him, my niece?"

"Lady Myrredith introduced us, Uncle."

The king leaned forward to see Lady Myrredith past the new husband of his heir. She bowed her head in greeting.

The king gave her a curt nod. "Myrredith of Cyndyn, what is this boy to you?"

"I am his patron, my lord … and his friend."

"Friend, eh?" The king paused for a cough. "We don't get too many of those here now."

"He's ever so clever, Uncle," the princess said.

"Clever?" her husband asked.

"Oh yes, he has quite a gift for juggling!"

"Juggling?" The king eyed Billy. "Are you any good?"

"Well–I–that is…"

"Quite good, Your Majesty," a voice cried from the crowd.

"And who might you be?" King William asked.

"I am known as Malcolm the Magnificent, Your Highness … your humble servant."

"Malcolm the Magnificent, of course. Come here, man. Come here."

Malcolm approached the dais. In an unexpected flash of movement and jingling of bells, Malcolm propelled himself feet over hands and back again. He landed next to Billy in a perfect two-point stance, which immediately became a bow.

The king's guards visibly tensed; however, everyone else on the dais, including the king, applauded the famous performer's entrance.

Still bowing, Malcolm glanced, to the side, at his amazed partner. "I'll teach ya that sometime," he whispered.

The king slapped the table. "Well done, Malcolm, I have often heard of your prowess in the courts of my lords. Your presence is most welcome."

Malcolm rose with another jingle. "It is an honor I have looked forward to for some time, Your Majesty."

"So, tell me, Malcolm, is William here a student of yours? I was told that you performed alone."

"You might say that Billy is my student, Your Majesty. You might also say that I am the student from time to time."

Billy looked in shock at his mentor, then to the king who had turned his attention back to Billy. Billy could see that the king was reevaluating his first assessment of him.

The king slapped the table again. "Well then, let us have some juggling!"

Malcolm produced Billy's juggling hat, seemingly out of thin air. "Remember what we practiced?" he whispered as he handed Billy his hat.

Billy artfully palmed several balls secreted in his hat and placed the hat on his head. He nodded to Malcolm, and they faced the head table. They bowed to the king and the new heir, and then to each other.

"One, two, three …" Billy said, and they began.

The crowd surged to its feet as the two jugglers transmuted the very air into small, brightly colored balls and began to shuffle them into amazing patterns. Billy's balls were all green, and Malcolm's yellow. In the short time it took Malcolm and Billy to synchronize, all other activity in the ward came to a stop. Now, regardless of Billy's wishes, all eyes were on him and Malcolm. Billy was aware of the attention he was under, but he only felt the weight of two eyes upon him: the eyes of his king.

Billy heard the pitter-patter of Malcolm's juggling change and realized that he had forgotten to add another ball to his own set. He was thinking too much. The king's presence was proving to be more of a distraction than Billy could handle. It was almost enough to bring down the lot.

Billy tried to refocus himself. *The only things that exist are the balls and Malcolm. The balls and Malcolm. The balls and Malcolm.* Gradually everything faded away except for the familiar pitter-patter and the balls in motion.

Billy regained his rhythm and started to walk towards Malcolm. Their patterns merged and meshed until they were in reaching distance. At that moment, Malcolm grabbed one of Billy's green balls and added it to his collection of yellow ones. Then Billy took one of Malcolm's. They set up a sequence of stealing each other's balls, creating a new array of yellow and green. The tempo began to increase. Faster and faster they went. Billy and Malcolm could sense the tension in the audience build. Slowly, they circled each other. When they reached halfway around, like magic, they were each juggling balls of a single color again. But now, Billy's balls were all yellow, and Malcolm's were all green. The audience cheered.

"And again!" Malcolm shouted.

Billy and Malcolm the Magnificent circled each other again, and again the patterns emerged having been changed—each juggling two yellow and two green. Billy looked Malcolm in the eyes as the crowd let out another cheer. Malcolm nodded, and they stepped closer together and turned to be side by side. Next, Billy stepped out and slid over in front of Malcolm. Their balls formed into one pattern that was too complex to grasp at a glance. They united into a single creature with four hands and one mind.

Suddenly Billy heard an odd sound. Malcolm was laughing. It was not just a little guffaw, as he often did while teaching Billy a new trick, but a good, strong belly laugh—a fat, frolicsome, contagious laugh. Billy had never heard such a laugh and started to laugh as well. Next, the whole audience laughed. It was obvious that the two jugglers were enjoying themselves completely.

Malcolm was nearly hysterical with laughter. Billy was afraid they would lose control and bring down their balls in a shower to the dais flooring. Malcolm seemed to have gone mad, but nothing changed. Their motions became automatic. They were in perfect synchronization. Even when Malcolm improvised new patterns with the balls, Billy was able to follow his lead.

Their act had progressed far beyond what they had rehearsed when Malcolm finally managed to control his laugh.

"Ready?" Malcolm said, as he sped up the rhythm.

"Ready for what?" Billy asked.

"The change."

Billy thought for a moment. *What change could Malcolm be talking about?* The only "change" he remembered from their practices, they had already performed. Billy became very nervous. He wasn't sure how much longer he could keep the balls aloft. The balls were a blur, even for him.

"What change?"

"One ..."

"What change?"

"Two ..."

"Oh, zounds," Billy muttered, remembering a trick Malcolm had mentioned that he wanted to attempt someday. *I guess "someday" is here. But why here – now – in front of the king?*

"Three!"

Very subtly the pattern of the flying balls changed. It really wasn't much at first, certainly not enough for a well-fed and wine-seasoned audience to catch. Malcolm started to make extraneous arm movements. Billy couldn't see them, but he could sense the brief pauses they created in the rhythm—pauses which then became part of a new, complex rhythm. Billy wished he knew more about the trick he was about to perform.

The change that occurred was completely unexpected by everyone who witnessed it, including Billy. Before their eyes the yellow and green balls started to change color. Within a matter of seconds all the balls were blue. Somehow, from somewhere, Malcolm had exchanged the yellow and green balls for blue ones, and even though he had handled them himself, Billy was at a loss.

Billy's mouth fell open, and he almost stopped juggling.

"One, two, three," Malcolm said again.

With trained expedience Billy snatched four balls out of the air. Malcolm continued to juggle his four as Billy removed his hat and sat on the ground. A moment later – one, two, three, four – all of Malcolm's balls landed in Billy's hat.

The audience erupted in cheers. Many banged their cups on the tables. Everyone went to his or her feet. Malcolm bowed humbly and helped his protégé to his feet. Then they both bowed several times to the crowd and the head table.

Billy looked at the king between bows. King William was grinning from ear to ear and banging the table with the handle of a cup, which had broken under his enthusiastic response.

Finally the crowd quieted and allowed the king to speak.

"Well done, William! Well done, Malcolm! I see now why you are called Magnificent. I've not seen anything like it ... ever!"

The crowd cheered its agreement.

"High praise indeed, Your Majesty." Malcolm bowed. Billy mimicked his juggling master.

"And you, William, I can see quite well why Malcolm has deigned to take on a student after all these years."

"Thank you, Sire." Billy bowed again.

"Malcolm, I want you to have this."

King William reached down to his side and pulled out an elegant dagger. At a glance, Billy estimated there were a dozen gems set into the intricate gold handle and sheath. It was a prize worth a king's ransom.

"Your Majesty ..." Malcolm said, "I cannot accept such a priceless—"

"Take it," the king ordered. "I don't hand out such bounty to just any-one, but you have earned my honest esteem. I offer it in homage to a great artist." The audience cheered and Malcolm swelled with pride. He stepped forward, bowed before King William, and graciously took the dagger.

Billy wondered if there would be a dagger for him. It didn't have to be a fancy one. An ordinary old knife would do. Just something that he could take home to the Valley of the Yew and say, "This was given to me by King William." However, it seemed like too much to hope for, after all he was just the apprentice.

The king then turned his eyes to Billy. He smiled appreciatively, and for a moment Billy thought that would be all.

"And as for you, young man. I am certain that the artistry we have just been witness to, would not have been possible without you."

Malcolm bowed. "Quite right, Your Majesty,"

"Therefore, I—" King William broke off his pronouncement as he glanced down at his vacant side. "I'm sorry. I don't have another dagger to give you."

"That's not necessary, Your Majesty," Billy said.

"Yes it is! I want to reward you somehow."

"It's enough to just be here, Your Majesty."

King William frowned. "It's not often that I have such loyal, unselfish guests." He made a point of looking around the crowd. "That in itself is worthy of reward."

Princess Kathryn leaned forward to touch the king's hand. "Aye, Uncle. He is good and honest."

The king looked at his niece and nodded. "William, it is obvious to me that you have won over my heir, in whom I have great faith. I therefore defer to her to devise a fitting reward for you."

The princess smiled to her uncle and then looked about thoughtfully. Then her eyes sparkled with an idea.

"Amongst our many marvelous wedding gifts, there is a glorious creation, which I was most taken with. However, it is a gift more fitting for someone with William's obvious talents."

Princess Kathryn leaned back and beckoned one of her maids to her side. Lady Myrredith appeared troubled by something. She looked at her childhood friend, the princess, with a questioning expression and whispered something. The princess simply held up her hand for patience.

The princess' servant arrived and knelt next to her. Billy watched the girl's face turn into a smile as her mistress whispered into her ear. Then suddenly the servant bowed and ran to one side of the dais. The secrecy of the princess' choice was making waves throughout the audience. Each one was wondering, "Is it my gift?" A low hum began to build in the crowd, as the gathered guests softly talked to one another.

At last the maid returned, carrying an oddly shaped package wrapped in cloth. She went to her princess' side and handed the object to her.

The princess stood. "Come forward, William."

Billy slowly stepped towards her. His eyes were on the object she held by her side—partially obscured. When he was a step away from the table, Billy bowed to the princess.

"This is the most fitting reward I could think of, William. And one I'm sure you will put to good use."

Billy stepped forward and took the package from her. Instantly he knew what it was. Even had the weight or size been completely wrong, the way it naturally fell into his arms gave everything away. Quickly he removed the cloth cover to reveal his reward.

A hush fell over the crowd as sunlight danced off the polished face of a beautifully crafted lute. Billy felt tears welling in his eyes as he examined the fabulous inlaid patterns along the wide neck and sound hole. Up to now, Lady Myrredith's gift of the clothes had been the most wonderful he had ever been given, but the gift of this fine musical instrument, especially from Princess Kathryn, made clothes seem altogether unimportant.

"Thank you," was all Billy could manage to say.

"Not at all, William. It is what you deserve."

"Does the boy play?" the king asked.

"He has an extraordinary way with song, Sire," Lady Myrredith said.

The king looked at her and then at Billy. "Is there no limit to your talents, young man?"

Billy bowed again to hide his embarrassment.

"Oh, Uncle," the princess said. "Let us hear a song from William. He has the most enchanting voice."

The king eyed his niece. "You too?"

"Aye!" shouted someone from the crowd. "We want to hear Billy!"

"Let's hear the boy," shouted another.

Other voices chimed in, until the ward was noisy with their exultation. Some simply cheered, while others requested specific songs. Billy turned to look them over and saw his new friends from Hillshire. The earl himself stood amongst them, a raised tankard in his hand. Old Finney nodded to Billy. Billy bowed to him and then turned to face the king.

The king crinkled his forehead and stared out at the large contingent of rowdy guests. He held up his wrinkled hands until they were finally quiet. He then turned his attention back to Billy. "I see you have a following."

Billy felt genuinely embarrassed. "I'm sorry, Your Majesty."

"Sorry? It seems to me that you should be!"

Billy bowed his head.

"You should be sorry, for not coming here before now."

Malcolm let out a laugh, and Billy looked up to see that his king was smiling at him. Billy returned the smile and again bowed to his ruler.

"So," the king said, "what songs do you know?"

"I know many songs, Your Majesty, but there is one song which I would most like to sing for you."

The king held out his hand and nodded for Billy to proceed. A cheer went up from the lower tables. Billy turned to Lady Myrredith and Sir Hugh, whose proud, encouraging smiles looked most parental.

While Malcolm quieted the crowd, Billy took a moment to tune his new instrument. It had a beautiful, round tone, more full and rich than Sir Hugh's instrument. The neck was a trifle larger than he was used to, to accommodate additional strings, but Billy didn't mind at all. The strings were right where they ought to be. He gave them a gentle strum, and they jumped to life under his touch. Billy couldn't help smiling even broader as he slipped the strap over his head and began.

The song Billy chose to perform for the king was one that he had heard most of his life. It was perhaps his favorite ballad, retelling King William's most famous battle, wherein he saved Lyonesse from an invasion. Billy sang the words, as he had never done before. Unfortunately he forgot, until it was too late, that the defeated army belonged to the father of the princess' new husband.

In the middle of the last stanza, Billy stopped. There was nothing but silence as he looked back over his shoulder to the head table. There he saw nearly every conceivable expression on the faces of the nobles.

"What's wrong?" the king asked with a smile.

"Uncle!" Kathryn exclaimed.

"I just ... I just realized that he—that I—that the song ..."

"I thought ya sung it quite well," the prince said.

Everyone stared at him in surprise, the odd sound of his accent stuck in their ears. The prince looked around and then rose to his feet.

"My friends. I, Prince Gaelyn, am now of Lyonesse. My wife, Kathryn, will someday be ruler of this land ... and then our children after. How could I ask ya to stop singin' your songs? The songs that fill your hearts with pride for this great nation?"

Silence hung over the ward and then was shattered by a sudden banging. Everyone turned to face the sound. The Earl of Hillshire stood in the midst of the crowd banging his tankard on the table. Forthwith, the entire crowd cheered their new prince.

"Hooray, Prince Gaelyn, hooray!" The attitude of their new prince was a sure sign that there would be peace and prosperity for all. Billy strummed the first chords of "Lyonesse, My Home"—a song long considered by the common folk to be their national anthem. When people, standing near the dais, heard his sweet, angelic voice over the din, they stopped their applause to listen. Soon everything was silent except for his soothing tones. Romantic images of their homeland rolled over the assembled guests and servants like warm honey.

When Billy reached the last chorus, the entire ward joined him. Without warning, Billy found tears rolling down his cheeks. From his vantage point he could see the entire ward, and so he cast his eye around the ward to forever record this moment in his heart.

Billy's eyes stopped short of the dais when they fell upon the brooding form of Don Miguel Scarosa. The scowling troubadour leaned against a flagpole at the edge of the crowd, his ruffled white shirt stained with wine and his lute hanging limp from his shoulder. He glared at Billy as they made eye contact, then he threw back his head to swill down the last of his wine. Billy, disturbed by the Spaniard's appearance, couldn't take his eyes off him.

Before Don Miguel could bring down his cup, a darkness enveloped him, which caused Billy to shudder. The pale face of Ergyfel appeared next to Don Miguel's and began whispering in his ear. Billy completely forgot about the song he was singing. As Scarosa brought his head back level, he sent Billy another black look. The magister continued to whisper, and the Spaniard's frown changed into a smile—a satisfied, menacing smile. Billy's blood ran cold.

The last notes of "Lyonesse, My Home" echoed through the ward, bringing Billy back to his senses. He glanced around and strummed the final cord of the song. Then he turned his attention back to the edge of the crowd. Don Miguel was still there, but he was now alone. Billy scanned the ward for the black attire of Ergyfel. He had vanished again.

"Billy! Hooray!" someone in the crowd shouted.

Others started to chant, "Billy! Billy! Billy!" Then more added their voices to Billy's praises.

Billy looked at the crowd and then to the head table, where his patron lady smiled knowingly. The entire table of nobles smiled at him.

Billy glanced back at Don Miguel. The angry troubadour dashed his empty cup to the ground and tromped off to the donjon. Billy wished that he could say something to him, but alas it would have to wait, for the crowd would not.

Billy was overwhelmed by the response of his audience. He stepped forward and bowed. He desperately wanted to go back next to Lady Myrredith and Sir Hugh behind the big table. In a moment of indecision, he started to bow and step back at the same time. It cost him his balance and sent his bottom to the dais decking with a thud. Billy's audience laughed but continued to applaud him.

Quickly Billy rolled up to his feet and faced the head table. King William was laughing appreciatively and clapping his hands. The others at the table were likewise applauding him. Billy felt the warmth of his blood rising in his face and bowed to hide his embarrassment.

"Rise, William. Rise."

Billy straightened and faced his namesake. King William grinned and gestured for Billy to approach.

"That was beautiful, William, simply beautiful. Now, it would please us if you would sing some more."

"If it pleases Your Majesty, I could never refuse."

The crowd let out another cheer, and immediately the Hillshire contingent began to shout requests. Billy, still flushed, turned to face them. He listened for a moment to their shouts and then held up his hands for quiet.

When the din had died down, Billy strummed on his lute and began with the song that had been such a great success at Earl Finney's court in Waru-Dunom. Gladly the revelers arose and responded to Billy's musical queries with the traditional shouts and dancing steps. Without hesitation, Billy went from one song to another, occasionally giving the dancers a chance to breathe by singing a ballad for them. His charm and music captivated them, and nearly everyone joined in the dancing, including Princess Kathryn. She and Prince Gaelyn were becoming very popular themselves.

After a dance, the princess and prince approached Billy. The newly-weds leaned over and requested a song. Billy, already into another tune, smiled and nodded in agreement.

Then Kathryn said, "My uncle hasn't been this happy in years, William! Myrredith is in agreement. In fact, I don't think I've ever seen him this carefree! Even his illness seems less severe today." With that, Prince Gaelyn grabbed her by the hand and took her for another dance.

Billy's heart was bursting. He looked to his patron and his king, who were enjoying the dance of the prince and princess. He couldn't imagine anywhere he'd rather be, or anything he'd rather be doing. Despite the rough start, it was turning out to be the perfect day.

* * *

This ends Book One.
The adventure continues with
The Jester,
Book Two of the
Jester King Fantasy Series.

I truly hope you enjoyed reading this book as much as I enjoyed writing it. If you did, I would greatly appreciate a short review on Amazon or your favorite book website. Reviews are crucial for any author, and even just a line or two can make a difference.

Thank you!
KC

The Jester King Fantasy Series
The Innkeeper's Son
The Jester
The Prince
The King

ABOUT K. C. HERBEL

I write stories about adventure, magic, intrigue, danger, defeat and triumph. I also write about things that really matter, like: friends, family, love, loyalty, right and wrong, good vs. evil, patriotism, bravery, duty and honor.

†

K. C. grew up in the American Southwest and spent two decades in Southern California. He has traveled much of the U.S. and Europe (both East and West) and has worked in France, Korea, Japan, and China. Now he lives in the woods near Richmond, Virginia with his family, which includes three dogs.

ACKNOWLEDGMENTS

It has been said, that it takes a village to raise a child. I suppose the same could be said for a book, and this one is no exception. My village contains those cunning, wise, foolish and fun around me. I leave it to you to decide where you fall in, but know that without each of your contributions, this book would not be what it is.

A special thank you to Mary Anne, Stella, Leslie, and Melanie for nurturing me with love and friendship in your own unique ways. I would be negligent to not mention Shane, Jack and Robert, whose hijinks, humor and imaginations abound and have helped to lighten my mental landscape. Thanks also to Mark, Raymond and Stiles for your teaching and mentoring, and to Tom who is no longer with us. My gratitude to J.R.R. Tolkien, without whom I might not have been inspired to write fantasy, and to C.S. Lewis whose work left a lasting impression on my heart. Lastly, to John DeChancie; thanks for your insightful advice and delightful encouragement.

K. C. Herbel
Richmond, Virginia
August 2015
God go with you!

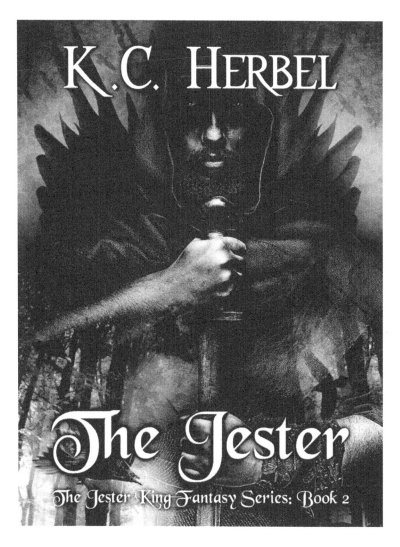

For a limited time, you can get a free copy of
The Jester!

Look for details at: www.kcherbel.com

Made in the USA
Monee, IL
02 June 2020

32332804R00184